LURED

The *Unrivaled* Serpent

iLOMILO
PRESS

ARIANA
KEDDIE

Lured – The Unrivaled Serpent.

Book 1 (Bound by Infidelity trilogy)

Published by Ilomilo Press 2020

Copyright © 2020 Ariana Keddie

ISBN: 9780648836742 (eBook Edition)

ISBN: 9780648836704 (Paperback Edition)

Ariana Keddie asserts her right to be identified as the author.

This book is a work of fiction derived from the imagination of the author. For the sake of realism certain locales, business names, events and places have been used, but have been done so in a fictitious manner. Any resemblance to a true event or business is purely coincidental. Any character or name resembling a person, alive or dead, is also purely coincidental.

The contents here within are explicit and adult in nature. Some scenes or themes may affect sensitive readers. Reader discretion is advised.

Draft edit – Chelsea Kuhel MS Editing Services

Final edit – Marni MacRae and Julia Davies

Final proof read – Amber Kleesh and Joanne Thompson

Cover design by David Prendergast @ Reedsy. Photo complements of Khusen Rustamov and @ Pixabay

ALSO BY ARIANA KEDDIE

(Bound by Infidelity Trilogy)

LURED - The Unrivaled Serpent
BOUND - The Catalytic Rose
FREE - The Luminous Pearl

For Mare.
Without your encouragement,
not one word of this novel would have been written.
Thanks for your admiration, and those kicks up the butt.

"The most beautiful stones have been tossed by the wind, crushed by the water and polished to brilliance by life's strongest storms."

- Tom Schaefer -

HER LIFE

When I first met Alex, he introduced himself as Alexander. I thought it was strange that he used the formal version of his name, given he arrived in worn jeans and a long-sleeve faded tee.

He arrived on a Sunday.

My husband Gerard and I had been out all morning playing golf with friends, and we didn't notice him at first. Gerard had gone inside with the golf bags leaving me to collect our sweaters from the back seat of the car. I sensed Alex before I saw him, causing me to spin on my soft spikes as he approached from behind.

"Do you need any help?" he asked.

Alex looked different from how I'd imagined him when Gerard told me he might drop by sometime. I'd pictured him with menacing features—a sharp nose, lots of piercings or tattoos crawling up his thick neck. A shaved head perhaps. Well, I got the thick neck right. But without a photo from my husband, I'd been at the mercy of my wild imagination, and I was sure his stepbrother would be someone to fear, even with assurance from Gerard that Alex was not that type of badass to land himself in prison.

"No thanks, I'm fine." I scanned our driveway and yard, confused how he had arrived. He later told us he'd been dropped off by a taxi, that he'd been waiting in the gazebo and had fallen asleep. I doubt that now. I can almost guarantee he'd been watching us from the moment we'd arrived. Assessing our life, calculating where and how he would pull it apart.

When I squared myself to address him, he cocked his head then frowned. Through dark, thick lashes, his intense green eyes searched mine—like he recognized me from somewhere or that I reminded him of someone. I wasn't sure if my heart skipped a beat because I felt nervous, or because I became intoxicated by the cologne he was wearing. A scent that was sweet, musky, and reeking of trouble.

"Christ, that's a crop of red hair. You must be Paige," he guessed, thrusting out a well-abused hand. "I'm Alexander, it's about time we met."

I was shaking his hand, still stunned by his blatant reference to my hair, when Gerard burst out the French doors, throwing his arms upward toward the clouding sky. "Aaaa-lex," he exclaimed, surprised by Alex's unexpected arrival.

"In the flesh," Alex sang out, squeezing my hand before dropping it and moving onward to meet Gerard halfway. I rubbed my palm where his touch still lingered, acutely aware of the chemical sensation his contact seemed to have left behind.

Gerard had spoken little of Alex before that day. I figured he was ashamed, perhaps embarrassed that his stepbrother had become incarcerated. It wasn't exactly something Gerard, a newly appointed attorney, needed overshadowing his career, and I doubt he wanted to risk me discussing Alex amongst our friends. Not that I ever would. And so, Alex was out and looking for work, and it seemed Gerard couldn't have been happier.

Ignoring me, they plunged into a conversation and made their way inside, leaving me to collect the last of our things from the car. I played hostess for a while, throwing together a platter of food for them to eat before I disappeared through the double doors into the living room, hoping to finish the novel I was reading. When Gerard needed to return calls that kept interrupting them, Alex was left wandering around the house until he found me.

I admit, I was curious about Alex and my imagination went wild as he entered the room. I'd never seen a man like him up close before, at least not in the flesh. His lightly tattooed forearms looked as though he'd spent his days doing chin-ups using the prison's overhead plumbing. I pictured him pinning down an inmate to beat the crap out of him, complete with blood and teeth scattered across a concrete floor. I shivered, but for some reason, I felt a strange desire to know how a woman would feel being caressed by his thick, strong hands. Did he even have a woman? Had there been one before he went to prison? Suddenly, I had so many questions; I found myself staring. My tongue was twitching, but my mind became frozen as fantasies of him banging a raven-haired beauty materialized in my mind's eye. Her face being pressed up against a wall not giving one iota of resistance, even though her skin would later look pockmarked from the brick indentations, his lust being worth both the pleasure and the pain.

He wore his boots inside—the type bikers' wear. I was hoping he wouldn't dirty the expensive rug as he made his way around the room, checking out our belongings. He looked scruffy—his shirt having seen better days. Tattered, it was missing almost all its buttons and was too small; by the way it molded itself over the contours of his chest, highlighting his muscular physique. Regardless of his unkempt appearance, Alex exuded a level of confidence I'd never sensed in anyone before. Strong yet unassuming, he was—intimidating.

"You guys have got a lot of nice stuff." Alex nodded, I gather in appreciation, while he picked up random knick-knacks before his hand caressed a large glass egg. A Jack Storm original, whose price tag could feed a small village rather than be collecting dust in our home. From out of nowhere, I began wondering if Alex was casing the place, causing more heat to find my face.

"Thanks, it's mostly Gerard's." I looked back down at my book and fiddled with the corners of the page as he continued to hover around the room. Out the corner of my eye, I watched him drift over to the bookshelf, where he bent to peer at the horizontal bottle, containing a model ship I'd bought Gerard when we first started dating, some five years earlier. Suddenly, Alex glanced back and startled me.

Having caught me watching, his mouth turned up at the corners and a wicked glint lit his eyes. I didn't know where to look. My focus darted around the room before falling on my book again, trying to gain control of my breathing.

He wandered over to the windows next, blocking out the sunshine with his dominating stance, crossing his arms and spreading his legs wide. I couldn't take my eyes off him. He was so confident, raw, and masculine.

"What are you reading?" he asked, his back still turned away from me, just staring out at the pool and yard. His question for some reason made me anxious, confused that he was interested in me at all. Then all I could smell was his cologne again. It was as if the rise and fall of his broad shoulders as he breathed, helped the scent permeate the room. I started to notice minute things about him. Like the way his dark hair was matted in places and the oddly shaped scar at the back of his neck. And the way he clenched and flexed his hands that were still folded against his chest, as though preparing to fight. The room became so thick of him, I could almost taste him.

"I beg your pardon?" came my stuttered reply, sounding more like a stupid whimper, as though it wasn't a reasonable question he was asking. But I was so bewildered by the effect he was having on me, I found it hard to formulate any rational thoughts.

"What are you reading?" he repeated, still transfixed by something outside.

"A book."

Finally, he turned around. "I can see that. But what's it about?"

"Oh. Um." Flustered, I then looked like a complete idiot because I turned the cover over to look at the title. I heard him chuckle. When I looked up, a smile was still lingering, a cheeky grin that softened what I first thought to be a harsh face.

I became so heated, I glanced up at the air conditioner, mentally willing it to turn itself on. "It's nonfiction, a memoir."

"I thought as much." He stuffed his hands in the pockets of his jeans and rocked on his heels, his head bobbing, just staring at me.

I didn't get to know what he meant by that, because Gerard came back and strangely, I felt like our conversation was too private to continue.

"Sorry, Alex. It seems the wicked never rest." Gerard looked at me and frowned. "Paige, don't we have any cold beers in the fridge?" He sounded a little annoyed that I hadn't been hospitable.

Uncurling my legs, I apologized then made my way to the

bar, all the while I could feel Alex's eyes following me. Even when I peeked over my shoulder, as Alex was led to view Gerard's prized collection of rare books, he was still watching me.

Squatting behind the bar and out of sight for a moment, I tried calming myself in front of the fridge. Wrapping my hands around the cold bottles, I placed them on my burning cheeks. Most likely I was warming the beer, but I didn't care —my face was on fire.

When I stood, Gerard was showing Alex something in a book he'd plucked off the shelf. I went over to them and held out the opened bottles. Gerard took the beer absently still chatting away, but when Alex took my offering, his hand covered mine; holding tightly for what seemed like the longest moment.

At first, I thought it was an accident because he was paying attention to Gerard, but when he didn't readjust his hold, I realized he meant to pin me in place. It both scared and thrilled me that Alex could be so bold, to make such a gesture with my husband right there.

Most people, when describing someone's touch, say it was electric, like heat or a buzz. That's not what it felt like when Alex held on to me, and it's most likely why I didn't jerk my hand away. His touch wasn't electrical; it was soothing and magnetic, like he couldn't or wouldn't let me go. I just stood there like a zombie until he finally moved his hand, his fingers taking hold of the neck of the bottle instead. Then he winked and held my gaze. He didn't speak, didn't utter one word. But in those few seconds as his eyes searched mine, I could feel him questioning me.

I eventually excused myself, saying I needed to take a shower. But really, I just needed to get away. Everything about Alex unsettled me. His actions, his deep voice. The way he kept trying to catch my eye. I knew that if Gerard hadn't been there that afternoon, Alex would have slowly and seductively drilled me. Found out everything he could. Studied my flaws, preyed on my weaknesses.

For the last five years I'd been living a blissful, happy life with the man of my dreams. But suddenly, Alex had me doubting myself. I felt like a fraud, and intuitively, I knew my life was about to get turned upside down.

2

LOSERS

Sitting at the dining table with my feet tucked up, my knees are pressing painfully against the wooden edge, but I don't shift my position. I'm trying, to no avail, to dull the nausea that's threatening to send me to the bathroom because outside, Alex doesn't seem to have a care in the world. Unfortunately, that's all about to change.

He's working in one of the garden beds amongst the shrubs with a shovel in his hand, but he stops to answer his phone. His jeans are well fitted, and when he mounts one foot on the shovel, his ass flexes. He certainly is something to look at, and it makes me question once again how a man can exude so much sexual energy, just by being alive.

When he throws back his head and laughs, he has me guessing at who he could be talking to. A buddy or his parole officer maybe. But a reality check has me suspecting it's most likely one of the many women I don't doubt he has.

Glancing down at a cold mug of coffee, I roll it between my palms. My stomach is a cluster of knots, and I've barely touched a drop. All the internal bantering I've been doing this morning while watching Alex has boiled down to one decision now. I need to let him know what happened last night. It's not right, not fair for him to be unprepared for what I expect is coming.

In an instant, I have a load of trash as an excuse, and I'm out the French doors.

Alex doesn't seem to notice I've come outside. Either that, or he's ignoring me, for which I can hardly blame him. For the last six weeks, I've been avoiding him like the plague.

After dumping the garbage bag, I slam the can lid and act as though I'm interested in the yard that looks like a golf green now. I can't deny Alex is good at what he does, but when my attention finally settles back on him, and his eyes dart my way, I'm filled with regret.

The baseball cap he has on, is the same one he's been wearing every day for the last four months, since he started working here. It's always turned the wrong way around and it makes him look boyish. But he is far from being a boy.

When his call is over, he shoves his cell phone in his back pocket, rearranges his hat and sunglasses, then strides my way. I search to see if anyone else notices him approaching, acutely aware that the nearer he gets, the farther south my pulsating heart seems to slide. "Christ," I mutter under my breath, and even though the temperature is already in the high nineties, with his attention now trained on me, I'm wrapping my dressing gown tighter.

"Hey," he greets, jutting his chin while chewing fiercely on gum.

"Hi. I'm glad you're here early." I take a step back when he tries to slip past me on his way toward his pickup truck. Parked beside the shed and shaded by a large jacaranda tree, the vehicle is dented, old, and loaded with gardening supplies.

Taking off his glasses and hooking them on the pocket of

his jeans, he locks eyes on me. "You sure about that? Seems to me you've been pretending I don't exist anymore."

Ignoring his comment, I step closer to his pickup and watch as he withdraws a box full of potted plants. They're not rose bushes as I'd hoped, but I don't comment. It's too late for that now.

Alex stalls, waiting for my reply. When there is none, he shakes the pots slightly. "Okay then. Well, I'm here early because I was trying to beat the heat."

Dirt is sticking to his sweaty brow and darkening his stubble, emphasizing his bow-shaped lips and reminding me where I'd allowed those masterful pieces of flesh to roam.

With his shirt open at least three buttons down, my gaze drops to linger on his glistening chest, shamefully, for a few seconds longer than it should, until I respond that he failed because it's already a scorcher.

When I look up, I'm met with an amused expression which sends heat rushing to my face.

"You've gotten that right," he says in a gruff voice. "Here, you can give me a hand carrying these." Alex thrusts dripping wet pots of hairy leaf and what I think are callistemon in my direction, smirking because he knows how ridiculous it is to suggest I help him right now.

I step back quickly so he doesn't ruin my slippers. "Alex!"

"Well, what are you doing out here like that?" he gestures at my clothing.

When I give him the stink eye, and tighten my arms over my chest, Alex laughs. "Best you go back inside, Princess. I can't have you getting all hot and dirty—or can I?" he adds winking.

He turns to walk away.

"Alex, Gerard knows about us."

Stopping dead in his tracks, he turns around and spits his gum out onto the gravel drive. He takes a step closer.

Instantly, I'm clutching at my burning neck, but I can't help screwing up my face that he just spat out his gum.

"What do you mean he knows? Don't tell me you fuckin' told him?" He dumps the box of pots on the ground as my eyes dart to the gum.

"You know, you could have spat that out in the trash, it's right there."

"Fuck the gum. Did you seriously tell him?" He glares at me before pulling off his hat to scratch his head and stare at his feet, looking for answers or questions or maybe planning out his escape route.

I shift my weight from one foot to the other, my stomach churning while he processes everything. Finally, he looks up.

"Shit," he cusses in disbelief, dragging a hand down the back of his neck before his eyes shoot to the upper story of my house. "What's he doing now?"

I glance up as well. "Still asleep, I hope. I just thought I should warn you."

"But why tell him?"

"Because I've been an absolute wreck since it happened, Alex. That's why. And because I love him."

"Yeah right."

"I do so," I snap. Staring down at my folded arms, I try calming myself before looking back at him. "I'm sorry, all right. But I just couldn't keep it in anymore."

"Obviously! Fuck!" He half turns away then squares himself and raises his voice. "I need this job, Paige."

"I know. It was just… Oh God, I don't know." I chew on a fingernail not knowing what to say.

"Suppose my job here goes to shit?" He slides his sunglasses back on and shakes his head. "Christ, I'm a fucking idiot."

I glance toward the French doors, praying Gerard hasn't overheard us arguing, then lower my voice. "He didn't say too much last night," I lie. "I begged him to sleep on it." God, now I sound like I'm chasing a medal. "But... I don't know—maybe you should just go before he gets up. He hardly slept, and you don't know what he's like when he's tired." Again, I tell him that I'm sorry.

Alex pushes his sweaty hair back before returning his cap to where it belongs. He juts his chin at me again. "And what about you. How come you're not out on your sorry ass then?"

"I don't know. He said he can forgive me, but do men usually do that kind of thing?"

"Fuck if I know, but I'd sure as shit kick your ass out the gate if you were mine."

"Seriously?" My tone rises again. "Why did I even bother telling you? So much for gratitude."

"Gratitude?"

"Well, I came out here to warn you, didn't I?"

"Gee, thanks then, Princess. For getting me fired."

"Christ, I just told you I was sorry."

"Yeah, so am I now. But I'm not leaving. If Gerard wants to have it out..." Alex bends to collect the pots. "I'll be right here waiting, and you can tell him I said that. He knows he had it coming."

My flinch causes one side of Alex's mouth to curl. What the hell was that supposed to mean? I open my mouth to ask, but he's already walking away. Then I remember what Gerard said last night about revenge, and by the time I've closed the French doors to our family room, Alex is back digging in the garden as if he couldn't care less.

With a still pounding heart and a cluster of nerves on overdrive, I go over to the sink and scrape last night's burned disaster down the garbage disposal before flushing it away. Wishing, praying it was that easy to dispose of the shame I feel inside.

3

ILOMILO

I want to blame the scent of the lilies. Make excuses because I had my monthly 'visitor.' Wish I could lay blame on anything other than myself. But there was no running from the mistakes I'd made in both cheating on Gerard and then telling him about it. The straw that broke the camel's back. What a stupid saying, and yet those damn flowers and Gerard's beautiful smile last night had done just that. After hours, days, and weeks of despising myself, I was ready to burst, and I had, literally, into tears. I then tore my husband's heart right out of his chest while he held out a bouquet, their scent overwhelming my better judgment to stay quiet and shoulder my shame until I died.

When he arrived home after work, he started telling me about some play that was coming to the Empire Theatre. He asked if I'd like to go.

"What's it called?" Reluctantly, I took the flowers from him, and in that exchange, I imagined a searing hot A burning its way through my chest, branding me forever as an adulteress.

"*No Man's Audience*, by some fellow called Byrne. I've

never heard of him, but the reviews are good," he said enthusiastically, knowing I'd love to go.

My lack of response because I'd been stewing on a confession all day, made Gerard look twice before I forced out a reply. "I guess. I mean—it has been some time since we've been on a date." I pulled a tight smile then picked at a dead leaf amongst the otherwise perfect bunch of lilies, wishing he wasn't always being so goddamn nice, that I had a legitimate reason for cheating on him. He frowned at me before meandering toward the counter to pick at the cut-up carrot from off the chopping board.

And then it was like he flicked open the confessional shutters, his voice all warm and buttery while his ridiculously iridescent-blue eyes softened and looked concerned. "Oh honey, what's the matter? I thought you'd be excited?"

It all came out in a groan when I slapped the bunch of lilies on the counter instead of putting them in a vase. Those damn flowers had become a weapon that crucified my soul. Why in the hell did Gerard have to ask Alex to work for us in the first place anyway? Make him our gardener. Here at our home, and then be there in the shed, acting all macho and seductive. Christ, it was like putting a cat in with a mouse. I loathed myself for being so vulnerable and naïve. The shame I was harboring made me pathetic. I even tried taking the easy way out.

"You need to divorce me, I'm leaving you, I need to go." I paced the kitchen, crossing and uncrossing my arms, stuffing my hands in my pockets, only to rip them out again to cover my face and slump in a chair.

"What?" He recoiled so fast you'd have sworn I slapped him. "Why on earth would I want to do that? You're the best cook around." He tried laughing through a mouthful of carrot, but when he noticed me wiping at my wet cheeks, he stepped closer and his smile slid away. Then he started ranting about his age.

"You're not old, Gerard. Stop saying that all the time. You know I'm not concerned about our age difference."

"Well, what is it then, why would you say something like that?"

I braced myself, took a deep breath before looking straight at him. "Because I cheated on you."

There it was, out, along with his heart which I may as well have tossed onto the floor for how quickly he looked down. He stood frozen, his beautiful eyes wide and staring at some space near my feet.

He came up slowly to search my face. "You mean—with another man?"

"No, at backgammon. Of course I mean with another man."

He frowned at my sarcasm, but I think I was deliberately baiting him to grab me, shake me, slap me across the face, and punish me. Instead, he lumbered off into the living room, shaking his head and going straight to the bar. I apologized over and over. Telling him I couldn't explain how it transpired. "It was a thoughtless and stupid thing to do. And it happened so fast. But I was just there, and suddenly I wasn't me anymore."

"Not you? What the hell does that mean?" He slammed a tumbler onto the wooden bar, making me jump.

I knew it was a lame excuse. I just shouldn't have been there. I was weak, that's all there was to it. And even though I didn't deserve it, I sought his understanding.

"I promise it was only the one time, Gerard, and it meant nothing. It was a dumb mistake." I stood behind the sofa, smoothing the suede fabric, hoping it would protect me in case he suddenly became enraged. But he took his anger out on the bar fridge instead, kicking the door shut with his foot before dropping ice in his glass and filling it to the brim with Scotch whiskey.

"And you think that makes it all right? Are you going to add that it won't happen again as well? Fucking women." He took a large gulp from his glass and glared at me, making me wonder if that was how he studied his clients before they went to trial. As though his silence would draw out any last thoughts, which seemed to work because then I blurted that I didn't even enjoy it, a blatant lie and another thing I'd never done to Gerard before.

After several minutes, he settled down on the overstuffed couch, rolling his glass between both palms and taking sips in quick succession, just staring at the floor. I used the opportunity to lower myself onto the sofa opposite him, pulling my legs beneath me and making myself small.

I waited.

After what seemed like an eternity of him smoothing his face, trying in vain to palm his grimace away, he placed his tumbler gently on the glass coffee table and locked eyes with me.

"Who was it?"

When I didn't answer, he leapt to his feet and paced in front of the couch. "When did it happen, was it recently? Was it that slimy, little waiter prick at Donovan's? He made it no secret he thought you were beautiful. Ogling you then asking if my daughter was single. I should have smashed his face there and then." Gerard rolled his eyes at the ceiling, lost in thought for a moment while I stayed silent.

"Where did it happen? Please tell me you didn't fuck someone in our bed. I'll burn it. Christ, I'll burn this house." He trod the carpet again.

"Six weeks ago, and no, it wasn't in here. Please, Gerard, stop. Stop pacing!" I reached out for him, but he ignored me and grabbed his drink, gulped down what remained before getting another.

"Who?" he demanded again.

I shook my head. "Just punish me. Tell me to leave, do whatever you need to do, but don't torture yourself with knowing everything."

He thumped his fist down on the bar. "Why damn well tell me if you're not going to fully confess?"

I agree, he had a point, but telling him the sickening truth? I knew it would kill him. So I stalled, hoping he'd give up, but he became manic.

"Christ," he exhaled. He slumped back on the sofa, then sat forward again, cradling his head in his hands for a moment, unable to console himself. "It was Nadal, wasn't it? He fucks everything in a goddamn skirt. I will fuck his wife if it was him, then burn his precious restaurant." He was referring to our neighbors up the road, and I groaned at the thought of Gerard screwing Jenna.

"Gerard. It wasn't him or the waiter," I said calmly.

He leapt to his feet and knocked the table, his drink splashing everywhere.

"Who—the fuck—was-it-then?"

He scared me so much. I began sobbing, couldn't answer even if I wanted to, which I didn't.

He went to the bar again to refill his scotch, waiting for me to calm down. When he returned, he was also carrying a glass of wine for me. He held it out; just out of my reach and glared at me. A gesture that screamed volumes.

"Paige, who was it? Tell me now or so help me…" His fixed jaw conveyed his seriousness.

I swallowed hard. "All right. But before I tell you, promise me you won't do anything about it tonight, that you'll sleep on it and let yourself calm down."

Gerard stepped back as though I'd pushed him. I'd said

nothing, but somehow—I'd implied everything. He started shaking his head and a wicked grin ruined his otherwise handsome face.

"No, I have a suggestion for you—Paige. You tell me exactly what happened, and I'll tell you who it was." He moved away and stood near the bar.

"What?"

Pushing his jacket front aside, he placed a hand on his waist, looking almost amused. "You heard me."

"Gerard! You do not want to know the details."

"Yes, I do, and you will tell me."

I grabbed my glass and took another large mouthful of wine. "No. You're angry, I get that. But telling you all the sordid details will only…"

"Sordid, that's a detail, now tell me more."

I pinched my nose, tried to ease the dripping. "You know what I mean, and no, I don't think I should tell you anything else. If you can't forgive me and you want me out, just say so."

I rose from the couch, already mentally packing a bag, thinking of accommodations and whether Gerard would let me at least leave with the Lexus when he said, "Well, there's something I need to tell you then. It was most likely a revenge fuck, Paige. That cocksucker Alex wanted his revenge." He strode over to the couch and sat on its edge.

"What do you mean revenge?"

"So, it was him."

My stomach lurched and I'm sure I turned pale.

Gerard reclined back into the couch and crossed his legs, then threw an arm over the top. I'd never seen him look so smug.

"I should go. I'll get a hotel or something," I said, making my way out of the room, intending to pack.

"No—I don't want you to go—it wasn't your fault. He was

just using you to punish me. I should have expected it really, the cunning little shit."

Stopping short of the doorway, I turned to face him, my tears drying instantly while he went on.

"I'm sorry I got mad at you. It was hurtful to hear but I'm not surprised. Alex is more your age, and look at him, he's built like a damn porn star, most likely he acted like one too."

I shook my head, but I couldn't answer him. All I could think about was what a mistake I'd made, what a complete fool I was. I became dizzy, found it hard to breathe. How could I have been so cruel, not to mention insane, risking everything I had?

"I don't expect you to forgive me." My voice, barely a whisper, drifted toward my feet. "I think I should just go. I'm sorry I had to tell you, it was just... I've been a complete wreck. Every day he's here, reminding me of what I'd done."

"Please, come and sit down," he suggested, coaxing a reluctant me back to the couch for further interrogation. "We'll talk about it, get everything off your chest. You made a mistake, that's all. I just need to understand why."

I tried to gloss over details, but he was insistent, demanding to know everything. Where had it taken place?

"In the shed," I replied, draining my glass.

"Why in the shed, did he fuck you standing? Did you arrange to meet, was he expecting you or did it just happen?"

"Gerard, stop. But if you must know, no, it wasn't planned. I was just there to ask him about roses."

"Roses?"

"Yes. I wanted him to plant roses instead of those ugly plants the both of you decided on."

He flinched at my remark but didn't miss a beat.

"So, what made the transition, did he just grab you or did you entice him?"

I buried my face in my hands, desperately wishing I could

just vanish. I couldn't understand why he was torturing himself, wanting to know every detail. Even when he got up to pour himself another drink, he continued badgering me.

"Well then, tell me this. Who, kissed who first?"

"Gerard, enough! Stop asking questions, I'd just want to forget about it."

"But I need to know. How did he excite you?" He gestured with a bottle of red, asking if I wanted another. I shook my head in both disbelief and refusal but watched as he poured himself another glass of scotch, a big one. He was onto his fourth, it was concerning. So was what he asked next.

"Did he make you come?"

"Gerard!"

"Well, I think I have a right to know—Paige."

"Please don't make this any uglier than it already is." Again, I was on the verge of leaving, but when he sat down next to me, he rested a reassuring hand on my knee.

"Are you in love with him? Have the two of you formed an attachment?" Looking high, he took small sips eyeing me over his glass.

"No! It was a mistake and I regret it. Gerard, Alex has nothing on you. I love you—I always have, you know that." I looked into his eyes, my hand cupping his face in assurance.

"You understand I will be having a word to Alex about this, but yes, I will wait until tomorrow like you suggested."

Relieved, I hugged into his chest, relishing the way his fingers then trailed up and down my spine as he sipped quietly on his drink.

Then, without another word about it, we made our way to bed. Turning off an oven, that until minutes ago, contained burned *Coq Au Vin. N*o doubt it's now a dish, that will never be Gerard's favorite again.

4

NATURAL

Disappointment radiates off him. It's in his footsteps, in the atmosphere. From the kitchen counter, where I'm now preparing breakfast, I turn to look as he strides down the tiled marble hall. Straightening his tie, briefcase in hand, Gerard still cuts an exceptional figure for a man of forty-two. His blond hair, now graying at the temples, is brushed to the side and he's chosen to shave his usual three-day stubble away. That should be an encouraging sign, but somehow, it doesn't make me feel any better.

Although eighteen years older than me, I still find Gerard dauntingly handsome, and I can't take my eyes off him as he hangs his suit jacket on the coatrack then drops his case to the floor. He enters the open plan area, and instantly he's searching outside.

Turning off the gas cooktop, I return the lid gently to the pan. "Good morning, I made scrambled eggs. How was your sleep?"

He snaps his head around. "How do you think it was?"

It's a rhetorical question that just gives him an excuse to glare at me.

"So, is he here?" he asks, coming closer.

Dropping my head and stepping forward, I mumble a reply before plunging my hands in scalding water, attempting to scrub the encrusted pot from last night, anything to avoid looking at him.

"And why were you up so early?"

"I couldn't sleep," I mumble again.

From off the counter, he snatches up the newspaper then pulls out a stool. "Well, you woke me. Carter wants to meet early, so do you mind dishing up. Please," he adds, shifting his eyes to me before hiding behind his paper. "And get me some juice while you're at it."

"Gerard!"

"What?" he snaps.

I stare at him gobsmacked, the small amount of coffee I drank earlier, curdling.

He lowers his paper. "Well, for shit's sake, Paige, how do you expect me to be? You fucked another man behind my back."

"But what about last night? I thought—I thought you'd forgiven me."

"I have. But that doesn't mean I need to be happy about it."

"Well no, but…"

"I need time, Paige. Just give me time. Now, can I *please* have some juice?" He gets up and moves over to the table to resume reading while I fuss about getting him his drink, realizing I should have kept my mouth shut about Alex.

Placing the glass in front of him, I summon the courage to reach out and smooth his hair. "I really am sorry. You do know that—don't you?" When he ignores me, I slide down and crouch by his side, begging him not to hate me.

After a moment of tension, his body slackens. "It's fine, I'll get over it. It's just raw right now. I've been thinking about it all night, trying to figure out where I went wrong."

"You did nothing wrong; it was me."

Wishing I could turn back the clock, I lay my head on his lap.

"Get up off the floor, Paige," Gerard says gently, lifting me up by the arm and pulling me onto his lap to play with my hair. "I just wanted you to be happy. I wanted to be the one to make you happy."

"You do! I am—happy."

"But he excited you like I haven't been able to. Didn't he?"

"No, it was a stupid lustful moment." I sit taller, grab his face and make him look at me. "You and I have something special—you know that. *You* make me happy."

Gerard nods. "But he was different, wasn't he? He had you panting with desire, you craved him nailing you. I bet he made you moan and even scream."

"Gerard!" I leap from his lap. "What are you doing? Are you trying to make this into something it's not? Just ask him to leave, and neither of us will have to see him again."

"Do you really think it's that easy?" The disdain in his tone is so harsh, I'm ashamed that I tried to blow it off as that simple. Turning away, I move toward the windows, let the tears come. He hates me; is disgusted. Suddenly he rises, his chair scraping. When I turn, he has his arms open wide, beckoning me. As soon as I bury my face into his chest, he is tilting my chin so he can look into my eyes. His expression has softened, and as he wipes away my tears, he shushes to stop me from crying.

"I'm just processing, trust me—everything will be fine. I'll have a word with Alex. All this means is we need to get to know each other better." Abruptly, he steps away and goes over to the cooktop.

"What do you mean, better? We know everything. I'm still

the same person." I join him at the island bench, snatch out a Kleenex and watch in a daze as he dishes up the eggs.

"Obviously, we don't, and you're not the same person." He gives me a quizzical look. "You don't know everything about me, and now—I understand, I don't know you like I thought. Do you mind getting the coffee?" He brushes past me, carrying two plates to the table.

What does he mean I don't know everything about him? My stomach churns from the uncertainty, making my skin prickle and become sensitive. I turn slowly and do as asked, taking cups down from the overhead cupboard to pour coffee, his into a favorite mug, mechanical and on autopilot because my mind has left me. What don't I know?

When I join Gerard at the table, I'm amazed that he's shoveling food into his mouth as though he hasn't eaten in months. Easing into a chair, I sit on my hands to stop them from shaking.

"So good, honey," he compliments, through a mouthful. "Come on, eat." He waves his knife at my plate. But I don't feel like eating. Something is wrong. He's hot, then cold. One minute he's looking as though he could kill me, the next he's calm.

Picking up a fork, I push the eggs around my plate. "Will you be asking Alex to leave?"

After a moment of regarding me, Gerard dabs at his mouth with a napkin then glances out the window again, as if the mention of Alex's name might make him appear. "I gather you spoke with him this morning?"

"Yes. I suggested he leave."

"Why?"

"I don't want the two of you fighting in front of me."

"What, you don't think I can take Alex, is that it? Scared he'll beat the crap out of me?"

"No, I just…"

"I assure you I could hurt Alex if I wanted to. Maybe not with my fists, it's obvious he's a lot stronger than me. But I can hurt him in other ways." He readies a fork full of eggs. "Just like I could crush you if I wanted to." His food disappears into his mouth. I stare at him wide-eyed.

"Don't look so scared, I'm only joking." He whacks the side of my knee then brings the coffee mug to his lips, studying me while he drinks. When he puts down his cup, he's smiling. "Look, I don't want to hate or punish you and Alex for what happened, but I can't just let this go as if it's no big deal." He picks up his utensils again and cuts into some toast.

He has me thinking about his comment from last night about revenge.

"I know Alex regrets what happened, and he's been keeping his distance from me. Honestly, he hasn't tried anything since."

"I doubt he regrets it, Paige. He knew exactly what he was doing. You were just his pawn, but I think I'm partly to blame there."

I blush. Does Gerard really think I'm that naïve? "You mean the revenge thing? What happened between you two?" I ask.

Gerard rests his elbow on the table and strokes his jaw, looking intent. "He thinks I stole a girlfriend from him, but I didn't, she offered herself to me because Alex was too busy screwing up his life and not paying attention to her." Whoa! And then he tries to gloss over the admission. "Listen, will you trust me on something?" In shock, I nod without a word. "I think we need to change some things to pull through this, do you agree?" He finishes his coffee and looks at his watch.

"That depends, I guess. What do you want to change?"

"For the moment, I'd like to think things over. What are you doing today?"

Frustration is starting to fray my nerves and it comes out in my tone.

"I don't know. Just preparations for the Brave Hearts fundraiser. Annabel is coming for lunch. Gerard, what do you need to think over?"

"And after that, anything?" he asks, taking his plate and standing, deliberately ignoring my question.

"No."

"Good. I'll call later, when I've sorted some things out." He walks over to the sink to get rid of his plate then returns to pull me to my feet. "I love you." He kisses me quickly.

I return his sentiment, but he can tell I'm bothered.

"What is it? Are you worried about the girlfriend thing? Because if you are, you don't need to be. It was a long time ago, well before you."

Somewhat relieved, I nod. But it's more than that. He's leaving me with unanswered questions.

"I've totally fucked up, haven't I? I should have just kept this to myself."

Gerard huffs, "Probably. But now that it's out, we need to deal with it." Then he's frowning and shaking his head. "And please don't swear, it makes you sound cheap."

His comment has me rubbing at my tingling neck. And then, with an enthusiasm I've never felt from Gerard before, he smiles with a primal growl and squeezes my ass in both hands before planting his lips firmly on mine.

I know I should be relieved, that Gerard is handling the indiscretion so well. I mean, if he and I can rise above my infidelity, I'm hoping we can survive anything.

But as I watch him leave for work, heading straight to his car, instinct tells me Gerard is most likely in denial, and I should brace myself for when he comes to his senses.

5

REASON

Determined to not let Gerard's odd behavior get to me, I busy myself with baking before sprinting up the stairs to get ready for Annabel's arrival. The moment my eyes land on our unmade bed however, I'm questioning Gerard all over again. I was expecting him to turn away from me when we got into bed last night. But the moment we were under the covers, his hands were all over me, clawing at my nightshirt to get me naked as fast as possible. Once I was undressed, he just sat there, looking over my body as though in some sort of despondent trance, making small circles and drawing imaginary lines from my breasts to between my thighs. Every time I tried to touch him, he shoved my hand away.

When his focus shifted and he began rubbing his thumb over my entrance, I had to look away. His actions made me feel dirty, like he was searching for any trace of Alex, or perhaps he was wondering how Alex had seen me. Maybe it was something else. Either way, his silence and penetrating gaze unnerved me, making it impossible to feel comfortable.

After minutes of fascination, he abruptly grabbed my legs

and flipped me over. Then he pulled me up onto all fours and spat on his palm, moistening me before thrusting himself inside my unprepared body. I consoled myself that I deserved his rough treatment. I'd betrayed him in the worst conceivable way, and that was his way of regaining his claim on me.

My stomach churns when I remember the begging that followed. Gerard's busy hands and urgent pleas for me to climax. Of course, it hadn't happened, the desperation in his voice alone had made my skin crawl. I try shaking the memory away, but then Alex just fills in the space.

Annoyed at myself for letting my mind wander, I snap on the shower head tap and turn the heat up, hopeful that the boiling water will banish any invading thoughts.

I try focusing on the mundane.

Annabel is coming over, and there are things I need to do. Laundry needs to be folded. Gerard's suits need to be taken to the cleaners, and... *Alex grabbing hold of my skirt.*

Shaking my head, I scrub harder with my loofah. Combined with the hot water, my flesh everywhere, is soon red raw. The distraction doesn't even help.

"You're just dying to be fucked aren't you, Paige?"

Sucking in a breath, I wipe the water off my face. Cursing at myself for mentally reliving what happened, and that I should have, in that moment, slapped Alex's hand and walked away. Why didn't I fight him off?

Shifting the tap handle to produce a more tepid stream, I support myself against the glass and allow the water to cascade over my head. Drowning out the present, I reluctantly let the overwhelming truth possess me. I had loved his seduction, that's why I didn't fight him off.

And then, I'm back there in the shed, watching Alex as he tinkered with the mower, feeling nervous because being alone and so close to him was making my heart gallop.

There was just something about him. How rugged and dirty he looked hovering over the mower, clearly trying to fix it. His effort was making him perspire. Sweat that trickled along his temples, he had to keep lifting one shoulder to wipe it away. He wasn't even aware I was there, just watching him.

"I was thinking." I announced my presence. When his head snapped around at lightning speed, I had to stifle a giggle because I'd actually made him jump.

"Christ, Paige. Sneak up on a guy why don't you?"

"I'm sorry. I just wanted to get your opinion on something." Pulling my braided hair over one shoulder, I stepped inside the shed and leaned against the open door.

"Oh, and what's that?" he said, tossing the screwdriver he was using back into the toolbox before slamming the metal lid closed. He wiped his hands and brow using the cloth that was hanging out his back pocket. I let him concentrate on lifting the mower off the bench and placing it on the floor before I continued.

"That garden bed Gerard asked you to work on, I thought of something else you could plant instead of plain old hairy leaf and golden yellow." Plants I truly thought were ugly.

"Oh, did you now, and what would that be?" Distracted by his still dirty hands and dripping forehead, he moved over to the small basin to wash away the sweat and grime before facing me for an answer.

"Roses."

"Roses?" His look of surprise got buried in the crook of his arm when he used it to dry off his face.

"Yeah, I thought you could plant different colors, make a real show of it. I know they're more expensive, so I wanted to get your opinion. Is the soil suitable for roses?"

Alex folded his arms and leaned against the workbench nodding, "Sure, pH. is good. The soil is a little acidic which is perfect, and it drains well." He shrugged his shoulders. "Should work."

"I'd love to see something amazing, special. Would different varieties work?"

His mouth twitched and puckered into a smirk.

At first, I thought I'd said something stupid. I stuffed my hands into the back pockets of my skirt, growing more nervous when Alex then pushed himself off the bench and took a step closer to me.

"Sure, it can be done. But... You might want to keep it simple though. A few different shades but just one color would work best."

"What color do you suggest?" I tried to keep my tone level and looked toward the garden bed that I could see from where I stood. Then Alex came nearer, so he too could look out the doorway toward the garden bed, imagining. But he was standing too close, half leaning over me, and my heart seemed to stall mid beat. The smell of him was so alluring, my breathing stopped.

He straightened and looked down at me, the slight grin still twitching at the corners of his mouth. "Coral."

"Coral," I repeated, letting out my trapped breath with an obvious exhale. "I'd never thought of coral."

"Yeah, and there's a nice one called Malibu."

"Sounds exotic."

"It's got a nice scent too. Light but spicy." He was sounding dangerously cocky and suddenly I felt gullible and vulnerable about what was transpiring, that I was imagining what I could read in his gaze that was fixated on me. A look that traveled all over my body as though he were taking me in for the first time or mentally undressing me.

"Well, that's good. Done, I'm sold," I said, pulling my hands out from my back pockets, getting ready to leave.

That's when he made his move. He snatched me by the waistband of my skirt and held tight.

"And you know what else?" He smiled and narrowed his eyes. "Coral roses symbolize... desire," he breathed out seductively.

"Well, aren't you just the gardener, Alex." I pushed on his hand, trying to make him release me.

"Oh, I know how to tend gardens all right." He winked and yanked me closer. "You're just dying to be fucked, aren't you, Paige?" He glared down at me with smoldering eyes.

His bluntness shocked me, but what embarrassed me most, my pussy clenched. Heat sped to my face. "What? No." I pulled against his hold. But he saw it in my eyes. I was sure of it. They were tingling with expectation as I familiarized myself with his features up close. And for the first time, I noticed the gold flecks in his green eyes. He clenched his jaw, drawing my attention to his bow-shaped lips that were pulled a little tight. He licked them loose, before smiling with his teeth and letting me go.

"Sure, about that? I think you're lying. You liked me touching you the day we first met, didn't you? That's why you're here all hot and in heat." His expression turned smug. "I bet you want my cock so bad—you're already wet."

His dirty talk had my mind racing. I couldn't move or speak. I just became acutely aware of my heaving chest and thumping heart, and I'm sure my face blushed a deeper shade of pink. He reached for the top of my skirt again, the line of his smile growing more extended as he drew me in. Inch by erotic inch, and he didn't let go.

"Please, Alex, don't," I'd pleaded, feeling vulnerable under his gaze.

"Don't what?" He dipped his head and breathed across my temple, his spare hand reaching around to cup my ass. I was fucking panting, just like he'd said, panting like a damn dog in heat.

Shamefully, I stood motionless, moaning when his hand slid under my skirt and between my thighs, letting out a whimper when his fingers grazed the crotch of my panties.

"Oh God, please don't do this to me, Alex," I groaned softly, pressing my hands half-heartedly against his broad chest. I was so aroused by what he was doing, I couldn't stop blinking and held my breath as his eyes studied mine. What I saw, kept me frozen me in place. He was pure lust, personified.

"Oh, fuck," I wailed when he slid his finger behind the fabric of my panties and touched my lips, brushing gently back and forth, making me tremble. Then he withdrew his hand and smelled my scent, right in front of me.

I'm sure I sucked in all the available oxygen between us, and my shock amused him. Leaning in close, he held my gaze then asked me point blank, "Do you want me to fuck you, Paige?"

I shook my head, but I made no attempt to get out of his hold.

"You sure as hell smell like you do," he murmured letting go of my skirt abruptly, watching me like prey as I tethered on the brink of stumbling backward. My breathing had become so rapid, I felt dizzy and had to steady myself against the door. Alex had me wound so tight, if he had said boo right then, I would have screamed.

Finally, I snapped out of the trance. "Jesus, Alex. That was sooo... inappropriate." I was looking down at my hands, smoothing down my skirt when he moved in so quickly, my head smashed against the wood as he forced me up against the shed door.

He splayed his palms above my head and pushed playfully

into me, thrusting and grinding his pelvis against me. "You're a dead-set fucking tease, Princess."

"Alex." I pushed on his chest. "Stop it and get off me." My concern swelled.

I looked straight at him, determined to give him a mouthful when his expression changed from menacing to something else. "Do you even know how fucking beautiful you are?" he said.

I blushed and looked down at our feet, only inches apart. "Stop it, don't say things like that." But his whispered admission was flattering, and I found myself relaxing the pressure I was applying to his chest.

"Feel how hard you make me," he whispered in my ear, pulling my hand down and forcing it against the large bulge in his jeans. He held my hand there and bore his sin-drenched eyes into mine again, searching for someone he knew was in there.

I felt myself caving. My sex swelling. I wanted to pull away, but at the same time I wanted to feel him, kiss him and bury myself in his chest. I wanted to squeeze what I held in my palm. He lowered his other arm and slipped it around my waist to draw me closer. Then he made me rub him gently.

"Alex, stop." But my command came out as a pitiful plea because I was losing control of my rational mind and my hand was obeying him.

"You know what I'd like to do, Princess?" he said, his rapid breathing matching mine.

I shook my head, disgusted with myself for wanting to know what he wanted to do instead of trying to get away. But I'd forgotten everything. What day it was, where I was, that I was married. I just hung there in his arm like a limp rag doll staring into his devouring eyes, knowing that from the strength in his body—he could do anything he damn well wanted to me. I quivered from the thought as my desire saturated my undies.

He playfully clacked his ivory teeth at me, making me jerk in his arms. He chuckled and flashed a suggestive grin. "I want to eat you out and make you scream." His words were tangled around a solid growl. I moaned and involuntarily slackened, shocking even Alex when he was burdened with my extra weight.

I became sticky between my thighs, and the throbbing between my legs became painful. My eyes must have been begging then, signaling Alex do whatever he pleased to me. Because when my hand fell away from his crotch, allowing my chest to splay wide for him, he seized the moment and cupped a breast, then brought his lips crashing down on my throat. Licking and kissing his way up and behind my ear then whispering, "I'm going to fuck you hard, Princess, so if you don't want it, you better tell me no."

"Oh God, Alex," I moaned loudly. "We can't. I can't." But our bodies wouldn't listen.

Alex had known exactly how to seduce me, and I loved every second.

His blue shirt reeked of musk, sweat and dirt with just a hint of soap. And as I dug my fingers into his rounded biceps, pumped from holding my weight, I morphed into someone I didn't recognize. Reaching up, I held onto Alex's face with both hands, greedy beyond belief. I desperately wanted to feel his lips and taste his minty-flavored tongue from the gum he was always chewing. I only meant to have a taste of him. But I got carried away, lost in the moment, and I let him screw me right there in the gardening shed, amongst the gas fumes and clippings, the pool cleaner, and old paint cans.

There was no slowing him down after that kiss either. His rough hands were urgent, pushing and pulling at the hem of my tan leather skirt, finally sliding the snug fabric up so it was scrunched and nestled around my waist. He tongued behind my ear, sucked on an earlobe, kissed his way along my jawbone before discovering my lips and searching my mouth with his tongue, like there was a pearl waiting for him to find.

Groaning and panting, he fondled my breasts and ass, then drove his hand down into my panties to caress the throbbing part of me. His fingers teased to quench me until I became breathy, helpless, and so wanton I spread my legs to allow his fingers in. Then it was my hands flailing in every direction, trying to get a hold of Alex, a table, any solid surface, as he pushed me back farther and farther into the shed. I ended up against the workbench, breathless, desperate, and eager for more.

I wanted him to slow down, had hoped to have some control over the situation, but he became so fervent, he tore my favorite lace undies clean off. They ended up on the concrete floor, alongside the foil wrapper of his condom, scuffed into the dirt and grease without care. I later had to throw them away, stuffing them deep down the side of the trash can where I hoped Gerard would never see them.

Oh God, why didn't I stop him? The memory of Alex sexing me was still haunting me daily, consuming all my idle moments. I could avoid Alex. Pretend that I didn't want him, that it was wrong and shouldn't have happened. And I had convinced Gerard it was a mistake, swore that it would never happen again. But I couldn't lie to myself. For the last six weeks I'd been reliving every single second in that shed, over and over, driving myself insane.

I squeezed my thighs together, trying to block the overwhelming urge to touch myself, knowing the moment I do, I would be allowing Alex to recapture what he'd wrongfully claimed.

I thought confessing to Gerard would rid me of my

anguish, put an end to what I considered a daily betraying ritual. But Alex was all over me and in me. Every moment of every day. I'd been satisfied with mine and Gerard's sex life, but now, there was no denying the exuberance I felt just getting lost in that memory.

Alex had barely touched my body. The sex had been rough and fast. But somehow, he affected me in a way Gerard never had. I felt free, lost in pure sensation. My mind ceased to function, and I've become hooked like an addict after their first rush, aware now that something else exists. I can't deny what happened with Alex was the most erotic experience of my life. Alex didn't just arouse my mind, he penetrated beyond it, had thrust himself right into my very soul, then pushed me over the edge. That had never happened before, ever.

I stay in the shower far too long, lost in my addictive thoughts. Angry at myself because I'm getting so turned on by memories I shouldn't be reliving.

Suddenly, there's a banging on the bathroom door and it opens an inch. Screaming, I uselessly cover myself with my shaking hands until I get the sense to reach for a towel.

"Whoa, calm down it's just me." A hand, palm up, comes around the corner of the door.

"Alex?"

Thinking it's an invite to enter, he opens the door entirely just as I'm flicking off the tap and securing the towel tighter.

"Christ, what have you been doing in here? I've been waiting in your room for the last fifteen minutes. Are you trying to drain the water supply or something?"

Stepping out from behind the screen, I take possession of the door then close it partway on him. "Do you mind? I'm half naked here."

Alex's cap has returned to its backward position and his sunglasses are stuffed in his slack shirt pocket. I notice he has removed his work boots and socks. I'm not sure if I'm grateful or concerned. When he glances at my feet, I notice I'm dripping all over the floor. Stretching out a leg, I pull the bathmat nearer, but when my pressure slackens on the door, Alex pushes it open and I almost lose my towel. "What do you want, Alex?" I snap. My attention darts between him and my towel, and I try to push past him, Alex leans against the doorframe blocking my way out.

"I heard you calling for me, Princess."

"Stop calling me Princess, and you did not hear me calling. Because I wasn't. Now move."

"Maybe not from this." Alex smirks then drags his thumb along my bottom lip before pushing the tip inside my mouth. I jerk my head back and slap at his hand. "But from here," he adds, tapping my temple.

It takes a moment for me to respond, my brow creasing so firmly, he raises his eyebrows and cocks his head, realizing he's onto the truth.

"Cut it out, Alex. What are you even still doing here, didn't Gerard talk to you before he left?"

"Nope. Just drove past and gave me the finger."

Frowning, I push him away. "Move. If you want to talk, wait for me downstairs." When he goes to grab me, I sidestep him and head for the safety of my walk-in closet.

"What did Gerard say when you told him?"

"That's between him and me, Alex. Go downstairs. No, better yet, just go, period!" I shut the closet door in his face and lean against it, forcing myself to stop desiring a repeat of our escapade in the shed and concentrate instead on what I should wear.

"Fuck, that's harsh," Alex says through the wooden door. Turning, I rest my head against the door. I swear I can feel him on the other side, waiting for an apology or an explanation from me. But what do I say? That I need him to go because I'm constantly lusting after him. That I watch him inconspicuously from the living room while I pretend to read. That I touch myself, imagining his fingers tracing my lip, his hand caressing my neck. I hate being that person. He needs to go.

Alex taps lightly on the door. An insistent little tap, tap, tapping, and cooing.

"Paige," he sings, "What did Gerard say?"

"Look. What happened, happened. All I can say is thank God he forgave me."

Alex stops tapping. I pull on some underwear then jerk a white cotton summer dress off the hanger and slip it on. Finding my tan strappy heels, I clasp them in one hand then pull the door open.

"Christ, Alex," I screech, because even after several minutes of silence I find him still in my room and blocking my way. I sigh noisily. "What do you want?"

Dropping his arms from the doorway, his hands go into his back pockets. "Do you really think he's forgiven you?"

"Yes. But why do you even care? I was just a revenge fuck, right?" I push past him and back into the bathroom to comb my hair, which is futile. It's full of knots because I didn't have time to wash or condition it before Alex interrupted me.

"A what?" Alex leans against the bathroom opening and chuckles.

"Gerard said you wanted your revenge. Is that true?"

The corner of his mouth twitches then he lets out a huff. "No doubt that's what he'd like to believe."

"Well, is that what I was?" I turn away from my reflection. "Gerard steals a girlfriend off you years ago, so you think it's okay to seduce me?"

"I don't know maybe, partly. Mostly I think we both wanted it. But shit, I didn't expect you to just stand there. I was waiting for a sneaky low blow to my nuts. A Kung Fu hit to my throat before walking away. But you just stood there. Fuck, you made me hard." He pulls at the crotch of his jeans, the memory seeming to arouse him.

I toss the comb I've been attempting to use back into the drawer then slam it shut. "I should have stopped you. I honestly don't know why I let you do that to me." I inhale and shake my head, annoyed that my body is responding in places I seem to have such little control over when around Alex. "I'm not a cheater, Alex. I don't want to be a cheater. Even standing here talking to you feels wrong. You need to go."

Ignoring my request, Alex straightens to his full height and folds his arms over his chest, trying to look serious. "Why? Don't you trust yourself around me, Princess?"

"Stop flattering yourself. I'm happily married. You were a momentary lapse in my better judgment."

"Christ! Now, who's getting on her high horse? So, how did he react?"

Gathering my hair, I turn away from him to face the mirror to re-clip my tangled mess. "Who, Gerard?

"Yes, Gerard."

"Hurt, angry, curious, forgiving."

"Sounds like a fucking shopping list, a predictable one."

"What's that supposed to mean?"

"That, is probably Gerard. Predictable, boring. I bet you fuck missionary once a week."

"Alex, stop it." I brush past him and over to my dresser. "We're the ones in the wrong, not Gerard, so don't start attacking him, or is he right? You want revenge? Is that why you're here? You want to ruin what Gerard and I have? What else did he do to piss you off?"

Alex meanders over to the window and pulls back the curtain to look outside. "Are you actually happy with Gerard?"

"What? Are you deaf or something? I just finished telling you I was." I turn away from my dresser after securing my earrings and taking my contraception pill. "Yes, I'm happy. Look at the life I have. I'm sorry you've lost your job here, but this is no good." I wave my finger between us.

Suddenly, his hand goes around his back, and there is a quiet buzzing. Alex withdraws his phone and looks at the screen.

"Speak of the devil." He waves his cell at me. "Ten bucks I'll get to keep my job."

"I highly doubt that," I scoff.

Ignoring his phone, Alex takes a step closer. "You shouldn't have told him, you know. I honestly thought we'd keep it to ourselves, that it was just a quick fuck. I could have kept my hands off you."

But it's not his hands I'm afraid of. It's my own. I don't want to be one of those women. I love my husband, my marriage. Alex was, no—is a distraction. He needs to go.

"Anyway, best I call him back. Face the music." He waves the now silent phone. "See you around, Princess."

I watch him go then press my eyes shut. And as my arms wrap around for comfort, I start begging to God that something will happen to make Alex leave.

6

UNRAVEL ME

W ith my cell glued between my shoulder and ear, I manage to place some homemade multi-colored macaroons on a floral plate and start making iced tea.

"He's still here. In our yard still doing the fucking gardening." I seethe through clenched teeth. "Annabel is here, and I don't want to make a scene. You called him, didn't you? Told him to leave."

"Don't swear and how do you know I called him?" Gerard lowers his voice to a grumble because I've caught him in a meeting. I don't normally call him at work. In fact, it's kind of a taboo thing to do. He prefers a text so he can call back when it's convenient. That is unless it's an emergency. Well, when Alex passed the window moments ago and smiled smugly at me, I decided it is an emergency. After receiving the phone call from Gerard, I expected Alex to get his marching orders, not leer in the window like some sort of predator.

"Because he came into our bedroom, Gerard," I snap, aggravated because he doesn't get it? The man is a threat to us. "His phone rang right in front of me and he said it was you."

"Did he try anything?"

"No. Oh God no. I will not let him touch me ever again." I squat to get ice, huffing and puffing from trying to do two things at once. Annabel arrived early and is waiting for me by the pool. On her insistence, not mine. In the scorching heat. Not to mention being Alex's audience while he continues with the gardening as though nothing is wrong. But everything is wrong. I don't want him here.

"Calm down, Paige. He's still there because I haven't asked him to leave."

"What! Why not?"

"Because Alex isn't my problem, you are."

"What?" I put the glass jug down and climb onto a stool. "How can you say that, when he…"

"When he what? He forced himself on you. Is that how it was?" he questions, in a firm, irritated whisper and I imagine he has had to leave the conference room by now, go down the hall, maybe even into the men's room to get some privacy.

"No. No, of course not."

"Well then, you obviously wanted it."

"Gerard."

"Paige, take ownership damn it! Look, I need to go. The team is waiting for me. I will call you later. Don't worry about Alex, he will not cause you any trouble, he's given me his word."

"His word, are you fucking serious?"

"Goddamn it, Paige, stop using foul language. You sound disgusting. I will call you later. Now is not the time."

I want to scream at him and throw the phone. He doesn't even say goodbye, just disconnects, and I'm left with a silent phone, a headache, and a crick in my neck. I take a deep breath. I need to pull myself together or Annabel will know something is up.

Picking up the tray and ice-filled jug, I continue preparing morning tea, then go back outside, putting on my damn happy face so I can play the I've-got-all-my-shit-together hostess. When clearly, going by my mounting migraine, on the inside I don't have it all together.

The day is unbearably hot. Why Annabel wanted to review the fundraiser list by the pool is beyond me. I'm getting more annoyed by the second that she insisted we sit outside rather than enjoying the air-conditioning. But I'm gathering by the itty-bitty bikini she's wearing under her sheer colorful cover-up, she anticipated a dip in our pool. I'd like to say I shared her enthusiasm for a swim, and normally I would, but not with Alex here. Prowling around like a bobcat. All right, that's me being overly dramatic. In fact, Alex isn't doing anything out of the norm. He's raking up leaves at least twenty yards away, not even looking our way. But how come I can feel him so strongly? Is it me or is he sending out a silent signal? Even at this distance, he reeks of pheromones. *Look at me, look at me* is just oozing out of him. But still I won't look. Unlike Annabel, who can't stop staring at our *'gardener'* as her fingers air quoted earlier when first spotting him.

"Golly gosh, that man is hot. I can practically smell his sweat from here." Annabel lets out a dreamy sigh.

I refill Annabel's pitcher, hoping to get her attention back.

"Well," she drawls. "I bet you're happier than a pig in mud when you're sitting in that living room feasting your eyes." Annabel reaches for her glass and motions toward the house before taking a sip.

"Annabel, stop it. He's Gerard's brother," I retort, though my sudden flushed face must be a dead giveaway that her air quote might have true meaning.

"Well, I reckon he's doing an amazing job, isn't he?" She pulls her cute Chanel glasses down and peeks at him over the frame. "Do you loan him out?" she adds with a seductive murmur, her mouth slowly curling. She becomes enthralled with whatever he is doing, curiosity gets the better of me and I steal a look myself.

My gasp causes Annabel to chuckle and glance at me. Then she's back to watching Alex. He's peeled off his shirt to give his forehead and neck a good wipe. Marching half-naked over to the tap, he wets the garment down then puts the dripping thing back on. We can't stop staring.

"He's doing that on purpose, the devil of a man," Annabel laughs, turning her attention back to her notes. I can't seem to stop watching him though. I think I'm waiting to see if he looks our way, to get confirmation that Annabel is right, that this is all a show for our benefit. He is such a snake. He knows what he's doing to me, pressing buttons I'd rather he didn't.

Annabel snaps her fingers in my face. "Hello, how about some eyes here now? I know it's been painful, but we're almost done for the day."

Her clicking attracts Alex's attention. Twisting, he makes the obvious gesture of smoothing his shirt over his well-defined pecks and smiles.

I look away. "Sorry. I'm away with the fairies."

"Yeah right. I know he's eye candy and tempting, but you're not allowed. That wouldn't be fair. You've already got one drop-dead gorgeous man at your knees. Me on the other hand?"

"That is not what I meant. But anyway... You on the other hand what? Is something going on with Stuart again?" I know I sound a little more confounded than I mean to, and I'm not being judgmental, it's just their relationship seems… overly complicated at times, when it needn't be. Like I'm one to judge. I let out a questionable huff at myself.

Annabel leans in on her elbows, a tight smile sharpening her already defined cheekbones.

"Nothing, I suppose." She taps her pen, stalling.

"Come on, out with it."

Annabel thrusts herself backward into the chair. "Two words. Jenna-bloody-Martín." She tosses the pen then smooths her highlighted brown hair that's pulled tight into a bun.

Grabbing my iced tea, I try hiding my amusement behind my glass.

"What? She's a man-eater and you know it," Annabel says.

"That was three words and no way. Stuart would never do that to you, Annabel." Knowing exactly what she means because every woman in our circle of friends had gone down Jealousy Lane because of Jenna Martín at one time or another. Jenna with her short platinum blonde bob, looking like a Stepford wife at her worst, and a damn Hollywood movie star at her best. The fact she is flirtatious, a superb host, and ridiculously organized doesn't help her cause either. Nor does the fact that many of the husbands use Jenna as a shining example of what, 'One could do, if one put in some effort,' which is obviously the hand Annabel was dealt this morning.

"Stuart compared me to her this morning." Annabel leans forward again. "I was getting Katie ready for school when she handed me a note. You know, the school we pay *lots* of money for, asking parents for help in the cafeteria because they've decided the children might like to see Mommy or Daddy more involved. I work!" she practically screams.

Which is true, some of the time. Online journalism is a fickle thing.

"I said, 'Oh right, not likely, I'm too busy' and I tossed the note in the bin," she goes on. "Then precious little Katie's face fell like Humpty off the bloody wall, so Stuart said, 'Come on, surely you can spare one or two days a month. I bet Jenna has already signed up for once a week, and she works at the restaurant all the time.' Can you believe he said that to me?"

"Oh, sweetie. Just because he said that doesn't mean he's sleeping with her." I smile and reach for her hand.

"I know. I'm just pissed because he makes me feel guilty. But God, it's not like *I* pushed Katie out. Aren't I already doing enough by letting her call me Mom?" Annabel becomes somber, and I know that she honestly feels bad that she isn't exactly maternal. It must be tough inheriting your husband's dead ex-lover's child. Especially when you didn't know she existed until *after* you drove off together with cans trailing and a 'Just Married' sign.

"Well, if it's any consolation, Annie, I think you're doing an amazing job as a mom."

"Thanks. I know, I'll get over it." She tries shrugging it off. But when I let go of her hand, I notice her nails are bitten to the quick and hope there's not more to Annabel's little outburst this morning than what she's telling me.

"Maybe the two of you need to get away, leave Katie with Maude and Trevor.".

"No. Stuart's folks don't need us weighing them down." She fidgets with her earring. "Besides, we've got this fundraiser to organize." She taps the pile of paperwork between us. "See! Work. This is work, right? I shouldn't feel guilty, should I?" she asks, trying to reclaim her confidence.

I shake my head.

"Speaking of Jenna. Are you and Gerard going to their

soirée?" she air quotes again. "I'm dying to meet the newbies, aren't you?"

Annabel sees I'm puzzled.

"Didn't you get the text from Jenna last night? It was a group one, so I know she sent it." She pushes her glasses onto her head.

My phone was inside, and to be truthful I hadn't checked messages since my confession to Gerard. That seemed to take up all my headspace.

"No. What did it say?" I sip from my glass, then rolling the cold surface against my forehead, hoping to keep the oncoming migraine away. Then I notice Alex is on the move with a wheelbarrow full of garden debris he's been raking up. He glances our way. When my stomach flutters, my eyes snap back to Annabel.

"Dinner party next month. She wants to introduce the McEwans. Six o'clock. Sharp," she adds pulling a face to mock Jenna. "I like her, but gosh, sometimes I'm sure she'll drown in the next rainstorm."

When I frown, Annabel pushes her nose up. "You know? She's stuck up, is what I mean."

Nodding, I let out a heavy sigh. When it came to Jenna, that was my pet peeve. Whenever anyone new arrived in the neighborhood, she seemed to make it her mission to be the first to acquaint herself. The problem was, although Jenna could be the perfect hostess, she was also known to fill heads with gossip, tainting everyone's reputation before they got a look in. I wouldn't be surprised if Gerard and I were already painted a subtle shade of snob or dubbed children haters. Which would be unfair. Children just weren't in the cards for Gerard and me and we aren't snobs. Gerard just likes to keep a lower profile than most.

"I'll check my phone later for details," I tell her.

"Let me know what you plan on wearing. I hate it when

you look gorgeous without me. You know, us girls need to stick together to give Jenna a run for her money," she laughs, and I chuckle along with her.

"Hello, Alex," Annabel greets, jarring me. Her southern drawl thick with suggestion. Hopeful he's just passing by, I don't panic until his wheelbarrow comes to a scrapping halt and his heavy boots march our way.

"Mind if I grab a cold drink?" he asks, looking down at me, his shirt still wet and clinging to his body.

"Oh, please do," Annabel answers quickly, her eyes roving and her face lighting up. She taps my hand. "Paige, Alex will be needing a glass."

"Um, yeah, sure," I reply, pushing out my chair. "I'll go get one."

"Nah this'ill do." He grabs my half empty glass and reaches for the ice-filled jug of tea.

"Where you from, Alex, and how do you know so much about gardening? Did you study horticulture or something?" Annabel asks.

"No," Alex and I chorus. I could kick myself. That question was *not*, directed at me and Annabel gives me a curious look. Not missing a beat or giving any thought to the fact he's using my glass, Alex gives Annabel his attention. Now *I'm* sweating all over. Taking a reprieve, I look around the yard acting disinterested and hoping my feelings aren't melting the makeup off my face. As if the humidity wouldn't already be doing that job.

"I just like nature. Grew up in Portland mostly. Why, where are you from?"

My head snaps around in time to see Annabel straighten. "Oh, you're funny." She waggles a finger at him. "What? You mean you can't tell by my accent."

"Yeah, I just wanted to hear you admit it." Alex chuckles.

"Cute and funny. South Carolina and proud, I'll have you know." Annabel raises her curved brows.

"I can tell," Alex chuckles, and I assume he means because of the heavy accent she seems to ramp up rather than down.

"What took you so long coming to acquaint yourself with the friendly folk here at Point Dume, Alex?"

Alex shrugs. "Timing, I guess." He guzzles down his drink and puts the glass on the table between my resting hands. "It's hot, ladies. I might need to cool off in the pool later," he says, deviating from the conversation. "Would that be all right with you, Paige?"

I clear my throat. "Um, I'm not so sure that would be appropriate, Alex. You're just here to work, aren't you?" I smirk and push the glass away.

"Paige!" Annabel slaps my hand. "Of course, that would be all right, Alex. But why wait. Cool off now, we won't mind." She bats her thick eyelashes, and with a smirk, her almond-shaped eyes turn into seductive caramel portals.

Alex laughs. "It's cool. I'll wait until you're finished."

"Why, you're just a spoilsport, Alex." Annabel pouts at him.

"Annabel," I gasp. "God, don't mind my friend here. I think she needs tossing in the pool." Despite myself, we all start laughing.

"Thanks for the drink." Alex gives me a wink before walking away.

"My goodness, just as well he's your brother-in-law," Annabel whispers, leaning in on her elbows, still watching him.

I act as though I'm busy with my notes. "Not to mention I'm married, Annabel."

"Well, yes, I guess there's that too." She sits back, her hands getting busy with papers making me wish I could concentrate on what we're here to do.

But through my peripheral vision I keep watching Alex, and all I can think about is spying on him from the living room later while he swims. Will he still have a swim? Would he have taken my comment seriously? Had I been serious? Should I be serious? Christ, this is bad; he needs to leave. I don't know right from wrong anymore.

"What's his deal anyways?" Annabel asks, breaking through my reverie.

"Sorry?"

"Alex. How did he just drop in from nowhere and end up working here? Is he hitched? A guy that sexy has to be seeing someone, doesn't he?" She's inquisitive because I've never talked about him. I'd clammed up tighter than a fish's butt because only months after he first arrived here, I'd done the unthinkable. All Annabel knows is that Alex comes from up north and he is Gerard's stepbrother. I'd neglected to tell her he'd done time.

"I don't think so, at least I've never seen him with anyone." I pick up my pen and start jotting down notes, hoping she'll drop the subject of Alex.

She doesn't.

Leaning forward, she taps the top of my hand. "Paige, fill me in."

I steal a look to make sure Alex is well out of hearing range. "He's done time, all right, but don't go getting paranoid or telling anyone. He was only twenty-four at the time, and he must have been going through his stupid stage, because he was armed as well."

"Really?" Annabel eyes him all over again. I roll my eyes when she looks back at me. "What? Ain't I allowed to look?"

"Like you haven't been." I crinkle my brow. "Anyway, Gerard offered to help by giving him the gardening job."

"Gosh, that's generous and trusting." She smooths her

hair again then rests her chin on her knuckles hanging on to my every word.

"I guess. Honestly, I would have been happy to keep doing the gardening."

"What for?"

"Why not? It's not that hard."

"Not hard. Did you notice all that sweat dripping off him? Besides, aren't you still tied up with Harper's Bazaar, three days a week?"

"Yeah, but it's sporadic."

"That's a shame. Still, I think you're lucky, Paige, sometimes I'm jealous of you."

"I am lucky." I put my head down and pretend I'm working, silently praying that I haven't in fact blown my marriage, secretly wishing I could talk to Annabel about Alex and Gerard and the mess I've created. But I can't, I'm too ashamed. Not that Annabel would condemn me, she proved that when I told her about my alcoholic mother and how poor we were after my father left. I expected she might judge or at the very least gossip, but she hadn't. *"We've all got a past, sweetie,"* she reassured meat the time.

Annabel looks at her phone, I assume for the time. "Next week I hope to have the list of sponsors for you."

"Okay. What about the Everette committee, are they still interested in helping?"

Over the next hour, we go over what still needs doing in preparation for the Brave Hearts Foundation's success. Our aim is to raise funds for extra staff and equipment for the cardiac ward at the LA Children's Hospital.

Annabel stops riffling and looks up briefly. Shoving her notepad to the side, she reaches for the pitcher of iced tea. "Paige, when you get a chance, can you ask Gerard if he's heard of a man named Ronald Klaneski?" She refills our glasses and hands one to me. "He's been coming around our place talking with Stuart about some business venture. He's also into construction. Stuart says he doesn't want to talk about it with me just yet because it might all fall through, but there's just something that doesn't feel right about this guy."

"Let me write his name down so I don't forget." I jot a note on my pad. "I'll ask him when he gets home. What makes you think Gerard might know of him?"

"Well, firstly, he's an attorney and they hear stuff most of us don't, and secondly, I overheard one of their conversations and Gerard's law firm got a mention. I'm not sure why, but I think maybe Ronald uses them."

"You know most stuff is confidential."

"I know, I'd just like Gerard's thoughts on his character, that's all."

"I'll see what I can find out. I'll text you if he knows anything."

"No. Call me, please. Stuart has a habit of looking at my phone and heaven forbid I put a passcode on it. That's a surefire sign, you've got something to hide," she says, making me feel extremely uncomfortable because I realize she is right. I never lock my phone and yet I never ever thought about the fact that Gerard did, he has always locked his phone and I'm not talking about his work phone either, that's always unlocked, but for as long as we've been together, Gerard has always locked his private phone. Suddenly I'm questioning why.

After a quick lunch and seeing Annabel off, I go to the strip mall to get away from the temptation that is Alex. While I'm out, Gerard finally calls like he said he would.

"Sorry it took me so long to get back to you. How are you feeling now?"

"Not much better, so I'm in town getting drinks. Do you need anything? I know I do." My tone is short because I'm still angry and questioning Gerard's sanity.

"What's the matter?"

"Why haven't you asked Alex to leave? He was there flaunting himself in front of me and Annabel today, stripping off his shirt and asking if he can go for a swim." I snatch up some potato chips. But when Gerard doesn't answer straight away, I put them back and grab an extra bottle of wine instead.

Gerard chuckles. "Well, it is in the nineties today, Paige. Are you forgetting he's out in the heat working on a pretty garden for your enjoyment? Why didn't you just go inside?"

"Why are you siding with Alex, and why aren't you asking him to leave?"

"Like I said this morning," he says calmly. "Alex is not the problem, you are."

"What?" My shoulders slump. "You've changed your mind about us, about me." I put down the bottles of alcohol I'm holding because I'm starting to feel lightheaded.

"No, Paige, I haven't changed my mind about us, but you understand I married you, not Alex. He can do whatever the hell he likes. You, on the other hand, are my concern. You wanted something I wasn't giving you. That's what our problem is. Not Alex."

I look around the convenience store, feeling like we're on loudspeaker. Then I'm searching for a chair. I need to sit before I fall. There are alarms bells going off and I can't think straight. Nothing is making sense. I want Alex gone. Gerard doesn't, even though he was betrayed by him.

"Now, unless you were lying last night, that you do in fact have feelings for Alex, then he's no longer a threat, is he?"

"No, but…"

"But what, Paige? You didn't want him. It was forced, but you don't want to tell me."

I groan when my heart lands in my bowels. Why does he keep saying that? "No." I whisper using the shelving to steady myself.

"So, these are the facts. Alex is a conniving cunt. Excuse my profanity, but he is. Regardless, we need him right now. You on the other hand are my wife. Rather than let you go, I'd like to understand what you need. Given the circumstances, I feel I'm entitled to figure this out my way, or is this going to become about you?"

I'm shaking my head, but he can't see me. He snaps out my name, startling me. "No," I reply quickly.

"Look, all I'm doing is giving you and Alex the benefit of the doubt, that's all. People make mistakes. Alex had his reason. I understand that. But what was your reason? That's what I'd like to know."

"There was no reason."

"Yes, there damn well was and you know it. Stop lying to yourself."

I can't speak, my heart is racing, and my head is pounding. There's no blood left to make my vocal cords respond.

"Paige?"

"I don't know, it just doesn't seem right. How can you let him get away with it?"

"So, you want me to punish him?"

"Yes. He betrayed you."

"No, you betrayed me. You're the one who is bound to fidelity. Alex made no such promise to me."

Holy fuck. Has he gone insane? I don't know what else to say.

"Paige, if you don't trust yourself around Alex, then maybe you're the one who needs to leave."

He's right. He is so damn right. My bottom lip quivers. I can't believe this is how he's handling my cheating on him. He's handing me the ball, the chain, the lock, the key.

"I've asked Alex to have dinner with us tonight."

Now I need a bucket, my eyes scan the shelves, the room is spinning. Dinner, fucking dinner, like we're all good friends. "No," I snap.

"Yes. I want to talk with the both of you. Together."

"About what? Gerard, please don't ask me to sit down with the both of you. It will be awkward. I can't do it. God, how many times do I have to say it was a mistake? I think I'm going to be sick," I ramble on, making my way out of the convenience store and into the fresh air in search of a bench seat.

"Paige, calm down. Your life is not about to end. It's just dinner."

"But why?" I wail, drawing attention to myself before sinking onto an already occupied bench seat. But I don't care if I'm overheard anymore.

"I want to discuss something with the two of you."

Something is wrong. This is not normal. Why did I confess? How do other husbands handle infidelity? I think of my father, how he slapped my mother in front of me when he found out she was cheating. How he packed his bags and left that same night. Left me alone with her and her best friend the bottle. Alex was right. I should have just kept my mouth shut.

"Paige, are you still there?"

"Yes."

"Look, I just think it's important that we talk."

After a long pause, I finally agree. "Fine, but I'm not speaking about any of it. I've told you what I have to say."

"That's fine, I'd just like you to be there. Oh, and if you wouldn't mind cooking a nice meal."

I screw up my face and shake my head. "So, what should I cook then, a banquet?" I ask flatly. He ignores my sarcasm.

"Seafood. Let's have seafood, and you know what my favorite is."

I did. Oysters Kilpatrick. And make that—by the dozen!

7

PERSONAL

The drive back to Point Dume is painfully slow. Peak hour traffic has congested the highway, and it's not until I take my exit that I can pick up speed. When I arrive home, as expected, Alex's truck is no longer in the drive. I'm relieved he's gone, but the large parcel of seafood and a bag of alcohol I carry inside is just a big fat reminder he'll be returning later tonight. Alex. Alexander and me, together in front of my husband. I groan aloud and kick the French door shut with the heel of my wedge sandal.

After unpacking the groceries, I put away the packet of cigarettes I purchased. It would disgust Gerard if he found out I'd bought them, and I'm questioning why I did, since I haven't smoked in years.

I hide them in the back of the laundry cupboard, certain I'll be digging them out later tonight and chain smoking; while I sit on my suitcase waiting for a taxi.

For the rest of the afternoon, I attempt to get some assignments finished. I have three photographs that need re-touching before I forward them on to my editor and a proposal to write for an international advertising firm I'm aspiring to work for.

After two hours, having only completed one touch-up and my proposal, I hit send and relax, taking in the office Gerard and I share. His side consists of shelves laden with thickly bound leather books, numerous pinboards and neat stacks of folders balancing on his beechwood office desk. Everything is orderly. Twisting my chair, I glance around my side of the room that Gerard graciously cleared for me the first day I moved in. It's dominated by my large Apple computer on a glass desk. The top is messy, which Gerard is forever pissed about, with printouts, Manila folders, markers and reference books for inspiration.

I have one photo adorning a wall—a blown-up picture of me and Gerard in Dublin. Taken the night Gerard surprised me with tickets to see Snow Patrol, my favorite band at the time. It was the first and last time I humiliated myself by jumping up and down squealing like the schoolgirl I was, shocking Gerard and clearly showing my age. I screw up my face at how underdressed I am compared to Gerard. Him in a blue polo and me in a sloppy gray sweater that I bought from the merchandise stand.

I took the selfie to mark the beginning of my new life with an incredibly handsome and generous man. It's grainy and a poor example of my work, but I love it. My eyes sting knowing I've triggered something, and now our life, well, *my* life, feels unpredictable. I don't like unpredictable. I took comfort knowing what was next. I think about Alex's comment this morning. "I bet you fuck missionary once a week." Christ, how transparent are we? But it's more like three times. So there, Alex.

Turning off my computer, I do some household chores to keep my mind busy then start on dinner. By six, I'm done. I've showered and changed into cargo pants and a loose-fitting top, something comfortable and unflattering. I find my cozy spot in my chair and look at my phone, staring at the home screen for a few seconds before my thumb activates the contact list. Scrolling through, I chew on my thumbnail, still undecided if I should call Sheree when her miniature face appears. No matter how many years pass, looking at her still gives me an ill feeling, settling like a doughy bun threatening to repeat. I'm not sure if it's the fear of Gerard finding out I've kept in contact with her, or that it's getting harder every time we speak to sensor what I tell her about my life. I'd already confessed to her about Alex, only days after it happened. Which I should have kept to myself. If only she knew the enormity of my betrayal. I push the thought away, and regardless that my heart is thudding against my ribs, I press dial.

"Hello, Sheree speaking." Her voice sounds flat and there's a moment's pause from me until I surmise she must not have looked at the screen before answering.

"Hi, it's me."

"Hey, sweet pea, what's going on?" She sounds like she is on the move.

"Have I caught you at a bad time?"

"No, but just hang on one sec."

I can hear her talking to someone then laughing. Drawing my legs beneath me in my chair, I pick at the polish on my toenails and make a mental note to get them redone soon.

"Sorry, I was just saying goodbye to Darby. He's heading out to Cameron's stables to pick up a horse."

"How is he?"

"Still gorgeous and amazing in bed. So, what are you up to, please tell me you can come and meet him soon? Did I tell you I've moved in with him?"

"No! God, I only spoke to you two weeks ago. Isn't that a bit quick? I mean you've only just met him."

"Well, I haven't exactly moved all my stuff in yet, but I'm staying there more than at Mom's now. When are you coming back to visit?" I can almost see her pouting like she did when we were kids, complete with hands on her hips.

"I'm busy with a fundraiser, and well, work's still crazy. Besides, I don't think Gerard would appreciate me leaving home right now." I make yet another new excuse.

"Why?" She sounds confused and I don't blame her. Sheree doesn't know about my life with Gerard. But if there was one person who would judge me for marrying an older man, it would be Sheree.

I pause for a moment before I answer, and as always, she doesn't rush me but gathers by the length I hold my silence that it's big.

"You're not in danger, are you?"

I think about that for a moment. Am I in danger?

"No, not really."

"Oh, come on, what kind of answer is that?"

With a thickening throat, I ask after her mom, hoping to steer the conversation away from me.

Both only children, Sheree has been my best friend since childhood. More like a sister to me, she had the life I dreamed of, and to this day, I can never understand why she befriended me when we were thrown into the same class in third grade. She lived on the right side of town. The side my mother was always criticizing because that community took care of their perfect nuclear families, which put her to shame.

"Mom's fine, don't change the subject."

"I don't know. I'm confused, and I don't want you to judge me."

"When have I ever judged you?" she says in sharp syllables.

I clamp my eyes shut and silently wince then sigh. "Sorry,

it's just... you would never do something as ridiculous as I've done."

"What's that supposed to mean? Come on, pea, what's going on?" she prods forcefully. Then it hits her and she gasps, "Oh no. Gerard found out about Alex, didn't he?" As soon as the words spill from her mouth, my innards are in knots.

"Yes, but only because I told him," I blurt.

When she gasps, I need to move the phone away from my ear. "Why would you tell him?"

"How could I not? God, I don't even understand why I let Alex near me. It's not as though my husband is an asshole, and Alex is a knight. If anything, it's the other way around, I think." I second guess myself.

"Well, what happened? Does Gerard want a divorce, do you need to get out? He didn't hit you, did he?"

Sheree fires one question after another, not letting me get a word in. I half suspect she's packing an overnight bag while using her work phone to get time off as we speak. Me being in danger is the only thing that would get her within a ten-mile radius of the city.

Her last comment makes me scowl. "Why would you think he'd hit me?"

"I don't know, the way you keep the man a secret I have no idea what he's capable of."

"It's not like that, Gerard's just a private person and you know I'm ashamed about who I am. Where I came from." It might sound like I'm ashamed of Sheree, but it's the only thing I can think to say to explain why I never wanted to introduce them or invite Sheree to our wedding. If only she knew the truth. I rub my forehead and shift in the oversized chair.

"Gosh, you're hard on yourself Paige. I'm sure Gerard

loves you regardless of your upbringing," she consoles, obviously not offended.

And she's right that Gerard accepts me, but then, Gerard has no idea I'm still in contact with Sheree, and if he knew, he'd be furious and most likely not speak to me for days. But Sheree is my rock. The only person I trust and keeping her friendship is worth the risk of getting caught. It's just such a shame I need to keep our lives separate for that friendship to work.

"So, what's the verdict then? Silent treatment?" she asks, as if reading my mind. "He wants to level the score, cheat on you in return? What kind of man is he, Paige? Not the forgiving type I bet."

Again, I'm surprised by her comment and ask why she'd think that.

"I don't know, maybe it's the memory of how my parents worked. Dad was jealous as hell and gave Mom the cold shoulder if she ever went against his opinion. I can't even imagine what he would have done if she even looked sideways at another man. Men can be such assholes, I'm glad they separated."

I uncurl my legs and cross them instead, swallow hard to remove the lump that's formed in my throat.

"Well, thankfully Gerard's not like that. I'm not exactly sure yet, but we're all having dinner tonight. He wants to discuss something."

"What's there to discuss?"

"I'm not sure, that's why I'm calling you. What do you think he's thinking?"

"How would I know? I don't even know what the man looks like. For God's sake, get more active on Facebook, will you? At least post the wedding photos you keep saying you will. How am I meant to keep up with your life if you don't post stuff except those crappy cute cat memes you seem to like?"

"What? I love cats, so shoot me," I joke.

Over the next half an hour, I fill Sheree in on the details of the last couple of days, then talk about the mundane. I learn she's starting a new job doing admin work for an online firm and hear more about Darby, who runs a racehorse spelling ranch and ironically is packed like a mule himself.

"Too much information but I can't wait to meet him," I state, not for the first time, as if I'm jotting down a date on my calendar.

"Yeah well, I've given up on meeting your elusive husband. I can't believe in five years you've never brought him home to meet me."

"Well, you could always come here," I taunt, though I know she never would. Since getting lost as a child on a school excursion, Sheree hates the city.

Then we are back on discussing why Gerard wants a meeting, throwing theories around that have us in hysterics.

"Maybe Gerard wants you to measure them both and make a verdict," she suggests with a chuckle.

"Hilarious."

"Well, we better not put Darby in that comp, he'd win hands down," Sheree goads, making me laugh again. I'm glad she manages to ease some of my tension with her light-hearted comedy.

"Bragger."

"Oh, pea," Sheree sighs. "I hope it all works out okay. You've been so happy. I need to go, but keep me in the loop."

Just then, I notice headlights pointing up our driveway.

"I will. Have fun with your mule." I hang up hastily, satisfied that I called.

Finding the remote, I turn on the news. It's what Gerard

likes to watch when we share drinks before dinner. The usual information spreads across the screen, boring me immediately. Lowering the volume, I get up and pace for a second, then sit down again. Then I'm berating myself for being nervous. It's just dinner and talking, right?

Expecting Gerard to come through any second, I'm surprised when there is a knock on the front door. Uncurling from my comfortable position, my bare feet welcome the cool tiles as I stride from the carpeted living area and down the entry hall.

"Coming," I call out when the fist on the door becomes demanding.

Just as I'm reaching for the handle, it twists, and the door is thrust wide, knocking me off balance when the wood collides with my forehead.

Immediately, I slap both hands on my forehead. "Holy mother fucking shit!" I wail, cradling my throbbing head.

Looking between my forearms, a stunned Alex stands in front of me and it takes a few seconds for him to respond. I figure he doesn't know whether to apologize or reprimand me because of my vulgar language. Looking amused, he addresses the latter.

"From the mouth of a princess comes gutter talk. Sorry, I thought you said come in." He pulls my hands away to inspect the damage. He screws up his face, then rubs a gentle thumb over the wound while apologizing. His genuine concern acts as a ripcord to my heart, alarming me. Twisting away, I rub where a large egg is beginning to form and head for the kitchen.

"Don't worry about it. I just need to ice it. What are you even doing here so early, anyway?" I ask, as he follows me. Suddenly, his hand is pressing into the small of my back, making me jump.

"Gerard said to come whenever," he states pulling open

the freezer drawer for me and extracting a handful of crushed ice. I search for a Ziploc bag, holding it open so he can pour in the shards.

"Thanks," I mutter, avoiding looking at him directly. Taking the bag of ice to my head, I turn to check on the small marinara cob loaf that's warming. "You can wait in the living room if you like, I've still got some things to do in here," I lie, hoping to send him away.

"Do you need any help?"

"No." I pull open the oven door, still avoiding his gaze, the bag of ice firm against my forehead. Then Alex is slipping up behind me as though he's interested in what's cooking. When he grazes himself against my ass, I go rigid.

"Something smells good," he states close to my ear.

"Alex, don't." I slam the oven closed and push him away with my back. Putting more distance between us, I pretend to be busy with dishes. He's amused by my sense of unease because he chuckles before leaving the room.

After only a few short minutes of me pretending to be busy, question why I'm disappointed he left the room, I know I'm being stupid trying to avoid him. Taking the ice with me, I go back through the double doors where I find Alex holding the one framed photo of Gerard and me on our wedding day. He looks up when I enter, then puts the photo down and without an invitation, heads toward the bar like he suddenly owns the place.

"Sure, help yourself," I say sarcastically, coming farther into the room. I take up what seems to be my preferred position lately, behind the couch, and watch him intently.

"Thanks, I will." Reaching the bar, he holds up the bottle of Glengoyne. "Nice," he murmurs turning to me.

"That's for Gerard."

"I see." Alex puts the bottle down and goes for a beer from the fridge. There's the sound of gas escaping when he twists off the cap, followed by clinking when he tosses it in the sink. "Any idea what this is all about?"

"No, and I'm not comfortable about it either. I feel like a complete idiot. I shouldn't have told him."

"No. You shouldn't have," Alex agrees. "Mind if I sit?" he's suddenly cordial. "Knowing Gerard though, he'll make a big show of how powerful he is or some shit. Make us feel like assholes who need to grovel for his forgiveness or something."

Huffing, I take a seat on the opposite couch to him "I thought I'd already groveled. I figured he'd forgiven me last night. Now I've got to put up with this bullshit of walking on eggshells now more than ever. God, why did you have to go and seduce me in the shed?" I bring the ice bag back to my head while Alex nearly chokes on his beer. Composing himself, he wipes his mouth with the back of his hand.

"Me, seduce you?" He fails at pulling an innocent face.

"You're not going to deny you grabbed me then tore my undies off."

"Well, you didn't exactly tell me to stop, and telling Gerard was your idea, not mine. I wouldn't have said jack shit to him. It could have been our little secret, Princess." He winks then takes another gulp of beer. It's only now that I notice he's rather dressed up, at least compared to his work clothes, which is how I've mostly seen him. His long-sleeved shirt is rolled up to the elbow, showing off his thick tanned forearms, and is tucked into his belted jeans. The oval buckle he's wearing is tarnished and old and the only word I can make out on it is 'Colt' but I have no idea what it means. When he hears the ice jangle in my hands as I bring it to my head, he flinches.

"It's gonna bruise."

"I'll be fine," I reply dryly, then make my way to the bar,

banishing the bag of ice to the sink. "I wasn't expecting you to be here before Gerard. I don't even get why you're here."

"Thanks?"

"Well God, I mean, what's there to discuss? What did he say to you this morning when he called?" I pour myself a glass of red wine, locking eyes on him as I make my way back to the couch.

"Well now, I guess that one's between him and me isn't it?" He cocks his head, suggesting two can play at the game of 'I'm not going to tell.' Taking a sip of beer, he leans forward on the couch and adds, "But if you beg, I might tell you."

"Ha, ha, like that will ever happen."

When he flops backward into the couch, I catch a whiff of his cologne I didn't smell before, it's faint and smells musky with a hint of floral and spice. The same one he wore the day we first met; I think.

"You smell nice," I blurt before I have time to sensor myself, and instantly my face catches fire.

Alex smiles. "I'd want to smell good. This shit costs a bloody fortune just because it's got some French bitch's name on it."

I know instantly he's referring to Chanel.

"So why buy it then?" I raise my brows, challenging his pique.

One corner of his mouth curls and his eyes turn on the heat. I shift on the couch, curling my legs beneath me and taking my eyes off him and on to the news broadcast because he's starting to have that effect on me I both love and truly hate.

"Why do you think?" he challenges.

"I don't know, you're the one telling the story." I take another sip of wine, hoping to look uninterested. I can feel his eyes boring into me, but I refuse to look his way. I know he's trying to play with me, and I hate how easily I become engaged.

"Because I like it, and so do—the laadiees," he brags, sitting back against the couch and bringing his ankle up to rest on his knee.

"Well, there you go then." I steal a quick look at him, then watch as he fiddles with the buckle of his boot.

"What time is Gerard getting home? Doesn't he realize I've also got shit to do?"

I shrug, then look down into my empty glass, surprised I've drained the wine in record time. Alex gets up and holds out his hand for my empty glass. Staring up at him, I can't help being mesmerized. His rugged face and penetrating eyes say so much without him even speaking.

"Want another one?" he asks, smiling salaciously at me.

I nod. My body responding to his proximity in an instant so that the hand holding my glass becomes sweaty, and I worry I might drop it. When he takes the glass but doesn't move away, my lips involuntarily curl to bite themselves and my breath stills.

"And what about a wine?" he clarifies, making my eyes widen and breathe out his name.

"You know what I need to do, Princess?" he asks crouching in front of me, pushing the coffee table away with his back, then running a hand along my thigh. I watch his movements and I'm sure I look like a stunned deer, because I act like one. Miraculously, I'm able to shake my head and meet his gaze.

"Finger fuck you before Gerard gets home."

"Jesus Christ, Alex." I push on his shoulders. Hard.

He stands and starts laughing. Then shakes his head. "It's so easy to get you fucking panting, Princess. What the fuck are you doing with an old fart like Gerard?"

"You're an asshole, Alex." Exasperated, I rise to go check

on the cob, pushing him farther out of my way as he tries to grab a hold of me. "Stop it, what are you doing?" I twist and squirm trying to free myself.

Squaring me to face him, he attempts to make me look at him, but I can't. I can feel my eyes glassing over and ready to spill. He is deliberately tormenting me, and I don't understand why.

"Why are you here, Paige? Are you just one of those tarty little gold diggers out to get his money? Is that what you're doing here?"

"Stop it, you know nothing about me, or Gerard for that matter. I'm in love, asshole. That's what I'm doing here."

"Pfft, yeah right," he shoves me backward, and it takes a moment to right myself.

"Why are you being so mean to me?"

"Me! Mean to you? You let me fuck you, and then you try throwing me under the trainwreck that is your life thinking that will make it better, when clearly, you're fucking hot for me."

"I am not. It was a mistake. Just because it happened doesn't mean I love you."

"Who said anything about love? But if you were in love with Gerard, I wouldn't even be on your radar. You're so easy to read. I'm surprised this is the first time you've fucked someone else. Wait, maybe I'm not the first." He twists his head, his eyebrows arching, and I could slap off the smug look that crawls across his face.

"Stop it, just shut up. You don't know anything. You're just a jerk who wants to ruin my marriage. I love Gerard, adore him. He is the only man I've ever been in love with, so you, you just stay the hell away from me." I storm out of the room before my tears confirm he's affected me on a much deeper level.

Suddenly, I'm shaking, furious that I let him get to me this way. Abruptly I turn around, intent on having it out with him. But then he's there. Standing against the doorway of the kitchen, his hands in his pockets just looking at me. A look of pain and sadness that I can't understand. I purse my lips but the tears slip over anyway. Regardless, or maybe it's because he has rattled me, I want to fall against his chest. I want him to hold me and tell me that everything will be all right. That it's normal what I'm feeling, that I shouldn't be scared, that it's not a crime to suddenly feel so damn alive when he's around. But then blinding and sobering, there are headlights coming up the driveway, and for the first time in my married life, I'm disappointed my husband is finally home.

8

WICKED GAMES

A s soon as Gerard enters the house, the atmosphere becomes thick with conflicting energy. Coming from the kitchen, having checked on the cob loaf, I'm fidgety and nervous. Alex approaches from the living room with a fresh beer in hand. He doesn't smile, just acts indifferent as though he's stumbled onto something, he can't work out yet, and Gerard seems charged like a new Copper Top battery.

Gerard first greets Alex then puts down his briefcase by the doorway. He leans in quickly to plant a kiss on my lips. Uncomfortable by his display of affection in front of Alex, I pull away abruptly and reach for the bruise on my head.

"Christ, what happened to your head?" Gerard asks, throwing a look at Alex before turning back to me. Gerard misses the frown that crosses Alex's brow before he retreats into the room with a huff and the shake of his head.

Lifting my chin, Gerard examines my bruise in better lighting.

"Door," I tell him.

"Nasty." Gerard kisses the bump gently then takes in what

I'm wearing. "You're not planning on staying in those clothes, are you?" he whispers, glancing around for Alex.

I look down quickly as though I've forgotten what I have on, then pull my ponytail through my palm.

"Well, yes. It's not like it's a formal dinner or anything."

"Maybe not, but you know I like you looking nice when we have guests," he argues.

My heart races. Wouldn't it be better if I didn't look nice? Gerard takes hold of my elbow and guides me toward the stairs.

"Alex, would you excuse us while I take a quick shower? Help yourself to another beer," he calls offhandedly over his shoulder as we pass the double doors. "Sorry, I'm so late. Carter has a new client. He wanted me to sit in on the meeting," Gerard tells me of his day. "Has Alex been here long?"

"No." My voice comes out high-pitched.

"No, no, that's not what I mean." He pulls me onto the top landing in front of our bedroom, then turns me to face him. Taking my hands in his, he looks again at the bump on my forehead. "I hope you put ice on that?"

I nod.

"What I meant to say was, I hope you weren't feeling uncomfortable being alone with him. After our talk this afternoon, I realized I should have been more sensitive given your past. I hope you can forgive me." He drops my hands and enters our bedroom. Not bothering with a response from me he adds, "I should have called to let you know I would be late."

"No. You should have given Alex a time when you'd be here as well instead of telling him to come whenever because actually—I was feeling uncomfortable." I cross my arms over my chest then follow him.

"Paige, please drop the attitude. I just apologized, didn't

I?" Gerard makes straight for the shower leaving me to sort through my wardrobe looking for something casual yet nice to wear. Gerard's out in no time at all followed by a cloud of soap. Naked, he is still drying his hair, and water is beading on his lean body. His long legs are solid at the top but pale, almost iridescent. Gerard is still fit and firm, most likely because of his daily squash matches with work colleagues he's continued over the years.

"So, despite our arguments, did you have a good day?" he asks loud enough for me to hear him in the closet.

"It was all right I guess." I glance out the doorway at him in the bedroom before returning to my task.

Too hot, too skimpy, too big. I push past my jeans and skirts, then pull out a silk shirt but put it back immediately when I consider the seafood meal ahead of us.

"How was your lunch with Annabel then, aside from the entertainment?" he chuckles, tossing his towel on the bed.

"Ha, ha, very funny. I'm trying to do the right thing here, so I don't understand why you're not taking me seriously."

"Am I allowed to say life's too short?" He shrugs, pulling open a drawer to find underwear from the dresser before coming into the walk-in closet with me to select something to wear. He goes for his cream easy-fit slacks and a long-sleeved navy shirt. How come he gets to wear something comfortable and unassuming? I shove the hangers roughly aside. With a quick spray of cologne, he's done but I'm still sorting through clothes. It's the first time in ever that I can't decide what to wear. I'm concerned that anything I put on will send the wrong message, I'm just not sure who to.

"What's the matter?" Gerard asks, rolling up his sleeves.

"I don't know what to wear."

Gerard strokes my jawline with his thumb. "Wear something sexy," he suggests grabbing hold and kissing my pouting lips.

Why? I want to scream. Is he hoping to make Alex jealous? Rub his nose with the fact that I am his wife, that he can look but don't dare think about touching me again? I hate this. It feels like it's all a game to him. Standing on tiptoes, I wrap my arms around his neck and kiss him, nuzzle my nose into his cheek, inviting him to mess with me, to reassure me he has truly forgiven me.

"I already feel sexy, right here with you."

Gerard grabs my wrists and forces me away.

"Alex is waiting for us, Paige." He pulls a playful scowl.

He's up to something I'm certain of it now. But what?

"Why do we have to have Alex over for dinner, anyway? I don't like this. Being reminded of hurting you," I snap, falling away from him and sorting through my clothes again.

Gerard stands taller. Grabs a firm hold of my arms and turns me to face him. "After dinner, we will talk, the three of us. I'd like some things explained, and then I might propose something."

"Like what?"

"That's for later, but please if you can do one thing tonight, Paige, it's hear me out. It might sound strange at first, but... well, let's just wait until after we've eaten and I have my answer?"

"Answer to what? What's this all about? Why can't we just talk, just you and me, why do we need Alex here?"

"Because I want to give him a piece of my mind for starters, and I need to ask him something."

Gerard must notice my face pale because he pulls me closer trying to soothe me.

"What are you so worried about?"

"I don't know. It just doesn't seem normal. It's like you think we're children who need a talking to."

"Well, are you?"

"No!"

"Then stop acting like one. Dry your eyes, put on something nice, then come downstairs. I think we all need to eat—it's getting late and we've a lot to discuss."

"Please promise me you won't fight."

Gerard reaches forward, strokes my hair until he reaches the clip then undoes it, letting my long hair spill loose.

"There, that's better. And that will depend on Alex. Will you be down soon, then?"

"Do I have a choice?"

"No. Not really." His tone is very matter of fact. He brushes my cheek before leaving me and heading downstairs, his answer confirming what has changed between us. He now sees me as immature and irresponsible. Not his wife. Not his equal.

Five minutes later, I come down the stairs and go straight into the kitchen. I'm determined to get dinner over with as quickly as possible. Pulling the marinara cob loaf from out of the oven, I place it on a dish and then take it through to the living room. I've slipped into my knee-length, backless, black and gold dress. It's a little more playful than I'd like, much too sexy, but I'm hoping my choice will appease Gerard. I've left my hair down as Gerard implied, and when I walk through the door carrying the dish, both men turn to look at me.

I lock eyes on Gerard first, standing at the bar facing Alex who is sitting on the sofa. A smile and an eager nod from Gerard tell me he appreciates my appearance. Alex, on the other hand looks tense, making me wonder what they were discussing before I arrived. Grooming his facial hair, Alex gets to his feet.

"Mind if I grab another beer? " He's at the bar before

Gerard even has time to respond, cracking open a Budweiser and taking large gulps like he's just arrived from the Nevada Desert. He tosses the cap into the small sink again and glares at me. Freezing me on the spot.

"Just help yourself tonight, Alex." Gerard comes toward me. "Honey, would you like a wine?" He places a hand on my bare back, getting first dibs on the cob loaf.

"Maybe later," I murmur. I need to keep my wits about me in case things blow out of proportion. But within moments Alex is already in front of me, holding the wine I poured earlier but neglected because of Gerard's arrival.

"Let's get on with this then, Gerard." Alex thrusts the wine at me. Seeing my hands full, he snatches the platter from under Gerard's face and plonks it on the table. "If you've invited me here so I can watch you play happy couple, I'm bored already," Alex cuts through any and all pleasantries.

"Alex," I gasp nearly dropping my glass.

"The dip is delicious, Paige, perfect as always. Alex, you should try some," he suggests unfazed by Alex's outburst and not answering him. Gerard winks at me before setting himself on the couch and reaching for the remote to change it from television viewing to the sound system. I take a seat beside him, hoping to show my support, even though I'm still questioning whether he deserves it. Soon, music is playing quietly in the background, but still the tension in the room is so thick, it's palpable.

Alex gives me a look I can't decipher. Is it annoyance, concern, or is he just uncomfortable? "Well?" he badgers.

Gerard sits forward and tucks into the dip platter again, washes it down with his scotch, taking his sweet time before answering.

"Like I told you. I just want to talk, that's all." He looks around for a napkin. Leaping to my feet, I'm grateful for the excuse to get away briefly. It's nearly unbearable the feeling of angst coming from Alex. I'm sensing any minute now their voices will rise along with their fists.

"So, get on with it then," Alex is saying when I come back in the room, serviettes in hand.

"Thank you, Paige." Gerard pats my knee when I take a seat next to him and uses the napkin. Then Alex is shaking his head and rolling his eyes like he's disgusted. I'm feeling more nauseous by the second. There is something strange going on. I can't tell whether Gerard is giving us a false sense of security or he legitimately wants everyone relaxed about the situation. And why is Alex so angry now?

"Alex," Gerard starts. "You know what you did was a low act. And if it was revenge you were going for, what happened between us was years ago."

The balls of muscle on Alex's jawbone flex. "Well, I had plenty of time to think things over, you know."

"I understand that. So, are you admitting you acted out of spite then?" Gerard squeezes my knee.

Bitting the inside of his mouth, Alex looks to me then rubs his jaw. Please say yes. Please, please say yes. I beg with my eyes. He turns away and looks at the couch as if deciding whether to sit back down. He doesn't; instead, he crosses his arms.

"Yes, all right then, that's how it was. Now what?"

"I'd like you to admit that to Paige and I think you owe her an apology for using her to get back at me."

Gerard sits back into the couch and sips on his scotch eyeing Alex.

Alex purses his lips but can't stifle his amusement. I can't believe he's covering for me. I gulp my wine and wait.

"I could do that, but as you once said, 'shit happens.'" He cocks his head to the side. "I haven't heard an apology from you yet."

"That it does, Alex. Shit does happen, and sometimes it happens to innocent people." I look down at Gerard's hand when he rubs my leg but his eyes are still fixed on Alex. I look from one to the other, acutely aware that they are having a pissing competition or something. "And as far as an apology from me, I had hoped that employing you was enough. There are other handymen out there, you know."

"So, you asked me here tonight to give me a piece of your fucking mind in front of your wife? So she can see how much of a man you are? Well get to it, tell me I'm a cunt and to fuck off and I'll be on my way. Thank you for helping me out, Gerard, but I don't play games."

Alex places his beer on the coffee table then looks at me. "Thank you for your hospitality, Paige, and yes I am sorry for what I did to you."

A inferno surges through my entire being. He's prepared to take all the heat and his genuine apology punches me straight in the solar plexus. My fingers creep to cover my mouth. I don't want to accidentally say anything to make things worse. I look at Gerard, wondering if this is enough for him to forget about what we've done. Gerard nods, looking thoughtful.

Hooking his thumbs on either side of his buckle Alex waits for Gerard's rebuttal. When it doesn't come, he presses, "So am I to pack my shit up and get out of your life then?"

"You haven't finished the gardening yet," Gerard replies, reaching for more food. Alex pulls his head back and frowns, no doubt curious, like I am, why the sudden change in tone, not to mention topic.

"What?" Alex's short reply is dripping with impatience.

"How far along are you?"

"What does it fuckin' matter?"

"I'd like to know."

After a short pause, Alex gushes out that apart from

building the pergola over the fishpond and trimming some bushes, he's almost down to maintenance only.

"But I guess you'll need to find someone else to do that now," he rushes, shifting his weight and crossing his arms again.

"No, you'll be doing it. I'm not asking you to leave, Alex."

I snap my head around and grip his arm. Ignoring my shock, Gerard takes another sip from his glass and continues assessing Alex.

Alex juts his head. "What the fuck is all this about then if it not to send me on my way?"

"I need your help with something else now." Gerard states.

Alex glides his hand across his jaw, looking from Gerard to me. I give a little shrug.

"Is that right?" Alex bends to reclaim his beer. I take another sip of wine, intrigued, now that the worst part of their conversation seems over with.

Gerard leans forward, helping himself to more dip, slopping some on the table. I reach for a napkin and clean it up.

"Can I trust you to be honest with me, Alex?" asks Gerard.

My head pops up and my eyes go wide. Alex frowns that I'm cleaning up Gerard's mess before he averts his attention back on him.

"Sure. It's not like the cat ain't out the bag."

I toss the napkin on the table and prepare myself behind my glass of wine.

"Can we agree that I've looked out for you since you got out?" Gerard asks.

"Yes, yes, you have." Alex tilts his bottle in a kind of salute.

"So, I'd like you to stay for dinner. I'd like us to be comfortable with each other again because I suspect what happened may have actually been a godsend."

A godsend, it wasn't a godsend; it was a mistake.

Alex lets out a hearty chuckle. "All right, if you say so."

"I'm serious. There's something that's been bothering me for a long time now and I think you may be the answer."

I'm looking at the side of Gerard's face. My expression is fixed, watching his jaw move as he speaks while one thousand questions race through my mind, but I can only latch on to one. How can our betrayal be a godsend?

My heart pounds. The whooshing in my ears is deafening. Then Gerard is turning to me inquiring about our meal. "What?"

"Are we ready to eat?" He looks from me to Alex. His face placid, his eyes sparkling.

"I g-guess s-so," I stammer.

Gerard squeezes my thigh in reassurance.

"Sure." Alex gives a shrug. "Why the fuck not?"

"Alex. Please. Language," Gerard says.

Then to my dismay—Alex apologizes.

9

BREAK MY BABY

Over a meal of oysters Kilpatrick, deep fried calamari, garlic prawns and fresh oven-baked cod, we sip our drinks and make small talk. With the lights down low and a candle flickering, the atmosphere became relaxed. Gerard and Alex have reverted to easy conversation, retelling stories from their childhood and filling me in on details I never knew. When the conversation drifts to the why and how Alex ended up in prison, he tells stories from his six-year stint on the inside. I find myself riveted then laughing out of pure astonishment, or maybe it's the wine.

"Was it really that bad?" I ask, referring to the pranks the inmates got up to just to amuse themselves.

"Put it this way, Princess, if the warden hadn't found Tresidder duct taped, buck naked the next morning and fired his ass, he woulda got iced." Alex says, referring to the then newly recruited officer. "Christ, he was just too young for that kind of work. Seriously, at best he would have ended up someone's bitch and I'm not talking about just the dudes behind bars getting to him either," he adds, nodding his head. "The screws are just as fucking bad." He throws Gerard a look that tells me he doesn't respect the hierarchical system Gerard is affiliated with.

Pushing myself back in the chair, I nod that I understand. Well, almost. "What's iced mean?"

"Killed, Princess."

"Wow. I can't believe you've been through that, Alex. It sounds horrible." I let out a small huff and then smile because after weeks of anxiety, I'm finally letting go of the shame I've been carrying around. It seems Gerard's idea to have dinner wasn't so bad after all. Despite the betrayal, Gerard and Alex are civil. I watch Alex quench his thirst from all the talking then turn toward my husband, feeling warm and elated that he's been able to rise above it all.

He's been watching me, waiting until I've heard enough and now there's a pause in the conversation and without warning, Gerard becomes serious.

"Alex?" he says, his gaze slowly shifting to the swiveling glass in his hand. "Earlier, you agreed to be honest with me." He looks up from the vortex he created in his tumbler.

"Yes. Yes, I did." Alex smiles my way and whips his eyebrows up.

"Well, I'm hoping that when you fucked my wife, you at least made her orgasm?"

Alex nearly spits his gulp of beer over the table.

My smile evaporates, my breathing halts, and my heart freezes in my chest. Like literally stops for a micro-second.

Alex palms away the beer that escaped his clamped lips and my breath stays caught, horrified now that Alex is looking amused. He clears his throat. No, no, no, no. Please don't tell him.

"Yes. I mean, isn't that half the aim of the game," he answers proudly, believing his consideration in giving me pleasure was why Gerard asked.

"I did not," I interject.

"I knew it!" whoops Gerard, slapping his hand lightly on the table, dismissing my admission completely.

My face falls into my hands. The room becomes small and oxygen depleted, silent except for the soft music playing in the living room. Gerard rubs my back.

"Thank you for telling me the truth, Alex. Paige was never going to."

With my face still in my hands I shake my head, slow at first then faster. Looking up at Alex, I say with conviction, "I faked it."

Then I look at Gerard and repeat myself, "Seriously, I faked, it."

"No, you did not." Gerard rubs at my leg. "Why would you?"

Alex looks confused. Gerard just smiles.

"It sure didn't feel like you faked it," Alex says, not helping.

My face falls into my hands again and I groan.

"Am—I—missing something here?" Alex frowns.

Feeling sick to the stomach, I get up from the table. "I'm going to bed," I announce. But Gerard grabs my hand.

"Please, Paige. We need to deal with this." He holds onto my hand tightly, looking up at me with pleading eyes. Sinking slowly back into my seat, and not knowing where to look, I stare at the dirty dishes in front of us. I should clean up, sober up, and go to bed, but he's been so forgiving, surely I owe him my allegiance.

Folding my arms over the table I look from one set of expectant eyes to the other. Expressing that I'm not impressed with this sudden turn in the conversation. Gerard touches my hand, then looks at Alex.

"How did you make her climax? Did she come more than once?"

Alex sits back, folding his arms over his chest, finally taking us seriously. "What's going on?"

"Just tell me how you made her get off, Alex," Gerard asks again, a little more forceful.

I can't speak, can't think. I'm so embarrassed I'm close to laughing about it. Gerard deceived us. He lured us into admitting more than I ever wanted to share and now he wants the details. The cocktail of emotions raging bring on an instant headache. This will destroy our marriage.

Alex reaches for his beer and takes a long pull. Avoiding all eye contact, he cradles the bottle between two hands and begins peeling at the label. "I don't know. I was just fucking her and played with her clit. Isn't that how you do it?" he mumbles slowly looking up, his eyes darting from me to Gerard.

"Yes, but Paige has never come for me."

"What?"

Now it was out. The ugly truth. Right there at our dinner table over leftover oyster shells and empty beer bottles.

"I'm going to bed, Gerard." I shove my chair out, past horrified now. Gerard reaches for my face and pulls me in, so our foreheads connect. I wince when he presses on my bruise.

"But, Paige, this is a good thing. Don't you see? He made you come. You had an orgasm!" Gerard sounds excited, as though I've been accepted into some stupid sorority or something.

"So, are you guys telling me... Paige has *never* come before? Fuck, man. I mean shit! What a fuck." Alex sucks in an extra deep breath and runs his hand back and forth over his head, making his hair stand in all the wrong places. Then he's rising to his feet. "I'll get going, let you two talk it out. Gerard, I'm sorry, man. Paige? Shit, I don't know what to say, sorry, I guess."

"Can you sit down, Alex? That's only half of the reason I wanted you to come here tonight."

Alex looks to me for a clue, but I'm motionless, disgusted, ashamed. I take another sip of wine and stare back down at the table, find a stain on the cloth, wonder whether it will come out in the wash. Did I fold that load earlier? I try detracting myself with the mundane, but the moment Alex speaks, I'm drawn to his face through up-turned eyes.

"Go on then. What else is on your mind?" Alex asks, not sitting but opting to rest his hands on the table and lean in.

Gerard turns to me. "You promised to hear me out, Paige, so don't interrupt until I'm done." There's a firmness to his tone, making it sound more like an order than a request.

My heart has become a loud repetitive thud, and I'm sweating everywhere. This talk is unnerving me in all the wrong ways, and there's a pulsing between my thighs that I can't explain.

"I'd like to make it clear that Paige and I have regular sex."

Alex frowns then looks at me.

"Gerard, please," I interject quickly, "Alex doesn't need to…" Gerard's hand snaps up in front of my face to silence me. I shake my head and stare at the table. Hello, dying of shame here.

"And by no means is it boring. But I've tried many techniques and toys trying to make her climax and nothing seems to work."

"Seriously Gerard, this is embarrassing," I moan. "Can't you swap tips and tricks over a beer at some club when I'm not around? God!"

"No, you need to be here for this, Paige, and you promised to hear me out, so stop interrupting. Please," he adds, noticing my lips pucker and my jaw clench. "As I was saying. We've tried many things with no results, and well, I'd like to see how you made her climax."

"Are you fucking serious right now?" My eyebrows, I imagine, may have joined my hairline in mortification.

"Please don't swear, Paige." Gerard snaps.

"You do." I glare at him.

Gerard shakes his head looking exasperated, but he's not deterred. He turns to Alex again. "I'd like us to have a three-way, you know a ménage à trois," Gerard explains, perhaps thinking saying it in French will somehow glorify it.

Alex nods, looking a little humbled.

"Would you be willing, Alex?" asks Gerard.

"Sure. It's not like I haven't had a three-way before—it's just usually with two chicks."

"Of course, you'd agree," I snap.

Alex stands fully upright, his palms outward in surrender. "Shit, sorry. No, I mean only if you want to Paige. I ain't doing anything unless Paige agrees. No fucking forcing her or any of that shit."

"No, of course not." Gerard turns to me again, taking both my hands in his. "Paige. I want to watch you have an orgasm, honey. I want to see you lose yourself, lose control. I want to see your eyes when you climax. I want to know how he did it."

I feel sorry for him. He's lost his mind. My betrayal has pushed him over, turned him into a crazy person.

"Please, for us. It will make us stronger as a couple I'm sure of it." He sounds so desperate, so excited at the prospect but I just can't. I'm too afraid it will ruin our marriage. I figure if we cross that line, there will be no going back. Once is manageable, in time we'd forget what I'd done. But if I go back again and he sees me enjoying myself at the hands of another man, I'm certain it will eat him alive.

"No."

"But Paige." Gerard stands, his chair scraping loudly across the floor and almost toppling over. "It's been almost five fucking years, five years! Ever since we first started dating, I've been trying to make you come. Then Alex comes along, and you're wet from just looking at him. I want to watch my wife have an orgasm."

"Don't cuss, Gerard."

"Don't get smart with me. You think it's all right to have sex with another man and then the minute I want something in return you decide to have a bloody conscious."

"That's because what you're asking for is insane. What husband wants to see his wife getting screwed by another man? It will eat at you. Don't you realize that?"

"Don't assume to know me and what I might or might not like, you don't know a thing."

"Obviously."

"Christ! Calm the hell down you two. And Gerard, stop trying to guilt her into it. This is my fault, not hers. It's all right, Paige. I'll just go. I'm the one who fucked this up."

"You didn't fuck it up, Alex. It was already fucked up. I was just being too pretentious to admit it," Gerard snaps out, shoving his chair into the table before walking out of the room.

My mouth drops open and my eyes sting. "Gerard," I groan, but within seconds our bedroom door slams.

"Man, I sure didn't see that coming. Paige, I'm sorry. If I'd known I wouldn't have said anything."

I burst into tears.

"Aw shit." Alex runs his hand over his head and drains his beer, then moves as though to console me. I try waving him off. I want my husband not Alex. But Alex walks around the table, rests a hand on my shoulder, and sighs. "I'll talk to Gerard. Maybe I can give him some pointers or something, shit I don't know."

"Do you know how lame that sounds?" I brush my tears

away. Alex crouches, twists my chair, so he's eye level with me. "What's wrong with me, Alex?"

"There's nothing wrong with you, or Gerard. Some women just can't get off." He wipes a stray tear off my jaw and smiles. "Although I've yet to come across one," he says, trying to make a joke. My mouth curls just slightly. "Nah, seriously, there's been a couple, I'll admit that. Often it's something in here." He taps my temple like he did this morning. Standing, he squeezes my shoulder again.

"But there is something wrong with me, Alex. I know there is."

"Don't say that, Paige."

So I'm not overheard; I reach for his hand and pull him back down.

"But there is." My stomach flip-flops that I'm admitting this to him, but I want to understand it myself, so I go on. "What you did to me in the shed—I can't stop thinking about it. You were rough. And at times, you hurt me, but you made me have an orgasm."

Alex grimaces. "Shit, I'm sorry. I thought you liked it." He reaches out to wipe more tears from my face.

"That's the problem, Alex. Obviously, I did like it. In fact, I loved it," I say through a congested nose. "I love Gerard, I really do with all my heart, so why haven't I been able to orgasm with him?"

"Like I said, Princess, it's all in here." He taps his own temple then stands. "You've got to work this shit out with Gerard, he's your man." He smooths my hair. "Go see a shrink or something, I dunno, but I should go. Let you guys get some sleep."

"I guess you got your revenge?" I reach for my used napkin and blow my nose.

"This is not what I wanted, Paige, and revenge has got nothing to do with it. I'm a guy, I like to fuck. You seemed to want it and I honestly thought it would be something that we'd keep to ourselves. I meant what I said this morning. I had no intention of getting between the two of you."

For some reason, his last statement hurts. It's as though he wants to wash his hands of me now. He came into my life and shook it up. Saw the loose wingnuts and decided a little fiddle wouldn't hurt. And now the stupid wheels have fallen off. Back away from the mess, Alex, get away now, I can imagine him thinking.

"I hate you, Alex."

There's a minute flinch from him as he stares down into my face. "Good. Maybe it's best we keep it that way then," Alex says, walking away. Leaving not just my eyes burning, but also my chest, because it feels like he just broke off a piece of my heart.

BRIEF ENCOUNTER

I went to a psychiatrist just after I married Gerard. Only once. As soon as I mentioned my husband was eighteen years my senior, she told me I had dependency issues that most likely stemmed from my childhood. It felt like I was standing in front of an X-ray machine. I'd only been in her office for a little over fifteen minutes. It shocked me she figured me out so quickly. I never went back. I had no desire to relive a past where my adoring father abandons me, leaving me alone to look after a self-destructive alcoholic mother. I should have gone back, though, and worked through my issues. But sometimes, the past is just too dark to revisit. Instead, I ran away. From everything, including myself. Mostly myself.

I'd gone because I'd started having nightmares, and because Gerard encouraged me to go. My nightmares always revolved around a car accident. The car I'm in gets launched into the air. The next thing I'm aware of is the black swirling water as I submerge. When I panic that I might drown, the vehicle floats to the surface. Then I'm standing on the roof as it bobs in the middle of a lake that has no banks that I can see. I know it's a lake because people are water-skiing past me with the feeling of a memory attached to the scene. I want to swim to shore, but I understand that I don't know how to swim. I always wake up screaming. But I never know why.

I haven't slept a wink all night. Gerard managed to, but only after many hours of tossing and turning, finally succumbing around three. Watching him sleep, I'm clueless to what's in store for us now. I'm sure in Gerard's mind, last night should have resulted in a positive outcome, but I've disappointed him—again. I stare at his slightly parted lips, imagine angry words spewing forth from now on and forever. I can feel it radiate off his warm body. He'd been able to forgive me because he thought there was an answer to our problem. That he could somehow turn the incident into a positive thing. But a three-way with Alex. That's insane. I ask myself why, but I don't go looking for the answer.

Morning is pressing behind the curtains, some light slipping between the cracks. Slowly, it works its way along our wall and then our bed until it highlights the contours of Gerard beneath the blankets. I think about the Snow Patrol's song "Crack the Shutters." Remember how Gerard had whispered, well yelled, into my ear during the concert that it was his favorite song of theirs. That it resembled how he felt about me. More tears slide down my face. Gerard is my everything, my life, and I can't imagine a world where he doesn't adore me anymore.

I search his face as the room becomes brighter. His hair is tussled from what little sleep he had but his breathing is relaxed, for now. I want to run my fingers along his full lips, kiss them. I want to make love but question, will he ever want to again? My pillow gets soggier by the second and I imagine I must look a mess. I roll onto my back and stare at the ceiling. I haven't shut my eyes all night. Running through the night over and over and then thinking about the sex with Alex. Every time I imagine myself with him, I pulse inside. I think about how I tried to lie. Saying that I faked the orgasm and then wondering why on earth I've never just faked it with Gerard? I should have done that. What an idiot. All those times I could have soothed his ego just by moaning and wailing like Meg Ryan.

Encouraged by the thought, I roll back over to face him and find him awake. My hand instantly reaches to cover his cheek.

"Hi," I smile warmly.

When he doesn't return my smile, a lump constricts my throat, and my eyes burn again. I stroke his stubbled cheek faster, desperate to get a reaction from him. I bring my face closer to kiss him, to make up for last night, but he grabs my wrist.

"Stop it, Paige."

"Please Gerard, I'm sorry. Don't you realize I said no because of how much I love you?"

"Do you?"

"Yes, yes, I do. You know I do." I reach for his face again, straining my hand in his tight grip. For a moment, he just stares straight at me, holding my hand away and contemplating something. When he releases my hand, I snatch his face between both hands and kiss his lips, over and over telling him I love him over and over. When his hand finally rests on my hip, I slow down my frantic pursuit. Subdued, I stare longingly in his eyes. He's still not smiling, and it's shredding my heart to pieces. "You said you forgave me?" I remind him.

"I've forgiven you for cheating, Paige. I've already told

you that. But I can't forgive you for denying me what you gave Alex."

A loud groan escapes before I have time to stifle it. "But I don't want to deny you that pleasure Gerard, I just don't think we should do it with Alex."

"Who then? Pick someone else. We can go online and join a group. There would be hundreds of men who would love to make love to you."

"No, Gerard, don't be insane. You, I pick you. I want you to make me come. Please, let's keep trying. I just never realized how much it bothered you. You never said anything to me. Make love to me. Please, I know I can climax for you."

Gerard's phone vibrates and sings out a tune that is his alarm. He goes to move away from me, but I wrap my legs around his. Tangle myself around so we can talk things through. I hate the thought of him going to work thinking I don't love him anymore. We need to work through this. I need to know I'm forgiven.

"Paige, stop it. I need to get up." He tries freeing himself from my vice-like legs. "And you've known it bothers me. You can't even climax when I go down on you. Now let me up."

"No."

"Paige."

"No. I want you to make love to me. I'll get myself off."

"Paige, you're being irrational and that's never worked before either. Now let me go."

Gerard's phone bumps into the glass of water amplifying the sounds. He wrenches himself away, rolling so he can silence his phone. I still have my legs entwined in his, making it impossible for him to get away without a real struggle. Once his phone is quiet, he turns back to me.

We lay side-by-side facing each other.

"I can come. I know I can. Please don't leave this morning

without trying. Last night brought it home to me just how much it matters to you."

"But doesn't it bother you?"

"No!"

"Oh, come on, seriously?"

"It's never bothered me, I swear."

"Then why did you fuck Alex? What were you looking for?"

"I wasn't looking for anything. It was a stupid thing to do. A stupid, ridiculous mistake, he's not even as good as you. It was quick and rough."

"Pfft, yeah right."

"Gerard, it's true. You're more handsome to me than anyone. Ever!" I add.

He lets out a sigh and shakes his head at me. "Is that right?"

Relief floods me when his body slackens, and his hand snakes up so he can run his thumb across my bottom lip. "I don't want to do anything that would destroy our marriage, Paige, but I have to be honest. The fact that I can't make you orgasm so hard you scream and quiver—it makes me feel old."

"You're not old. You're sexy and a good lover. It's me, it's me." I whisper, stroking his face, trying to make him understand that he's not to blame.

Slipping my silky nightie up and over my head, I expose my breasts, then climb to straddle him between my thighs

"I really need to go to work," he smiles, fixing the sheets I'm getting tangled up in.

"I think you should call in sick," I tell him, twirling his chest hairs between my fingers, relief flooding me when his hands run up my sides until he brings them around to cup my breasts. My nipples respond instantly, puckering beneath his fingers and he swells beneath me, his cock finding a resting place between my folds. Grabbing my ass and rocking me gently, he tries helping me along, still talking, eager to have himself understood.

"You know I love you, and would do anything for you?" Nodding, I tell him that I know, and I think of all the times he has showered me with love and gifts and surprises. Random bunches of flowers being delivered. Arriving home to find an outfit laying on the bed and an invitation to meet him at a restaurant, a driver already arranged. "Having you in my life answered my prayers. You made me happy and I'm just sorry that for whatever reason it was, I wasn't enough. Is it my age? Is that what you don't like, do I repulse you?"

My tears spill over and I've stopped trying to arouse him or myself. He said, *made* him happy, past tense.

Outside, I can hear birds chirping, a neighbor's child shouting out, and then a distant mower. The sound reminds me of the weekends I'd spent at Sheree's as a teen. Us sunbathing in her backyard while her father mowed the lawn. The hot sun bronzing our bodies until her father snuck up and threw a bucket of icy water on us, sending us squealing around the backyard. Gerard's words just now feel like that bucket of freezing water, except I'm not laughing and squealing. The biggest ache finds a home behind my rib cage.

I search his concerned eyes, my lip trembling. I've hurt him. Slowly I lower myself over him and nestle into his neck. My stupid moment of weakness, and I've crushed the confidence out of this adoring man, whom I owe so much. "You could never repulse me, Gerard. I love you. I always have."

Gerard makes small circles on my back with light fingertips, kissing my temple and ears. "Don't get upset, honey. Just tell me what you need. How can I excite you? Is there something you would enjoy that you're afraid to tell me?"

"No." I mumble into his neck, wiping my tears away. Lying because how I can tell him I came with Alex because he pinned my hands, and just took what he wanted? That his unchecked passion sent my mind into a spin until I couldn't process a single thought? That I became 120 pounds of putty that fell apart around his hands, his knee, his cock, his lust for me.

"Are you sure? Because you know you can tell me anything. I mean I might have my own desires that I've never told you about and together we can make it work."

I lift myself off him and stare into his face. "Like what?"

Pushing me over, Gerard is on top of me in a flash. Wedging himself between my legs and pressing himself against me.

"Well, I've always fantasized about you sitting in a chair and playing with yourself while I watch."

I give a little shrug and smile. "That's do-able," I say, taking hold of his moving hips, feeling him swell between my legs.

"What about using a toy on yourself, like really fuck yourself with it?"

I grimace a little, never quite liking dildos. "They're so—plastic though."

"I suppose that wouldn't make you come anyway." He sounds a little childish and reminding me why we are having this conversation. His rubbing increases in speed, getting himself harder. Then he leans in for a kiss, firm and demanding before reaching for his phone to check the time. "That's why I think a real cock would work," he continues. "And I get to watch. I keep imagining you in the throes of lust and ecstasy, that I'm there just staring into your beautiful eyes, watching your lips swell and turn bright pink." Gerard slides himself gently inside until I'm full, and gasping. "Alex can lick your pussy, make you suck in your breath, hard, like you did just then," Gerard keeps commentating excitedly, his rhythm slowing down. I wrap my legs around him, my finger digging into his sides. "While Alex fucks you," Gerard says, thrusting roughly into me. "I want you to moan and pant into my mouth as I kiss you." He lets out a growl before diving onto my lips.

But his references to Alex while inside me is unsettling. I want to be present, but he's sending me into the past. Reliving Alex's touch, his greedy rough hands. His gentle lips but threatening teeth on my earlobes whispering how horny I make him feel. I press my eyes closed, wishing away the conflict until Gerard thrusts roughly between my legs again. Where is this aggression coming from?

"I want him to fuck you hard and for you to be looking at me. To truly draw me inside when you climax. Oh Christ, that would turn me on." With a throaty moan, Gerard closes his eyes and throws back his head, pushing deeper with his arching body. A little unprepared, I let out another gasp trying to accommodate his enthusiasm, my body protesting slightly. He smiles at his prowess, his eyes turning their deepest shade of blue whenever he gets aroused. I whimper when he grows even harder. He is the perfect man, really. So handsome, so smart and mine. I reach between us to stimulate myself, desperate to bring myself closer to climax.

"I love you, Gerard, please never doubt it."

"I know because you're getting wet, aren't you? Try to come for me," he coaxes.

I shut my eyes and murmur, just allowing myself to fantasize, imagining Alex is looking me up and down. He's not saying anything, just looking at me, wetting his lips then smirking. *You want me to fuck you don't you, Paige?* I relive him saying, making me heat up. But I can hear the mower in the distance again, it's annoying and distracting because it's making me remember Sheree's dad staring at me, and I can't work out if it's the sun or him that's making me hotter, and then I felt the moisture pooling, my pussy swelling. I force my imagination back onto Alex watching me.

Gerard pumps slowly as I massage vigorously. Faster. I scream in my head. Fuck me like you can't get enough. With my eyes still firmly closed I grind myself against Gerard, wishing he wasn't behaving so controlled. Then I'm picturing Alex again. He's walking around me, eyeing me up and down then stops behind me and crouches down. I don't turn around, just stay perfectly still as he runs his hand, his thumb leading the way, slowly up between my thighs. My leg wiggles a little like he is an annoying fly, and I imagine him slapping my ass, making it sting, but my pussy clenches in anticipation of where he wants to put his thumb.

I whimper aloud, then moan and begin my impression of the female orgasm. Allowing myself to fantasize, try to recapture the moments in the shed with Alex, just before I came undone.

"Oh, yes. Oh God, yes."

"Are you getting close? Just let yourself go. You're safe here with me, just let it come. Open your eyes. I want to see your beautiful green eyes," Gerard begs. "Come with me. Christ, you're so wet. I make you wet. You love me fucking you don't you?" he breathes out in a heady rush, impaling me with another thrust, closing in on his release. My eyes open and chills run through me, causing my insides to twist and a numbing to spread through me. Not wanting to let Gerard down or the frustrated tears to come, I keep moaning my award-winning act.

"Oh God, yes. You feel so good, you're so deep and hard. Oh God, yes, I like that," I coo.

"Yes, oh yes. Ah huh, hmmm, yes." There's a gasp, a moan, and I close my eyes readying for the finale.

Gerard holds still. When I open my eyes, he's looking at me. His expression is dark.

"What?"

"You were going to fake it."

"Nooo, God, don't stop." I grab his hips, pulling him closer, trying to make him thrust. But he's become rigid and his erection is waning.

For a moment he smiles, but there must be something in my expression.

"You won't come," he states.

"Yes, I will. Keep going. It doesn't matter if I don't climax, anyway. I'm still enjoying it." I reach out and touch his face but his hand comes flying between us, slapping my hand, then roughly pulling away from me.

"It does damn well matter."

He has pulled the blankets back with him and is crouching between my legs, leaving me feeling exposed. I try pulling some blanket toward myself, but Gerard stays firmly in the way. He places a palm between my legs and begins rubbing.

"Please, honey I need you to have an orgasm for me, even just once," he pleas, his thumb finding my clit.

"Gerard, honestly, I still love it. I don't need a climax to enjoy it."

"I just don't understand," he says, inserting a finger inside me, still massaging my sensitive spot. "You were right there—I could feel it."

"You're putting too much pressure on me Gerard." I halt his overactive hands before he's snatching them away from me.

"Well, doesn't this tell you we need help?"

I pull myself up into a sitting position and glare at him.

"Stop it. You've become obsessed. Thousands of women don't climax. It's not a big deal."

"You came with Alex," he shouts back. "It's me, isn't it?"

"No, Gerard, it's not you." From nowhere, heat seems to rush up my neck, forcing me to cover my eyes.

"Well, did you get off with your boyfriends before me?"

"No." I mumble, still hiding beneath my hands. I don't admit that that's because there weren't any before him. That would only confirm how inexperienced I am.

"Are you telling the truth?"

"Yes. I promise." I join him on my knees so I can throw my arms around his neck and hug him. Then I'm grabbing his face between my hands, pulling him down to meet my lips. "It's me, Gerard, it's me that has the problem." I peck his lips over and over. "Something just happens when I get close, it's like I go numb, down there," I say, kissing him again. "In all honestly, I think it was a rare fluke that I came with Alex, I really do." Sounding a little too nonchalant, I rub the top of his thighs in reassurance, then glance around the room, almost forgetting that it's a weekday, and he needs to get ready for work.

Gerard pulls back, shaking his head. "No. You don't love me."

"What? Of course I love you. Don't say that."

Gerard maneuvers himself off the bed. I'm quick to follow, wrapping my arms around him as he tries retreating to the bathroom, pressing my face against his back. "Please don't be angry."

He goes stiff and pries himself free.

"Gerard."

"I love you, I really do," he says, his head hung low and staring at the carpet, his back is still to me. "But I need to know."

"Know what?"

He sucks in a lungful of air. "How he made you come, and whether you can do it with me there."

"Gerard." I place a hand in the middle of his back, hoping he'll face me. He doesn't. Instead, he walks away mumbling,

"Otherwise, Paige, I think our marriage is in trouble."

11

BROKEN

Gerard doesn't eat breakfast, but that's because I don't cook him any. I watch as he moves about the kitchen getting coffee. He goes between his office and the living room, carrying his cup, acting busy as though gathering things he needs to take to work. He comes through to the kitchen from the office with folders, then returns them and comes out with different ones. He makes calls I know aren't necessary and I can't stop my eyes from stinging. Trying to work out how Gerard's comment can make any sense at all. I'm damned if I do and I'm damned if I don't. What the hell does he want from me? I'm so angry now, I could punch him.

I'm sitting at the dining table, shivering. The air conditioning is too cold, but I can't be bothered turning it off. I'm holding a cup of cold coffee with my feet pulled up off the cold tiled floor. Everything is cold, including Gerard. Including me.

"What time will you be home tonight?" I ask when he returns once more to the kitchen, making out he is searching for something, which I know he isn't because he's never disorganized.

"Why do you need to know?"

"No reason, I was just wondering."

"You have special plans, do you?" He's dripping in sarcasm.

I don't even bother answering him because I know he's just being an ass. Suddenly, my phone springs to life. I leap to my feet, only just reaching it before Gerard does.

"Who is it?"

I glance at the screen. "No-one," I reply, silencing it.

"You understand by not telling me you're digging a huge hole for yourself. So, I'll ask again. Who was it?"

I stare at him for the longest time, deciding whether to be honest. If I tell him the truth, maybe it will shock some sense into him. Make him realize that what we have is special. Remind him of the sacrifices we made to be together.

Gerard is clenching and unclenching his jaw, waiting.

"Sheree."

Gerard pales slightly, his mouth drawing into a thin line. He shakes his head. "Why the hell are you still in contact with her? Christ, Paige. I thought we agreed…"

"She doesn't know anything about us. Gerard she was, is, my best friend, you know that."

"We agreed to leave all that behind, Paige. And I thought I was your best friend—besides, you have new friends here now, you don't need her. Christ, what in the hell have I gotten myself into with you?" His words are so cutting, my face burns with shame.

Gerard picks up his briefcase then finds his keys on the counter. When he's at the French doors, he turns around and stares at me as though contemplating.

"What, Gerard? Just come out and say it."

"Don't you dare fuck him today. You know, finish yourself off."

"Argh, you bastard!" I hurl my half-full coffee cup through

the air. From where I'm standing it barely makes it as far as Gerard's feet, but he steps back to avoid the tidal wave that's soon following the porcelain missile that shatters all over the floor.

"Real smart." Gerard steps around the mess before exiting. I'm too angry to even respond. I flop onto a chair. I already told him I didn't want to fuck Alex again. He's just being a jerk because he's not getting his own way. I force myself to get up, grabbing an old cloth and some paper towels from under the sink to clean up the mess I made.

On my hands and knees, I wipe the floor then catch Gerard coming back out of the garage on foot, calling out to Alex who I didn't even realize was there. He looks up from raking under the jacaranda trees that have been steadily dropping leaves now that summer is on its way.

Sitting on my haunches, I watch as the two talk. Gerard has his back to me, so I can't see his expression, but his arms seem to do plenty of explaining and Alex looks forlorn. Then Gerard gestures toward the shed. My stomach clenches. Not taking my eyes off them for one second, I drop the sopping paper towel and get to my feet.

Alex places his hands on his hips and stares at the ground, then removes his hat and glasses, clasping them in one hand. Using his sleeve to wipe his brow, he shakes his head then looks toward the house and nods several times. They're so far away I don't have a clue what they are talking about or whether Alex sees that I'm watching. Running his hand through his hair, Alex must say something that makes Gerard look to the ground. Then without warning, Gerard punches Alex in the face. Gasping, my hands fly to my mouth "Shit," I breathe through my fingers. My instinct is to run outside and calm Gerard, but before I have time to step over the mess and reach for the door handle, he is walking away flicking his hand from the impact.

Alex stands for a moment watching after him, then slowly puts his hat and glasses back on and takes hold of the rake he left leaning against the tree.

When Gerard gets close enough, he looks straight at me. I reach for the door, but his grim expression stops me. A look that tells me how shattered he must feel. He turns sharply back into the garage and within seconds he's backing out his car.

I can't tear myself away from the door, not until Gerard's car has traveled down the drive and out of sight. Alex doesn't look his way or mine; just keeps raking up leaves. Looking down, I assess the mess I've made on the floor and think of the irony.

Although I'm bone tired, I know I need to run—to get out of the house, away from myself. I need to get out of my head. I change in record time and throw my hair up into a ponytail.

On my way out the door, I grab the bag of broken pottery and sodden paper towels to throw it into the trash. After adjusting my hat and slipping on sunglasses, I put my airpods in to drown out my internal chatter and listen to my favorite songs instead.

Jogging, I'm halfway down our long-curved driveway when I reach Alex. He hears the crunching gravel beneath my feet and turns toward me. I slow into a walk. He stops raking. For a moment, we just stare at each other. Pocketing my airpods, I give him a small smile and take a step toward him. Ten strides later still carrying his rake, which he uses to lean on, Alex is standing a meter away. I can tell Gerard connected well with Alex's left cheek, noting he broke the skin.

"Are you all right?" we ask in unison. Surprised, I huff out a chuckle. Alex looks to the ground briefly and when he looks up, his eyes seem to ice over. It's cooler this morning than yesterday and being shaded by the trees, Alex has removed his hat and glasses and left them at the base of one of the largest Jacaranda trees.

"I suppose you saw that?" he asks.

I nod then look around, unsure if I should get personal. When I look back at him, his expression is stoic. I point to his face.

"You should ice that. I'm going for a run, but you're welcome to get some, you'll find…"

"I'm fine," Alex cuts me off. He swaps the rake into his other hand and sweeps a few leaves in no particular direction.

"All right, well I'll get going. I plan on doing the six, so I'll be gone at least an hour."

"What's the six?"

"Oh. I just mean the route I take. Along Carnegie's Creek and around the boulevard. It's six miles, meaning it's safe for you to go inside, you know, in case Gerard comes home and finds you there, at least I won't be with you," I say, paying homage to Gerard's idiocy.

I turn to leave, but Alex launches forward to grab my arm. The second I look at the hand holding my arm he lets go.

"I'm not attempting to influence your decision Paige, and I sure as shit don't condone Gerard bullying you either, especially into doing something you're uncomfortable with, but I just need to say something."

My arms cross my chest, and I suddenly find something interesting about my shoes, uncertain if I want Alex to contribute to my personal life at all. He waits for a few seconds before moving closer, causing me to step back and glare at him. He holds his hands up, then shoves them in his front pockets and rolls his shoulders forward.

"He feels emasculated, Paige. Imagine what it's like for him. Every time he gets off, he's thinking how fucking amazing it feels. Then he sees you smiling at him, happy you've been able to do that thing, that women do. He wants you to experience it; he wants to *see* you experience it. That's ballsy if you ask me."

"Well, haven't you changed your tune now? Yesterday you were rubbing in how old he is and how lame in bed he most likely is."

"Yeah, maybe, but as far as that shit goes, he must love you plenty if he's willing to do anything, just so you can have that pleasure. I sure as shit wouldn't be able to. But then, like I said, most women I do—I see to the end. That's not having a go at him. Personally, I think it's what I said last night; it's in here with you." He taps his head again, something I'm getting sick of him referring to.

"Doesn't he realize, it doesn't matter though? Love isn't about sex and damn orgasms. It's about trust and mutual respect, friendship and having things in common. I'm so angry at myself for confessing. I should have just kept quiet. Things were fine until you came along."

Alex brings his arms around and folds them over his chest, scrutinizing me.

"What?"

At first, he doesn't answer, just keeps staring.

"What?" I pester, "What did I say? Don't you think that's what love should be about?"

"Oh, for sure! Abso-fucking-lutely."

"So—what? What did I say wrong?"

"You said, you wish you hadn't told him."

"Yeah and?"

"I would have thought you'd say, you wish it never happened."

I'm staring at him for too long, my eyes darting from one

of his to the other, my fluttering heart turning me into a puddle of sweat.

"I think you better think about that, Princess." He turns away. "Enjoy your run," he shoots back over his shoulder, leaving me feeling stupid in the middle of our yard.

"I still hate you," I shout at his back.

He knew what I meant to say. Cocky prick. I walk on down the driveway, glancing back over my shoulder several times before I realize what I'm doing. I need to sort this shit out. I can't let my culpability ruin my marriage.

When I get to the gate, I pause and look at what has become my life sprawled out in front of me. I live on Rye Court in a prestigious area of Point Dume. It's a beautiful house and I have my own car. My career is solid, and I'm married to a man most women drool over. The best part, it's a million miles from my trailer-trash past. Growing up in a small town where everyone knew me wasn't the problem, it was who they associated me with. When your mother turns tricks right under your nose, with men whose children attend the same school as me. I was both mocked by my peers and threatened by the parent to keep quiet. Most girls like me, end up with men they don't love in exchange for a better life, many even staying in abusive relationships just to keep the status quo. I have it all, but am I on the brink of messing it all up by pushing Gerard away? I need to run. To dispel any stupid thoughts away.

I was good at cross-country running in school. Often, I'd even beat the boys. I loved running, I guess I still do I surmise, as my feet hit the bitumen with such force my shins ache.

Back at school, the route for the students went past the length of the town's golf course. There was a cluster of trees that lined the fence, and sometimes golfers would stop their game beneath them and watch as we jogged by in groups of maybe six or seven at a time, except for me. I jogged alone. Sheree hated running, she hated most sports except horse riding, which I never took an interest in after getting bucked off.

Sometimes, when our school was training for a meet and we did the track daily, I would pass by the golf green alone, and spot the same man sitting in a buggy watching.

At first, I was excited thinking he might be a scout, looking for talented runners and I might get the chance of being discovered, get a scholarship handed to me, seeing I was always leading the pack. That seemed like the only prospect I had of getting out of Ponderosa Park and into a college, that's for sure. Unless by some miracle I won the lottery, which I was too young to enter anyway. No, when I was done with school, I was destined to go straight to work in either the Country Store, the only grocery store in town, or the jeans factory in the old mill that employed almost every female, including some from the outskirts of town.

When every day, for over two weeks, I kept seeing the same man with a bright green cap in the same spot, I started imagining he was my dad. That he was secretly watching me train and I started running faster. I wanted to make him proud, hoping he'd rally behind me, get excited to see me at the state championships because it's not like my mom ever gave a shit. My fantasy had me running and crying at the same time.

One day during summer, long after the cross-country races were through and I'd placed fourth, Sheree and I were sunbathing at her place. It was the end of our freshman year. We were celebrating by getting darker than the prettiest and most popular girl in school, Suzanna Evanston. Although, I honestly thought Sheree was the better looking of the two.

Sheree and I were chatting, reading magazines and working on blistering, when Sheree's dad started up the lawn mower. We both sighed, annoyed that he was wrecking our tranquil moment. Sheree shouted out to him, something rude. I remember blushing and feeling sorry for him because he was always nice to me and the comment, I think it was something like, "Go back inside and play with your stupid boats" because he liked making those model boats in bottles. I liked them and thought he was clever. But Sheree was often embarrassed by him. All I kept thinking was at least she had a father.

We were laying there trying to ignore the mower in the background when suddenly, we were doused in icy water, sending us squealing around the backyard in fits of laughter, until Sheree got pissed off because the water had splashed all over her new magazines. She stormed off, wailing to her mother how stupid her father was, and "look what he'd done," which caused another fit of laughter from me. When I stopped giggling and threw my dripping wet hair back, I saw him, Sheree's dad. He was back over at the mower pretending he hadn't done anything wrong, except he was wearing a bright green cap on his head and grinning from ear to ear.

Startling me out of my reverie, my phone vibrates in my hand. Ignoring it, I keep running. A minute later, it goes off again. Christ, can a girl get no peace? Stopping, I look at the screen and see I have messages from Sheree.

I'm free this morning if you need to talk. In other words, let me know what happened.

Then a second text.

Dying here.

Then a third.

Call me back! Attached is a scowling emoji.

I stare at the screen, regretting I mentioned the dinner at all. It was bad enough I told her about cheating on Gerard but Christ, a three-way so he could watch me have an orgasm. She does not need to know those details about Gerard and me. I relive my morning with Gerard; that he now knows I'm still in contact with Sheree. No, I just can't tell her anything else. Anyway, I don't even know what to tell her. I text back that I'm out jogging and will call later. I press send then turn my music up louder and jog on.

I'm only a few hundred yards along before I'm greeted by the first of our neighbors. Delilah Newton throws a quick wave at me. Out watering her garden, she seems to take great pride in her patch of petunias, and I can't think of one day that I haven't seen her in her front yard when I've been out for a run. A quick glance to my left to check for traffic and I cross the road. My brow is perspiring but my heart rate remains steady. It feels good to clear my head, and with the help of Spotify belting out tunes, I'm soon lost in my own little world.

By the time I'm two miles along, I've reached Jenna and Nadal Martín's home where I always slow my pace. She's the one and only person on our road who thoroughly intrigues me. To my surprise, she is standing by her front gate with her hands on her hips, looking up the road. As always, she is impeccable, and I can't help but admire her taste in clothing. No matter what the occasion, she always seems to find the perfect outfit. This morning she is wearing what I would assume to be the classiest pair of dress pants to exist. Black with a flared bottom, and a band that rests gently over her slender hips, clings just enough to turn her ass into a ski slope. The top she complements the pants with, is a cream, collared shirt that's tucked in. It's crease-less and has cuffs with large ties dangling at her wrists. She is stunning even with her house slippers on. When she hears my pounding feet, she turns. I silence my music before I get to her.

"Oh, Paige here you are. Again," she adds, as though an afterthought.

I pull up in front of her. "Hey, how's things? I got your text," I tell her, jogging on the spot. "Is everything all right?" I look up the road to where she appeared to be focusing.

"Oh, everything is fine." She waves a hand. "I was just watching—Nadal drive away." She smiles. A little falsely I might add.

"He's leaving late, isn't he?" I glance at the time on my phone frowning. Nadal Martín, an entrepreneur restaurateur, is known to always leave 'At sparrow fart' as Jenna so eloquently put it. It seems to be her favorite line whenever she speaks about their business. Nadal, a fifty-five-year old immigrant from Spain, married Jenna, in her thirties and it was suspected for a green card. With plenty of money and a passion for food, Nadal was destined for success, and no doubt Jenna foresaw it too. But hey, who am I to judge. I suppose she hadn't thought owning and running a restaurant required Nadal to actually work though, because it's a constant complaint of hers to anyone willing to listen. Nadal looks like a taller version of Sean Penn with olive complexion. How they managed two gorgeous children, no one will ever know. I'm wondering now, maybe she jumped the fence and got it on with her yoga instructor, who, now that I think about it—looks similar to her children. Hmm interesting. I smirk at my own wayward thoughts.

"Yes, he was running late this morning."

I wait for her to offer more of an explanation, but when she doesn't, I take the hint.

"Okay, well I better keep moving. I'd like to be home by ten." I glance again at my phone. Then turn to leave.

"Oh, and I was thinking of asking Gerard's brother if he'd like to come to our dinner party," she catches me after a few strides. "Would you like to mention it, or should I? I know he's been in prison and all, but well, he is Gerard's brother."

"Stepbrother," I correct. And how does she know he's been in prison?

"Same thing," she waves a hand again. "I'm inviting the McEwans. You haven't met them yet, have you?" She doesn't wait for a reply because she doesn't really care. She just wants to brag. "They're an interesting couple. I'm sure you'll like Ariel, she seems..." she pauses looking for the right word. Smart, funny, curious. I don't know—how about just plain old nice, if she is trying to draw up a comparison to me.

"Casual," she concludes, and I scowl. "Oh, don't get me wrong, she's pleasant enough, it's just, I don't know... They've got three children, all boys and well let's just say, they could use some hired help."

And that's Jenna, out with her paintbrush again. I draw in a deep breath.

"I see. Well, it will be lovely to meet them. I'll let you know by the end of this week if we're coming. I better go. I'll pass on your invite to Alex. I'm not sure if he'll come, but I'll let him know."

Jenna smiles. "Oh, I think he might. Anyway, sorry to hold you up," she apologizes before waving me off.

Oh, might he?

Now that I have cooled, I walk to begin, then ease into a jog again. I'm only six house blocks farther along when I come upon the new neighbors, the McEwan house. The previous owners were a fastidious gay couple who kept their garden and yard immaculate. Both doctors, one a surgeon, the other an ophthalmologist; no one knew them that well because aside from working ridiculous hours, they kept mainly to themselves. It seems odd now seeing a multitude of toys strewn around the front yard, and I secretly hope they will be getting a sitter for Jenna's dinner party. I can already sense Gerard's disapproval when I picture him watching three terrors running around destroying the Martíns' immaculate home and yard.

When the rocks that are my ovaries twang, I leap up a gear and begin jogging again. Hopeful we can enjoy a night out by then. I mentally go through my wardrobe deciding on what to wear, the music seducing me again.

By nine fifty I'm cooling down along our driveway after first stopping by the box out front to retrieve our mail. There's a pile of bills and some mysterious letters for Gerard and then, my subscription from *O*. I can't help it I'm addicted. I worship the woman and am enthralled by her articles. Looking around, I'm half hoping to catch sight of Alex, but his truck is no longer parked. I also notice he has left the shed door wide open, and in both our absences find that careless of him. When I reach the shed to shut it up, I peer inside. For a moment, a ghostly image of myself and Alex appears. Him pushing me farther in, his hands desperate. But no sooner has the memory surfaced it fades, feeling well and truly tarnished now. Well, I got my wish, I suppose. It no longer feels erotic but sordid. There are some things out of place. Picking a bucket up from off the floor, I return it to the open cupboard then lean against it, sighing because I'm questioning if I'm being fair to Gerard. I mean I'm not a prude; I suspect lots of people have threesomes, so why did I shut him down so abruptly?

My eyes settle on a blanket spread over the ride-on mower. Pushing myself off the cupboard, I fold it absentmindedly and put it back on the shelf where it belongs. Then shut the door on my memories, and any further analysis safely away.

By the time I come down from my shower, I am famished. A feast is in order, followed by a mug of coffee as I page through my O magazine. Then I have work to do. With four retouches due before Friday, three days away, I am cutting it close to my deadline, something new to me.

It's only when I've settled onto the couch with my cup and magazine in hand, do I remember Sheree. No doubt worried sick by now. Confirming I'm right, once I've connected, she is on the other end in a nanosecond.

"What the hell, Paige?"

I apologize profusely.

"I called like five times."

"What?" I turn my phone to the side. "Oh shit, I'm sorry, I must have hit the silence switch,"

"Is everything all right? What happened last night? Was he still angry?"

My mind is racing to concoct something to say. "No, he wasn't angry. Just—himself, I suppose."

"So, did Alex turn up? What did Gerard want to talk about?"

"Just the obvious. That we disappointed him. Shocked we could do that to him." I cringe at my lie. I hadn't even given it thought, it just came straight out. Confirming to myself that I knew deep down, I was rethinking things. I had no intention of letting anyone, not even my lifelong "rational" friend, tell me I was insane for giving this situation a second thought. The fact was, I'd never told Sheree about my inadequacies between the sheets.

"So, what's Alex going to do now?"

"Gerard told him he could stay."

"Really? How are you going to cope with having him around?"

"Having him around won't be a problem. It was a mistake. I regret it."

"Well, I've got to say, Paige, you hit the jackpot with that man of yours. Not many men would be as forgiving as him."

"I know. That's what makes what I've done worse," I say, staving off tears because she doesn't know the half of it.

There's a long pause while I think of something more to talk about. "Have you seen my mom at all, or heard anything from her?" Then it's Sheree's turn to pause.

"Sheree?"

"She got kicked out of the pub last Friday night. I was there. I'm sorry, pea, but why doesn't she just die." Suddenly, Sheree can't hold back, and each sentence punches me in the stomach even though I hate my mother. "She's so unkempt now, she smells damn awful. Guys at the bar were throwing empty cans at her. For some reason she seemed to interpret it as though they were trying to hit on her. God, it was embarrassing to watch. Sorry, but it's true."

"You don't have to be sorry. Some parents should not be parents. No, let me correct that, some people should just never be born." I wince, hearing my own harsh words.

As much as my mother was a desperate and tragic person, she is my mother and on some primal level my heart knew it, and strangely I felt sorry for her. I only wish I knew what had turned a nice little girl into such a self-destructive adult. Then I get an instant headache when a voice in my head whispers, "An apple never falls far from the tree, Paige."

"Ree, I've got to go. I'll call you later." And without letting her say goodbye, I hang up, leap to my feet and go sprinting down the hall. Past the office and through the laundry and into the little back room toilet. Falling to my knees, I cradle the bowl and without a moment's pause, heave up all my breakfast. Then sob hysterically.

NOT SO BAD IN LA

"People like him ought to be hung and quartered. At least extradite the filthy bastard." Jeremy's cussing comes out in an explosion which has Gerard reaching for my hand. It's not as though I'm unaccustomed to his colleagues' outbursts whenever we get together for one of Gerard's Friday meet-and-greets at his office, but tonight, Jeremy Morgan, Gerard's boss, seems heavily intoxicated and instead of saying it, is spraying it. Right at us.

Gerard gives me a tug, his elbow catching my arm, so I fall in behind and use him as a shield. Loosening his tie, I can tell my husband is getting annoyed that not only is his boss cussing in front of me, but he's been rambling on about a case for over an hour now and mostly repeating himself.

A plump man with rounded shoulders and a receding hairline, it seems he's ditched his suit for the day in favor of a loud shirt. It's covered in African birds in multiple hues of the rainbow and hangs loose over his linen pants, making him look somewhat eccentric, even if he looks cool and comfortable compared to me and Gerard in our formal wear.

"Sounds like you've lost faith in the system, Jeremy," Gerard says.

"Not at all. I just know from experience the low life will never be convicted." Jeremy upends his glass.

Bored out of my mind, because I have no idea who they are even talking about, I fan the top of my blouse and look around the room, hoping to spot any latecomers with whom I can relate to. Gerard gives my hand a little squeeze. He knows I hate these social get-togethers where everyone's conversation is focused on court hearings, litigation, legislation, acquittals, and the stupidity of all those involved. It was draining just trying to process the correct pronunciation of the terms Gerard and his colleagues use, let alone understand them.

Mostly I just hang off Gerard's arm like a man-bag being thankful these gatherings only take place when a new face needs introducing. Like tonight, it was for some young fellow whose parents must have had high aspirations from the moment he was born. Naming him after some fancy lawyer. I'd learned this, when Jeremy asked us to toast John Archibald Campbell. He had apparently graduated, *'Harvard with honors, and a list of recommendations longer than the justices of the Supreme Court list itself,'* Jeremy announced, earning him a chorus of laughter. Or maybe it was the shirt they were all laughing at. I know I was.

Well, good for John. But I found it hard relating to the over-educated people at these functions, since I'd only been privy to completing high school. Nothing as prestigious as Harvard, Yale, or Columbia. Secretly, I hope to be absorbing everyone else's smarts as I stand around looking and feeling like an accessory.

"Subpoena the daughter then." Gerard winks at me, making me smile because every suggestion he's offered so far Jeremy has argued away.

"The bastard will just enter a plea." Jeremy balks, and Gerard squeezes my hand again. "Why is this room so damn hot? Where's the fairness in paying six figures per annum in rent when they skimp on the bloody electricity? Damn corporate body, they all need shooting too," Jeremy snaps, "Excuse me, Paige, Gerard." Spotting someone, Jeremy struts off raising his empty tumbler and calling out someone's name.

"Pleasant as always." Gerard smiles down at me and releases my sweaty hand. "I think he just likes the sound of his own voice. But he's right, it's a sauna in here," he states, looking around and I notice the sweat beading his brow, which is no surprise. The high-rise conference room is facing west, and the afternoon sun is so intense that even behind the tinted windows, heat waves are notable against the glass. "How about I get us a drink? See if I can find someone to turn up the air conditioner," he suggests. "I'm sure it must be on the blink."

"Can't we just go?" I ask.

"One more hour. Is that all right?"

Sighing, I tell Gerard, it's fine. That I'm okay, that it's bearable. "Just barely," I add, pulling a face, then smile.

"Good, because I have something to show you. But not until seven." He glances at his watch. "Are you all right here? If you see Carter arrive, can you let him know I need to speak with him?" He walks away before I can answer, then gets caught between me and the bar by another associate that needs to have a word, leaving me fidgeting with my purse and wondering what he wants to show me. Feeling nervous that it could likely be the door. It had taken Gerard several days after the heated morning with both me and Alex for him to drop the debate about a three-way, regurgitating over and over that my infidelity was far worse than him suggesting what he had. Thank God, Alex was keeping an extra low profile. It's only now, two weeks later, that things are getting back to normal. And normal is what I want. Alex makes me feel vulnerable. The complete opposite to how I feel with Gerard.

Gerard is the only man I've ever loved. Aside from my father, that is. Protective, adoring, driven, and ridiculously good-looking, what's not to love? But we didn't have a normal courtship. Our coming together came out of need. He'd kept coming to the café where I worked. A few times we sat and chatted over coffee, but mostly he was just there with his colleagues. He'd always say hello and leave me big tips, but he'd had his world, and I was in mine.

Mine comprised not much, really. Work, study, go home. Or study, work, go home. Occasionally I went out to the movies with Josh and Amity from work. Both around the same age as me and Josh perfectly gay. But I was never much for partying per se. I liked to read and watch TV series. Eat Oreos by the packet and paint my toenails in front of the little electric heater that I huddled around during the winter with my flatmate Kelsey.

The first time Gerard had come into the café he was with Carter. Together, they stood in the doorway and shook off the soaking rain. Noticing Gerard first, I almost died, my heart raced so hard. Carter, a man with the same basic stature as Gerard, tall and athletic though far more hyperactive, had paled into the background as the door slammed shut behind them.

Stuck behind the espresso machine making coffees, it surprised me Gerard even noticed me at all. But after wading through the sea of cocky corporate honchos, many he appeared to know, he stood at the counter and peeked around the coffee machine, pushing his wet, dark-blond hair away from his eyes. Glancing first at my name badge, he looked up and smiled, his sapphire-blue eyes igniting.

Incredibly sexy wouldn't suffice what he exuded to me that day or any other day since.

"My treat today, Gerard. What will you have?" Carter asked him, his face inches from the cake cabinet.

Gerard. I mouthed his name, stifling a grin as I continued frothing milk. Gerard gave me a playful glare before answering Carter.

"Coffee and an apple slice, thanks. It's the best around," he stated, in a matter of fact tone; as though he'd been in dozens of times before. Which could have been possible because I'd only been working there a little over three weeks. Still finding my way around, I hadn't even tried the apple pie, let alone acquaint myself with the regulars.

"Done. Make that two, thank you, young lady," Carter said. "I'll find us a table up front, Gerard." He slapped a twenty on the counter. "Keep the change," he offered before marching off, briefcase in hand and unbuttoning his suit jacket.

Gerard lingered behind, making me blush as he pawed, as though interested, through a box of handmade gift cards on top of the cake cabinet. A lame attempt for recognition by a nineteen-year-old me.

"Were you just smirking because of my name?" Gerard asked, grinning.

"Maybe." I laughed, my eyes shifting between him and what I was doing.

Not insulted, Gerard just kept smiling and looking at me. Eventually, he pulled out a card—a photograph of the County Arboretum & Botanical Gardens at dawn. Flipping it over, he studied the little sticker placed on the back, and then his eyes flicked up.

"I study photography and work here," I answered his quizzical look.

"Well, Paige, seems you found your calling. They're good."

Again, he smiled. Adoring and familiar and I admit, I felt all warm and fuzzy, as silly as that sounds. After arriving in LA with nothing more than a backpack and high hopes on my side, his attention felt nice.

A week later, I got a call from Morgan & Cartwright law firm asking if I'd be interested in taking corporate headshots for their firm's new website. I didn't know it was where Gerard worked, and it wasn't until he took his turn on the stool in front of my lens, did I surmise my assignment was because of him.

I'll admit, I was infatuated with Gerard. It wasn't anything he did, but it was the way he looked at me whenever he showed up at the café, making my heart thud and my palms clammy. Looking back, I guess you could say I was flirting whenever he handed over those large tips, but I honestly didn't know how to decline them because I was grateful. I was struggling weekly to pay my share of the rent and trade school tuition. There was no family to call on for help and Gerard made me feel special. It felt natural to be playful around him.

"Got anything smaller?" I'd say. Or, "Don't you need this to fuel your jet-boat or something?" Then one day I had the cheek to say, "A few more of these, and I'll be able to pay my rent, Mr. Whitmyer" before sliding the twenty in my back pocket.

"How many more?" he asked, deadpan, causing my heart to forget which direction the blood was meant to flow. I laughed it off. But a few nights later after my shift at the café, Gerard was waiting for me in his car. He pushed open the passenger side door as I walked past. I wouldn't have known it was him otherwise.

"Can we talk, I'd like to ask you something?" he said, leaning across the passenger seat and staring up at me.

I looked up and down the almost deserted street,

deciding. With the sun not long gone, and gray clouds promising a light show and no doubt a symphony to match, it felt a little ominous. I hesitated, making silly "Um," sounds as I gathered my jacket in around me, and shuffled in my flats.

He smiled at my awkwardness. "Would it make you feel more comfortable if we met at the Dragon's Den later? You could bring a friend," he suggested, still leaning on an elbow and watching me through the open passenger-side door.

"No, it's okay," I relented, taking a deep breath before getting into his Mercedes. I placed my bag on the clean carpet and shifted in my seat, praying I hadn't trekked in any dirt.

"All right, fire away," I encouraged.

To my surprise, he didn't pull away from the curb. Instead, he switched off the engine and unclipped his belt. The way his eyes drank me in, I thought he was going to ask me on a date. Ask if I'd consider accompanying him to some office party or something casual like that, which alone was making me nervous. No. Yes. Maybe. I don't know, and why? All answers I was mentally lining up.

Flooring me right off the bat, he didn't mince his words. "How would you like to move in with me?" he asked.

"Excuse me?" I'm sure my face depicted I thought he was insane. I was not expecting that and said as much.

"No, I imagine you wouldn't have." He looked out the windshield briefly, took a deep breath, then rationalized his idea, saying he could help with my tuition fees in exchange for my company as a house mate.

"Don't you already live with someone?" I asked.

"No, I don't, and I think the house is a waste on just me. It's too large and lonely. I thought we could coexist, get to know one another better, and in time you might find me pleasant enough to, well, perhaps you'll let me take you out on a date," he said.

A date? Pleasant enough? I'd always found him pleasant enough. Although a lot older than me, he was handsome, and it was hard keeping my eyes off him. Even there, in the front seat of his car between our awkward silence as it grew darker outside, I was still trying to drink in his good looks.

In a flash, the streetlights had come on making my heart flutter and questioning whether it was a sign. Then it started to drizzle. And in the confines of the car, our nervousness was fogging up the windshield. I thought about the long walk to the station, the boring train ride home. The empty apartment because Kelsey, was staying at her boyfriend's place for the night. I covered my mouth with the tips of my fingers just looking at him, scanning his eyes. I couldn't believe I was considering his proposal. Rightfully, I began shaking my head.

"No way. I just can't," I stammered, not sparing his feeling at all. I mean it was an insane offer.

He looked surprised. I felt ungrateful.

"Will you at least let me take you out to dinner sometime?"

Sitting on my hands, I looked out the window, watching as people darted for cover. Their umbrellas threatening to turn hostile in their own fight against the wind.

I reached for my bag, my hand going for the door. "I can't. I'm sorry Gerard but it just doesn't feel right, and to be honest, I think I'd get on your nerves," I admitted, feeling more naïve the longer I sat there.

He disagreed. Told me I was passing up a fantastic opportunity, and I knew he was right. But it was something I wouldn't jump into no matter how easy it could have been.

Then as if God disagreed, the rain took vengeance. Massive drops of rain splattered against the windshield and found their way between the small crack of my partially opened door. Pulling it shut, I cursed the weather and my predicament. Gerard's proposal could be so right if it weren't so wrong. He offered to drive me home and against my better judgment, I agreed. We drove in silence for most of the way, but my stomach was alive with activity. I think he was allowing me to think things over, hoping that maybe I'd change my mind.

When he pulled up outside my apartment block, he reached for my hand and squeezed it. "Please think about it, and if you change your mind…"

"I won't," I promised, cutting him off then easing my hand reluctantly away.

Two months later I considered breaking that promise when Kelsey suddenly decided she needed to move in with her boyfriend, leaving me with the lease. Four months later, I did break my promise when someone broke into my apartment. He ransacked the place first, then waited for me to arrive home. The masked intruder held me at knifepoint. Stole my wallet and what few precious possessions I owned, including a small gold cat pendant with onyx eyes my father sent me on my thirteenth birthday. I was devastated and petrified. I needed to take on extra shifts at work, which meant giving up many of my photography classes, just to recoup my loss.

I became a wreck, and Gerard noticed. When I told him what happened, he insisted on calling the police which I hadn't bothered to do, thinking it pointless. Which it was.

For a solid week he insisted on spending the night at my apartment, in Kelsey's old room. After he left, I jumped at the slightest sound. His absence felt like I had no walls, that every window was open, and every lock broken. My imagination started rehashing every scary movie I'd ever seen until I was cowering under my bed with a blanket and pillow. So, when he asked me again if I'd move in with him, I agreed. I only meant it to be temporary, a safe place until I found a more pleasant neighborhood, one I could afford.

The years that followed those days, Gerard had given me everything my heart desired, and I fell in love. Contrary to what I first thought, we developed common interests, and when he introduced me to his friends, they accepted me, regardless of my age.

After scanning the sweltering room, I don't find Carter, but my roving eyes soon land on Gerard again. Standing at the bar, two champagne flutes in hand, he is talking with a suited lady. I chew on my lip just watching them. He must feel my eyes on him because he looks my way then smiles, showing me he has scored some drinks, his mouth still on the move.

Everything about Gerard is alluring, and I'm not surprised when the lady reaches out to touch his forearm, followed by a giggle directed at the ceiling. Apparently, he's sharing some joke. One I most likely would never get, and it makes me question for the millionth time, what on earth he is doing with me.

Ending their conversation, Gerard saunters back over with the champagne dancing in his hands, smiling seductively at me and no one else. His ridiculously captivating eyes sparkle and devour my entire being, causing a flurry of butterflies to make me giddy. Last month marked eighteen months of marriage, and every day I thank Kelsey for moving out, and even the burglar for scaring the crap out of me. Because there's not a day that goes by that I don't feel like the luckiest woman alive. Even if I do feel oddly out of place.

13

TRAMPOLINE

On our way home from the meet-and-greet at Gerard's law firm in the city, Gerard decides to pull up outside a tired brick building. Just inside Las Flores Canyon, the abandoned surf club looks out over the ocean and is deserted, and I'm wondering what this has to do with the surprise he mentioned earlier.

Reaching into the back seat of the car, Gerard pulls forward a simple shopping bag and hands it to me.

"What's this?" I ask.

"Swimwear."

I dig my fingers through my thick hair and into my itchy scalp then take the bag from him. Peering inside, I see he has brought along my black bikini, a towel, and a beach dress.

"Let's go. And bring that bag." Gerard pushes open his door and gets out of the car.

"Really?"

I'd been looking forward to going home and a cool shower, not some romp in the ocean. I indulge him by following him down the wooden steps until we are at the doors of the building's public toilets. "You want to go for a swim? Here, now?"

Gerard nods enthusiastically, his smile taking over his face. "Absolutely. I think it will be nice, don't you?"

"You're crazy. You—do—know we have a pool at home, right?"

"Yes, but look at that ocean." He sweeps his arm across the orange horizon. "And I'm only crazy in the best of ways. You'll see. Now quick, get changed and I'll meet you out there on the sand." He nods toward the beach where the odd person is wandering about on the small stretch of sand, mostly with pets on a leash, navigating the rocks.

Ten minutes later, Gerard and I are walking hand in hand along the craggy shoreline enjoying the coolness of the ocean on our feet as the sun sets. To my surprise, Las Flores Canyon is beautiful this time of night. With the tide receding, more of the beach becomes exposed, and we can walk quite a distance from where we left our car. The breeze is warm and carries the aroma of some nearby cooking, reminding me I have chicken thawing in the fridge. I was planning on cooking something nice, but somehow, I think we will end up with take-out instead.

I look around at the mansions perched up on the rocky incline, trying to locate where the smell is coming from.

"They're amazing, aren't they?" Gerard comments.

"Sorry?"

"The houses. How they're built right on the cliff edge. You know when the tide is high, the water comes right up, and the beach disappears."

"Really?" I study the mansions in more detail, stare in awe at the floor-to-ceiling windows that look out over the view, following what I imagine the occupant's line of sight to be. "Ahh, for the rich and shameless," I mock, then clear my throat, self-conscious because I'm referring to myself as that lately. "Aren't they worried about tsunamis though?"

"Maybe." Gerard comes to a halt and lets go of my hand. "Here will do."

Braving the cold water against our overheated bodies, we soak up the sea salt and sunset, making small talk between kisses and small gropes beneath the water.

Then Gerard is plunging his head under before flipping his head back and shaking his wet hair wildly. I squeal when he deliberately sprays me.

Pushing his hair back, he squints and looks mischievous, taking lunging steps toward me.

"Don't you dare," I protest, trying to wade through the waist-high water away from him. "I don't want to get my hair wet, Gerard," I hold out my hand trying to keep him at bay. He tries grabbing me but I'm slippery and manage to get away laughing at his weak attempt.

He halts and then smiles, his eyes sparkling against the ocean, turning them vivid blue that makes him look just drop-dead gorgeous. Sometimes, it annoys me he is so good-looking. I'm sure he'd get away with murder with a face like his.

"I won't wet your hair, I promise," he reassures, reaching out a hand. I scrutinize him for a moment before letting him take hold. Pulling me close, he lifts my legs until I'm nestled around his waist. "See, that's better. Now I've got you," he murmurs against my cool cheek, squatting so our bodies submerge to our chins, our faces and pelvises only an inch apart.

"You realize you just got my hair wet, don't you?" I chastise with a faux menacing glare when my thick hair that's in a loose bun acts as a sponge.

"Sorry," he whispers against my ready lips, kissing me

deep and lasting, salty and sweet. My arms loop around his neck, my fingers running up through his wet hair.

When our lips part I tell him he's forgiven. Then he's spinning me in the water. "Do you remember that day I walked into that café you were working at? What was it called again?"

"Seriously?"

"What? It was years ago, I can't remember."

"No, I mean, I was just thinking about that earlier. It was called, The Belletristic Café," I say in a posh tone. "You and Carter walked in off the street shaking yourself off like drowned rats in suits." I chuckle from the memory.

Gerard threatens to dunk me in the water. Lunging me backward, which has me frantically trying to keep hold of his slippery rib cage until I'm steady on my feet again, the ocean gently slapping at my sides.

"I can't believe you bought one of those silly cards," I remind him.

"I still have that card," Gerard replies smugly, pinching my ass like he's got something over me. I splash at him.

"Really?"

"Yes, and they were not silly. That's why I kept it. A token to remind me of the day I spotted you. Your talent got you that gig at my work remember?"

"That it did." My attention gets drawn to a group of teens jostling and hooting as they throw a football around. I reach for Gerard's hand, deciding we're wrinkled sufficiently to get out. Not to mention the sun has begun its rapid decent, making the air just that little bit chilly.

Gerard playfully slaps my hand away and splashes me with water then follows my lead—drying off and slipping beach clothes over wet swimwear.

"It's getting late. I was going to cook chicken. Do you

think we should stop somewhere and get take-out instead?" I ask, toweling my hair dry as I follow him along the beach.

"We can do that. But first, I want you to meet someone." Gerard stretches his hand out to me. We begin walking along the beach in the opposite direction to our car, following in the footsteps of the rowdy boys who are still playing ball ahead of us. Their cheers and laughter drift away when they decide to sprint up a flight of pedestrian stairs that lead onto the main road.

Once they are out of sight Gerard comes to an abrupt halt and faces me. "You love me, don't you Paige?"

"Of course I do." My chest tightens, and I shake my head, frowning sadly. Gerard has always doubted it, and now that I cheated on him, I've made it worse.

"Because I would do anything and everything for you. You must know that by now," he goes on, making me feel guilty that I didn't give in to his proposal. And now it seems Alex is mostly off the scene, only coming once this week to maintain the garden. He's even stopped working on the pergola over the fishpond.

"I'm going to propose an idea that might make our life a little more exciting. But if—you're thinking of leaving me I…"

"I'm not going to leave you, Gerard, but what idea? I mean, last time you suggested something, we ended up fighting."

"I know, but I think you might feel differently after tonight." He takes my hand again and keeps us walking. "You see, I realized the other day that mostly we do things I like. You know golf, yachting and the theater. I imagine women your age finds those things rather boring."

Gerard stops walking and faces one of the mansions on the hill. Following his gaze, I realize he is looking at a middle-aged lady standing on a cabled deck. Out of place in a suit, the ocean breeze is whipping at her dark hair. She's quite stunning and Gerard can't seem to take his eyes off her. It makes me wonder if he's trying to tell me he's been pining for someone closer to his own age. That I should find someone closer to my age. That we are on different waves lengths with our sexual taste and experiences. Or maybe... Oh God, is she some kind of sexual expert or something? Like the lady I watched on the Goop Lap who taught women how to explore their own bodies and pleasure themselves. Suddenly I feel nervous. Is this what I've driven my husband to?

"Come up this way, Paige. We'll go along the road on the way back," Gerard nods toward a flight of stairs to the side of the house we are staring at.

I notice a private property sign. "I don't think we can go that way Gerard."

"Trust me, it will be fine."

Mounting maybe twenty concrete steps, Gerard leads me to the top where we come upon the entrance of the decking.

"Gerard, stop." I jerk my hand out of his. The lady is standing over the far end of the deck on her cell phone now and oblivious to us but still I whisper, "It's private property."

"Paige, honey, trust me, it's fine." I search Gerard's eyes, trying to understand the mounting joy emanating from him.

"What's going on?"

"Did I ever tell you about the small inheritance my mother left me when she died?"

"I don't think so. No."

"Hmm, I thought I would have told you that. She died quite young you know. Anyway, I bought some cheap shares with my inheritance. I've been sitting on them for years, and I mean years. Christ, I probably bought them back when you were a child."

I flinch at his remark in our age difference. Annoyed that

he keeps reminding me like I'm supposed to one day say, Oh, oops wow, you know what? You're actually a geriatric old fart, how did I not notice before? And poof, blow out the flame of love I have for him.

Gerard gazes down at me wearing a broad grin then steps back to pull me up the last few steps. I take in the expansive decking as he spoons me from behind and rests his chin on my shoulder.

"I bought this house for us, for you," he announces.

"What!" I spin in his arm then look between him and the lady still chatting on the phone. Finally, it sinks in. This woman is a real estate agent. Relief extinguishes the lava heating me, and in an instant, I'm fighting the butterflies that have sprung to life.

"Isn't it amazing? Are you happy?" Gerard pulls away from me so he can gauge my reaction then starts moving about, running his hand along a windowsill and tapping on the glass. "It needs a lot of work and it will take some time to renovate, but I've got an idea for you." Gerard is babbling on so excitedly I can barely concentrate on what he's saying as well as register the amazing building in front of us.

Glass and weathered boards. Polished floorboards inside, and the ocean, and the sand, and the rocks. It's hardly modern, but oh! The potential is right there. Our home at Point Dume is beyond amazing but this, this beach house is —is, too much.

"Oh, Gerard, it's beautiful and you've bought it? You've actually paid for it, not just thinking about it?"

"Oh, I bought it all right." He comes beside me and puts an arm around my shoulders, encouraging me farther onto the deck. My head sweeps around, trying to absorb it all.

"It's two apartments, really. The lower one as you imagine is at street level. I thought you could turn it into a gallery."

"A gallery?" I squeal.

"Yes. Just wait until you see downstairs, it's huge. Plenty of room for a studio and an office."

I'm so shocked I can hardly keep up with what he is saying. Then my eyes are locking onto the lady who now has her phone by her side. With the nod of his head, Gerard cues her to approach us.

"Hello, Paige, I'm Sarina Lewis. I can tell by your smile you're happy with your husband's purchase." She pauses for a moment, giving me time to look around, then thrusts her hand out. I shake it briefly before she is carving her arm through the air. "Will you just look at this large outdoor entertaining area."

Still in disbelief, my eyes and smile go so wide, she laughs. I turn to Gerard and grip onto his arm, unable to hold back the little squeal of delight. My heart is racing so fast—it feels like I might pee.

"And inside, you have two large bedrooms on this level, and downstairs another two. Both floors have huge living areas and are self-contained. The original owners rented the lower apartment out, so it has its own entrance. They requested the build focus on large living areas rather than lots of unused bedrooms. Childless, I'd say."

She misses the look Gerard and I share and continues with our tour, coaxing us with her clacking heels as she shows us around the entire interior. It is large, but I can see what Gerard means by needing work. The vaulted ceiling, supported by large polished wooden posts is breathtaking, but the kitchen is outdated as are the two bathrooms. The bedrooms are a generous size and have built-in closets, which is a plus. We go down a short passage, and the whole time Sarina is giving us a redundant sale pitch before leading us to the front door and down another flight of stairs to the front of the building. Once there, Sarina opens the front door to the lower apartment, and we enter a living room first then through to the kitchen.

"See, we can knock down this wall here and open it all up." Gerard slaps his hand on the dividing wall between the kitchen and living room. "We can do away with the kitchen and just have a small kitchenette behind a low wall so the gallery can take in the view of the ocean. What do you think?"

"A gallery?" I repeat hardly believing my ears.

"Yes, Paige. Your photos are beautiful. You should hone your craft."

"Gerard, it's too much." My hands go to my head and I spin around to drink in the essence, my mind going wild with decorating, fixture, and furnishing ideas. Thoughts of commissioning artists' work to display. Oh, the possibilities. Suddenly, I'm squealing with excitement again, running to him, and throwing my arms around his neck, raining kisses on his handsome face.

"Really, you mean it. I can work from here, have a gallery, no more being stuck at home?" I search his eyes, mine filling with happy tears. Gerard's slight flinch gives way to a smile, then he turns and heads back upstairs into the main house leaving me to follow.

Lunging into my ideas to deflect my insensitive comment, we leave Sarina to slink off somewhere so we can explore.

I can't contain my excitement. A project, a renovation. Me in control. It's not that I don't like our home in Point Dume, I do. But when I moved in, everything was Gerard's, and I was content with accepting it as it was. I mean, I added the odd thing here and there, but everything was how Gerard wanted it.

"When can we start, where do we start?" I ask, still excited and exploring the main house again.

"Oh, renovating isn't my kind of thing I thought we'd get someone else to do that," Gerard says.

"No, it'll be perfect because I'd re…"

"Hey! How's it going?"

My mouth halts mid-sentence, the same instant my heart jolts. Alex's voice is unmistakable.

"Hi, Alex, thanks for coming." Gerard turns away from me as Alex comes in from the back decking. My smile disappears as I slip behind Gerard. I've barely seen Alex in the last weeks let alone spoken with him. He looks devilish, his hair is a mess, and he's got those big biker boots on again.

"Hello, Alex," I whisper when he looks at me.

He nods to acknowledge me. "So, this is it?" he asks addressing Gerard, his curious eyes turning upward like he is searching the sky for stars. When I follow his gaze, I'm surprised to realize he's doing just that. Above us through a huge skylight that dominates the formal dining area is the night sky in all its glory.

"Yes. The work needed seems superficial. Structurally it's sound, just some cosmetic surgery, really. I had a builder's inspection done. I'd like to put in a new kitchen on both levels, and you would have noticed the outside is desperate for a paint job."

The men talk on as we go from room to room. I think I know what's going on, but I don't want to ask to be certain. Is Gerard thinking of letting Alex tackle the renovations? On this house, our new home, my supposed gallery? I was hoping it would be my project to supervise. How will Alex know where I want things? I try to remain interested, smile when Gerard turns to ask my opinion, but I can feel my enthusiasm slipping further away by the second.

"Don't you think, Paige?" Gerard asks.

"What? Sorry I wasn't listening." I tear my gaze from the beautiful view outside.

"The master bedroom and bathroom. Alex just suggested moving them back here, to take in the ocean."

"I suppose that would make sense."

Alex furrows his brow. "You don't sound convinced, Paige. Did you have a different idea?"

"Oh no, not really. I haven't wrapped my head around the surprise. I got lost after Gerard suggested a gallery in the lower apartment." I flash Gerard a warm smile just as Sarina pokes her head around the door.

"Gerard, if I can steal you for a moment? There are things I need to run through with you before I leave. Regarding the outside lighting and remote security system. Is now okay?"

"Certainly. Paige, while I'm gone, why don't you give Alex some ideas on the gallery and kitchens?"

"Oh. Um. I don't really know. I mean…"

"You'll figure it out. I'll be back in a minute." He follows Sarina out the door. And as they pass by the window on their way to the side of the house, I notice how Sarina is graciously escorting Gerard by his bare elbow. I turn away and try swallowing the lump that just formed in my throat.

"Exciting purchase," Alex says, stuffing his hands in the pockets of his jeans.

"It is. I'm overwhelmed to be honest. He surprised me with it just now. Obviously, he told *you* about it though?"

"He mentioned it." Alex nods saying little else, making me feel awkward and walking around the room without a purpose.

"How have you been?" I finally break the silence.

"I'm fine, how about you?" He comes closer to where I'm standing, makes out he's interested in the view out the window. "Have you and Gerard sorted your shit out?" Alex throws me a sideward glance.

"What's there to sort out?" I look around the empty room avoiding eye contact, shrug, then walk out the room, touching walls and picking at the peeling paint as I go. "Have you found work somewhere else? You haven't been around much," I ask, glancing back to check if he is following me. When I realize he isn't, I stop in the hall, fold my arms and rest against the wall and watch as he opens and closes windows. When he's done testing them all, he saunters toward me until he's resting against the doorframe a few feet away.

"Nope. Thought I'd give you and Gerard space. But if I heard him right last night, Gerard was offering this contract to me. Unless you're not cool with that," he asks, catching me off guard and searching my face.

"What? Oh no, that's fine. I don't have a problem. I don't think." I reach up to pick a pushpin out of the wall.

"You don't think? Well, now is the time to decide. It's either a yes or a no."

I shake my head. "Fine, it's a yes then." I widen my eyes at him then meander down the hall. Alex follows me, both of us looking around at the work that needs doing. "Are you a builder?" I ask over my shoulder, curious if he knows what he's taking on.

Alex huffs. "Am I a builder? Let's just say I'm good with my hands and I give everything a go."

I screw my face at his cocky tone, but he just winks at me. "Really. Jack of all trades but master of none, then? I hope you don't destroy our house, Alex."

Alex laughs. It's a nice laugh, genuine, and he follows it with a broad grin then tries to palm it away.

"White," he says, looking serious again.

"White what?"

"Everything."

"Everything?" I question, leaning against the chipped and cracked laminated kitchen bench, my hand running over the gritty surface.

"Yeah. You know? Fresh start, purity. Take your pick." Alex looks directly at me. I turn away and move over to the sink to test the water pressure like I know what I'm doing. Anything to stall my racing heart and quickening breath.

"Small kitchen considering the size of the place," Alex notes following me. Why is he following me? Shouldn't he be checking the basement? Is there a basement?

"Maybe they hated cooking," I offer, turning on the tap. The stream coughs and sputters, making me jump back. "Shit!" I yelp, as water hits the sink and splashes up at me.

Alex is beside me in a flash helping me with the tap, bumping into me slightly and his soapy scent wafts between us. He quickly twists off the faucet.

"Lack of use, Princess. Happens a lot when houses are locked up for too long. The water just slowly seeps away, leaving it air locked." He steps back, cornering me between the benches. But is he, or am I just feeling cornered? And why is he being so familiar and calling me that all the time? Like it's a term of endearment?

"Good to know," I try sounding casual, but the smell of him and the word 'Princess' is burning a speeding path to all seven of my erogenous zones. No, make that eight. I think it just hit my pituitary gland, which awakens some deeper part of me, and now I'm buzzing all over. I go to slip past him, get out of his space. But he steps in front of me and then Gerard and Sarina are entering the room, chatting about the neighbors, garbage day, the high tides, the debris that gets washed ashore and the treasures the local kids seem to find. The whole time, Gerard keeps looking at Alex and me standing together behind the counter, and my heart is having a seizure inside my chest. I feel I have guilt written all over my face, but I don't know why. It's not as though we were doing anything. And then—Gerard smiles. A big grin that fires up the intense blue color of his eyes when he becomes excited.

"Getting some ideas?" he asks when Sarina finally stops chatting. His question comes out sounding like an innuendo, making me hotter.

"A few," Alex replies, suddenly bobbing to inspect the plumbing.

Then everything happens so fast.

I'm looking down at the top of Alex's head as he reaches into the cupboard. My thoughts are spinning with him down so low and close to the wanton part of me. There's a loud knock at the front door. Gerard, Sarina and I, all look in the direction of the sound. But then, as if my body has a will of its own, I slide my leg closer to Alex, press my calf ever so subtly against his solid jean-clad thigh, desperate to feel him but praying he doesn't notice. Then Alex is standing again. Standing so close I can feel the heat coming off his body. Sarina is telling us it's her ride, that she is planning on drinking on her dinner date. "Why drive when there's Uber?" she says, making everyone laugh but me. We are all listening to her explain that she needs to find her purse so she can call the sitter, ask if she can stay late, that she plans to help us celebrate.

But everything is a blur behind my glazed eyes, a jumble of words that I can't hear past the pounding in my ears. My breathing is shallow, and the room goes out of focus. Why did I do that? I look down at my hands, pressing down on the laminate countertop, my fingers curling, trying to grip and I know I should move. But even when Gerard walks away to see Sarina out, I remain frozen in place. Standing motionless yet quivering because when Alex stood up, his hand had glided all the way up my inner thigh and pressed against the desperate, combustible part of me. Leaving me paralyzed and mute while Alex—just walks away.

14

RUSHING BACK

When I turned eleven, my dad bought me my first diary. It had a rainbow and a unicorn on it, which was a little babyish for a girl my age, but I loved it anyway. I remember rubbing my palm over the glossy cover to feel the glued-on fairy dust then checking my palm to see if any sparkles came off. They hadn't. It became the second most precious thing I owned as a child. Alongside the cat necklace he would send two years later.

Looking up, I smiled my biggest smile thanking him.

"See, it's even got a lock on it so no one but you will know your secrets," he whispered, tapping the little padlock. When he bent down to peck my cheek, he twisted his head, so he was looking at my mother, and said, "Not even her." He winked and patted my head when he stood. He wasn't a handsome man, my father, but he had kind eyes that reflected what was in his heart, and a strong jawline for what wasn't. I never saw him in anything other than his work clothes. He was always in his work clothes.

"You have a good day. Make sure you save me some of

that cake I brought home for you. Keep some in the freezer for me, Pumpkin. Will you do that?" he asked.

I'd nodded. I loved keeping my promises to my dad because he always kept his to me.

"I was gonna make her one," my mother intervened, in a tone that often started arguments.

"Sure, you were, Mavis, just like you were, 'giving up the booze,'" he mocked, almost ignoring her standing by the sink in her dressing gown, smoking.

"Go fuck yourself, Lorry," she cussed. "I'd like to see you make one."

"I did. That one," he winked at me again.

My mother just turned her back on him and stared out the window, tapping the cigarette ash in the sink until he left. When she finished her smoke, she jabbed the hot butt in the sink and tossed it out the window. From the way she chuckled, I was certain she was aiming it at my father. I hated their arguments and the stench of smoke that permeated our entire house, even seeping into my pores. Every time I went to Sheree's, her mom would douse me in her latest fragrance no doubt hoping the rank smell wouldn't invade their home.

That night, the night of my birthday, I remember clutching onto my book with pride before sliding it under my leg so my mother wouldn't pay too much attention. I already knew a good hiding place.

Sheree and I had a clubhouse at her place, in their garage, right at the back, made using a big fridge box that was to be thrown away. We put cushions and blankets in it, then brought in all Sheree's coloring books and pencils and years later, other things.

Behind the big cardboard box, tucked beneath a shelf, was an old toolbox that we surmised her dad never used. It was old and empty, so it became our secret spot. We cut a hole in the side of the box, like a flap that we could reach through to access our treasures that were stowed inside. Most of the time I kept my diary there, but sometimes, when I wanted to write about Sheree, I brought it home so she couldn't watch me write. My hiding place for my diary when it was in our house was right under my mom's nose. In a hat box that she stowed on the top shelf of my closet.

Sheree and I loved our clubhouse, and the best times were when it was raining. We'd stay in there for hours sometimes, until her mother called her inside, then I'd have to go home. I hated leaving. There were never any nice smells coming from our place, only Sheree's, because her mom was always cooking. My mom hated cooking.

Picking up his duffel bag and slinging it over his shoulder that day of my eleventh birthday, my dad turned to me again and winked. "Make sure you let 'em all know it's your birthday at school today, Pumpkin—that it's your special day, okay?"

I nodded, then blew a kiss off my palm.

When he came home two weeks later from his shift job building rail lines, he slapped my mother as soon as he walked in the door, accusing her of sleeping around behind his back.

"What, you think I go working for days on end just so you can throw parties and get fresh with other men?" he yelled, hitting her repeatedly. Adding, "My brother warned me about you, said you were easy. I should have listened to him, dumb-ass man I am."

It was one of the few times I felt sorry for my mother because I knew she had put in an effort. Knowing he was coming home, she'd cleaned the house and put on a nice dress that day. She was even cooking some fancy casserole. I remember because she was using a recipe.

I cowered in the corner of the kitchen, wrapping my

golden yellow cardigan around my face, just peeking between the folds of nylon as the scene played out before me, my mother's howls and then her bloody lip and nose were all very real and frightening. I don't think he knew I was there because when he saw me; he stopped shouting and sang out,

"Hey, Pumpkin, come here and give your dad a squeeze."

When I leapt to my feet and sped from the room, he growled at my mother again, accusing her of poisoning me against him, saying it was all her fault I didn't love him. That she most likely said things about him that weren't true. I started crying into my pillow because it wasn't true. I did love him. He just scared me that day.

He moved about the house later that night, slamming cupboards and stuffing things into his duffle bag. I stayed in my room until he came in and told me he had to go back to work. When I argued that he only just got back, he just shrugged. "I love you, Pumpkin," he said tapping my nose with his finger. "I'm sorry I scared you before, but your mom makes me wild sometimes," he said smiling and showing off his crooked teeth.

I nodded, agreeing with him, telling him she made me mad all the time and he laughed. I'd asked him how many days he would be away, so I could write it in my diary, but when he told me he didn't know. I knew right then something was wrong, and a sickness gnawed at my stomach. I never saw him again. He left me with her and never came back.

It's been four days since the incident at the beach house with Alex, and with each passing day I've noticed Gerard's in a mood. He's barely touching me, and apart from daily pleasantries over meals and between commercial breaks when we watch TV, he isn't talking much at all. Not even about the beach house, which he had been so excited about until then. I've been constantly replaying the scene in my mind, wondering if it was possible that Gerard saw something? In a reflection or maybe the counter was lower than I imagined. Then I started believing Gerard was testing me, that Alex touching me was a setup, which became my cover-up because either way, I haven't told him about it. So, contrary to the promise I made myself to never bringing up the subject of a three-way, I've been obsessing over his proposal and desperate to know the truth.

I mean, had Alex acted independently, or God forbid, in response to me brushing my leg against his, as if I were asking for his attention. Had I asked for it? No, no way. That could've been accidental it was so slight. Anyway, just leaning against someone doesn't give them permission to do what Alex had done, slide his big, meaty hand all the way up and press against me. I clench below from the thoughts that follow. Alex had been unbelievably reckless, as if he didn't care about getting caught. I nod to myself as I wipe the kitchen counter. That's typically Alex. Then I'm doubting myself again. I'm now certain that Gerard put him up to it. I need to know the truth, but that means bringing up the idea of a three-way. At least that's what I am convincing myself that I'm doing when I ask him to come sit at the table so we can talk.

"You're the best thing that has ever happened to me, Gerard. I hope you believe that. I'm lucky to be married to a man like you and I'm grateful you were able to forgive me with Alex and you know—anything else that's happened." I pay special attention to his reaction, but I'm picking at my fingernails beneath the table. I stop myself by folding my hands on the table.

My compliment makes him smile. He reaches for my

hands then entwines my fingers with his. "I'm glad to hear you say that. To be honest, I thought you must have been mad at me about something. Ever since I showed you the beach house, you've been quiet."

"I thought you were angry at me!"

"Why would I be angry at you?"

My checks catch fire. "I don't know. It's just that… Well the last time I saw you around Alex was after the dinner night, and you were angry and then… well, then you invited him to fix up the beach house. I admit I was a little annoyed you asked him without consulting me and I guess I was sulking, but then you left us alone and we got talking and…" It's right there on the tip of my tongue but then I deviate. "Argh. Gerard, there are things about me I don't understand."

"Do you want to see a psychiatrist again, is that what you're saying?"

"No. What I'm saying is that I haven't been completely honest with myself or truthful with you."

Gerard pulls his hands away. Sitting straight he nods. "Go on."

"I think there is something wrong with the way my mind works. Like wires get crossed. What I think is good or feels right might be bad and wrong. And what I think is bad may be good. Because of that, I get confused, end up not trusting what I feel."

"Do you think that's exclusive to you? Because it's not. Many people don't trust their own feelings. I see plenty of that, I can assure you." He gets up from the table to get himself water.

"I know," I say, clasping my hands and wrestling my thumbs. "This is different though. You know I had a messed-up childhood."

Gerard sits again then rests his chin on his fist, one that's still sporting slightly skinned knuckles, and exhales loudly. When it comes to my mother, he has zero tolerance.

"This is hard, Gerard, hard for me because I'm anxious. I'm so scared of messing things up because of what's lurking beneath my problem. But I can't function knowing I've disappointed you somehow and... well—I was thinking about—you know that thing you want to do, and well, is not doing it, going to turn..."

"It's okay, Paige. I was being selfish and pressuring you. We can drop it. Forget, I suggested it." Gerard pushes back his chair and stands. Resting his hands on the table he smiles down at me. "You not being able to climax is not my business, really. If it doesn't bother you, it doesn't bother me. All right?"

His willingness to drop it should have made me feel better, but now I'm more curious than ever. Why has he been sulking all week if not because of my reluctance?

"I'm fine with everything. Let's have a drink, we'll watch a movie, maybe have an early night." He arches an eyebrow, making me smile. "Friday night we have that play organized. Do you still want to go?" he asks, making his way through to the living room. I get up and follow him.

"Yes, I do, it will be nice, but I haven't finished yet. I want to ask you some things."

"What more is there to know? We have different sexual tastes—we can only continue on and hope it doesn't put a strain on our relationship at some point."

Gerard pours a scotch, tosses in ice, then stirs it with a swivel. My face drains of blood. There it is. The truth.

"No wine for me thanks, Gerard," I say when he goes to pour one.

"Water?"

I nod.

Taking a seat, I tuck my legs beneath me. This is not how I thought the conversation would go. It feels like he's playing me somehow but then—not, because everything he's saying is true!

"Gerard. There's not too many men who would forgive their wife for cheating, why did you?"

"I love you."

He hands me the water then sits beside me. My mouth is so dry I drink almost half in one go.

"And when you asked to have a three-way, did you honestly think you could handle seeing Alex have sex with me? I mean wouldn't that eat at you?"

"I suppose if I knew he was going to steal you away, but I thought long and hard about it before I suggested it. Alex may have had sex with you, but he wouldn't take you away from this." He gestures around. "He knows who he is, and I don't mean that unfairly, it's just, he's not exactly marriage material, is he?" He raises an eyebrow then takes a sip of his drink. He seems to be smirking behind his glass.

"But he betrayed you. Why aren't you angry at him?"

"I was at first, but the more I thought about why he did it, the less it felt like a betrayal. Paige, he wanted to get back at me. He chose to do it that way. I think I know how he operates."

"But it could have destroyed our marriage."

"Only if I let it. Why are we talking about this, anyway?"

"Because I was thinking of reconsidering what you asked of us, if that's what you really want."

"Why the sudden change of heart?" he asks, eyeing me over the rim of his glass as he sips.

Is he smirking behind his glass? He must have set it up. "Isn't—that... I mean, only if that's what you want?" I stammer, realizing it's too late to back out. "I meant what I said the other morning. I don't need to have an orgasm to enjoy sex with you. I've read it's common and all the women say they still enjoy sex. If you don't believe me, I can look up the site for you. That's if you're interested," I ramble on.

Gerard indulges me with a smile. "I'm sure there are other women out there who can't climax, Paige, but I don't love or care about them. I'll be honest, I suppose it's not just entirely about you. It's about me too because I'd love to watch you climax. You know I've tried."

I look down, feeling ashamed and inadequate.

"It's not as though you haven't already had sex with Alex, I just want to watch," Gerard says, making me feel confused, vulnerable and—maybe a little too aroused.

I get up, deciding I need a wine after all. Gerard grabs my hand and tugs me onto his lap before I have time to get away and plonks his glass on the coffee table.

"I will do anything for you, Paige." He pulls me to his lips. His breath is hot, the familiar taste of scotch welcoming as I run my fingers through his hair. But suddenly I'm thinking of Alex, that it's his hair I'm combing through with my fingers, that it's his hand snaking its way under my dress. I'm so torn. There's one part of me that desperately wants to be everything to Gerard and another part that's craving Alex, that I'm waning in my decision, fearing we will ruin everything we have.

Gerard's hand reaches the lace of my underwear, his fingers teasing me through the fabric, fiddling with the side until he gains access. I spread my legs to make it easier for him and bury his face against my breasts. I love that he's touching me again, but hate myself because shamefully I'm imagining he's Alex, caressing my sweet spot. My confusion makes me want to cry. Then Gerard snaps me out of my reverie by reading my mind.

"Alex could stick his fingers in here. Is that what he did?" Gerard pushes inside me. "Hmm. You're already turned on."

I grab Gerard's face in both hands and nudge him back gently. His hand comes away to steady himself, gripping onto my waist, and I look at him for the longest time, searching his eyes. His face is passive, but his eyes radiate pure desire.

"Do you really want to see me with another man?" My heart is thudding away from the prospect but concerned by what I register in Gerard's eyes. Fixated on me, there's an elated yearning there, like the thought of a fix to an addict, that he wants it whatever the cost.

Gerard nods.

I get to my feet, dawdle over to the bar, thinking. Gerard switches the television on. I turn to see him press back into the couch, his eyes glued on the news, his scotch at his lips. Slowly I pour the wine, watching him, one arm thrown over the top of the couch, relaxed and nonchalant by our discussion.

"And what if I can't come, what then?"

"What? Oh, are we still talking about that?" He tries sounding coy and making an obvious display of tearing his eyes away from the news. Looking at me in faux surprise beneath arched brows.

I pull a face that makes him smile then repeat myself. "I'm being serious. What if we do it and it doesn't happen?"

"Well, at least we tried."

"So, you're saying, Alex is a means to an end then?"

"I guess. Yes. That's one way to look at it. But don't worry about it anymore. I was just teasing you about it."

"What, now you don't want to do it?"

"Look. Of course, it's something I fantasize about, will most likely always think about, but the idea doesn't sit well with you, so let's just forget it."

Sipping wine, I study Gerard over the bar as he watches the news. Reacting vocally to the baseball replays that are showing. Once. I could do it once. Alex most likely won't be able to make me climax again, anyway. But Gerard will be happy we tried, and things can go back to normal.

Oh, who am I kidding? Nothing has been normal since Alex arrived.

Sitting beside Gerard, I nurse my wine and watch the television with him. He rests his hand on my knee and smiles. "Minnesota won against the Angels."

"Is that good?"

"Well, I think it is, I had money riding on them." He drains his glass then rises. "I think I might go to bed. I have an early start tomorrow. Are you coming?"

I grab a hold of his hand before he has time to move away.

"What?"

"I'll do it, Gerard. Just once. That's if Alex is still willing."

He frowns. "Willing? Why wouldn't he be?"

"You did—punch him in the face the other week."

Gerard straightens and draws in a breath. "Yes, I did that didn't I? But no, you're only agreeing because of me. Let's go to bed."

I roll my eyes at him. "Yes, it's because you asked, but I'll do it if it will make you happy." My internal lie detector punishes me with a zap causing electrical mayhem to my heart. "I'm not sure if it will work," I continue, "But like you said, at least we would have tried."

Studying me, he chews on the inside of his mouth then pulls me to my feet. "All right, then. I'll ask Alex again, see if he's interested."

"Just promise you'll never hold it against me though. This is your idea."

Smiling, Gerard takes my face in his hands. "Let's say it's —our idea. But yes, I promise to never hold it against you. But that goes for you too." He taps my nose with a finger then comes in closer to kiss me fully on the mouth.

I sigh as all the tension leaves me. Content now that I just made my husband a very happy man.

15

GIVE ME LOVE

E very time I look at my hands hovering over my keyboard, they're shaking. At first, I thought it was because of the four cups of coffee I'd drunk this morning, but now I realize, as I stare at my Mac watching time tick over, it's because I am nervous about tonight. Gerard is planning on asking Alex to join us to the theater.

Getting up from my chair, I wander over to the window, deluding myself that I might spot Alex out in the yard but knowing full well, he's not even here. He's been spending his time moving into the beach house, so Gerard tells me, because Alex and I haven't spoken a word to each other since the night he rode his hand up my thigh. Christ, what am I doing?

Leaving the office I make my way into the living room to tidy up. But before I know it, the radio has lulled me into my favorite chair by the window where, after our romp in the shed, I was often sitting so I could watch Alex. Now all I'm doing is watching the grass grow, along with my anxiety because I'm desperate to know if Gerard has called him—yet I'm too afraid to text and ask. I don't want to give Gerard any reason to think a three-way is anything other than a bit of extra marital exploration. That I don't care about it one way or the other. But truthfully, I'm dying to know if Alex has agreed to this ridiculous idea. What if he says no? There is that possibility. Maybe that would be better. If Alex just says no, then all problems are solved. But he won't say no. Why else would he be sliding his hand where it has no business going if it wasn't because he wanted me?

Running my fingernails along the fabric surface of the chair, I mimic the script style writing that adorns the fabric, lost in my thoughts. Picturing Gerard in his office, phone in hand and pacing. Questioning whether letting another man sleep with his wife is the right thing to do after all. How can he honestly want this? I know for certain I couldn't bear to watch Gerard make love to another woman right in front of me. Groaning, I rise. I need to call him—tell him I've changed my mind. Protect him from himself. I'm certain now that he doesn't know what he's doing.

Frantic, I rush back to the office to get my phone when there's a knock at the front door. I come to an abrupt halt, my heart racing. Maybe it's Alex, coming to discuss the night with me. I try composing myself as I make my way slowly to the front door, pausing to steady my shaking hands. The knocking resumes, startling me.

Steeling myself expecting to see Alex. I'm surprised when I pull the door wide and there's a tall skinny man in a black uniform and cap with a logo embroidered on the front. His van in the driveway carries the same logo.

"Afternoon, I have a delivery for Paige Whitmyer." He holds out a clipboard for me to sign, juggling a large white box that he then tucks under his arm.

After signing and sharing pleasantries with him, he hands me the carton. "I have something else too." Darting away, he returns with an enormous floral arrangement that's stunning. My hand goes to my mouth and I can't help the tears, making the delivery man slightly uncomfortable when he offers them to me.

After thanking him, I close the door and head to the kitchen, my nose buried and inhaling the beautiful scent coming from at least thirty long stem roses. Coral roses—desire. I actually swoon and get butterflies. Alex must have agreed. The fluttering then seems to migrate between my legs.

Digging around, I find the card and read, 'To my beautiful wife, I don't want to tell you how much I love you, I want to show you how much I love you. Thank you for doing this for me, for us. You may be my wife, but more than that, you are my life. Love always. Gerard x.'

I can't believe the man I married. How can he be so forgiving then trusting? I fall into the chair and cradle my face. Stare at the unopened box. I'm ashamed of myself. Seeing the flowers, knowing Alex had agreed. I felt relief, when only moments ago I was ready to call the whole thing off. The reality that I have given in because I have feelings for Alex is shaking me to the core. But how? I don't even know him that well. Gerard's words come back to haunt me. His insistence to know why I cheated. He had a right to ask, I understand that now. I just wish I knew the answer. What is it I seem to need? Alex is just a man. A guy with basic needs who ravished me in a shed to get his rocks off. What am I infatuated with? I glare at the parcel through blurred vision for what seems like minutes, then finally pull myself together and find a Kleenex to clean my face. Then I become pissed off that Gerard is being so nice. I should be punished not rewarded. How can he be so trusting? Why didn't he just kick me to the curb like Alex thought I should have been? I don't deserve this kind of love.

I rip off the lid to the box and toss it to the floor, pull

back the tissue paper and see a gown. Resting on top of the gown is a small box. Clasping it, I open the lid and catch my breath. Inside is a gold necklace shaped like an octopus with two diamonds for eyes. It's stunning. The embossed writing on the lid tells me it's a designer piece and I imagine it must have cost a fortune.

Gerard, what are you doing? There is a folded piece of paper. When I unfold it, I read that Alex will pick me up at six. My heart jumps into my throat, and my hand goes to steady the butterflies that seem to multiply in my stomach. I pull the gown out of its box and hold it in front of me. It's a gorgeous sleek mermaid gown made from a shimmering stretch crepe fabric. The halter neck gives way to a plunging neckline, it looks so small in the waist I'm afraid it won't fit, but it's amazing.

Placing it back it the box, I survey my gifts. It's obvious he has thought long and hard over tonight and my earlier trepidation dissipates. Just one night, it's just one night. I love my husband and it's natural that I feel something for Alex because... because we shared a moment and he's hot and sexy. It makes sense to be attracted to him. It doesn't mean I don't love my husband, right? I keep chatting to myself as I mount the stairs with my gifts.

At four-thirty I shower, wash my hair and pluck my eyebrows. Thankfully, my trips to the salon have kept me hairless so I have plenty of time to apply a face mask and meander around the house aimlessly until it dries. The whole time I'm wandering around I need to resist the urge to bite my nails to the quick whenever my fingers find their way inside my mouth. I'm ping-ponging between feeling excited and sick. What if Gerard thinks I'm enjoying it too much? Will Alex even be able to perform with his stepbrother right there? What if I come in an instant, and Gerard knows I have feelings for Alex. God, he'll see right through me. This is a mistake. Why did I agree?

I surprise myself by applying flawless makeup even though my hands are shaking like a detox patient. Lastly, I blow-dry my hair then spray on some oil to calm the frizz and give it a sheen. Then I'm pace the living area for half an hour, sipping on a glass of wine to calm myself down. I'm still shaking but manage to paint my nails with nude polish as I listening to music. Shortly after, I'm in a trance wondering why Alex is picking me up instead of my husband.

When I check my phone for the time, I text Gerard to find out where he plans on getting ready. He replies after a few minutes, telling me he has a late meeting with a client. That it would be pointless to travel home just to go back into the city, and that he brought his suit, just in case. I end our texting thanking him for my gifts and laying on at least a dozen kisses.

It's five forty-five when Alex arrives in his pickup truck. I don't even wait for him to come to the door. The second he shuts off the engine, I grab my keys, clutch and overnight bag then meet him outside. I'll have as little alone time as possible. We'll be traveling all the way into the city together, I know. But I figure it's easier to be distracted in a car, besides, if I'd stay any longer in the house, I'd finish the bottle of wine I started and I'm already well on my way to tipsy.

"Hi," I say as he gets out the truck with his bag. He's wearing dark jeans and a pale gray shirt which looks poorly pressed, but because it's fitted to his bulky form, it's only noticeable up close. But still, I have the urge to press my hand against his chest to smooth the wrinkles out. Alex must notice me staring and looks down.

"What, not to your liking?"

I meet his steely gaze, feeling awkward. "No, you look fine. How have you been?" I unlock the car and we both toss our bags onto the bag seat then I hand over the key, preferring he drive.

"Good. What about you?" He pulls open the door and we both clip ourselves in. "I wanted to call you earlier, but I don't have your number. Gerard didn't pressure you into doing this, did he?"

In the confined space, his cologne becomes overwhelmingly seductive that I don't answer right away. My palms get sweaty, and my mind races around collecting memories of our time in the shed. His rough hands and pounding thrusts. Now my heart is like a jackhammer causing a whooshing sound in my head.

"Paige?" he questions, firing up the engine before it relaxes into a purr. His hand hovers on the gear stick waiting for my reply, his concerned expression filling me with doubt.

"No, he didn't. But I want you to know tonight is for Gerard, you understand that, right?"

"Oh, is that right?" He puts the gear stick into reverse. Smiling, he throws his arm over the seat and twists his body as he backs out of the garage. "And here I was thinking it was about you." He looks straight at me then puts the stick in drive and accelerates. "About making you come that is," he laughs and winks.

"Alex," I groan.

"Come on, Paige, lighten the hell up. We're going to fuck, so what if your husband is there watching—right?"

My hands wring at my clutch. "Oh God, let me out. This is a mistake."

Alex slams on the brakes. "I thought so. That's how you

honestly feel isn't it? Because I do not want to do this if you will regret it. Paige, you can say no."

My stomach is clenching and I'm feeling claustrophobic. I fling open the door. "I just need to get out for a minute." Leaving my clutch, I climb out of the car and walk around to the back of the vehicle and pace. I don't know what I'm doing. Is this a mistake or am I making this into something it's not? I try consoling myself that thousands, if not millions of people do this all the time. Wild orgies and swingers. Sex clubs and fulfilling fetishes. I'm not naïve about the sexual cesspool that is life, but shit! Two men, hungry and pawing at me. Resting my hands on the trunk of the car, I get as low as I can without lying down. Just so I can get some blood to my head.

"Shit, Paige."

My head bobs up.

Alex swoops in and wraps his arms around me, holding tight when I try to step back. His unexpected concern triggers a reaction from my eyes and the next thing I know, I'm sobbing in his arms like a baby. When I calm down and pull away, I notice the mess I've made of his shirt.

"Sorry." I step back and smooth the wet patch that has traces of mascara then meet his gaze. "I'm fine. I don't even know why I'm crying."

Alex nods and pulls out his phone from his back pocket. "Do you want me to call Gerard, tell him you've changed your mind?

I shake my head.

"*No.* But you're upset. Obviously, you don't want to do it."

"That's not why I'm upset, Alex. I'm stressed because… because of how I feel about you."

"What do you mean?" He shoves his phone back in his pocket and crosses his arms.

"I'm confused. How can I be in love with my husband but still want to do this with you?"

"Easy. We're basically animals with urges," Alex says, moving around to the driver's side and standing by his open door. Waiting to see what I want to do. Is it really that simple?

Getting back in the car, we repeat our earlier movements and get on the way. Alex keeps looking over at me.

"So, that's how it is for you, tonight is just an urge to fulfill?" I ask.

"Yes."

"Okay. Good," I mumble against the glass, trying not to feel hurt but questioning why I don't feel it's better that way. After all, I don't want Alex pursuing me. Do I? I steal little glances as he navigates down the driveway and onto the road. As soon as Alex has the car in top gear, he switches on the radio and starts tapping his fingers on the steering wheel in time to the music. I stare out my window, watching as people go about their evening, dragging in trash bins, walking dogs and playing with their children. All very normal. Making what we are doing even more surreal. When we are nearing Jenna and Nadal Martín's house, I'm reminded of Jenna's extended invitation to Alex, and I break the silence.

"Where?" he sounds confused after I tell him.

"The Martíns'. That's their place, just back there." I point uselessly out my window because we've already gone way past their pristine house. "Jenna told me to pass on the invite."

"Did she now?" Alex nods.

"What, do you already know her?"

Alex turns to me briefly before looking back at the road ahead, his expression passive. "Sort of," he adds but doesn't elaborate.

"Well, let me know if you'd like to go, and I'll tell her you're coming."

"Oh, I'll be coming all right, later tonight that is." He looks at me again and smirks.

"Alex." I smack his leg then turn to look out my window again, to hide my smile. His innuendos are wicked and what got me in trouble in the first place.

"You can do that later." He wiggles his eyebrows when I face him again. "You know, slap me. I'll enjoy being slapped on the ass while I drive my cock into you."

"Alex stop being so crude."

"Oh, you love it. Come on, admit you're looking forward to tonight?"

"What, the play? Sure, I'm looking forward to that. They say it's good."

"Ha, ha, whatever, Princess, act coy. I'll just make you pay for it later," he says. Shamefully I squirm in my seat and Alex notices.

"Want me to pull over and warm you up now?"

"Christ, Alex, will you just drive?" I turn my head away, ignoring him, taking deep breaths to calm the inferno that's already overwhelming me. I don't know how he does it, but everything he says just turns me to Jell-O making me want to jump him. God, it's embarrassing how easy I am for him.

"You know what you did the other night at the beach house wasn't right." I growl and fold my arms over my chest and stare straight at him.

"Oh, come on. I was just messing around."

"Were you, or did Gerard put you up to it? Was it an attempt to get tonight to happen?"

"No. But it sounds like it might have been your excuse to make tonight happen. And what do you mean, Gerard put…"

"I'm just doing this for him all right. You and Gerard

played me. It worked. We'll do this and get it out of his system."

"Right," he draws the syllable out, then turns his attention back to the road.

Thankfully, for the better part of the journey, we drive in silence, but when we are almost there, Alex contradicts that he's blasé about the impending arrangement.

"You know there's a risk in what Gerard wants, and I just hope you both realize that side of it."

"How do you mean?" Although I know quite well what he means, I just want to hear him say it.

"Been there done that. People can get hurt."

Oh! I wasn't expecting him to say that. "Why did you agree then?" I ask, pushing away what he'd said because I'd rather not be reminded he's done this before.

"Didn't say it would be me that gets hurt, Princess."

"Oh."

"Yeah, 'oh.' Paige, are you sure you want to do this? I mean, I know you say you love Gerard, and I'm sure you do on some fucked up level, but... aren't you doing this for the wrong reason? I know you two have issues and it's most likely my fault that it all came out, but—I didn't realize you were..." he pauses, looking outside to form a word that fits.

"You didn't know I was what? Broken?"

His head snaps around. "A nice person, not a gold digger and just some slut after my brother's money. I admit, I used you to get back at Gerard, and for that I'm sorry. But I'm not sorry I had sex with you, making it pretty darn hard to say no when your brother asks if I'd like to try it again."

I'm stunned into silence, still staring at him. Even in the darkness I can tell he is blushing.

"I just need you to know that all right?" he adds when I remain quiet.

"Okay." I look away, my face flushing from his admission. "No, I'm not a gold digger, Alex, but I am damaged."

"I wouldn't say that, just lost maybe," he ends, making a few final turns before finding the underground parking garage. I'm still staring out my window, pressing my eyes closed, hoping to hold back stupid tears that want to come. How does he know so much about me when he doesn't even know me? I'm reminded of our first meeting and how he stared at me, like right at me, or through me, or maybe he was seeing behind me, to that person who is lost.

We remain silent as we walk together to the entrance. When we spot Gerard, Alex grabs my wrist to stop me from rushing off.

"Paige, at any time you want to stop you say so."

I look toward Gerard. He has seen us and is walking our way. I twist my hand free. "I will. I promise."

Alex nods before stepping away and we close the gap toward Gerard. He's wearing suit pants and a sky-blue shirt that brings out the extreme color of his eyes. A jacket but no tie. His hair is styled, and he has shaven. It's no surprise he draws looks from the ladies entering the entertainment area as he walks our way. Fixated on me, he doesn't even notice the attention he gets.

"Honey, you look stunning. Doesn't she, Alex?"

Alex just raises his eyebrows, appearing blasé.

"Thank you." I smooth his lapels with both hands then rise on tiptoes to give him a quick kiss.

Stepping back, Gerard plays with my necklace, admiring it before searching my eyes. "Do you like it?" he whispers, our foreheads touching.

"I love it. And the dress, and the flowers. It was all a beautiful surprise, but you really didn't need to."

"Well, I wanted tonight to be special," he says loudly,

standing straight and taking my hand. "Alex helped with the flowers," he informs, offhandedly.

Behind Gerard's back, I mouth a thank you to Alex who winks and twists off a forced smile.

Gerard leads the way into the building with Alex following just slightly behind. Although I know we are only here to see a show and to get comfortable with each other, I'm as nervous as if it were a first date. Everywhere I look, people are in their finest, and I'm wondering if Alex is now feeling underdressed. If he is uncomfortable in this environment, he doesn't let on, instead he keeps pace as we march up the many stairs to the front entrance of the Empire Theatre.

Inside, there is a large bar to one side of the foyer that's packed with people wrestling for drinks. There are at least six staff members buzzing about behind the opulent bar that makes me wish I'd brought my camera. The sepia mirrored wall behind the workers is stocked with bottles galore, and with miniature overhead lighting it looks like they're standing below the stars. It would make an excellent advert shot.

People are milling around in groups, chatting and drinking, and it takes effort for us to find a space to make our own. Music is playing rather loudly, making the conversation a roar as everyone tries competing with it.

Gerard lets go of my hand, and the three of us stand in a tight circle, deciding what to do.

"Should we get a drink first, or would you like to go straight in and find our seats?" Gerard shouts.

"Drinks," I reply, loud enough for him to hear, clenching and twisting my clutch.

"I'm just goin' with the flow, bro." Alex shrugs, taking in the crowd. I look to see what seems to have caught his attention and notice he is watching a group of ladies holding champagne flutes. They are attractive in their short bodycon dresses that show off their long, toned legs and Alex seems to enjoy an eyeful.

"I'll get us a drink then," Gerard offers, touching the small of my back to move me so he can pass, momentarily pressing me into Alex and drawing his attention back on us.

"A Budweiser, thanks, Ger," he shouts after Gerard, then looks down at me.

"Would you rather be mingling over there, Alex?" I ask, rising on tiptoes so I can be closer to his ear, then nodding toward the group of young ladies he was watching. He follows my gaze, then looks back at me, his mouth curling.

"No. I'm serious," I say. "Are you sure you want to be here, with us? I mean this isn't exactly your scene is it?" I glance around again at the variety of faces before settling back on Alex. He slips an arm around my waist, thrilling me from the unexpected contact. When he pulls me toward him, I realize he is moving me so some people can get past. His arm falls away once they've moved on in an explosion of chatter, but the absence of his touch is so pronounced, I unconsciously lean into him.

"I'm fine right where I am, Princess. There's a time and a place for everything," he concedes, looking down at himself, brushing and straightening the front of his gray shirt, maybe aware now that he should have ironed it. His sleeves are rolled, showing off strong forearms, appendages I seem to have become enthralled with these days. With his head bent, I see he's used product to make his hair stand. The heavenly scent he's wearing seems to be a sedative, making me hallucinate and my insides flutter at the prospect of my naked body writhing against his. He looks up and catches me staring. Our eyes lock for a moment making me conscious of my breathing. My lips curl slightly before his face is breaking apart with a cheeky grin like he has read my mind.

"Here," Gerard calls, making us turn and breaking the spell.

We wrestle the drink from him and take a sip in unison, Gerard trying to catch my eye. But the heat coursing through me has decided to exit via my face so I turn away.

After some time and composing myself I link my arm through Gerard's. "You were quick, considering the crowd."

He puts a hand in one pocket and leans forward. "I knew one of the bar staff," he says, taking another sip from his tumbler, eyeing me over his glass and winking. He seems so happy, excited and I'm hoping for his sake that what Alex fears will not be his undoing. The three of us are quiet for a moment, sipping our drinks and people watching, making the odd comment or nod at each other as amusing characters pass by.

"I'm surprised at the turnout. It's not as though this Byrne is well-known. What do you think, Alex, are you going to be able to sit through it?" Gerard grins at his brother.

"You make out I'm not very cultured, Ger. I'll have you know I've been to a show or two in my time."

"You don't say," Gerard nods, looking doubtful.

"I saw a few with an ex, actually. She was into this type of thing—remember?"

The smile that graced Gerard's face falters slightly.

"You're right. I'd forgotten that." Gerard drains his glass. "Your turn to get drinks, Alex. Paige, would you like another?"

"No. I'll stick with the one, so I can drive." I upend the glass to finish the wine, then hand it to Alex. He takes Gerard's empty glass also then heads to the bar. Gerard puts an arm around me and pulls me close then rests his chin on my head.

"I love you," he tells me with a squeeze, his voice barely audible over the crowd. There is an announcement over the

PA that the show is about to begin that hushes everyone to a murmur. The music quiets and my senses become astute again just as Ed Sheeran sings out, "Give Me Love." My heart pounds to the lyrics and my eyes unconsciously search for Alex. He's walking back toward us carrying beers and, thoughtfully, water for me. He stands close so I can remove it carefully from the cluster he carries. With Gerard spooning me from behind and Alex in front of me, my imagination goes wild, causing a rush of heat I'm sure both men can sense from their proximity. I want this, no, I need this. Downing my water, the men sip their drinks and we all get shuffled along with the moving crowd.

Gerard has managed second level box seats. It appears to normally cater for six, but no-one seems to join us, so we reorganize ourselves to take up the center of the six chairs and I nestle in between the two men, finding and clasping tightly onto Gerard's hand, interlocking his fingers with mine.

When the lights dim and the stage is illuminated, I get the first flutter of excitement that accompanies a live show, feeling cultivated in the anonymity. The audience becomes mesmerized, and our unity thickens the atmosphere with energy.

The curtains are drawn. The stage is set. Two men sit opposite each other at a table. One wears a suit and the other a pair of jeans and a plain sweater. The suited man pushes glasses up his nose and taps his pen against a notebook in front of him. The other man has his hands, one on top of the other, resting on the table in front of him. He's hunched and looks tired. I conclude it's some sort of interrogation. The obvious thing, a recording device placed right in the center of the table between them. Apart from that, the stage is bare.

"You say you killed a man?" The suited man says.

"I did."

"Why?"

"For a reason," the tired man replies.

"Doesn't everyone capable of killing have a reason?"

"I did it for a very important reason. To protect someone I didn't want to lose."

Gerard squeezes my hand, but when I glance at him, he stays focused ahead. A lump congeals in my throat that I struggle to swallow down. Unhooking our hands, I grab around his arm instead and lean into him, concerned the dialogue on stage has a cryptic meaning that I'm supposed to understand. I steal a peek at him, feel relieved when he smiles. He then whispers in my ear. "I want you to feel at ease tonight. Just let whatever transpires, happen, all right? There's no need to check in with me."

His permission sends my heart into a frenzy. I don't know why he said what he said right then, but I nod, then turn my attention back to the stage, releasing the death grip I have on him, and slip my palm into his again.

By the time Act III is in progress, we've learned that the interrogation is an interview. That the lead character is presumably homophobic, and someone has been killed, a tenant in his shared accommodation. As the interview transpires, the back scenes come to life, depicting what has happened in the lead up to the crime. It's captivating, and I am so engrossed in the production that I barely notice Alex's hand move until he grazes my leg. Instantly my eyes dart downward, watching as he slowly draws my long gown up toward my knee, gathering the fabric into his palm. My head snaps up. He is watching me intently. I swivel to look at Gerard, but his attention is on the stage. The only sign that he knows something is going on is the salacious expression he wears.

"Watch the show, Princess, you're missing the good parts," Alex leans in to whisper. I become light-headed as I face the stage again, doing as I'm told while adrenaline and horny hormones flood my veins, making me so hot, the perfume I'm wearing becomes overwhelming.

My hand squeezes Gerard's and when I do, he shifts his, unhooking our fingers so he can press my open palm against his confined erection, letting me know he is getting immensely turned on, and with the curling of his fingers, he begs for me to squeeze.

I'm so aroused, I can't focus on the show anymore. I'm massaging Gerard's rock-hard cock as Alex continues gathering my dress until at last, he connects with the bare flesh of my inner thigh. The moment he does, my leg falls shamelessly against his. Shocked that I'm so wanton in public, I quickly pull my legs closed, but when I do, capturing Alex's finger between my knees, he glances at Gerard who then slides his hand onto my other thigh so both he and Alex can pry my legs gently apart.

"Oh my God," I sigh, throwing my head back in pure arousal, sucking in a lungful of air and holding onto it. I'm pulsating so hard it takes effort for me to gain balance. I try putting my focus back on the stage, letting my breath out in a controlled quiver through my pursed lips. I can feel both Alex and Gerard smile, though I don't dare look at them for fear of losing it completely. Instead, I shut my eyes as both men caress the inside of my thighs, traveling up and down in slow delightful strokes, using just their fingertips, climbing higher and higher with each pass. My chest is heaving and my eyes prickle with heat when I open them to watch their movements. I glance at Gerard before I'm reaching over and placing my other hand on Alex's cock. He's so hard the firmness of him is straining against the seams of his jeans. I gasp from the thrill of being so naughty and my legs fall farther apart, desperate for one of them to touch, right where I'm most vulnerable. But I'm getting wet, too wet.

"Gerard," I whisper, and he offers me his ear. "I'm getting so wet, I'm afraid I'll spoil my dress."

Facing me, Gerard smiles then looks to Alex. "Then I think we should take this little game elsewhere. Wouldn't you both agree?"

16

GOOD FOR YOU

"Well, this is embarrassing," I comment, looking at the hotel clerk behind the desk. "He's checking the bed configuration and counting our heads."

I'm relieved when Alex laughs, stepping closer he encircles my waist. "Don't stress, I'm certain they've seen it all before. I can guarantee you that," he says, kissing my temple. "Are you sure you want to do this? It's not too late to back out." He's so close to my ear, his words tickle, giving me goose bumps that cause my nipples to harden beneath my gown. I look up at him and smile, my eyes roaming over his closely trimmed facial hair until I'm staring at those bow-shaped lips I've been dying to kiss all night.

"Yes, I'm sure." I nod meeting his gaze.

"Good, because I intend doing you so thoroughly tonight, you're gonna feel me for the next two days." A smile takes over his face, and there's a shadow of a dimple on his left cheek that I've never noticed before.

I giggle when he pinches my ass. "Alex, stop, everyone will see." Placing a palm on his chest, I become serious. "Just promise me you won't hurt Gerard—you know, make him feel excluded."

We glance at the desk to see if Gerard is done checking us in. He turns and then gestures for us to come closer.

"You just worry about yourself, Princess. I've got the rest under control."

And with his hand firmly clasping mine, I don't doubt it for a second.

We have a sweeping one hundred and eighty-degree view of Los Angeles with the billion plus lights below, painting an extraordinary vista. Soft music is playing, and the lighting from the corner lamps are low, and I'm sure the sheets have been turned down, a mint or two on the pillows. But not three.

"It's amazing, Gerard. Look, you can see right across the city." Placing my bag on the floor, I move over to the widows and stare at the night life below. I'm curious if Alex is equally affected. When I catch his attention, he nods.

"Looks like you spared no expense, Gerard. I'm impressed."

"Thank you. I've arranged for room service to bring up a platter later and," Gerard pauses, then moves over to the lounging area and finds the ice bucket, "we have champagne." He holds up a dripping bottle of Dom Perignon.

Alex throws his bag against the wall under a beautiful photo of a snow-covered Nepal. "I'll just have beer." He wanders closer just as Gerard pops the champagne. I find some glasses, trying to hold them steady as he pours. I'm so nervous I jump when Alex rips open the bar fridge and takes out a beer. Twisting off the cap, he does what he always does, tosses it in the sink with a clang then leans against the marble island as though he is calculating what the next move might be.

Gerard puts a protective arm around my waist and pulls me in tightly. There's an awkward moment of silent staring, then he's holding up his glass.

"Well, here's to a good night. Thank you, Alex, for agreeing, and of course you, Paige," he toasts taking a sip.

"Hard not to." Alex glances at Gerard. I giggle, but then... did Gerard just flinch?

"I hope we can be relaxed about this. But I just want to say, for tonight, I mostly want to watch. I might join in some of the time, but please, don't think anything negative if I seem distant. All right?" Gerard says mostly to me.

"But I thought you said a three-way?" Hang on. Did he just say for tonight, as if there will be other nights?

"I did. I'll be here." Gerard puts down his glass and peels off his jacket. "Like I said, Alex has my permission to seduce you, so you don't need to worry about me." He walks off toward the bedroom. I assume to hang his jacket but he picks up his overnight bag, that he retrieved earlier from his car.

"Works for me," Alex casually agrees. I scowl at him before chasing after Gerard, my heels tapping loudly against the marble floor, stopping Gerard in his tracks. He turns to face me with a confused look.

"Gerard, I want you to be right there. This is meant to be an *us* thing."

He resumes walking, "Paige, relax and have a drink, nothing bad is going to happen." I watch Gerard disappear into the bedroom, then make my way back to the kitchen where Alex is waiting. He holds out my champagne for me.

Taking a deep breath, I reclaim my glass then drink down the bubbles and pour myself another.

"You seem relaxed about the whole thing, Alex. What's your secret?" Maybe all the other ménage à trois may have helped, I uncomfortably surmise. He doesn't answer at first, just studies my face. Then, when I'm half done with my drink, he relieves me of it, placing it gently on the counter.

"The secret," Alex pulls me in so he can whisper in my ear before dropping a light kiss behind my lobe, "is to stop thinking so much." His fingers trail little circles all the way down the length of my back, causing me to shiver and hold my breath. He lingers over my ass, teasing until he grabs both cheeks and jerks me, a powerful thrust that knocks the trapped air out of my lungs. He's already aroused. I can feel him against my stomach and when his lips taste mine, he grows stiffer, harder, and hotter. The heat radiating off him near scorches through the sheer fabric of my dress, making my breasts feel suddenly achy.

When our lips part, Alex strokes my neck and holds my jaw, pushing me away slowly until I'm pressed up against the bench. I grab the edge of the cold surface to steady myself, my eyes bound to his, held captive by the size and depth of his desire and his firm hand around my throat. Fuck! My arousal is so instant, I feel vulnerable and at his mercy as he holds me carefully by the face still searching my eyes. My chest is heaving, my legs quivering, and before I even understand what is happening, my dress is falling to the floor, becoming a black puddle at my feet. My sharp intake of air makes Alex smile. Letting me go, he dives onto my lips again, his arm going around my waist, almost double because he's so big compared to me. I take hold of his waist, his shirt, his jeans into two fistfuls trying to stay upright. We kiss urgently like we've been starved of the privilege for years. His hot hands over my naked flesh feel everywhere, his scent permeates the air like a cloud, a cocoon that I almost forget where and who we are until I'm reminded.

"Paige."

My heart leaps to my throat in the same instant Alex

turns me and I'm looking at Gerard, sitting casually with one arm slung over the back of the oversized leather armchair. I'm shocked because I didn't even realize he'd come back into the room.

I go to step away, but Alex holds on. Pulling me back so he can press himself against me and paw between my legs, the fabric of his jeans rough against the small of my back and I imagine he is boring his eyes into Gerard's, taunting him. The audacity of him is making me pant and feel giddy.

"Could you bring me more champagne, please?" Gerard holds out his glass, sounding authoritative. Alex's arms slacken but when I try to step away, he snaps me back. "Make sure you come back, Princess, or I'll have to come and get you." I shiver all over from the whispering against my ear, or is it his threat that heightens my desire even more?

Letting me go, I almost stumble on my heels before righting myself in search of the bottle. I only become aware of the game Gerard is playing when his smile appears. It's so lascivious, I giggle from being ogled as I strut across the room wearing nothing but heels and a red lacy thong. My whole body volcanic because I'm aware that I have become the center of their attention. I turn briefly, catch Alex undoing his zipper, then tremble as the reality settles in. My husband is going to watch another man fuck me. He's going to see me aroused and greedy and I can't seem to stop the excitement from reaching my eyes. I stifle another giggle but the corners of my mouth still twitch because I can't believe I'm actually going ahead with this.

As I pour the frothy liquid in Gerard's glass, his eyes never leave me. It's like he's seeing me like never before. What's scary, I don't know if he likes what he sees. When I'm done, he asks me to sit on his knee. I look toward Alex, remembering his warning, but Gerard tugs on my hand until I'm sitting.

"How do you feel?" he asks, pushing my hair away and nuzzling my neck. His cool hand slides between my thighs, gliding up until his fingers are brushing against the warm wetness from my pussy.

"All right, I think. A little nervous maybe." I quiver against him, search his eyes that have become a deep blue color. When he tilts his face toward me, I kiss him. It's soft, familiar and comforting, reminding me of the time we first kissed. Gerard's expert lips coaxing my inexperienced ones, gently probing with his tongue to taste me, as the back of his hand caressed my check.

"Do you know how sexy you look right now? Look over there at Alex, see how badly he wants to have sex with you. But you're mine. Aren't you?"

I nod almost hypnotically before tearing my eyes away to look at Alex. His naked muscled body leaning against the bench, watching us. The highlight of his desire held in his palm, comfortably pleasuring himself. The sight makes me throb and clench. Tattoos cover more of his body than I ever imagined, and every inch of him is hard. His pectorals are like sculptured bronze and his shoulders are everything they felt like the morning he grabbed me in the shed, massive and round. For a man his height, he's built solid with a six-pack so ripped, you'd swear he'd been doing hanging crunches every day of his life. He is beautiful to look at, and any second thoughts I have are tossed away.

The music becomes louder, and when I search for the cause, Gerard is placing the remote down. When my gaze drifts back to Alex, Gerard starts caressing my bare breasts, brushing a palm over, then pinching my nipples gently. The song becomes intoxicating. Selena Gomez cooing out sexily how she wants to look good but vocalizes it so seductively we know she really means to be bad. Like me, a bad little slut who is going to have both these men. I want to let go. Want them to want me so badly, they grab and pull and fight over me. Take me so high I'll never be afraid to let go again. It's only when I notice Gerard looking at my heaving breast, do I realize I'm panting—hard.

"He turns you on, doesn't he?" Gerard murmurs against my shoulder blade, his hand pressing against my pleasure zone, his fingers trying to pry me apart and find a way past my panties. "He has a fit body, is that what attracted you?" he whispers in my ear, then sucks on my lobe. When I don't respond, Gerard nips me. "Paige, I asked you a question."

I don't know how I should answer. There's still a part of me that's unsure and untrusting that this is for real, not some setup to humiliate me. Regardless of my inner conflict, I'm still breathy and becoming almost too aroused by the situation. Gerard squeezes my inner thigh.

"Answer me. I want to hear you say it. Does looking at him turn you on?"

"Yes," I breathe, throwing caution to the wind, then quickly looking at him. He pulls me down and kisses me hard, almost too rough, grabbing my jaw and holding me as he feasts on my mouth, his fingers sliding inside me. Soon I'm moaning and squirming on his lap with pleasure. Oh God, help me—I'm so horny, I'm aching all over. Unaware of anything else, I gasp when I'm abruptly yanked off Gerard.

Pulling me to my feet, Alex takes a turn at tasting me. Gentle at first until little nips take over and his tongue darts in. When he sets my mouth free, I press my face against his chest and look at Gerard.

"Just pretend I'm not here, honey." He smiles and motions with his glass before reclining, taking small sips from his glass as though completely at ease to have me taken. It looks as if he's savoring the drink as much as this moment, as another man excites his wife.

Moving us away, Alex pushes me backward until we are

nearer to the coffee table. "I want you to take me in your mouth, Paige." His thumb and fingers feel my lips before he kisses me, sliding his tongue along seductively. Then he's grabbing me roughly by the ass again, snatching a breath between kissing. "I want those lips straining around my cock." In one hand he grabs my throat again and bores his stare into my eyes to the point of me getting lost. Then he's kissing me again. Hard at first, then softening. "Fuck you're gorgeous." His eyes sweep over every inch of my face, letting go when I swoon, my head lolling backward with a moan. In an instant, and without hesitation, I'm sliding down to my knees before him.

My peripheral vision catches movement. I try to snap my head around. Gerard is on the move, but Alex grabs my face with both hands and tilts me so I'm looking at only him.

"Keep going, Paige, he's just getting a drink. Suck me, Princess, and suck—hard." Alex smooths my hair, gazing at me in lust and wonder. The way he makes me feel. His eyes, the way they reveal his hunger as though he intends on devouring me, it's erotic and could so easily become addictive that it frightens me.

But I take him, my eyes staring up at him and I forget about Gerard, forget that tonight is meant for him. This is everything I was afraid of, but I don't care anymore, and I become so prurient and uninhibited about the fierce piece of man meat I hold in my hand that I lick, suck and stroke with such eagerness, my own arousal trickles down my legs. Taking him down deep over and over, he moans, then grabs my head to still me. I'm out of breath and feverish when he pulls away. "Fuck, Princess." He looks to his left, shaking his head. "That's some seriously good sucking, you lucky bastard."

Gerard just smiles. He's back. Naked and in his chair. Now I'm the only one wearing clothing, as scant as it is. Alex lifts me to my feet and kisses me before instructing me to bend over and place my hands on the coffee table. When I do, Gerard has a full view of my ass and wet panties which Alex takes hold of and tugs, splicing me so wickedly, I yelp and shudder. And then Alex is there between my cheeks, his face, his prickles. Smelling me and growling playfully at my crotch.

"Holy hell," I sing out just as my knees buckle, forcing Alex to dig his fingers into my thigh to keep me steady before one hand finds its way to my aching pussy, pulling urgently at the fabric until he can plunge his tongue inside. His fingers, thumb, and tongue, all swirling, grabbing, and digging in so deep I lurch forward, not really wanting to, but trying to get away, to slow him down. But he doesn't. Standing, he wraps an arm around my waist and carries me, marches straight toward the bedroom and tosses me on the bed. I'm aroused and frightened all at once.

"Are you all right?" Alex wipes the evidence of me from off his face, his eyes wide, his chest heaving, his cock rigid and ready. Disorientated and puffing, I look around the room, then nod. Then Gerard is in the room.

"Gerard." I reach out, and he comes to take my hand. Sitting, he pulls me down so I'm lying down on the bed beside him. Kissing my eyes closed first, he then draws his tongue along my lips, his mouth covering mine. Passion and heat. Wet lips and biting. I'm lost. I only pull away because Alex starts tugging at my panties. I'm so hot and slick between my legs I'm embarrassed when Alex just stares down at me before running his palm over my bare pussy, his thumb stroking my folds.

"I think you like all this attention don't you, honey?"

I look into Gerard's eyes, the electric blue color eclipsed by his pupils, his breathing is heavy but controlled.

I nod and look down. Gerard is pumping himself, precum glistening on his tip, making me lick my lips, enticing him to offer his cock to me.

"Do you, Paige, do you like this attention?" he repeats pinching a nipple.

Alex slides down then pushes my legs up so I'm wider apart and he can bury his face into me.

I'm so heavily turned on, my "Yes," comes out as one elongated wail and I'm reaching for Alex's head to steady him. "Are—you?" I pant, causing Gerard's magnetic smile to light up his face.

"Very much, I'm learning a lot about you right now." Feeling a little self-conscious, I screw up my face to hide. Then Gerard whispers, "And I like what I see." Taking my face in both hands, his tongue licks and tastes my lips again, desperate and urgent before he's cupping a breast and he's on my nipples, swirling and sucking the peaks. I'm heating up everywhere, can feel sweat down my neck and between my breasts.

Alex jerks my legs, pulling me away from my husband and making me squeal. Gerard sits back a little, watches what Alex is doing which is blowing on my pussy, that's wet and hot and hungry, but his breath feels cool and teasing. I'm becoming so desperate, I beg him. "Please, Alex, I need you inside me." He glances at Gerard, then rewards me by pushing a finger inside, sliding in achingly slow then thumbing my clit, making me arch.

"I love you for doing this, Paige," Gerard says, smoothing damp hair away from my sweaty face.

I snatch hold of Gerard's arm, nodding again, then moan loudly as Alex inserts another finger. He feels so different to Gerard. Whatever he's doing, it makes my pussy clench and beg for more penetration.

"I want to see you climax, Paige. I want to see your eyes come alive, so keep them open, keep looking at me."

I nod again, feeling myself climb higher.

Alex becomes relentless with his fingers, pushing in and out quickly, then achingly slow and then fast again, driving me insane with the unpredictability of his movements. I can feel myself drawing so close to an orgasm that my eyes are on fire when I look toward him, see him watching me as I'm panting in ecstasy from what he's doing. Then he removes his fingers and I groan out a "No."

Alex smiles then lowers himself, his eyes holding mine as he buries his face into my pussy, taking one long lick along my slit, then grinning up at me.

"Oh God," I moan deeply from the soothing sensation of his tongue. He does it again, long and slow.

"Fuck you taste good," Alex murmurs. I grip onto the bedspread, twisting and pulling at it until it's bunched up in my fists, something to ground me. It's all so surreal that I struggle to focus my eyes. When I do, it's on Gerard. He keeps stroking his cock while his penetrating eyes bore right to my dirty little soul, hungrily waiting for my release.

"Christ," I wail when Alex flattens his tongue and begins licking the length of my folds over and over before he dips in. Closing my eyes and throwing my head back, I'm so close, and for a moment I falter, wondering if my rapture concerns Gerard. Never in all our years of marriage have I been so shameless, so deliriously orgasmic.

"Gerard let me suck you." Again, I reach for his pulsating cock that's veiny and delightfully engorged but then I'm snatching at the bedspread again when Alex inserts another finger, then another. I don't know how many. I'm so wet it's possible he has slid all of them inside. I'm on the cusp of both pleasure and pain, causing me to moan and thrash my head, I'm almost there. "Please. Let me suck your cock Gerard."

"No, not this time. I want to watch you, this is about your pleasure, honey," he replies, stroking my head then gripping onto my face so he can govern where I look, which is straight into his eyes. I groan and try to twist away but he keeps me captive in his hands, his eyes so blue and lustful and, then it happens, I come back, my mind sharpening and I'm thinking things. There's something there, it's dark and I'm growing cold. My body numbs and tears well, then slide down the side of my face. It's not going to happen. Alex is not going to get me over the edge. All this for nothing. I twist my head to the side away from Gerard.

"Paige, what's the matter?"

Alex stops what he's doing. Then Gerard is moving away.

"Pin her hands."

"What?"

Alex doesn't say it again, but in the next moment, Gerard grabs my hands and pins them above my head, pressing down firmly. I moan loudly and lift my body, a warmth returning and pooling at my core.

"Look at me, Paige."

But I can't. Something feels wrong when I open my eyes and look at him. "Paige." He grabs my face and turns me to look at him. I feel disorientated for a moment. Then Alex is back between my legs pleasuring me. A surge of heat travels through my center and I force my mind to focus on nothing but what Alex is doing. I clamp my eyes. Shut out the sight of Gerard even though he's begging me to open them. When I relent, I'm somehow able to see right past his desire-drenched eyes until I'm in my mind's eye. It's Alex that I'm staring at, as he plays my clit with his tongue.

"Oh God yes." The words come out in a rush. "Yes, hold me tight." With one hand, Gerard presses me harder into the bed almost snapping my wrists. His other hand takes a firm hold of my face by the jaw.

"I love you," I pant. "I really, really love you, so please don't hate me for liking this."

Gerard frowns, then drops kisses all over me. "I'm not going to hate you. Just let yourself go." He stares into my eyes. "Come for me, honey."

Alex is sucking, then licking then sucking again, he's sucking so hard, right on my clit, pulling the orgasm right out of me.

"Oh, my fucking God," I scream out as Alex drives his fingers deep inside me, sending me over the edge, and into a convulsion, gasping and sucking sharp breaths as I stare into my loving husband's eyes. "Fuck, fuck, fuck," I repeat over and over as Alex keeps swirling his fingers inside me, his tongue soothing and calming until my shuddering stops.

"Christ, that was beautiful to see." Gerard releases my hands, kisses my mouth, my eyes, my cheeks, smothering me in his elation that he has, for the first time, finally seen me climax.

"Gerard," Alex calls, jerking his head to the side, motioning Gerard to move away and as soon as he does, Alex closes my legs and flips me over in one quick motion. My arms splay out, and then he's pulling me up by the hips and onto all fours. "Come here and fuck your wife," he says, swapping position, so Gerard is now behind me, taking a hold of my hips. He guides himself in slowly, reveling, with a moan, the slickness and no doubt soft fullness of muscles that grip him firmly from the rapture of finally having an instrument of love to hold.

With Alex kneeling in front of me offering his hard dick, I become salacious, taking him greedily with gratitude. He allows me to set the pace as my husband thrusts in and out, his rhythm so calm, and controlled and familiar to me. I murmur in delight because not only do I have two men here satisfying me, but I'm so wicked yet brazen to be satisfying them. This is not just sex, it's love. I love these men—they are divine and beautiful with their pleasuring abilities.

Gerard's growls of desire, make me work harder at satisfying Alex, taking him deep down my throat with each thrust Gerard delivers. But after only a minute or so, Alex can no longer control himself, he takes my face in his hands and directs the depth and pace in which I take him, pushing so far down my throat that when he pulls back, I gasp for air.

"Can you come again?" asks Gerard, gliding a hand down my back before leaning over me to reawaken my clit. His touch sends shock waves of post orgasmic heights. I wiggle and squirm, it's too much, too many sensations. I push at his hand, but he keeps coming back.

"Come with me, Paige," he begs. But I don't think I can. When Alex lets out a throaty moan, then lets go of my face and leans back, I know he's about to come undone. I run my tongue along his shaft before my lips clamp down, causing him to explode and thrust himself into my mouth. His vocal release arouses Gerard, and it seems he too can't hold off any longer. Aborting his mission at trying to make me climax for a second time, he takes my hips in both hands and pounds into me. When my mouth detaches from Alex's waning cock, Gerard presses on my back so my arms give way and he can get deeper penetration. I wish I could climax again for him. His pounding cock is so hard and relentless he fills me completely, and in seconds, he thickens before erupting inside me, pressing into me with all his might then milking himself with gentle pulses until he's satisfied.

"Oh, Paige, honey, that was amazing. I don't think I've ever come so hard in my life." He kisses my neck and shoulders and his greedy hands roam everywhere. I watch Alex sprawl out on the bed, his arms going under his head, his chest still working out. I want to crawl on top of him, to smother him in kisses. I need him to hold me. I want his cock inside me. Why didn't he fuck me?

When Gerard pulls away from me, I roll onto my back

next to Alex. Look at him briefly and smile. When he just winks, I feel like bursting into tears. Say something, Alex. I look straight up at the ceiling. My thumb grazing his side. Touch me, Alex.

Then Gerard is lying beside me, putting an arm under me and pulling me tight, causing me to roll away from Alex who then gets up, makes his way to the bathroom. I can't look, don't want to see him walk away. Even when my stomach tightens, and I get light-headed. Instead, I wrap myself over Gerard. Grip him tightly, too afraid to look in his eyes. I'm scared now that it's all over he will realize what we've just done. He lifts my chin off his chest and smiles. "Christ, that was good, wasn't it?"

"Yes, yes it was," I agree, laying my face on him again.

So why do I feel so empty?

17

WAY DOWN WE GO

It's the sound of running water that wakes me. I pretend to stay asleep while I fully absorb my surroundings. I have a body pressed against me and an arm thrown over, pinning me down. The moment I'm conscious of whose arm it is, my stomach flutters. From our positioning when we all fell asleep, I know it's Alex next to me so it's Gerard who's taking a shower. I wonder whether Alex knows what he's doing, getting all cozy with me. His breathing is steady, so I press into him just the slightest, hoping to get closer but without waking him up. He'd been distant last night. Eating with us in near silence, then sitting out on the balcony on a call until late. He was going to leave until Gerard had a word with him outside. What they spoke about, I don't know. All I know, I felt relieved when he decided to stay.

Alex takes a deep breath and stirs but I keep my eyes closed. I'm hoping he thinks I'm still sleeping and doesn't want to disturb me either. I don't want him to pull away, his embrace is the closest thing I get to assurance that he feels something, anything toward me. That I wasn't just a deed that needed to be done; because when Gerard fell asleep, he didn't even try to make a move on me.

"Morning, Princess," Alex whispers into my neck, then kisses my shoulder. I don't answer at first, just squeeze his arm that's pulling me in tighter against his morning erection and I can't help grinning to myself.

"Did you sleep all right?" I ask.

"Shit, yeah." He slides a hand straight down my body to caress my thigh and gives me a squeeze. Then he's rolling away. I turn quickly, watching as he gets out of bed. Why is he getting out? Lay with me, Alex. Hug me. Talk to me. At least try to have sex with me.

"And I know another thing. I'm starving." He scratches through his hair then pulls on his jeans without bothering with underwear. Just like he did last night. "You guys thinking of having breakfast here?"

I pull myself up into a sitting position, watching him walk around the room looking for his shirt.

"I don't know, maybe."

Alex looks at me as he pulls on his shirt, his fingers getting busy with the buttons. "Are you okay?"

No. I shift around in the bed and straighten the sheets. Why are you getting out of bed? What was wrong last night? Did I do something wrong? What did Gerard say to you to make you stay? Why did you stay if it wasn't to have sex with me again? But I don't voice any of these thoughts. Instead, I act like a coward and hide behind my fake concern.

"Yeah, I'm just worried Gerard will have regrets now."

"I doubt it, but maybe you should check on him. I'm going to make coffee. Want one?"

"No, thanks."

Alex nods, leaving me watching his back as he exits the room humming. For a moment, I just sit there, nursing my disappointment before I finally climb out the bed. Why am I worried what he feels for me anyway? I'm married. To the most amazing man. A man women are constantly gushing over. Last night was—a means to an end. It's over now, done with.

Gerard doesn't notice me entering the bathroom because he is leaning on one hand and staring at the floor tiles. Letting the water overwhelm his head and face. I clutch my stomach, certain it's because he's fighting the morning-after demons that I instinctively knew would come but played ignorant to. Finding a band, I tie up my hair then peel off my nightie. Slipping quietly in behind him, I press my cheek against his back. Gerard jerks upright and clasps a hand over mine when I startle him, and it's only then that I realize he's been stroking himself. Embarrassed that I unintentionally invaded his privacy, I pretend I didn't notice.

"Good Morning," I say.

For a moment he stays where he is, letting me hug him, then slowly he turns in my arms and looks down, searching my eyes. When he doesn't say anything, my hands reach up to take his face. "Please tell me you're okay, Gerard. You know I didn't really want to do this because I knew it would hurt you all over again."

Gerard gives me a small smile then plants a kiss on my head. "I'm all right with everything. I'm just thinking things over, that's all." He hugs me tightly and mutters over my head.

"Like what?" I ask, nudging him away so I can reach for the soap. He moves from under the water, trades places, and offers the powerful jets of warmth to me.

"Like how funny love is. I thought I loved you before, but after last night, watching you like that, with Alex, I don't know how to describe it. It was like—I loved you on a whole other level, it became a selfless love I suppose you'd say."

"Well, I guess that's a good thing, then." But it sounds like he's building up to say more.

"You enjoyed it, didn't you?" Gerard takes the soapy washcloth from me, making me turn so he can wash my back.

"It was good. I'm happy you're happy about it—and now, hopefully, things can go back to normal."

Gerard leans over me, rests his chin on my head. "But I don't want things to go back to normal. I loved watching you last night. I've never been so turned on in my life." He turns me to face him. Washing the suds off and looking for my response. But my insides are tightening. I can't decide whether it's an ill feeling or excitement.

"But, it's not right."

"Says who?" Gerard frowns, but a grin spreads across his face.

"Me."

"Are you saying you wouldn't like to do it again? But didn't you feel excited having another man while I was there? Didn't it feel better than cheating on me?"

That was a low blow.

"Yes, but I meant for it to be a one-time thing. Something like that isn't sustainable. Someone always gets hurt."

"What, so you've done this type of thing before?" He turns me again and re-scrubs my back,

"Well, no, but…"

"So, you don't know that it can't work?" he says, cutting me off. "I think if we talked about it, set down some ground rules, it could work. So long as you keep it a 'we' thing. No sneaking around behind my back with any of the men we choose, then I think it could work."

Any other men we choose? When I spin around abruptly, Gerard gets out the shower and finds a towel, then offers me one. "I mean, I'm not saying we become a thruple with anyone. I just mean, every so often I'd like to see you with someone else."

I turn off the faucet and wrap the towel around myself, eyeballing him in shock. When I shake my head, he pulls me closer.

"Paige, there was something different about you last night. I don't want to lose you, so if sharing you gives you, and me, for that matter, something more in this relationship, well then..." He leaves the rest unsaid.

I'm still shaking my head, knowing we can't do this regularly, it will blow up in our faces, or at the very least, mine.

"You think pushing me to be with other men will be good for *our* relationship? That it will stop you from losing me. How does that even make sense, Gerard?" Pulling away, I lean against the vanity, folding my arms and staring at him. "You're going to ruin what we have, Gerard. I can't believe you think sleeping with Alex, no wait, did I hear you right when you said, other men? What other men? I don't want other men touching me. I only meant for this to be a once off thing, so you could see me climax because that seemed to be something *you* needed. It will look and feel the same every time, so what's the point."

"The point is, you'll be getting satisfied, and you being satisfied, satisfies me."

"I don't get it. I'm sorry but it just doesn't make sense."

"What he means to say is," Alex meanders into the bathroom, "it'll get him off watching other men fuck you. That's Gerard's new thing." Alex lifts the toilet lid then reaches inside his jeans. "He's discovered he is a closet cuckold. Just tell it to her straight, man."

I'm stunned for a moment because then Alex pees in front of us. Blinking and shaking my head clear, I turn my attention back to Gerard who gives a shrug, looking wide eyed.

"Humph. I didn't know they had a name for it."

"You like to watch? You don't want to have sex with me anymore, you just want to watch me get laid by other men?" I'm hurt, and when my face falls and the tears spring, Gerard moves in and gathers me in his arms.

"No, I didn't say that. Of course, I still want to make love to you."

I step away from him and pull the towel tighter around me. "I was everything to you, now you're not even slightly jealous, which means you don't care anymore. I ruined it. This is my punishment, isn't it? Next you'll be saying you want other women and then everything we have together will go down the drain."

"No, that's not going to happen." Gerard reaches out for me, but I step away, turning my head when Alex flushes the toilet and washes his hands right next to us, preening his face with his wet palm. It feels weird. Alex is so casual and calm around us, like it's the most natural thing for him to be here as we have this discussion. In fact, I think he's smirking slightly as though enjoying our dilemma. I need to get out, get away from them. I hastily wipe at my face, pushing Gerard out the way and brushing between them.

"If you like to watch so much Gerard, try watching porn," I spit, storming out of the bathroom.

Alex laughs "That went down well."

"Well, you were no help."

"Hey, this is between you two," Alex says, before I'm at my overnight bag, digging out my colorful maxi dress and slipping it on. Gerard is soon following suit, rummaging through his clothes, not speaking to me. Alex closes the bathroom door, giving us some privacy or maybe himself.

I glare at Gerard as he pulls his pants on, then uses the

towel on his head. He's ignoring me deliberately, I know it. I don't move until he notices me glaring at him and stops.

"What? Look, don't worry about it."

"But you're upset now."

"No. I'm not." He stuffs his clothes roughly in his bag.

"I'm sorry I cheated in the first place, but come on, does me not agreeing to fulfill your fetish mean our relationship is doomed now?" I babble, then attack my hair with a brush before gathering it into a messy bun.

Gerard buttons his shirt, shaking his head slightly. "I'd hardly call it a fetish, Paige, and I'm sorry too." There's no trace of sincerity in his tone. "I just thought last night was amazing. I also thought our marriage was strong enough to do something like this. But, like I said, if it will upset you so much, forget about it."

"Thank you." I go over to him and put my arms around his waist. "It would just get too messy, you must know that—right?" Gerard smiles tightly before extracting me off him. "Should we go have breakfast soon?" I ask trying to lighten the mood.

"If it doesn't bother you too much, I'd like to get going. There are a few things I need to do this morning. I'll need to stop by the office."

Yes, it bothers me. I wanted to end this on a pleasant note. "Can't we have breakfast first, Gerard, surely you don't need to work today?"

Ignoring me, he leaves the room mumbling, "Did you see where I put my watch last night?" He doesn't even wait for my answer, making it painfully clear he's angry Alex comes out the bathroom. When he notices Gerard is no longer in the room, he coaxes me over, gesturing with his finger.

"Maybe it's on the kitchen counter," I call out, frowning at Alex. When he continues motioning for me, I roll my eyes and move closer.

"Yes."

"Tell me what you didn't like about last night?"

"I didn't say I didn't like it. I just don't want to do it again."

Alex shrugs. "Why not though? You looked like you were enjoying yourself."

"I just don't want to, that's all."

"Isn't this something that you'd like more of?" He grabs his crotch making me look down.

"Stop it, Alex." My shoulders slump and I let out a groan.

"Thought so."

"What's that mean?"

"Why did you agree to last night, Paige?"

"Because it was something Gerard wanted. I hurt him. He didn't deserve that from me, us, and he wanted to see me... well, you know why."

Alex smirks and shakes his head. Then he's nodding. "You're lying."

"What? How is that lying? Or are you just pissed because it's something you'd like to keep doing now, but I won't agree? What was your little pow wow last night with Gerard all about, Alex?"

"Hey! Don't flatter yourself. I'll admit I liked it, because I like to fuck but I'm not short on women to do, Paige. It doesn't bother me either way, for all I care, get someone else then."

"I don't want you or anyone else," I snap.

"But I know you're lying. I just don't understand why."

"You don't need to understand why, Alex." I clamp my teeth and ball my fists.

Alex pulls his head back, shocked by my venom.

"But don't you think you should tell Gerard the real reason why you don't want to do it again. I mean, you just said you enjoyed it, and hey, it might just make your marriage stronger, right?"

"Maybe it scares me because I liked it too damn much, Alex, did you ever consider that?"

It's only after I make my admission that Alex looks toward the doorway and instinctively, I know Gerard is standing there, no doubt having heard the entire banter, which I assume now, is exactly what Alex intended.

I don't want to turn around. I don't want to see Gerard's expression.

"Fair enough then." Alex moves past me looking smug.

Sensing Gerard coming toward me, I slowly turn to face him. He has found his watch which I study before my eyes rise to meet his.

"You're scared of feeling too much, liking it too much, what's wrong with that?"

Gerard has missed the point completely. "What? Nothing. I mean I'm not comfortable showing that side of myself. It's scary. I'll scare you."

"You're not going to scare me. What, you think last night scared me? Christ, Paige. I haven't been that turned on in my life." Gerard pulls me in for a hug. Over his shoulder, I see Alex turns back from the doorway smirking then shaking his head at the ceiling. Why is he suddenly trying to wedge himself between me and Gerard?

"Can we please just have breakfast and think about this another day? It's all too overwhelming for me right now."

"Of course, honey, anything you want."

Really, I think sarcastically, but only if it's what you want, right, Gerard?

"Like you suggested. I'll catch up with work another time, right now let's just settle and have something to eat. Alex, have breakfast with us." He calls out, exuberant again.

Grabbing my cardigan, I take the lead down to breakfast,

desperate now to put this whole experience behind us, to make life normal again.

It's still early, and quite fresh outside in the marquee overlooking the pool where breakfast is being served, and despite the full length of my maxi dress, it's lightweight and does nothing to help keep me warm. I pull my small cardigan tighter as we follow the waitress to a table. She is a petite little thing that seems to hold Alex's attention quite well until he looks around the eatery to take in the few guests that have beaten us down.

Gerard slips an arm around my waist and leans into me. "How about we sit over there in the sun?" he suggests, pointing to a secluded table as far away as possible from a noisy family that seem to struggle with three small children, all of whom look to be under three, making me wonder if they are triplets.

"You're welcome to sit anywhere," the well-spoken woman offers, turning and smiling at my husband then blushing when her eyes dart to Alex who gives her a wink. Snapping her head back around, I can only imagine what she thinks. She shows us to a table and places menus down. "Feel free to order off the menu or help yourself to the buffet. Can I offer anyone tea or coffee?" she continues, in an efficient manner, shifting her long ponytail back over her shoulder and again smiling at Gerard.

Alex is quick to pull out a chair for me which I take, and I catch a look of surprise, or maybe it's hope, from the waitress when she looks between Alex and Gerard. I'm not a stranger to people's judgment. They've always been quick to assume Gerard is my father and not my husband, but it still takes all my effort to hold back my embarrassment from the awkwardness of the situation when Gerard then takes hold of the chair to sit next to me.

"Three coffees please," I say, putting her out of her misery so she can leave us.

"So, do you have any plans today, Alex?" Gerard asks, as they take their seats. Wearing a loose blue striped shirt that he has left half unbuttoned over jeans, Alex looks like he's ready for the beach. Gerard on the other hand looks ready for work.

"Just a day at home."

"Don't you mean the beach house? It's not your home, Alex." Gerard fusses with his cutlery, spreading them wider apart.

"Gerard!"

"Well it's not." Gerard states innocently looking at me.

"Right. Beach house. Anyway, I was going to rip down that creeping vine out front," Alex replies, handing us each a menu. He studies it briefly then places his down. "I'll have the full buffet seeing you're paying Ger," Alex smirks, resting his elbows on the table and weaving his fingers, his thumbs supporting his chin as he takes in the scenery. I look down at the menu and read what's available but jerk involuntarily when Alex brushes a foot against mine. I'm already struggling to stay focused because of the obvious power struggle between them and Alex flirting with me under the table, which is so typical of him, is not helping. I slide my foot away.

"Sounds good, what about you, Paige?" Gerard asks, putting down his menu, the same moment Alex decides to run his whole calf against my leg. I slowly lift my head and glare at him. Smirking, Alex pulls his leg away.

"I think I'll order off the menu. You two go, I'll order when the waitress brings our coffees over." I watch them walk away. One man tall, lean and dressed smartly—the other muscular, casual and oh, God, that ass. I shift in my seat and try to focus elsewhere, but within seconds, I'm elbowing the table and cradling my chin as those two men, the same men who just last night, were naked and worshiping my body, get their food. Stop it. It's done, it's over. I sit taller and fix the napkin over my lap then look around at the other diners who have begun filling the tables. I catch some of them watching me, causing my face to heat before I look away. They know, they can see what's going on. I suddenly feel sick and disgusted in myself and when the waitress comes with our coffees, I order something lighter than the Eggs Benedict I was planning on having. I shouldn't have done it. It was wrong. What if Annabel or even Jenna find out? Will Alex keep his mouth shut? I sneak another look and see they've loaded their plates. And here I was concerned Gerard would have regrets. I'm a slut. My face falls into my hands for a moment, embarrassed about how uninhibited I became, right there in front of my husband, letting Alex do things to me as I thrashed about on the bed.

"Paige?" Gerard rests a hand on my back and places his meal down beside me. I look up and around at the other diners, all seemingly back to their own business.

"I'm fine, I think I'm just tired." My eyes move over to Alex for a moment until I feel a tightening in my chest, then look away. I want him gone because it feels so wrong to have done what we did, but at the same time, I also want him to stay because of how electrified he makes me feel. Argh this is bad. I've started something I'm not sure I can live with and there's no way of making it go away. The awareness that no matter what happens, Alex is always going to be there, be part of what Gerard and I have makes me anxious. Where is this going to take us?

"Paige, do you think you can spare any time next week and drop in at the beach house?" Alex asks catching me off guard.

"What? No. Why?"

Alex sits back in his seat. "Um, how about for some input, or aren't you interested in having any?"

I look away when the waitress places a poached egg on toast in front of me, thankful for the distraction which allows me time to think and compose myself. Deciding I'm being ridiculous and assuming that he's asked for any other reason than it's my project just as much as his and Gerard's.

"I do."

Hovering over his meal, Gerard gives me a sideways glance, his hands still busy pushing scrambled eggs together.

"I'm hoping to have a lot of input because, to be honest, I was a little disappointed Gerard handed the job of renovating over to you." I pick up my cutlery, warming up to suggesting we all go to the beach house for another look after breakfast.

Alex's response is nonverbal, but supportive, raising his eyebrows and nodding. Gerard turns to me, looking surprised.

"You were?" He cuts into his chipotle sausage sounding surprised.

"Yes. I would love to help renovate. Especially when it comes time to paint."

"You?" Gerard frowns. "I wouldn't have thought that was your type of thing. When have you even picked up a paintbrush?"

Shrugging, I tuck my hair away and begin eating. "It's not rocket science."

Gerard laughs. "No, I suppose it's not. Still, it's not my sort of thing and I think Alex can manage without you."

"Nah, I can always use an extra hand." Alex looks from me to Gerard, then picks up a piece of bacon and shoves it in his mouth.

I gather from the look they share it is a challenge, rather than a blasé invitation, like whether Gerard is honestly fine with what happened last night, that he could confidently leave me alone with Alex and it wouldn't compromise the trust. I need to nip this in the bud straight away.

"No. I'd just get in your way, besides—I think maybe I was feeling overly confident. But I would like to see the progress now and then. Maybe once we leave here, we could stop by and have another look?" I suggest looking at Gerard and placing a hand on his leg. "I've only been there once so far."

Gerard clears his throat and pulls a tight smile. "We could, honey, but I really need to get some paperwork emailed through to Carter before tomorrow morning. Maybe another time."

Alex smirks. "You know, you arrived in separate cars, so you're still welcome to *come*, Paige."

I smirk at his innuendo and Gerard looks up quickly from his meal.

"What, now you don't trust us? Make up your mind, Gerard," Alex says.

"What, you don't think I have cause for that?"

"Hey, you're the one who pulled me into this, and now the thought of Paige and me being alone worries you. What, you think *I'm* going to swoop her away from you? I don't think so. I can get my own women, Gerard, I don't need to *steal* yours."

"Um, hello. Right here." Both men look but stare right through me.

"Don't start, Alex." Gerard looks around the eatery and lowers his voice. "I just mean I don't want this to become a free-for-all. If it's going to happen again, I want to be there to watch. That's fair." He pushes more food onto his fork. "Look, I'm okay with what happened last night, but you've got to see it from my side. I mean I've been trusting enough already don't you think?" Gerard looks between me and

Alex. Now I'm concerned. He really thinks it will happen again.

"That or stupid. I'm still undecided," Alex huffs and shoves a mouthful of food in.

"Alex!" I gasp, jerking back.

"Fuck you, Alex," Gerard mumbles, through gritted teeth, staring at his food and shaking his head.

I cower into the center of the table and whisper, "Stop it you two. See Gerard, this is what I'm talking about. You think we can all get together in bed and it's fine, but then the minute there's the threat of Alex and I being alone you're jealous. How would that ever work? Last night better not turn you two against each other. I was just making conversation about the house, all right?"

"I'm not worried. If you want to help Alex with the house, Paige, then go right ahead."

I roll my eyes at him, then Gerard tosses his napkin over his meal and reaches for his coffee cup.

Alex looks between the two of us and smiles. "Listen to that, Paige, you have his *permission*."

I feel nauseous. "I'm going back up to the room to pack. You two need to talk it out without me around. And Gerard, stop assuming I've agreed to do this again. I never said yes." Pushing back my chair, I rise then scrunch up my napkin and throw it onto my seat. Both men remain quiet, but I notice we've drawn a little attention.

Striding across the marble foyer, I jab at the elevator button impatiently, my breakfast curdling in my stomach. Things are going to go south I just know it. Shit, shit, shit. What have I started? I groan aloud, turn to see if anyone has heard me, then notice Alex is hurrying toward me.

"Paige, wait."

I stab at the elevator button again. I really don't want to be around anyone, especially Alex, if he keeps being so antagonistic. He's deliberately poking the hornet's nest and I don't understand why.

"I'll come upstairs and grab my bag and get going."

"What, why? Didn't you two sort it out?"

"It's sorted. This is yours and Gerard's shit, I did my bit."

"You did your bit." I screw up my face and fold my arms over my chest. "Well how are you going to get home?"

Now Alex is jabbing at the elevator button. "I've got a friend who lives here. She'll give me a lift back to you place to get my car, later today or in the morning." He steals a look at me.

"You have a fucking girlfriend?" I step back from him. Feeling even more disgusted with myself. Alex huffs, a scowl crossing his face. I turn away, my face flushing because the situation is so ridiculous. Of course, he has other women, but I still feel like a jilted lover.

The elevator doors open. Alex steps inside then holds the doors in for me. When I don't move, he prompts,

"Getting in?"

I stay in the lobby, unable to conceal my disappointment, hurt, and disgust.

"Paige?"

"No, you go, I think I'll wait for my husband." I rub my goosefleshed arms to stop me from shivering.

Alex's mouth draws into a straight line before he's letting his hand fall away from the door. "Fine," he says through tight lips, and stands tall. I watch as the doors close then twist my neck to look down the lobby for Gerard. But suddenly there is a "ding" and in a flash, Alex reaches out and pulls me in.

18

DIRTY MIND

"**A**lex," I yelp, "What are you doing?" Holding his arm against the closing panel of stainless steel, he pulls me into the elevator. When he releases the door, they instantly close.

"No. What are you doing?" He pushes an open palm against my chest, pressing me back against the elevator wall. "Don't you dare turn into a dead-set bitch and give me the cold shoulder."

"Ouch, you're hurting me." I pull on his arm that's pinning me, trying to relieve the pressure he's placing on my sternum.

"Good, then you know how it feels." He lets go and faces the door.

"What's up with you? I wasn't being a bitch. I just said I'd wait for Gerard."

Alex crosses his arms, still staring straight ahead. "Yeah, well, he got busy on his phone."

I stay pressed up against the wall, praying for the elevator to move faster. At the sixth floor, the elevator doors open and an elderly couple are waiting. When they notice Alex standing in the center dominating the space, and me hunched against the wall, they lose their smiles. Alex takes a step to the right and away from me.

"Morning." Alex nods. His voice sounds hoarse and there's not even a glimmer of a smile.

Grabbing hold of each other and stepping in, the couple force a smile and mumble a curt reply. I can't help feeling ashamed because of the tense atmosphere the poor couple have walked in on, and when the elevator moves on, everyone is pensive. Alex remains locked in his defensive pose as the couple murmur to each other about their plans for the day. The woman stays locked firmly around her husband's arm, and I notice he keeps patting her hand. No doubt in reassurance because Alex's attention is still locked on the doors as if he's about to bust in on a hostage scene on the next floor. All he's missing are the big guns. But, by the look of his tense biceps, they could easily suffice, I'm sure.

The couple exit at the twentieth floor and as soon as the doors slide shut, I poke a finger into Alex's back.

"Why did you have to start arguing with Gerard, and why are you angry at me?"

Alex ignores my questions. His eyes staying focused on his reflection against the stainless steel doors. "Alex, what happened?" I grab his arm and make him face me. "Did Gerard say something else, tell me?"

"I think you know why," he says, glaring. His green eyes now menacing, but still he seems to search my soul.

"No. I really don't."

The elevator doors open again, and because I'm fixated on Alex, I haven't noticed if we are at the correct level yet or whether someone has pressed at their floor. I look around confused until Alex grabs my hand and drags me out.

"Let go of me. I know the way." I stumble behind him,

trying to jerk out of his clasp. "What have I done, why are you so angry at me?"

Alex marches off in front of me but waits at the door when he realizes he doesn't have a key card to get in. Thinking it's a way to make him talk, I stand back, reluctant to open the door.

"Are you going to open the door?"

"Are you going to stop being an ass and tell me why you're angry?"

Alex holds out his hand. "Give it to me."

"No." I tuck the card behind my back. "Talk to me first."

Alex snatches hold of my free hand and bends it back. Yelping out his name, I instantly hand him the card which he uses. Then he lets go of the door before I have time to go through it, almost slamming it in my face because I'm too busy rubbing my wrist.

I stand baffled as he paces the living room floor.

"Alex, stop. What's wrong?"

He quits pacing. "You really don't know?"

"No."

Then Alex is charging at me. Backing me up so quickly, I nearly trip over my own feet as I try to retreat. He looks like he's ready to kill. When I'm pressed up against the kitchen counter with nowhere left to go, I pull myself tall in defense. My heart is hammering against my ribs. The reality hitting me square in the face. I have no idea what Alex is capable of. I don't know him at all. Shaking, I take hold of the counter behind me. Where the heck is Gerard?

"You're asking me what you did wrong? What I'd like to know is, what the fuck did I do wrong? Gerard suddenly treats me like I'm fucking disposable and then you've got the audacity to show contempt when I say I'm going to visit a friend. Fuck the both of you."

"Well, I'm sorry for being selfish. It just hurts to know

you have someone else in your life." My eyes sting and glaze over.

"Damn right you're being selfish. You're married to my stepbrother remember?" He turns away, muttering that Gerard can get fucked too. "If you only knew who he really was, you wouldn't think of him as so high and fuckin' mighty anymore," he calls out over his shoulder.

I stare after him as he walks off into the master bedroom. Feeling sick to my stomach that he's now speaking about Gerard that way. I'm devastated that it's all gone wrong. Last night was amazing and beautiful, but now Alex is angry, and Gerard is jealous. I'm nauseous. I need to right things. I can't bear the thought of ending everything this way.

When I approach the bedroom, Alex is carrying around his bag looking as if he has forgotten something.

"Alex, don't go like this. I'm sorry and I apologize for Gerard."

Alex stops moving about the room and looks to me.

"What do you fucking see in him anyway? Do you even see what he is doing to you?"

"I love him and he's not doing anything to me. He loves me, he's given me everything I've ever wanted," I don't hesitate in answering.

Alex huffs, looks at me for the longest time shaking his head slightly. "He might give you everything you want, Paige, but he doesn't give you what you *need*, and you know it."

"And what. Next you're going to tell me *you* know what I need?" I pull my cashmere sweater around my front and cross my arms.

"Fucking A, I know what you need. I knew what you needed the first day I laid my eyes on you. You were just screaming for me to pay you attention."

"What?" I screw up my face. "I was not."

"Bullshit," he replies, putting his bag on the bed and

zipping it up. "You're going to spend the rest of your life just keeping the status quo and for what, stability, the predictable. Why are you so afraid of being who you are and saying what you want?"

"I'm not."

"Yes, you are. Yes, Gerard. No, Gerard. How high would you like me to jump, Gerard? What are you, a fuckin' mail-order bride?" Alex smirks and shakes his head, then moves around the bed coming closer to stand near me. He starts tapping his finger into my chest.

"You are a liar. But then—maybe you just don't know who you are. Yeah that's it. You haven't got a clue what you really want because you don't know who the fuck you are. You've been with Gerard for what? Four, five years? Nineteen, you were fucking nineteen years old when you hooked up with him. You haven't even had a chance to know who you are."

"Alex, stop it." I slap at his hand but he just keeps tapping until I'm losing balance and I end up sitting on the bed. He's getting that look in his eyes I recognize, one that I'm both afraid and aroused by. I need to get up. Where is Gerard? My eyes dart to the main door.

"Oh, don't worry about Gerard, he's back to business, said he had some calls to make—it's just you and me here. So, tell me, Paige, what do you really want?" He traces a finger along my jawline tilting my face so he can study my eyes, which dart everywhere to avoid looking into those green gateways. I jerk my face away.

"Nothing. I don't want anything. I just wanted you to calm down and now that we've given Gerard what he wanted, I just want things to go back to the way they were."

"It's too late for that now, Princess, on fucking *Solsbury Hill*." He leans over me, forcing me back onto my elbows.

"What are you talking about, what's *Solsbury Hill*?"

"Did you miss my cock in you last night?"

I freeze. Then flop back, my arm covering my eyes for a moment.

"I thought so. You didn't do that last night for Gerard, you did it for yourself. You do want more of this." When I remove my arm, he grabs his crotch.

"Don't make me regret last night," I groan, pushing on his chest, shaking my head when he hovers closer—begging with my eyes he doesn't do what I know he is thinking of doing. I just don't have the strength to resist him. I hate him for knowing me so well. He pulls back and I think he's going to leave me alone, but he doesn't. Sliding down, he kneels in front of me and pushes my maxi dress up. Sitting up, I'm quick to stop his hands.

"We can't do anything." I push myself farther up the bed, trying to get away from him.

"Why fight it, Paige?" He crawls after me smirking.

"Because I don't really want it. I only think I want it. I love Gerard."

"Liar. Why do you keep lying to yourself?"

"What makes you so sure I'm lying?"

"Because I can feel it. You're not who you're meant to be. You think you love Gerard but that's not love. You feel obligated to him. Don't you know you're just a toy to him?"

"What?" I huff out.

I go to pull myself off the bed, but Alex grabs my ankle and pulls me back then crawls quickly over the top to me, pinning my hands above my head.

"Alex, don't."

"I could take you right now if I wanted to."

"Stop it, Alex, you're scaring me. Gerard could walk in any minute." I wiggle and plea, in a pathetic voice that carries no conviction because I can feel myself warming up, getting aroused by his insistence that he knows what I want.

Then my stupid eyes get wet. Not because I'm scared, but

because I'm disgusted that I'm secretly loving this. Alex is right. I'm a liar who doesn't know what she wants. Alex kisses my tears away then plants a hard one on my mouth, then resumes fumbling with my dress, pushing it up again until he finds the tops of my undies. He takes hold with one hand and yanks my underwear down roughly; the fabric cutting into my hips and a sneaky moan escapes me.

I should fight him off, this is wrong, Gerard is not here, it's a betrayal. But my breathing becomes labored and every cell of mine tingles. How can I be getting aroused by this?

I try kicking him but with my undies halfway down my legs, I'm only assisting him in getting me naked. I stop struggling, but keep my eyes closed so he can't see my desire. I let his hand roam freely over my abdomen and breasts, gasping when his fingers pinch my nipple.

"Alex, please don't do this," I groan, opening my eyes and searching his for the gentle Alex from last night and this morning. But he's not there, only a taunting stranger who is trying to unravel me.

His eyes squint. "Well, if you don't want it, Princess, why are you laying there instead of fighting me off?" he challenges in a smug voice.

He's right. Why aren't I fighting him? I want Gerard. I want my marriage. This is not love, this is just sex, dirty sex. Wrong sex. "Let me go," I snap, surprising even myself.

He slackens for a moment, letting go of my hands as though questioning what he is doing, but then changes his mind. In an instant he's pulling at my panties again until they are all the way off, then drives his knee between my legs to spread me. In seconds he has his jeans undone and at his knees. I can't help it. I moan. I damn well moan and I'm getting aroused because he's so primal in taking me. I cover my eyes with my hands, feeling scattered and confused. Then

I'm peeking through my fingers at his hard jawline, but his eyes are all concern. I reach out and stroke his face.

"I don't understand why you're being like this. Last night was nice. You made me come for Gerard."

Alex jerks his face away. "I didn't make you come for Gerard. I made you come for me. He just happened to be in the fucking room."

What?

Alex sits back on his haunches and pulls my dress down to cover me.

"What are you doing?"

"Leaving."

"What, why?"

Alex stands, pulls his jeans up, but leaves his fly undone. "What do you want, Paige?" he asks staring down at me.

"What do you mean what do I want? You're the one pushing yourself on me."

"Yeah because that's what you want. Because you're too gutless to go after what you need."

"How the hell do you know what I want?"

"Because I know women like you. And I sure as shit know men like Gerard. He keeps you all locked up in that pretty palace of his. Swooning you with gifts and fake fucking love."

"What are you trying to do, Alex?"

For a moment he just stares at me, the hard line of his jaw becoming more defined. "Nothing." He half turns away then snaps around again. "Tell me you didn't want me to fuck you just now. That you didn't want me to force you, so I take the decision away from you because that's how you want it?"

"I don't know what you're talking about. I'm not asking for you to do anything."

"Christ, you must think I'm stupid. I see the way you look at me."

I slide myself to the edge of the bed, look around for my panties, and ready myself to get to my feet.

"Leave me alone, Alex. You don't know me, and I have no idea what you're talking about."

"Like fuck you don't."

In a split-second Alex grabs me under the arms and tosses me in the middle of the bed. Pushing his jeans away he kicks them off and in the same instance he's crawling toward me as I scamper back. My breathing becomes labored. Fuck, what's he doing? What am I doing? Because just watching his determination and lust-drenched eyes is turning me into a glow stick. I'm hot everywhere and not going anywhere. Shoving my dress up, he pulls me roughly by the hips and positions himself between my legs. Oh God, he's going to do it. My body responds. Clenching and pulsing in all the right places making me flood in an instant when his hands, like heated gloves, scorch my already hot skin. My whole surface becomes hypersensitive, so sensitive I can even feel the hairs of his thighs, his breath in my hair, and the pulse in his wrists as it thumps softly against the top of my legs. We're both staring, searching as if for the green light.

He's there, right there at my opening, waiting for me, pressing into my tender outer folds. I want to say stop, but I can't make my mouth move. I don't want him to stop but I know letting him go on is wrong. Why does wrong feel so alluring?

"I don't want this. Not like this," I mumble under my hands that are covering my eyes again, trying to block out reality.

"Yes, you do."

"But I shouldn't."

"Yes, you fuckin' should," he says matter-of-factly, pressing himself against me, pushing on my folds, causing me to moan and snatch at the bedspread in preparation of his thrust. A weird mind muddle overwhelms me, which happens every time I'm with Alex, and makes no sense. I get overly intoxicated when he pushes me to the edge like this. He's right, he's so damn right. I want him to just take me, so I become blameless, shameless but my wicked desires will be fulfilled.

I'm spineless.

"You don't even have a condom."

"Fuck the condom, I'm clean. This time you need to really fucking feel me," he growls.

"No. You need to stop now."

Alex looks stunned, and for a moment he doesn't move, just his eyes searching mine, determining my seriousness. He nods and pulls away, but in a heartbeat, I'm reacting to the yearning ache that's betraying my rational mind. Because as if they have a will of their own, my calves tense and curl behind his knees. I want him. Need him to impale me, to punish me, to process me, to numb my chaotic mind. The core of me clenches, trying to draw him back toward me. Alex looks down at my rising pelvis and my chest that's heaving with desire.

"You still want this don't you?" he asks, grabbing his cock and boring his eyes into mine. "You're just a little tease who wants to be fucked senseless, aren't you, Princess?" He smiles knowingly at me.

A million thoughts run through my head at once causing me to become dizzy, but there's one screaming command, 'say no!' Because I shouldn't be wanting this, allowing this, it's another betrayal. I won't be able to live with myself. But my eyes I know are begging him to take the decision away from me, which is stupid and wrong. Why would I want him to take me by force?

I shake my head slowly, but my panting chest and hot eyes are silently daring him.

He narrows his eyes and tilts his head. "Why are you still lying?" He jabs himself at me, rougher and startles me. My arms flail out with a gasp. "Say you want it." He clenches his teeth. "Do you want me to do it, Paige?"

After what seems like forever, my head spinning and my arousal climbing, I finally admit it.

"Yes." That single word ignites in his eyes with lust, but I shut mine in shame. I'm so going to hell for this.

Alex doesn't wait a second longer before he slides into me, full tilt and hard, quenching my whole body, making me quiver then instantly climax into an arch around his cock, locking onto him tightly as if life depended on it, then humping to soothe myself, the release burning away every thought I own.

Alex groans with my climax, throwing his head back, his eyes tightly closed. I can feel him resisting the urge to fuck me with all he has. Gripping my hips, he makes small minute pulses, rubbing against my pelvis whispering, "Fuck" repeatedly in time with his gentle flexes, allowing my body to do the work—knowing, feeling, understanding, that he barely needs to move inside me when our sex is combined, because we feel electrified and addicted to this sinful act. I close my eyes, feeling him, absorbing his passion, and to my surprise, I climax again to his gentle rhythm. I don't understand how it happens so easily with Alex and seconds later, he erupts. Moaning my appreciation but needing him deeper, my fingers dig into his hard butt muscles making him wince through gritted teeth. Alex obliges my need, pushing my legs back and pressing into me with several hard thrusts, making me quiver. I open my eyes and stare at him with a mixture of gratitude and disgust, warring it out in my mind until a sheepish grin widens across his face. Then I quickly come to my senses and shame wins out.

"Fuck, fuck, fuck," I scream straightening myself and watching as Alex pulls on his pants.

"We just did," he chuckles.

"No, I mean shit. How am I going to live with this now?"

"Just leave him." He tucks in his shirt.

"Leave him? I don't want to leave him."

"Are you serious right now?" Alex's face contorts. "You just let me fuck you again. You said we couldn't do it in front of him, but you'll do it behind his back. Think about that." Alex the ass starts tapping his damn temple again. What have I done?

He shakes his head and sighs. "Look. Don't worry about it, just think of that as—a continuation of last night, forget about it, all right? You just need to understand all this. Nobody owns anybody around here and I don't fucking appreciate being used, and well… You obviously needed a good fucking, and that's something you need to think about." He runs his fingers through his hair looking as cool as a cucumber then feels his stubble and eyes me.

Christ, my head is spinning so fast I'm speechless. How in the space of fifteen minutes has Alex managed to not only have sex with me but also make me question everything I know?

"I gotta go. I imagine Gerard will be up here soon. I wanted to be gone by the time he got here—it will make him feel better about everything. Trust me on that."

Grabbing his bag, Alex comes closer, standing just a foot away, looking down at me still sitting on the bed struck dumb. He lowers his bag and offers me his hand then draws me to my feet.

"You and me, that shit's complicated?" He nods, trying to get me to agree. When I nod in return, he kisses me softly on the forehead. "That's why we gotta keep it simple. If you're unhappy with Gerard, get out, find someone else. You don't owe him anything, Paige. There are plenty of guys out there who are young and fun. You're beautiful. You should chase your dreams. Don't get old before your time." When I don't respond, he tilts my chin with his finger. "Stop pretending you don't want something else."

I take hold of the front of his shirt and pull him into me. I don't want him to leave. I suddenly accept how much I need him around. I fiddle with the buttons of his shirt.

"You wanted that, didn't you, Princess?" he asks quietly, perhaps second-guessing his actions and feeling bad now I've got nothing to fight back with, nor the desire. When I finally look up, he looks concerned.

I nod but shy away. "But I don't want to need it like that though, Alex. What's wrong with me? And are you sure you're clean? I mean, shit!" I let go of his shirt and step back. My hands cover my cheeks attempting to cool down my flushed stupidity.

Alex pinches my arm gently, making me look up. He winks and juts his chin. "Mandatory testing. I'm clean, I promise." Then he shrugs. "And I don't know, some of us just like it rough, I guess."

Just as he's about to turn away I take hold of his shirt again, gather the soft fabric into fists.

"Alex, what's her name?"

"Who?" He frowns.

"Your girlfriend." I ask, looking at his tanned chest, then running a hand over the small patch of hair there.

Lifting my chin, he smiles. "She's not a girlfriend, Paige. She's just someone I know."

Kissing me once more, Alex turns and walks out of the suite, leaving me alone and carrying a new secret. One that binds us again, just this time, for me, it's even tighter.

19

DO YOU REMEMBER

I t's Friday night. We've agreed to go to Jenna and Nadal's dinner party but there's no sign of Gerard. I tried calling his cell and even his receptionist to no avail. I wouldn't normally be concerned, but Gerard is usually compulsively punctual. Topping that off, Alex is also MIA. I haven't seen or heard from him since last weekend at the hotel. After three days, I couldn't pretend I didn't care any longer. But when I inquired about him, Gerard seemed annoyed.

"He's fine. He just wanted a few days off. Besides, Alex isn't your concern, is he? You married me. Unless that is, you want it otherwise?" He'd raised both eyebrows, questioning me. I turned around to get a baking tray I didn't even need, scared because I was sure my eyes would give me away.

"No, but I was just wondering if he is okay about everything?" I asked weakly, my head down and washing the tray. I couldn't help thinking it was because of me though. Had I scared Alex off with my freaky 'dominate me' or was he filled with contempt because I hadn't left Gerard? As if it's that easy to leave.

"I expect so," Gerard said tossing down the pile of mail

he'd been sorting and ending our conversation when he went off to get himself a scotch.

He was right. Just because Gerard invited Alex into a three-way didn't mean I should suddenly become concerned about him. After all, it was me who was adamant a repeat would never happen again. But there was an uncomfortable knot in my stomach that just wouldn't go away. Then two days later when I mentioned the rotting leaves under the trees were becoming a problem, Gerard snapped again, saying I should have thought about that before I fucked the hired help, leaving me reeling in shame and wondering if he knew what Alex and I had done behind his back.

But then Gerard seemed to realize his outburst was out of line. Reaching for me he apologized over and over, telling me he was just annoyed that he couldn't get me off the way the two of them had the previous weekend and he couldn't understand why I wouldn't agree to another three-way.

I couldn't tell him I was petrified of falling for Alex and ruining everything we have. What if I became dependent on Alex? I was already feeling way too much, and I couldn't be trusted around him anymore. Where Gerard is the perfect husband, Alex is my perfect lover. But for the life of me I can't understand why. No, Gerard needed to battle it out in his own mind because I was still trying to figure it out myself.

The remainder of our week had been filled with a slight tension, only broken up by the mundane. Annabel popped over twice to go over further details for the fundraiser I had suddenly lost all interest in. I told her that Gerard hadn't heard of Ronald Klaneski but she didn't seem to care anymore and was in a mood as she stuffed her paperwork back in her bag getting ready to leave. The fact she was fighting a cold didn't help. "Kids and Jenna and their bloody germs," Annabel grumbled because Jenna has a, 'have germs, stay away' policy and Annabel knew her infectious presence would not be appreciated. "Trust Katie to bring home germs from that private school she shouldn't be going to in the first goddamn place because we can't afford it," she said. It was a concern to hear the level of resentment Annabel was having toward her stepdaughter. Rather than the two getting closer, I could sense Annabel pulling away from both Katie and Stuart.

Sheree on the other hand, sounded more in love than ever when she rang to inform me that she and Darby were taking a quick trip to Thailand. Her excitement at getting away was contagious, and I considered asking if I could go along, just to escape from everything here. But there wasn't a hope in hell Gerard would agree to that.

By seven o'clock there is still no sign of Gerard. Now I'm feeling concerned and anxious. I text Jenna, apologizing for being late and suggest they start without us. After pouring myself another wine, I call Gerard but again it rings out before going to his voicemail. It's so unlike him I decide it's time to contact the hospitals. Suddenly, when I'm just about to hit call, headlights flash across the living room wall. Finally! Putting my glass and phone down, I head toward the French doors to let him in, but then there is a knock at the front door. Changing direction, I pull open the front door and Alex is standing there. "Hey." He smiles.

"Alex!" I look past him, expecting to see Gerard "Where's Gerard, is he with you?"

I step aside to let him in. Alex looks different. Nothing obvious, maybe it's just his body language. He's wearing the same designer jeans he was wearing the other night that hug his ass. The short-sleeved shirt he's wearing, strangles his biceps and shows off his forearms and then—there's that cologne which instantly serenades my nether region, again!

Whatever the subtle change is, my lady bits don't seem to mind one bit.

"No. But he's fine. You can stop worrying."

"Who said I was worrying?"

Alex huffs and pulls a face. "As if you wouldn't be worrying."

"Do you know where he is then? It's getting late, the party started an hour ago." I lead the way back to the living room, because now—I really do need a drink.

"He's at the Dragon's Den. He asked if I'd take you to the party and he'll meet us there, and here," he says, making me turn and face him. "He said to give you this," he adds, thrusting a brown paper package at me.

"What is it?"

Alex shrugs.

"Did you say he's at the Dragon's Den? Is it work related?"

Alex shrugs and makes his way toward the bar. "Mind if I grab a beer?"

I nod. "Help yourself." I follow him absentmindedly. "That seems odd that he'd be there. The Dragon's Den is hardly the place for a meeting, more like a gathering and an excuse to drink, I bet." My bullshit radar tells me there's something more going on. Gerard's behavior is out of character.

Alex looks like he's thinking for a moment but doesn't ease my curiosity. "You look nice." He cracks the beer, throws the cap in the small sink, and takes a sip.

I stare down at the simple flared black jumpsuit that hides comfortable pumps that keep the hem from scraping the floor. With a plunging neckline reaching my navel, it frames the beautiful gold octopus necklace whose diamond eyes keep getting caught by the lighting. Oddly, it now gives me the feeling Gerard is someone spying on us. As though his desire to watch me can transmit through space. I push my long hair away and over my shoulder.

"Thanks. Where have you been this week?" I tousle the natural waves with one hand. Secretly I was hoping Alex would still go to the party and now he's here, with me. Alone.

"Nowhere in particular." He looks around the room, sipping the beer before looking back at me. "You going to open that thing?" He gestures with his beer bottle at the package I'm still holding.

"Why, is it important? What's going on, Alex?"

"I swear, I know nothing. He rang, asked if I was still going to Jenna's and if I could meet him outside the Dragon's Den. Then he gave me that." He nods at the parcel.

"He's playing at something. He's been shitty all week and now you're here alone with me." I start unwrapping the package in my hand. "I think he's trying to catch us doing something." I shot him a surreptitious glance. "Maybe so he can use it and make me agree to his kinky 'I like to watch' shit."

Alex chuckles at my dramatics. "You could just agree. Poor bastard, I think deep down he knows he's a pussy in bed and he wants a real man to show him how it's done."

I pause with unwrapping and scoff at him, waiting until he sinks into the sofa then looks up at me again. I shake my head. "You're so conceited, Alex. Gerard is fine in bed."

"But you don't want fine, do you, Princess? You want sensational. You like to be fucked, not made love to." He takes a sip of beer, looking smug with one arm draped along the top of the couch.

I can't help laughing at his cockiness and my laughter makes Alex laugh. I take a seat on the armrest of the opposite couch. "So, you think you're sensational, do you?"

"I made you moan, didn't I? How's Ger going with that then?" He takes another sip.

I look at the package in my hand and push at the paper.

"Well now, that's none of your business is it, Mr. Sensational?"

"So, that's a no then. I thought he might have learned a few tricks from last week."

I don't answer him, instead; I rip off the last of the paper and reveal a box with a picture on it. Alex sits taller, hoping to see what it is. I chuckle and show him.

"You're telling me you know nothing about this?"

"Swear to God, that's all Gerard. Maybe he learned something after all." Alex sinks back into the couch and takes another sip of beer.

I look down at the box that, going by the image on the outside, contains a black silicon vibrator. It looks as though it's already been opened because the seal is broken. I open the lid and see Gerard has left a note.

Alex watches me read it. When I finish, I huff.

"What? What does it say?"

"As if you don't know."

"I don't." He laughs. "Scout's honor."

"As if you were ever a scout. He wants me to use this at the party tonight. Well, that's a definite no."

"Aww come on, Paige. Let Gerard play with *pussy*. I hear from the ladies it can be quite a turn-on."

"You're funny, Alex." I wrap the paper around the box again and put it on the coffee table.

"How's your friend and the fundraiser thing going?"

I smile at his attempt to make small talk, feeling pleased he remembered my charity work from our conversation over the seafood dinner the other week. "Fine. You should come along."

"Pfft. Not likely. No offense, but it's not really my thing."

"What is your thing then?" I take a sip of wine.

"Clubs," he shrugs. "That's how most *young* people have fun, Princess." His cheeky smile pulls in his dimple, and even though he's having a direct dig at me, I can't help smiling.

"You'd call yourself young? Ha! Hate to break it to you, buddy, but I see wrinkles."

"I'm still under thirty-five." Alex drains his beer. "Should we get going then?"

"Yes," I say, standing then finishing my wine. "I'll just get my clutch, it's in the kitchen." I stride off ahead of him. When I come back into the hall, Alex is waiting with the unboxed vibrator in his hand.

"Don't forget your toy, or—are you the toy? Or maybe, he wants you to be everyone's toy," he questions slowly cocking his head, his mouth turning up at the corner.

"Shut up." I snatch it from him, look around, then decide to stuff it in my clutch and out of sight. "Let's just go."

Alex grabs me as I go to walk away. I try to tug free. "Let me go, you've had your fun."

"I'm sorry. That wasn't nice."

"No, it wasn't. Why are you mean to me? Like all those things you said last weekend."

He steps closer. "Because you frustrate the shit out of me."

I push a hand on his chest to keep him back. But as soon as I touch him, my fingers end up curling and gripping his shirt. Then he's pressing on my hand so I can't pull away and advances toward me.

"Why do I frustrate you?" I keep stepping backward until he has me pressed up against the wall, then he lets go of my hand and places both his on the wall, caging me in.

"Because I can see you're unhappy. You're trapped."

"No, I'm not."

He looks at how he has me between his arms. "I think you are." He smells the surrounding air, then focuses on my eyes. "I missed you this week," he says, in all sincerity, just inches from my face. "I didn't want to, but I did." His eyes dart over my features, taking in my nose, my hair and ears, then settling on my lips. "You should kiss me."

"Oh, should I?"

"You know you want to," Alex smirks and leans in closer.

"Why start something we can't finish, Alex? No, now please, move, we need to get going." I push on his chest but get nowhere.

"All week I could feel you. Smell you. Fuck, I can still taste you." He plays with my earring, then lets the back of his fingers trail down my neck until he's placing a gentle palm under my jaw, tilting my face upward.

In seconds I'm pulsating heat. How does he do it so easily? With so little effort he has me aroused. It's insane. My fingers clasp onto his shirt, and I'm staring at his lips, shaking my head, wishing I wasn't so vulnerable.

"I wish you wouldn't tease me like you do, Alex. You'll drive me insane." I re-establish eye contact, allowing myself to fall under his spell.

"Who's teasing who, Princess? But I have no intention of leaving you unsatisfied ever."

I get lost in his eyes. They've turned dark from arousal, but there's a soft yearning there which makes me melt. My heart is racing ridiculously fast, creating a mild delirium that sets in and makes me forget everything.

"But you know this can't go anywhere." My voice is so low it's barely a whisper.

"I know. But, there's just something about you, Páige."

One arm drops away from the wall to pull me in tight and cradling the back of my neck before he is pressing his lips on mine. Soft, moist lips caressing then growing hotter and more desperate as he groans out his hunger. My hands reach for his face, taking hold not wanting to let go until I have my fill, which I'm scared now will never be enough. He tastes sweet and spicy, and when his tongue plays with mine, my legs become shaky, and I moan into his mouth.

There's everything to lust over with Alex. His confidence. The way he stands, the way he holds me. And then there's everything to hate because he's both rough and gentle, mean then kind, inquisitive but also detached. Everything about him feels addictive because he's a contradiction that I can't figure out. I'm so turned on, I want him to crawl inside me. The yearning becomes so painful, I press myself against his leg, desperate for him to relieve the ache.

He pulls away too quickly, panting and looking lost for a moment.

"Shit." He shakes his head, trying to gain his senses. "I can't believe I forgot."

"What, what did you forget?"

He marches toward the front door and pulls it open, looks over his shoulder at a breathless me.

"I've got someone waiting in the car."

20

FUCK FEELINGS

I drive.

Alex keeps looking at me then reaches to stroke my inner thigh with light fingertips. I shove his hand away and peek in the mirror at his date, who looks not one second over eighteen and has her fucking head glued to her phone. What is it with men and young women and people with their phones?

Alex hangs onto the ceiling grab handle and looks out his side window. I'm thankful Jenna and Nadal's home is only a short distance away. I should have made them walk. At least Alex. I think Miss Innocent in the back doesn't even understand where she's going. I'm embarrassed for her. And me. What sort of idiot am I?

"You know, you left the shed door open last week."

"I did?"

"I'm not sure if you're *aware,* but this road has experienced its fair share of *criminal activity,* Alex. So, *we* would appreciate you being more careful."

Alex lets out a snide huff. "Right. And by 'we' you mean..."

"Yeah, you know, *my husband* and I." I catch a glimpse of Miss 'barely there' brown doe eyes in the mirror. Her name is Genevieve, but Alex likes to refer to her as Gena. What a snake. How could he do that to her? To Me? Argh, the man is insidious. All I want to do now is go home.

I turn toward the Martin's house and barrel up the driveway then find a spot to let them out. "I'm going home. You can tell Gerard for me." I'm about to push the gear stick into reverse and demand Alex get out, when we notice Gerard standing by his car and locking it. There is a gentleman with him whom he must have brought along. My heart races in panic and there's a bunch of worms squirming in my stomach because we—are extremely late.

"Shit," Alex exhales. "Looks like you can tell him yourself."

Gerard looks to his companion then at my car again, pausing for only a moment before he is striding toward us. I don't know whether to stay in the vehicle or get out and act like everything is fine. Before I even have time to decide, Gerard is pulling open my door.

Alex climbs out. "Hey. Looks like you beat us, anyway."

Gerard offers me his hand. "Are you getting out?"

"I… I'm not sure. I don't think so. I don't feel well."

"Oh?" Gerard straightens, letting his hand fall by his side then steps back expecting me to peel out. He looks over the roof of the car. "Why are you late?" I flinch at his tone toward Alex and grip the steering wheel.

Alex explains he had to pick up his date first, who manages a shy hello before Alex is whisking her away toward the house.

"Are you all right?" Gerard asks, helping me out the car. He then tilts my face and presses the back of his hand on my forehead before I flick it off.

"What's the matter?"

"I'm fine. But why did you send Alex around?" I bend to

retrieve my clutch from the dashboard before locking the car.

"I had a late appointment, then I needed to pick someone up on my way home and I didn't think you'd want to arrive on your own."

"You seem to enjoy throwing him at me lately." I march off ahead of him.

Gerard grabs my arm and spins me to face him. He looks over my head. "Why, what did he do?"

"Nothing. It's just," I try to think on my feet, searching for something that will make sense to him. "All this week, whenever I mention his name you get annoyed and then he arrives at our house without a word from you. You're confusing me. I don't know whether I'm supposed to be friendly toward him or not." Gerard smiles then weaves my hand through the crook of his arm and walks us onward.

"Don't mind me, you just be yourself. Everything is fine."

But it's not fine. I look up the long driveway ahead, watching as Alex walks hand in hand with his date. Jealousy and disappointment are warring it out in my veins until all I'm left with is a bitter taste in my mouth.

When we reach Gerard's car, the gentleman he arrived with joins us. Gerard quickly introduces me, informing me that Jamison has an interest in sailing and owns a small wildlife reserve in Texas. But I couldn't give a flying crap. All I can think about is getting hammered.

"You're here." Jenna holds the door wide for us to enter. "Come in, come in. Hello, Alex, I'm so glad you... Oh! And you brought a friend?" Alex introduces his date who is looking more uncomfortable by the second. This dinner party is not something I imagine a girl like her would enjoy. She looks as though she'd rather party in some flashy night club in the valley, sipping fancy named cocktails. It's most likely where Alex picked her up.

Jenna rests a hand on Alex's arm before sliding it beneath his elbow and guiding him inside. My fingers curl tighter around my clutch and there's a growl clawing up my throat that's threatening to pass my clamped lips. Moving along beside Gerard, with Jamison trailing behind, we head down the hall toward the yard where the party has gathered and sounds to be in full swing.

The outdoor entertaining area is ablaze with fairy lights and jazz can be heard just below the buzz of conversation. A champagne bottle corks off followed by a chorus of cheers and a barrel of laughter.

"Salud—'ere is to good friends," Nadal toasts in his heavy accent.

Just as we reach the back porch, Jenna slides up beside me and slips her arm through mine. "You know, for a while there I thought you weren't coming." She sounds carefree and I suspect she's had more than one champagne already, bottle that is.

"Didn't you get my text?"

"Oh, I don't carry my phone." She lets go of me and waves a hand through the air. "Come, let me get you some bubbles." She pulls me away from Gerard just as I notice the girl with Alex gripping his arm and whispering. "Gentlemen, care to follow?" Jenna invites, moving us forward so I can no longer hear what his date is saying. "Oh, and you too... um."

"Genevieve," I offer, but Jenna ignores me. Instead, she points out Nadal to Gerard's wildlife friend, whose name I've already forgotten, and he wanders off to greet him.

I take in the guests quickly, noting that I only know a handful of them, and instantly I'm wishing Annabel were here and not sick. I spot who I imagine are the McEwans, childless by the looks, and they look a little out of their comfort zone as well as Alex's date.

As I'm slipping away with Jenna, Gerard grabs my arm. "If

you don't mind, Jenna, I need to speak with Paige in private. Take Alex and his girlfriend, we'll be back in a minute."

Girlfriend!

"Oh. All right then. But please don't take too long. Nadal will want to serve dinner soon and we've been waiting on you." In an overly familiar manner that surprises me, Jenna takes Alex by the hand and leads him away to the large banquet table she has set up on the lawn. Her spare hand starts waving in the air and her mouth is on the move, leaving the poor girl Alex came with tagging behind like a lost puppy. Alex glances back, jerks his head for her to follow, then catches me eyeballing them. I'm feeling for Alex's date more by the second, not to mention I'm now experiencing a real glimpse down Jealousy Lane and he's not even my man. Latching on to Gerard's arm, I squeeze tighter, then quickly look away.

"Here, come with me." Gerard pulls me back through the hall and into the elegant guest powder room, I barely have time to take anything in before he is pushing me up against the vanity and burying his face into my hair. "I was hoping you'd wear a dress," he whispers, caressing my ass and admiring me in the mirror.

"Sorry." I stare at our reflection.

"Did you get my gift?" he asks close to my ear, his breath smelling of scotch. "Are you using it?"

"What!" I twist in his arms. "You were serious?"

"I've been thinking about it all day," he admits, digging into his pocket and retrieving the remote with a smile. When I don't return his look of excitement, he stands straight. "So, you don't like it?"

"Gerard, I'm not going to walk around all night with that thing in me. What were you thinking?"

"I was thinking we might have a bit of fun." He leans back and folds his arms. "Did you even bring it?"

"I'm not using it here. We can try it out at home later." I turn back toward the sink to check my makeup then wash my hands.

"Why were you and Alex late? Is he the reason you don't want to try the vibrator? Because you were screwing him behind my back again?"

Shame crawls along my neck and threatens to heat my cheeks. Regardless, I glare at him through the mirror. "Alex already told you why we were late. Didn't you see his *date*?" I snatch at the towel to dry my hands then take my time refolding it.

Gerard exhales loudly. "Come on, Paige, I'm trying here. You know, it's been hard getting past you cheating on me. And I just thought adding a little spice would help. What I don't understand, is why you're so reluctant to work with me? Unless of course, it's because you're lying."

"Lying about what?" The room is becoming claustrophobic and I'm beading sweat.

"About how much you love me. That you want to work on our marriage."

Now it's my turn to sigh. "Fine, it's in my purse. I'll use it, but I doubt it will be a turn-on. I'll be too self-conscious."

"Don't be silly." Excited again, he squeezes my arms and kisses the top of my head. "I'll see you at the table." He turns the doorknob getting ready to leave. "Oh, I believe this only has a short range," he informs, clutching the small black remote. "I'd like to set it up on my phone one day, but for now, this will do, won't it?"

I stare at Gerard deadpan, not knowing how to respond. I'm not sure I like this sudden twist in his sexual flavor. It's like I don't really know him anymore, and he's becoming obsessed with my pleasure. Alex's little seed takes root. No, this is for Gerard's pleasure while using me.

"What is it?" he asks seeing I'm concerned.

"It's just—well. Why this all of a sudden?" I ask, holding up the toy.

"Well, I figured if you didn't want to engage with anyone else again, why not try this? I can watch you get aroused from afar. Look." He takes my hand and pressing it onto his crotch, "I'm getting hard just thinking about it."

I shake my head but smile for him. "You're certainly not a boring run-of-the-mill man, are you?"

"No, but whoever said I was? I'm just pleased you're willing to experiment." He leans in and gives me a quick peck on the lips. "Now hurry. I believe Jenna the Great is waiting on us." He pulls a face, then opens the door and steps out, leaving me alone and staring at my reflection unsure whether I like this new side of Gerard.

I think about returning to the table alone, then quickly pull open the door. "Gerard," I catch him halfway down the hall, "Please, will you at least wait for me?"

He nods. "Hurry then."

Grabbing the bottle of red in front of me, I pour myself another glassful. Then I'm clenching my legs. *Gerard.* I look up at him seated opposite me and to the right. He's resting an elbow on the table, nursing his jawline and grinning but I'm wishing to God I hadn't been so stupid as to wear a thong. Right about now, only halfway through the night, it feels like I need a goddamn maxi pad. I haven't left my chair all night for fear I'll leave a puddle. I force a smile and raise my eyebrows at him before being drawn back to the person I've been seated next to.

"… shell-shocked. I guess that's why they train them before they go out. Blah, blah, blah," is all I take in from the guy with whom I've been stuck talking about war for the last hour. Not my favorite topic in the least.

I nod absently at him, distracted when Gerard gets up from the table to follow Max, who I'd learned when introduced was the builder responsible for the recent makeover at Nadal's restaurant. They take their drinks and head toward the seating on the landing so the man can smoke. I'm guessing Gerard is questioning him about the beach house and I wonder if Alex is aware. I look down the end of the table and see him chatting with a girl who is not his date. She had left no sooner than we arrived. It has me curious why Alex brought her in the first place and why he didn't leave with her.

I quiver to my core. Not because of Alex's sudden intense gaze when he looks my way, but from the vibrator that keeps going off at intervals. I look around for Gerard and see he has accepted a glass of wine Nadal is offering around, and has joined the man Gerard arrived with, who has been chain-smoking since we arrived.

Oh God. I just want to get off this chair. Please, you blabbering buffoon. Go away so I can get up. I direct a strained smile at the guy next to me then glance at the lady sitting on my other side who is engrossed with a friend of Jenna's whom I've never met before. Although I haven't been following their conversation, I think they are discussing nannies.

Taking a sip of wine, I decide I've had enough of the one-way conversation. Grabbing my clutch and tucking it under my arm, I excuse myself, but no sooner do I stand, I need to rest on the back of the chair because Gerard delivers another round of pulses. I push my hair away from my face, trying to look purposeful and wait him out. Finally, it stops. I throw him a scowl but he's not even looking my way, the ass. This is not a erotic, at all.

I walk the length of the table then pull up alongside Alex and his companion. They both look up.

"Paige, this is Issy."

"Hello," she chirps, "You're Gerard's wife, aren't you?"

I nod. "That's right. Do you know him?"

"Sure do. I'm Carter's assistant. Carter and Gerard are often on cases together and guess who's the bunny getting all the paperwork together? Me. Yay, go tiger." She waves her hands in fanfare, amusing me with the way she refers to herself.

"Have you worked there long?" I ask.

"Four years." With that knowledge, I guess her age to be closer to mine and I question why I've never met her before. "I avoid those boring 'meet and greets' like trains during flu season. Besides, I spend enough time at the office as it is." She tosses her blonde hair over her shoulder and glances around then leans in. "No, that's not entirely true. I hate to say it, but I don't go because there is a certain someone who gets way too touchy-feely once the old Dutch courage hits their veins." My stomach flip-flops and I glance at Gerard. "And it's bad enough I have to put up with it when that certain someone is sober, but when she's drunk, she's twice as bad." She sits back and looks at Alex. "Like, seriously, do I even look gay?" Alex just smiles then looks up at me. He shifts in his seat just as the device vibrates. My eyes dart over to Gerard again. But he has his arms folded over his chest, engrossed in conversation with someone else. Who has the remote? I look back at Alex who is focused on the blonde, but he's wearing a grin and I've lost track of the conversation. Feeling awkward, I decide it is time to leave.

"Well, it's nice meeting you. But I think it's time I get going. I have an early morning appointment." I cut her off with a high-pitched lie because the device in my pussy is still vibrating, and it seems to increase in power. Then Alex flashes a smile. Does he have it? Gerard glances at me then holds up a finger at the person he is talking with, indicating he needs a moment. He comes over to me.

"Paige, I'm just going home for a minute. I want to show the house plans to the builder we met earlier. Are you all right here?"

"I was thinking of leaving myself, actually."

"No. Stay," he says a little forcefully then looks down and greets the young assistant with a smile, inquiring how she is.

"Relaxed. But do you ever stop working, Gerard? You're as bad as Carter when it comes to chillin' out. Isn't he, Paige?"

It surprises me she addresses Gerard by his first name and I'm curious whether she is as informal at work. I shrug and pull a tight smile.

Ignoring her, Gerard informs me that he will be back soon then slips an arm around my waist. "Paige, please stay," he commands quietly and gives me a squeeze. Walking away, he slips both hands in his pockets and a moment later the vibration dies. So, he does have the remote.

"I need some water—will you excuse me?" I say to Alex, before I'm also walking away.

Inside, I help myself through Jenna's kitchen cupboards in search of a glass.

"Hello, it's Paige, right?" I turn around and see the gentleman Gerard introduced when I first arrived. I blush because I can't recall his name.

"Jamison," he reminds me, extending his hand and approaching me. His palm is clammy and tacky from the mixed drink he holds. He notices when I wipe my hands together. "I'm sorry, sticky shit, isn't it? Just can't seem to enjoy beer or wine I'm afraid."

"Is it scotch?"

"Rum."

My nose flares involuntarily.

"Not drinking?" he asks when I turn to fill a glass from the tap.

"Just pausing." I watch him out the corner of my eye as he leans back on the bench and crosses his feet. Hmm, predatory stance if ever there was one. At a guess he is nearing fifty. He's dressed smartly in suit pants and a faint pinstripe shirt open two buttons down. A round face, he looks friendly, and when he smiles, I notice his front teeth sport a gap. If that alone doesn't suggest he's wealthy, the gold bangles and chains around his wrist dismiss any doubt. He runs a hand through his thick, reddish-brown hair.

"So," he starts. "How do you fill your days?"

"Oh, just this and that," I reply, not really wanting to get into a conversation, he's Gerard's friend not mine.

"What is this, and what is that? Come on, I'm interested in knowing a little more about you." He juts his chin, encouraging me to divulge myself, then pushes a hand in his pocket and takes a sip of his drink.

I watch his eyes closely.

"Well, I work freelance for Harper's Bazaar and I'm also helping my friend Annabel, like I do every year, with a fundraiser event in aid of the cardiac ward at the Children's Hospital in LA. You should come," I suggest.

"Oh," he smiles, and I realize how poorly I termed the request. "I think I'd like that. When is it on?"

I twist away to refill my glass, hoping to hide my embarrassment. "July fifteenth. It's a Wednesday night. A little inconvenient being mid-week, but it was the only day we could secure Royal Park this year. Do you know the park? It's on the esplanade? The ocean view is beautiful."

When I turn back around Jamison is nodding. "I know it. I'll come, it's a date." He raises his glass then takes another sip. "So, tell me more, but we should get you a drink first?" he looks about the kitchen expectantly. "Maybe there is some in the fridge." He puts his glass down then goes to check.

"Please, it's fine. I'm not a big drinker to be honest."

"Oh look, I've scored." He holds up a bottle of wine he's found in the fridge. "Come on, just one."

I attempt an inconspicuous glance outside, but he is beside me in a heartbeat, peering into cupboards. I want someone to rescue me. Where the hell is Gerard?

"Here you go," Jamison hands me a glass of white wine. Then, reaching for his drink, he clinks my glass. "Cheers to a successful fundraiser."

"Thanks," I take a sip. "What about you, what do you do?"

He gets comfortable against the bench opposite me and fists his pocket again. "You mean, apart from overseeing the wildlife reserve," he says a little pompously. "Import and export."

"What do you import and export?" I take a gulp from my glass, hurrying the one drink along.

"Mostly I import white goods. Sometimes it's fabric and soft furnishing and on the odd occasion—furniture. You know, the usual stuff that comes into the country."

"Sure, sure, I've watched Border Patrol," I giggle at my own joke.

"So, you think I look like a drug lord, do you?" he asks, smiling and taking a sip of his drink, his eyes glinting over the top of his glass.

"That or a human trafficker." Gasping, my hand flies to cover my mouth. "I'm sorry, that was so rude. I didn't mean that. See, I told you I needed to stick to water," I stammer a lame apology and pull a face. I'm relieved when he chuckles.

"Well, sources tell me it can be quite a lucrative business, but no I'm not twisted, at least not in that way." He gives me a wink.

Whatever that means. I finish my drink and decide to

refill it. The conversation is going somewhere I don't like. I try thinking of an excuse to get me outside.

Deciding I don't need one I push off the bench. "Well, it's been nice talking but I miiiiiight just see..." Holy fucking Jesus. I look to the doorway expecting to see Gerard. I'm feeling like one of those dogs with an electric collar around its neck except mine is a piece of silicon stuffed in my pussy. It stops almost immediately. Jamison follows my gaze. Then we look back at each other.

"Ooh sorry, was that a bit too strong for you, poppet?" he drawls, then shifts his hand in his pocket to deliver me another pulse. I almost drop my glass. My hand reaches for the kitchen bench. I look up at Jamison horrified. He turns it off straightaway, blushing a little.

"Give it to me," I hold out my hand. Jamison hesitates.

"I don't think I've finished with it yet, Paige." He presses the button again. The sensation is sickening, and I close my eyes, fighting to drown my embarrassment. It truly is a weapon in the wrong hands.

"Give it to me." I thrust my hand out forcefully. I'm just about to lunge at him when Alex walks in the room.

"Paige, are you okay?"

"No," I almost burst into tears. "He has the remote." Both men look equally shocked. Alex, I assume because this man, this pervert, has a remote controlling a toy in my twat, and Jamison, because Alex seems to know about it. The toy dies in an instant. I shove out my hand again and thankfully, he drops the remote into it. Snatching up my purse, I rush out of the room and head for the powder room.

Oh my God, I can't believe Gerard did that to me. I clutch briefly at the vanity and stare at my mortified reflection before extracting the vibrator and throwing it in the bin. I don't know who to be angry at. Me for agreeing, or Gerard and Jamison. I cover my eyes and try to shake the realization away. How fucking humiliating. And now Alex even knows, just like he predicted, Gerard shared me like a toy.

My head snaps up and I'm looking at myself again, my tears evaporating off my heated face in an instant. Alex knew it was going to happen. They were all in on it. I double over and throw up in the toilet. In an instant my head is pounding. No, no, no. Please don't let it be true that Alex knew.

It takes at least ten minutes to compose myself and even then, I don't want to go back outside and face the other guests. I pace the small room, working myself up into a frenzy then decide I'm just going to slip away and go home.

"Tap, tap, tap"

Expecting to see Alex, I steal myself before a sweaty palm turns the knob and I peer out to find Jenna standing at the doorway looking concerned.

"Gerard is looking for you, Paige. Are you all right?" She pushes on the door gently. Moving aside, I allow her to come in.

"I'm fine." I stand in front of the mirror, pretending I need to fix my makeup. She closes the door, then her hand goes to my back and she stares into the mirror at me. She's wearing a teal-colored Gucci looking positively prim. She's opted for her Stepford housewife look tonight and it only amplifies the disgrace I have become. My eyes dart to the bin hoping the vibrator and control have buried themselves amongst the trash, which I'm surprised is even in there, Jenna being so fastidious.

"Well, come on, come back out and join the party."

"Is Jamison still out there or has he left?"

"Jamison! He's still here, why? Did he do something to upset you?"

"You could say that."

"Oh, don't pay any attention to him, he's a drunk. I don't

know why Gerard asked me to invite him anyway, we barely know the man. He dines at the restaurant quite frequently with colleagues and women he manages to get, but that's it. Do you have any idea why Gerard wanted him here?"

"Gerard asked *you* to invite him?"

"Yes." Now it seems it's Jenna's turn to fix her makeup. "Gerard popped in one afternoon at the restaurant and asked if I'd mind inviting Jamison. Anyway, who was that baby Alex brought tonight? Thank God he got rid of her. Now I just need to get that blonde to move along."

"Excuse me?"

She doesn't even need to answer me, she just bores her eyes straight to the center of my being and burns a path to my heart.

"Well, why should you get all the fun? He's young and oh so yummy and single, and he obviously loves doing the ladies who don't want to commit."

I look at her blankly for a moment, letting her words find a spongy spot somewhere in my brain where it can be buffered a little.

"You mean Alex?"

"Yes, Alex." She keeps staring at her reflection. Her fingers clearing the edges of her mouth from stray lipstick before she clamps her almost iridescent teeth and examines them.

"But—what—about Nadal?"

"Nadal? Are you kidding? He gets himself plenty of fresh meat at the restaurant he lives at and why even bother trying to keep him on a leash, he's a Spaniard for crying out loud. I just get my own. And anyway, what about Gerard, Paige?" She raises a perfectly shaped eyebrow and enlarges her sea-blue eyes.

"So, are you saying, you know about me and Alex?"

"That he did you in the shed? Yes. Seems to be Alex's

preferred man cave." She's fucking smiling like the Cheshire cat, the bitch.

Now I understand. The shed door, the picnic blanket. Jenna looking up the road. She'd been waiting for me to go past. I'm in shock but I need to know if Jenna knows anything else. I grab her forearm in a tight grip.

"Please don't tell Gerard about him and me."

"Oh, good God no, I wouldn't dream of it, Paige. Us girls need to stick together. Come on, now that's out of the way, let's get a drink. I'm glad we've got something in common now. I've always wanted to get closer to you." Something in common. Is she serious?

Opening the door as a pre-empt, I allow her to lead the way.

"I'll be out in a minute. Pour me that drink. A big one," I add, and she giggles like a schoolgirl, leaving me wondering if she'll even remember this conversation in the morning.

Gerard and Alex, Gerard and Jamison, Alex and Jenna and that...that girl...friend! How many more are there? A rage I never knew existed wells within me. What a trusting fool I've been.

So, it's turned into a free-for-all has it? Well, I think I need to teach some men a lesson then.

In less than thirty seconds, I'm ready and heading down the hall. My head held high and a little black remote held firmly in the palm of my hand.

"Hey! In here," Jenna calls when I stride past the kitchen. She's carrying two glasses filled to the brim with red wine. "I know I will regret this in the morning, but with Alex here," she whispers. "I really don't give a monkey's ass. I just pray

Nadal finds that cute little thing, Issy from Gerard's office, tempting enough to go for a drive."

Taking a glass from her, we start for the outdoors. "He always uses the restaurant as an excuse, you know. 'I'm just going to show such-and-such the restaurant, Jenna. We'll be back in an hour,'" she mimics Nadal. "Wish he'd give me an hour." She arches her perfectly penciled eyebrow again, and I take another few steps down Jealousy Lane. Jenna is beautiful, even drunk as a skunk. She tilts her head. "No, actually I don't. He can stay away from me with that pecker from now on. I'm quite satisfied. Were you?" She giggles, grabbing my arm and spilling my drink. "Oops sorry," she gasps.

"It's your floor." I huff out. I have never seen Jenna this drunk and despite the angst that's bubbling under my surface, I'm getting a good laugh out of her.

"People, we are back," Jenna toasts the air and wobbles on her heels when we arrive on the back landing.

"For Christ's sake, Jenna, take a seat before you fall," Nadal yells then laughs. I notice he is indeed chatting with the young blonde Issy who has now changed seats.

"Oh, phooey." She waves a drunken hand at him, and if I'm not mistaken, the party seems to have dwindled. There are maybe five couples still huddled in small groups with a few singles amongst them. Gerard makes a beeline for me after Jenna makes her announcement. I rush my wine to my lips and gulp down as much as possible before he reaches me.

"Gerard, you're back. How gallant, even if it's too little too late."

"What does that mean?" He offers his hand to help guide me down the stairs. When I don't take hold, he jerks his head back and goes rigid.

"Aww, so sweet," Jenna coos, obviously too drunk to notice the silent standoff. "Where's my knight? Oh, that's right—I don't have one." She pouts at Gerard who rolls his eyes and shakes his head at me before offering her a hand. When she becomes a handful, I use it as an escape and search for Jamison. He is sitting with the McEwans, the new neighbors under a huge sycamore tree on a paved area off the lawn. Spotlights surround the trunk, creating perfect ambiance, and any other night it would seem like a lovely spot to relax, but I'm seething under the surface and don't even give a shit how serene it looks, I'm just glad now Jamison is still around for my revenge. I head toward them without even looking at anyone else.

"Hello. Mind if I sit?" They all turn, but Jamison sits back in his chair and his smile morphs into a thin line.

"Paige, please do." He gestures to a chair next to him. I take another sip of wine then navigate myself to the other chair opposite him. "I think I'll sit here, thanks." Before I take a seat, I lean forward and hold out my hand to Jamison. "Oh, and I think you dropped your car key earlier." I know my smile must look fake because it sure as hell feels it.

Jamison holds out his hand, looking a little confused, but a flash of recognition soon lights up his face when the remote lands in his palm. With an overly appropriate smile for finding his key, he thanks me then slips it into his pocket.

Sitting, I address the McEwans. "I'm Paige, in case you'd forgotten my name." Gerard comes up behind me then places his hands on my shoulders.

"Oh, hello, honey, this is Ariel, Greg and Jam... Oh silly me, you already know Jamison. Don't you?" I tilt my head up at him. Ariel and Greg both shift in their seats, obviously feeling uncomfortable with my tone. They smile awkwardly in greeting.

"So, what are we talking about?" I ask, turning back to my audience.

"Ariel here is an airline stewardess. We've been sharing

places of interest," Jamison enlightens us. Ariel nods and smiles. Explains the messy house. Shame on you Jenna, judging a hard-working woman.

"You must love it," I say.

Gerard squeezes my shoulders and sighs.

"Sit down Gerard, join in, let's have some *fun*," I suggest patting his hand. I imagine my overly cheerful attitude is unnerving him because I've never been this assertive before. Expecting him to pull me to my feet and take me home, I'm surprised when Gerard decides to join the conversation and takes the last remaining seat beside Jamison.

"Have you been to Abu Dhabi," I ask Ariel softly, watching as Gerard takes his seat. Our eyes connect for a moment before I'm hiding behind my glass, my attention back on Ariel.

"Several times, and yes, it's as amazing as they depict in that *Sex and the City* movie," she laughs and reaches for Greg's hand. "It's the question everyone asks," she gushes.

"Gerard's been, haven't you Gerard? It was before we were married." I bring the glass to my lips to sip then change my mind because Jamison administers a wave of pulses causing me to grip the glass tighter and press my legs into the chair.

"What did you think, Gerard? Did you get a look around or was it all business? I've only been three times to Abu Dhabi as a tourist. Mostly it's just a layover in Dubai for me. Still, the service is amazing. Can you believe they make a point of remembering everything from what magazines I read, to whether I have skim or full cream milk on my cereal?" Ariel says.

"It was business. And no, I didn't see much. Did you go together on vacation?" Gerard asks, looking from Greg to Ariel, then me with a frown. He's extremely subdued and for a moment it's hard to swallow around the lump in my throat because of what I'm doing. But he handed the remote to Jamison in the first place, so let him suffer now thinking I'm loving it. Even though I'm not.

Jamison cranks up the power and I'm forced to put down my glass and press both hands on my knees. My heartbeat is escalating and now I do wish I was sitting on a cushioned chair from the banquet table, not this mesh outdoor one—I'm barely able to muffle the sound since we are so far away from the music source that's been turned down now it's getting late. I glance over at the few guests still at the banquet table and spot Alex. He looks at me immediately and I catch the concerned scowl. *Fuck him, too.* I look back to Gerard who is still speaking.

"Unfortunately, my work situation doesn't leave much free time. A day off here and there would hardly fit in the flying time. I will take Paige one day, though. I still owe her a honeymoon."

"Reeeally," I half yelp in response to both Gerard's sincerity and the cranked-up toy that keeps catching me off guard. I look at Gerard then Jamison, who seems to like the highest setting on the remote. The creep.

Greg, Ariel and Gerard all look at me. I'm gripping the armrests so hard I think they might bend.

"Aww, she sounds pleased about that. Gerard, you should do it," Ariel encourages sweetly and taps my hand.

"Speaking of going." Greg stands. "I think we better. Kids," he explains, zipping up his jacket.

"Yes, we should get going." Ariel agrees. "It's been a big day for us. First a christening then this. But it's been a pleasure meeting you all."

As soon as they are out of earshot Jamison presses the control again. I aim a moan straight at Gerard.

It's only then that what I assume Gerard suspects is

realized. His jaw clenches but I turn away and look directly at Jamison.

"More," I purr like the little tart he must think I am. "No, wait." I turn back to Gerard. "We need Alex over here too and then, maybe later you can all gangbang me," I fake an excited squeal.

"You are a greedy little thing aren't you Paige," Jamison tells me in a low growl. "Very nice Gerard, you have yourself a little tiger in disguise here." He then brings the remote into full view and presses the button again. I press my legs harder onto the seat. Jamison leans into Gerard still watching me.

"Mind if I make her come, Gerard?" he whispers.

Gerard doesn't answer, nor does he take his eyes off me, he just holds out his hand.

The second Jamison places the remote in Gerard's palm, I stand and retrieve the vibrator from in my clutch that's been pinned beneath my leg and slap the toy on the table in front of them.

"You two are disgusting," I say, leaning in so I don't make too much of a scene.

Looking up from the toy, Jamison chuckles. "Ouch. Look out, the kitten has claws."

I glare at Gerard—hard, before turning on my heel and leaving. Brushing past the table, I mumble, "And you're an asshole too Alex." Just loud enough for him and Jenna, whom he's talking with, to hear.

The second I'm inside and out of sight, I peel off my shoes and run through the house and out the front door. Straight to my car, I fire up the engine and push it into reverse. Backing up, I can't think of what to do or where to go. I look down to shift the stick into drive, my foot poised over the accelerator ready to floor it, when there's a loud bang on the hood. I let out a screech then see it's Alex standing in front of the car, his hands pressing down as though he has a hope in hell of holding the one plus ton of steel in place.

"Get out of the fucking way, Alex," I scream through the glass.

"What happened?"

"You know what happened. Now get out of the way."

I shove the stick into neutral and rev the engine. Alex straightens and his head darts up, as if he sees someone behind me. I turn to look and see Gerard out the back windshield standing on the front porch of the house. In the next moment, Alex has pulled open the door and is sitting beside me.

"Get out, Alex."

Alex juts his chin at the windshield. "Just go."

"No. Get out."

"Just fucking drive."

"Get the hell out of my car. You're as bad as all of them. I can't trust you or anyone anymore."

Without realizing, I've let the floodgates open and tears are drenching my face.

"Paige." Alex reaches out to touch my leg.

"Don't touch me!" I scream and slap his hand. "You knew, and you let it happen."

"I didn't know Paige." Alex gives me a concerned look before he glances out the rear window of the car again.

"If you want to talk, drive, but you better make it fast."

"Please, Alex just get out." I rest my head on the steering wheel.

"Paige, honest to God, I didn't know. I was only joking before." He rests his hand on my lap. The warmth radiating from him is soothing and begging me to believe him. I try to get control of my heart rate by slowing my breathing, when suddenly I'm startled again.

"Alex, get out." Gerard is standing at Alex's wrenched open door.

Great. So much for a fast getaway.

I let my forehead fall onto the back of my hands, still gripping the wheel and growl.

"I just—want—to be left alone."

"Alex, get out so Paige can leave. This is between her and I."

I twist my neck around, see Gerard step back to give Alex space, but Alex doesn't budge. He looks back at me.

"Paige, if you don't want to go home, you…"

"Alex, this is none of your God damn fucking business. Now get out of the car."

"Let Paige make up her own mind, you sick fuck." Alex challenges getting out the car. His bulky body puffed and ready to fight. He twists and lowers his face to peer inside at me.

"I'll come with you, Paige. Just…"

I don't hear the rest of what he has to say. Nor do I know whether I hurt Gerard who was holding onto the car door as I pressed my foot on the accelerator. Because the next thing I know, the passenger door slams shut as I tear down the Martíns driveway with no idea where to go.

21

IF YOU WANT LOVE

My mother once told me men needed sex to stay calm. That it was the surplus of testosterone coursing through their veins that turned nice men nasty. "I'm doing those men's wives a favor by letting their husbands visit me," she'd said, trying to justify her actions when I questioned why I recognized a few of her visitors as fathers from kids at my school. I asked why they were going into her bedroom even though she had Carlos, her boyfriend. It didn't take me long to figure out what they were doing.

I hated being home when she had men over, sometimes Carlos would even be in the living room watching television. It disgusted me so much; I started going to Sheree's and sleeping in the shed instead of sleeping in my bed. It scared me one of those men might one day come stumbling into my room, and I was sure my mom wouldn't bother stopping them.

I was never afraid at Sheree's, even in the pitch dark. Most times, Sheree's dad would come in and work at a desk he had set up. I'd stay so quiet he'd never know I was there but the comfort of him messing around, doing whatever it was he was doing, would always send me to sleep. I think it's why I didn't tell Sheree that I was secretly sleeping in our clubhouse. I didn't want her telling her mom and spoiling the comfort I felt in those moments of being protected, even if he didn't know I was there.

Finally, one day when I was around eleven or twelve, he caught me. It was late at night and I'd brought my homework along with me. Armed with a flashlight, I was working on a history project about the Pacific Railroad that joined the West and East of America in the eighteen hundreds when one minute I was concentrating and the next; the flap was being drawn, and he was poking his head in smiling at me with a plate of sandwiches. He hadn't even turned on the shed lights, and it made me wonder if he had known for some time I was hiding out in there, just waiting for the right moment to catch me.

I think that was the day I formed a crush on Sheree's dad. I used to tell Sheree her dad looked like an actor from the soap operas my mom used to watch. Sheree told me he was too smart for that because he was always studying. He was smart, and kind, and definitely patient. He helped me that night with my homework, which was something no one, apart from Sheree, had ever done, not even my father who I hadn't seen in almost two years by then. I begged him not to tell Sheree or his wife I was sleeping there, and I was afraid he would tell my mom, but he didn't. Instead, he seemed to care more about me from then on.

Whenever I was there, he brought out food and talked to me for hours. Telling me things about the world that I'd never heard before. Like what supernovas were and why the Northern Lights appear. He spoke about UFOs and government conspiracies. Most of it went over my head, and often he'd talk away while I just laid there listening until I fell asleep. He made me believe for once in my life I was important, more important than his wife and even his own daughter, my best friend, Sheree.

The bathroom door is slightly ajar when I wake the following morning, and I can smell the coconut scent of shower gel. Smacking my tongue to the roof on my mouth I try bringing about some moisture but fail, and the second I think about the previous night starring Jamison, I cringe and feel nauseous. What was I thinking giving him the remote? I should have just gone home, discussed it with Gerard rationally. I cover my face with my hands and groan then pull the sheet over my head to block it all out. But then I'm thinking of Alex. Was he telling the truth? Saying he didn't know. Then I'm wondering what he got up to last night. Most likely went back into the party and then Jenna would have gotten her claws into him again. A territorial growl crawls up my throat. I know I shouldn't care, but do.

I roll over onto my stomach to press out the horrid sensation there. Why did I fall for him? Why would I do that to myself? He has other girlfriends, and he screwed Jenna. Christ, why Jenna? Suddenly there's pressure placed on the bed, and I'm caressed across the ass and I realize the shower has stopped. Pulling back the sheet, Gerard is there wearing a towel, smiling at me.

Last night, after I'd driven off, all I did was drive around the corner and sit in my car. When I'd finally calmed down, I returned home to find Gerard a mess on the couch. The second I came through the doorway he was on his feet and hugging me, apologizing over and over. Begging me to forgive him. I hadn't, but I agreed that we were both tired and needed to sleep.

"Do you feel like breakfast?" he asks, brushing hair off my face.

"Not really. I still feel sick to my stomach." I pull myself up into a sitting position and tuck the sheet under my armpits.

"You know I am sorry, don't you? You were never meant to know he had the remote. He is a true cunt." He rises from the bed and I can sense in his tone that he's either disappointed at himself, or me, or maybe it's with Jamison. Perhaps it's all of us. Still, I dig the dagger in.

"And you're not?"

He flinches at my brutality, tosses his towel onto the bed, then walks naked to put his boxers on. "You're right I deserve that. But Jamison assured me he'd wait until I returned, so you wouldn't realize."

"Wouldn't realize? Why would you give a complete stranger access to my, my…" I struggle for the right word. "bits, anyway? You're still punishing me, Gerard?"

"Punishing you? I forgave you. I'm not punishing you at all." Gerard goes back into the bathroom, sprays on some deodorant then tosses the aerosol back in the drawer. He comes back to stand in the doorway—a confused look on his face. "Are you saying you thought having a three-way with Alex was a punishment?"

"I don't know. Sort of."

Supporting himself with the doorframe, Gerard studies the carpet, shaking his head seemingly lost for words. I think about Alex's warning, that I'm just a toy for my husband.

"What—am I to you?"

Snapping his head up, Gerard looks bewildered. "You're my wife." He scrunches up his face like it's the most stupid question he's ever heard.

"Your wife or your whore to pimp out to your work colleagues?" I swallow the lump of courage that forgot to stay in my heart. I've never challenged my husband like this before and honestly, from the look of his body language, I'm wishing I hadn't.

Gerard twists his mouth and studies the carpet again, looking surprisingly unashamed—more like, annoyed. He looks up. "I told you I get turned on watching you with other men. It just pisses me off that you can cheat on me and I'm big enough to forgive you and let you have more, but what turns me on, is considered too kinky or something. I'm just trying to turn a bad thing into something we can both benefit from." He folds his arms over his chest for a moment studying me.

I'm speechless. The truth is out. He has manipulated me from the beginning. Forgiving me for cheating was his way to get something he's been wanting all along.

"Men!" I roll my eyes, hoping to lighten the mood a little. "You're all about your dicks, aren't you?"

Gerard huffs and lets his arms fall to his side. "That and money."

"Why didn't you just talk to me about it first? You gave the damn thing to Alex to give to me. Was he in on it too?"

"I didn't discuss it with you because it was an afterthought. I was going to introduce the idea of Jamison later, see if you'd be interested in letting him come home with us, and if I'd asked you about the toy, it would have defeated the purpose. And no Alex was not in on it."

"Come home with us?" So, Alex was telling the truth. My heart gives an involuntary flutter and I can feel the corners of my mouth twitch.

"Yes."

"You wanted me to get it on with that creepy fucking

man? What happened last weekend with Alex doesn't mean I've agreed to this new fetish of yours."

Standing at the foot of the bed in his boxers, he glares at me then shakes his head. "Don't swear. I've told you how cheap it makes you sound."

That comment hurt and I'm pushing him. What's gotten into me?

"Well gee, Paige I'm sorry, but you seemed to enjoy your, 'punishment' last weekend," Gerard says, air quoting. "I thought maybe you'd change your mind. It's been said he has a big cock." He twitches his eyebrows and smirks.

"Gerard!"

"Look, forget about it. I don't want to argue. It was my stupidity not yours, and I'm sorry. It won't happen again. Now are you going to have breakfast with me or are you going to stay in here and wallow?"

"Wallow? I'm not wallowing. I'm humiliated and angry."

Gerard opens a drawer and pulls out track pants and a tee. "Why are women so set on making a drama out of life all the goddamn time?" he mumbles. "People mess up, all right. Now can we drop it?"

"Gerard."

"What?" He turns around to face me. His eyes are cold but glassy. I turn my hands up at him.

"I'm sorry, I don't share the same sexual..." I can't think of the right word to say. "Things," I end up using for lack of a better word.

"So, you keep saying." Shaking his head, he expels a deep breath. "I'm just hungry. I need breakfast." His tone is a little softer, but he turns and leaves looking somber, making me feel guilty.

"I'll be down soon," I call after him.

Christ. Will our life ever be normal again? Sliding back

down into the bed, I punch the mattress with both fists thinking about last night. I know I should stay angry at Gerard? It was wrong what he did. But with my head so full of Alex I'm racked with guilt. How can I be mad at Gerard when...I let out a sigh, Alex is still on my mind twenty-four seven?

Alex didn't know. He even came after me, tried to console me. But why? Stop. I'm married. I want things to go back to the way they were. I can't complicate my life now. I have everything I've ever dreamed of and more. But oh, God. The way Alex's eyes roamed all over my face. The way he grabbed me in the hall and that kiss. My fingers find their way to my lips, as if pressing them there will bring back the sensation. What am I thinking? He had a date in the car. I clamp my eyes shut and rub my face, growling and still arguing with myself. He obviously didn't care that much about his date. I mean she left without him. He let her leave—without him. No! The man is a player. I need to wake up to myself. Gerard is my husband. A good one. He has done everything for me. Alex is a passing fascination. I'm married. We took vows and made sacrifices to be together. End of story.

Coming to my senses, I toss back the sheets and go to the bathroom, flinching when I notice the sex toy left on the vanity. Walking over to it, I slide it straight off the bench and into the bin.

After having a shower, I follow Gerard's lead and slip into a pair of comfy sweatpants and a tee then pull my wet hair up into a bun. After applying a little moisturizer, I'm done and heading down the stairs, enticed by the smells Gerard is creating in the kitchen, determined to put everything behind us and move on.

But by the time I hit the bottom landing of the stairs, I can hear he is not alone. Amongst the clanging of dishes and utensils I think I can hear another male voice. Alex's voice. I approach as quietly as I can, along the tiled floor with my heart beating like crazy, to stand just outside the entrance to the kitchen and dining area, so I can listen in on their conversation.

"What did she want? And why didn't you tell me after you first saw her?" Gerard slams what I assume is a lid onto the pan.

"I'm telling you now, and she didn't want anything. She knew I was out and wanted to see me."

"Jolene needs to move on."

"Bit hard given her circumstances"

"That isn't my fault."

"Wasn't it?"

There's a moment of silence and I'm wondering if Gerard is busy or if he is giving Alex the death stare. I resist the urge to peek around the door.

"I don't know why she thinks she needs to get in contact with you anyway," Gerard's voice rings out.

"Maybe you should try answering your phone occasionally."

"Maybe she shouldn't be calling me either. Christ, what a pain in the ass she turned out to be."

"That's harsh. Anyway, despite what you put her through, she still looks good." There's a long stretch of silence which has me fidgeting and nervous that any second one of them will poke their head around the corner and catch me. I feel stupid and childish, but I can't seem to move. Who the hell is Jolene?

"You think so? Well, I guess that's why she's a model, Alex." Gerard, I assume, tosses something in the sink with a clang.

"Was," Alex corrects.

There's an uneasy twist in my gut that's not from hunger.

I should go in now. But it's like I'm on the edge of a busy highway waiting for a safe break in the traffic before I cross.

"I think you need to keep your distance from her, Alex. And for Christ's sake, if you care at all about Paige, you'll keep her out of it."

"Hmm." It sounds as though Alex is murmuring into his mug. "How was Paige this morning? After last night's shit show, I'm surprised to see her car here. What the fuck were you thinking handing a remote to numb nuts Jamison?"

"Don't even start on me about that mistake."

"Seriously. Poor fucking form, man."

"Don't sound so condescending, and I didn't appreciate *your form* last night either, weaseling yourself between me and my wife. And don't forget, you're not exactly a damn saint."

"At least I ask for consent. Who the fuck is this Jamison guy, anyway?"

"Just someone I met a couple of years ago in Santa Monica. At—a bar when I was away for work. He started talking about—his ex-wife and how they'd swap partners sometimes."

"What, and you hung onto his bloody phone number just in case?" Alex seems to miss the lie I pick up in what Gerard is saying. Because I got the distinct impression last night that Gerard seemed very familiar with Jamison.

"Don't be stupid. He came to our firm several months back looking for representation, and…"

"And you just thought you'd invite him to fuck with your wife. Jesus, Gerard. Paige isn't some slut you can use."

"Oh, so now you're the expert on my wife, are you? You don't consider her fucking you in my shed a slutty thing to do?"

I cover my mouth to stifle the loud gasp I suck in. He never really forgave me. I need to get away because I don't think I want to hear any more but my feet stay rooted when a subtle huff escapes Alex, before he goes on to flat out insult Gerard.

"You make out you're so selfless, Gerard, acting as though the other night was about Paige, but it wasn't, was it? You don't care who fucks her just so long as you get a fix, you're still the self-centered prick you've always been. Christ, I *should* take her away from you—you, arrogant bastard."

My eyes go wider even though my ears need to do all the work at trying to figure out what's going on. My mind's still spinning about this Jolene person and how she fits in to Gerard's life before me or is she still... Oh God, I'm feeling sicker by the second. Is Gerard living a double life? And Alex knows about it?

"Listen, you've had your revenge. If you want to keep your job, I suggest you pull your head back in. The women in my life are not yours to worry about. Are we clear?"

My stomach twists. He has another woman. I turn and press my back against the wall, resisting the urge to just slide to the floor.

"Stay calm," Alex says, then someone stirs a teaspoon and taps it loudly.

I can't take any more, they're discussing things I'm not sure I want to know, and it feels like there are frown lines cementing themselves permanently in my forehead.

What's surprising me the most is the way Alex is defending me, and my husband, the person I thought I knew so well, is making omissions that contradict the man I've spent the last five years with. The adoration I have for my husband, the stability, the trust. Argh! Up is down and down is up. And here I was thinking Alex was the one with integrity problems.

I slip away to the laundry and act as though I have been putting in washing, slamming the lid on the washer loud enough for them to hopefully hear. Then as casual as possible, given the fact I'm carrying a ten-pound boulder of knots in my stomach, I make my entrance into the family room and immediately look for Alex.

"Oh, Alex, it's you. I thought I heard someone else's voice. I didn't know you were coming for breakfast." I stand awkwardly in the doorway. Alex is sitting at the kitchen counter in front of Gerard, pretending he's interested in our junk mail next to the fruit basket.

"Morning, Paige. No, I'm just here to get my car."

"Oh," I nod, feeling my face flush.

"I'm nearly done," Gerard informs, rinsing dishes he used and stacking the dishwasher. "Coffee's ready, help yourself."

"I'll get you some, Paige, you sit," Alex offers, dropping the pile of mail.

I catch the pissed-off look Gerard throws Alex, but he sticks his head down without saying a word. I look from one to the other.

Thanking Alex, I take a seat and then Gerard grumbles something under his breath.

"Pardon?" I ask.

"Nothing, I just hope you're hungry."

Alex crosses the room with a coffee, then takes a seat at the table with me.

"You all right after last night?" Alex murmurs, pushing the cup toward me.

Nodding, I give him a small smile. "How did the party end up, did—you stay the night?"

Alex nods. "Jenna offered the guest house. I was too wasted to drive."

I nod then stare at my coffee, hating that my stomach is twisting into knots because I'm disappointed Jenna played the good hostess while I became the drama queen. Alex will most likely run a mile from me now. But then, maybe that's for the best.

"So," Alex turns to Gerard, who looks up briefly. "I know I need to catch up on the gardening here, but if it's all right with you guys, I'd rather spend next week preparing the outside of the beach house for painting." He takes a sip of coffee and raises a cryptic eyebrow at me.

"That's fine, which reminds me, that builder from last night, Max was his name. I gave him your number so you two can discuss what walls need to be taken out downstairs. He also has men to do the electrical."

"No problem. Well, I'm going to get going. Let you two eat breakfast." He rises from the chair, then drains his cup and leaves it on the table.

Instinctively my hand reaches out to grab his arm. "You don't want breakfast?"

"Nah, I don't usually eat breakfast." He pushes in his chair and comes to stand behind me. My eyes dart to Gerard who is getting cutlery and collecting the plates, and in an instant Alex bends to kiss the top of my head. "Sorry about last night," he murmurs into my hair, freezing my chest. My eyes fix on Gerard, unsure if he saw what Alex did or heard the comment. My heart is pounding so hard, I can't take a full breath. What is Alex thinking by doing that? Moving on, he pinches a piece of bacon as Gerard rounds the counter carrying plates.

Even though I should still be livid with Alex for coming on to me last night and having a date in the car, then finding out about him and Jenna, now a heaviness settles inside me that he is leaving so soon.

"Gerard, we should sit out front, it's a beautiful morning. Alex, stay, have another coffee with us. I'd love to hear what's planned for the house." I turn to Gerard as he settles the plates on the table.

Gerard pauses, his expression passive. "You can if you'd like." He shrugs.

"Nah, I gotta go. I need a shower and more sleep. I'm still hungover from last night." He makes his way to the door.

"Choose a nice color," I mumble as Gerard takes a seat. Slightly pissed off I've had absolutely nothing to do with the renovations so far.

"What's that?" Alex lets go of the door handle and rubs his forehead before pushing back his hair.

"I said, I hope you choose the right color."

"Hey, feel free to get samples and bring them around. It will save me the hassle."

I look between Gerard and Alex. "All right, I will. Tomorrow." My gaze settles on Gerard. "It's just—well, like I said the other morning. I was really hoping to help. And the other day, I saw this house…" I begin explaining myself but trail off because Gerard puts down his fork and takes a sip of coffee looking at me over the lip of his cup. When he goes back to eating without encouraging me to go on, my face catches fire. I swallow hard and look at Alex, then push on.

"I'll even be happy to help you prepare, if you still need an extra set of hands, that is." I pick up my fork and start stabbing into the eggs, ignoring the burning sensation on the side of my head and refusing to look at Gerard. When I can't take it anymore, I turn to face him.

"What?"

"Nothing, I just thought you had enough things to do around here. But if that's what you want to do." He lifts a shoulder. "I suppose you're always going on that you feel stuck at home." Gerard adds.

"That's not true. I just want to have some input that's all. You and Alex seem to make all the decisions without me." I put down my fork and shove my plate away.

"So, go. If you want to help, go help. I'm not sure I

understand why, but that's just me. I prefer to hire people to do the dirty work."

Gerard grabs his mug again, leaving me with no clear indication if he's baiting me, insulting Alex, or maybe even me. Perhaps he's being sincere, but I can't tell because my senses seem to be all over the place this morning.

I glance at Alex, who is looking tired and perplexed.

"Are you certain you're not going to mind?" I reach for Gerard's forearm, feeling a little guilty that I have an ulterior motive. But I need to know what secrets he is keeping from me. Who is this Jolene person they were talking about? I know I should confront Gerard, but the lack of oxygen getting to my lungs is telling me he would not be impressed to know I was eavesdropping. And Alex, well after learning what I heard, I think I can trust him to tell me. I hope.

Rising, Gerard collects his plate and looks down at me. "I don't mind. Just do what you need to do. I have to make some calls." He puts his dishes in the sink then heads off toward his office. I'm surprised he doesn't put up more of a debate. Then Jamison flashes though my mind and I suspect the change of heart might be because of his remorse over my humiliation and reaction last night.

"Oh, and Alex," Gerard stops at the doorway. "Will you keep me posted on your progress? I want to make sure we don't blow the budget and struggle to pay you or the tradesmen."

Alex looks to the floor agreeing, then rubs at his forehead again. Once Gerard leaves the room, he turns his attention back to me. "So, you'll be around in the morning then?" he asks, taking hold of the door, I imagine he's getting a little impatient to get going.

Pulling my plate back in front of me, I try acting unfrazzled by my act of rebellion. Secretly I'm hoping Alex is proud of me for standing up to Gerard this time.

"Yes." I scoop up some eggs I've suddenly got an appetite for.

"Okay. Well, you better brace yourself for what's in store for you then."

Frowning, I lift my head up only to find Alex has already left. Without so much as a goodbye.

22

WAVES

Gerard's phone vibrating on the bedside table the following morning drags me out of a peaceful sleep. Confused, I sit up and look around our room. Normally, Gerard is right there beside me silencing it in a flash, before cuddling up to me. Sometimes even making love before he gets ready for work. But this morning, he's gone. There's no sound from the bathroom and when I pick up his phone to silence it, I realize it's only four o'clock. Why would he set his alarm that early? I wonder, placing it down, then throwing back the blankets to look outside, see if it's still dark.

"Gerard."

When there's no answer, I make my way downstairs to see if I can find him. The ground level is near pitch black and there's no sight or sound of him. I move through the house quietly, but with each step my heart pounds harder. "Gerard, are you here?" I whisper, suddenly afraid he's heard an intruder and is hiding somewhere, getting ready to pounce. "Shit." Unsure if I should turn lights on, I press myself against the wall in the hall, straining my eyes and ears.

After a minute of—nothing, I go down the hall toward his

office, convinced now that he must be there with the door closed. But just as I reach the halfway point down the hall, I notice a faint stream of light coming from under the bathroom door. Feeling a little intrusive but curious, I breeze past the open office and then place my ear against the bathroom door. Suddenly there is a muffled scream causing me to shout out before I have time to clasp a hand over my mouth. I spin on bare feet ready to steal back down the hall, understanding the sound came from a device, not a person in real life. The cry wasn't coming from the bathroom either but up the hall toward the office. Two steps into my retreat however, I collide straight into Gerard who is now standing in the hall, his other cell phone clutched in his hand.

"Paige, what are you doing?"

"I didn't know where you were." My hand covers my racing heart. "I called out and… Well, I thought there might have been an intruder inside. Why are you awake so early? And I heard a scream. Were you watching a movie on your phone or something?"

Gerard smirks. "I guess you could call it that."

"Why did you leave all the lights off? You scared me," I cross my arms, coming down from my fright.

"Did I?" He turns and goes back into his office, switching on the light. "I didn't want to wake you that's all."

"Your alarm went off. Why did you set it so early?" Now that the lights are on my heart has returned to a normal rhythm, but every other part of me feels uneasy. Confused why Gerard would be sitting in the dark.

"Was it? Sorry. I must have set it wrong. I couldn't sleep so I thought I'd watch something."

He's behaving so sheepish it's a dead giveaway what he's been watching. He obviously took up my suggestion to watch porn, which is fine—I think. The thing I'm really struggling with though, is it sounded like the woman was screaming in pain not pleasure. Shivering, I turn away and give myself a little hug.

"Do you want some coffee?" I call out, now heading down the hall.

Suddenly, he's behind me wrapping his arms around my waist and growling into my neck. "I'd rather make love to you instead."

"Gerard," I giggle, squirming when his hand reaches down between my legs.

"Come back into my office and let me throw you over the desk."

"Oh gee, how romantic." Gerard must hear the hint of sarcasm because he releases me immediately. When I turn around to face him, he is strides back into his office then slams the door. I'm so stunned by his reaction, it takes a few seconds for me to follow, and when I open the door to make amends, he is staring at his phone with the volume turned up. This time, there's the distinct sound of a woman moaning.

Gerard lifts his eyes to me.

"Gerard?" My brows pinch together.

When he looks back down at his phone without a word, my stomach churns.

"Fine." I say, when he continues to ignore me. "Sulk all you like, but I was only joking."

"Whatever, Paige." His eyes remain fixed on his phone.

When I still don't leave, he looks up. Smirking and unperturbed that I'm in shock and shaking my head at him, he shoos me away with the flick of his fingers. My eyes burn with the threat of tears and it's not until I retreat and pull the door shut behind me, that he speaks up.

"Oh, and Paige."

I blink back the tears and push open the door. "Yes."

"I hope with all this work you plan on doing with Alex,

you'll still be home in time to cook me dinner. I mean, you're not here for nothing, you know."

I'm so hurt I can't even muster an eye roll at him. Not that he'd notice anyway because he immediately goes back to the entertainment on his phone. Then it's my turn to slam the door on him. But for all the false bravado, all I can do is climb back into bed and cry. His rejection cutting me to the core that when I finally fall back to sleep, it's filled with nightmares of a past I'd rather keep buried.

When I arrive at the beach house later that morning, I'm instantly intimidated by the hive of activity there. There are at least four trucks including Alex's and at least six men moving about the exterior of the house erecting scaffolding. I'm too busy looking for a place to park that I don't even notice Alex until he is banging on the roof of my car, startling me. When I lower my window, he tells me to park a little way up the road in the public parking area.

By the time I've killed the ignition, I've thought up at least three excuses to renege on my decision to help. Ranging from Annabel needs me to babysit. Donnie called with last-minute deadline changes and even, I think I'm coming down with the flu. All of which I knew wouldn't fly because I'm hopeless at lying. Instead, I sit in my car looking out at the ocean until Alex gets concerned or curious that I've lost my way, and walks the two hundred yards to find me.

"Time is money, Princess." Alex pulls open my door.

I let my hands fall from the steering wheel and look up at him. "I didn't know there would be so many people here. I feel a bit embarrassed to be honest."

"You're the owner, Paige. There's no reason you shouldn't be here. Anyway, we'll get paint samples first and most of those guys will finish up soon, they're only putting up the scaffolding. Out." He pulls my door wider.

Reaching behind me, I retrieve my bag as I brought my camera along, intending to get before and after shots I hope Gerard might appreciate.

An hour later, I'm trailing behind Alex in the hardware store after selecting the paint. And apart from throwing the occasional glance over his shoulder to make sure I was still following him, he's all business, almost oblivious to me as his eyes dart high, low, left and right in search of the things on his list. Making me question whether he wants me here at all. I remind myself why I'm with him, extinguishing the disappointment I feel that he seems cold and distant.

"Alex, who's Jolene?" I ask when he gathers some tape before throwing it in the shopping cart I'm pushing.

He looks down at his list again before shoving it in his back pocket. "I give in, who? Ah, I need one of these," he deflects without missing a beat, squatting in front of the lower shelves, giving me a provoking view of his thick thighs beneath his straining denim until he stands again and moves on.

"I know you know who I'm talking about, Alex."

I notice he takes a deep breath before stopping. Turning around, he elbows the shelf beside him, biting on his lower lip then clucking his tongue and assessing me.

"Are you sure you want to go there, Paige?"

"That depends on where there is, Alex. Is Gerard secretly seeing someone that I should know about?"

"It's my understanding he kept that little piece of information from you for a reason, and obviously you're too weak to confront him about it. So, if I tell you who she is— where exactly will that put me?"

"Um, in my good books." I shift my weight from one foot

to the other and look around, surprised at the amount of people in our aisle alone.

"You'll be driving the wedge—you get that right?"

"Oh, and keeping the fact that we had sex in the hotel without him isn't one?" My eyes dart about realizing my voice has risen.

"Yeah well, I'm thinking maybe you should have told him about that."

"What? Why would I want to do that?"

"Are you forgetting what he did to you?"

Looking around, I notice people are listening in on our conversation and a sweep of heat travels to my face.

"Look, just tell me who she is."

"You know, I tried warning you about him." He turns around and begins walking again, making a beeline for the checkout so fast I scurry to keep up.

"I know, but who is she?"

"Jolene was my ex. The one Gerard charmed away."

"And what? Is Gerard still seeing her?" I press into his side and whisper. "Does he still love her or something?"

Alex huffs. "I doubt that, but part of me wishes he fuckin' did." Alex dumps paint pots, tape, and the tarp on the belt, then heaves a sigh. After a moment of silent staring, he takes possession of the cart and unloads more goods. "Look, I think if you want to know more about her, I suggest you ask him. I need this job, Paige."

"I can't. The only reason I know is because I overheard your conversation the other morning. Please, Alex, I need to know. Is he having an affair? Is that why he wanted to get us together? Did he film us so he has proof and I can't get alimony if I leave?"

"So you're planning on leaving him then?"

"Well no, but...

"Paige, stop. Try to see this from my side for a minute. It's not that easy getting work when you've done time and I can't afford to fuck this up. Besides, I'm too fucking bias. There's always two sides, am I right? Let's just say the man has secrets Okay?" He raises his eyebrows.

"You don't know the half of it."

"So, wise up then, Princess, because it'll be better if you leave me out of it, don't you think?" He turns away to load up a box with our purchases, leaving no question that our conversation over Jolene is over.

Back at the beach house, we pull up on the narrow car space that faces the highway, now devoid of the other trucks, and I'm instantly impressed with the small but dynamic changes Alex has made now that I can see them. Although he has only just started on the renovations, I'm surprised by what he has already achieved in the three weeks since we took ownership.

"Alex," I almost squeal, climbing out of his truck. "It looks fantastic. I can't believe you've done this much. When did you find the time?" There is now a front entrance and a terraced rock garden with a spectacular display of succulents.

"Ahh, you know, weekends, late at night," he replies, offhandedly, loading himself with a box of paint cans and whatever he can manage.

"I love, love, love this. Did you build it?" I ask, running my hand along the highly lacquered, slatted wooden fence panel that feels like glass. There is a stainless steel mail slot with the number 21409 cut out.

"Yeah one of the first changes. That stupid seahorse mailbox had to go."

I laugh remembering it. "You really are handy, Alex."

"And you're surprised?" he questions, arms loaded and waiting for me.

"I am." My heart flutters a little and then some more

when I notice the large board above the letter box that has 'Name Your Gallery Here' painted in messy writing. I throw Alex a big grin.

"I can't wait to see inside," I say, showing my enthusiasm by grabbing the rest of the supplies from out of the truck.

"Have you thought of a name yet?" he asks, nudging at the sign.

"A few actually." Not prepared to divulge them, I only mentally run through them. 'Paige's Pics,' 'Tempt You Art Gallery,' 'Smashing Art,' 'Ocean View Art.' "But I'm not set on any yet. Got any ideas?"

"Just one, 'Future Holds.'"

The knowledge that Alex has even been thinking of a name is enough to move me, but what really pulls on my heartstrings is the name itself. Instantly, I stop following him. When he notices, he turns around. "What? Don't like it?"

I can't help it. My eyes and nose sting. I smile appreciatively at him. "No. It's perfect, I love it."

"Ah, I don't know about that, but I'm sure you'll think of a better one. Come on, stop getting all sappy and stalling."

Alex leads me to the external stairs around the side of the house but when we're halfway up, I pause and take in the ocean. Gentle waves are trying to reclaim seaweed, and I count four windsurfers with bright-colored sails. There are plenty of people out and about swimming, running with pets and simply lounging on the sand. An excited ripple runs through my body when I think about working here every day. "God, it's such a beautiful clear day. Have you met any neighbors yet?"

I close my eyes and let the ocean breeze caress my face, then inhale deeply, letting the last of my earlier tension with Gerard go. When I open my eyes, Alex is staring at me.

"Stalling again, I will have to take it out on your hide if

you keep this up." He chuckles then moves on to the top landing. "And in answer to your question, yes. Lawrence and Gabriela Fernandez, in there." He tilts his head at the house to the right of us.

"What are they like?" I quiz, hoping to get some insight into the people who will one day become my new neighbors.

"Lorry seems well educated and honest, considering."

"Considering?"

"Considering that's most likely him out there surfing," Alex figures, jutting his chin toward the ocean. "Gabriella seems to be the one who brings home the bacon. He does... whatever the fuck he wants. I think he's still being pampered by his folks," Alex guesses, unlocking the door and shouldering it open with a shove. Pale blue paint peelings sprinkle to the weathered doormat at his feet, some sticking to his shirt. "Should fix that, but it's a good alarm." He pulls a face and pushes harder with his hip, making me smile.

Once inside, I glance around in every direction trying to take in the story of his life, but there is barely anything to look at. I'd hoped to get an insight into the real Alex. Some pictures or classic bits of furniture even some books but all that's there is a crappy old couch, a coffee table that's made from scraps of wood and several cardboard boxes. The kitchen where he dumps our shopping is still as it was a few weeks ago. There are bits of paper on the counter that look like installation instructions, otherwise, not much else. I remember back to the night Alex broke down my resolve, right there behind that bench.

I turn to gaze out the glass sliding doors and onto a balcony to stop my wayward thoughts and notice a slim rectangle table, made in the same fashion as the coffee table, with a few old plastic chairs.

"Coffee?"

"No. I'm good." I move around to his side of the counter,

running my hand over the old laminate, until I'm caressing what is a new swan-neck waterspout.

"New tap? This will come in handy if you get too hot-headed with me today boss," I tease, pulling out the retractable spray nozzle and playfully aiming it at Alex.

Alex gives a little chuckle but turns away and switches on the coffee maker.

"The other one shit itself soon as I moved in."

My smile wavers a little. Alex seems to be slightly standoffish.

"Are you angry at me or something?" I ask, watching as he gets a cup down and puts a few stray dishes in the sink. He doesn't answer right away making me think he didn't hear me. I go over to the sliding doors and look outside again, my arms folded in front of me.

"Do you like living here?" I say louder.

"Yeah, it's all right, nice to wake up to. Gets a bit noisy with the traffic though," he admits.

When the machine signals, he pours his coffee. Remembering I'm here to work, I lunge in.

"Right, so while you're having your coffee, where should I start and where's the music?"

I spin around the room looking in the corners where I think a speaker might be. When I turn back to Alex, he's waving his phone.

"What? That's it? No sound system?"

"Take a good look around, Princess. I got a whole lot of nothing." He pulls himself up onto the kitchen counter and sips from his steaming cup looking at me. His passive expression saddens me because I realize the contrast in our lives.

"Where's all your stuff?"

"I was in prison remember."

"Yeah but that was six months ago, where were you staying before you moved in here?"

"With a buddy. Tony."

"Please tell me you at least have a bed?"

Alex smiles behind his mug.

"No, I don't mean it like that. I mean…" I move closer to him, have the urge to place my hands on his thighs, wanting to express my empathy for his situation. But I stop. Alex has let a seriousness cloud his face. Placing his mug to his right he grips the edge of the counter and leans forward, his eyes narrowing.

"Why did you go home?"

"Pardon."

"You asked if I was angry at you. Well, the other night at the party. Why did you go home?"

"Where else was I supposed to go?"

"Don't you have any friends? He fuckin' used you Paige." Alex pushes himself off the bench and takes a step toward me. When I stare at the floor instead of him, he reaches over his shoulder and scratches his back then folds his arms. I make eye contact for a brief second before surveying the room.

"Look, we should just get stuck into it. I'm here to work. I appreciate you worrying about me, but… you don't need to, and as you pointed out, I've got to figure this out myself."

Alex swipes a hand over his jaw. "That you do. Right then." He claps his hands loudly. "Work it is."

We work until four, which only sees one exterior wall sanded but already it's an improvement and, despite the earlier tension, we've held a conversation in intervals. Mostly we've kept to ourselves. I know it's because I'm vibing a force field because in truth, Alex's opinion matters way too much and I don't want to hear what he's preaching.

While Alex cleans paintbrushes outside, I wash up in the bathroom. Then curiosity gets the better of me when I pass the two bedrooms and I can't resist the urge to peek, to see which one he is using. Even though I know it's only temporary, and the house belongs to us, I still feel like I'm still intruding on his space. Gingerly I push open the door to the master bedroom and am surprised to find it empty. I go on to the second room and throw open the door, relieved to find a large bed with a duvet, pillows, bedside tables and even a lamp. I cover my chest with a hand, relieved because I was half expecting to find a sleeping bag. Knowing Alex was sleeping on the floor when Gerard and I get to sleep in a massive king-sized bed with all the comforts of a home would have done my head in.

Closing the door so he doesn't know I've been snooping, I go downstairs to look over what will one day be my art gallery. With the sun hanging lower in the sky, it bathes the rooms in a warm glow, making me wish I lived here already.

Suddenly, I'm startled by a noise coming from the laundry.

"Alex, is that you?"

"Yeah, just me," he calls back immediately.

I follow the sound of his voice then watch him silently from the doorway of the boiler room, my eyes taking in every damn inch of him as he makes room for the sample pots of paint and other supplies we brought back. I think back to the heat of our first encounter, our time in the hotel lobby. The wild sex and his seduction. I can't block it out and am so captivated in the memories, I don't realize he's stopped moving about and is staring at me until he leans against the water heater.

My eyes lift from somewhere around his waistband

to lock eyes on him, my sight drinking in his grubby face and outlined lips. His thick forearms cross over his chest and I can't help it, frustration wells up inside me at the unfairness of it all. This strong desire I have toward a man when I'm unavailable is infuriating because I'm stuck with a wanting that I shouldn't. There's no agenda to Alex, no condition. He is what he is.

"I hate you Alex." I mumble, starring at the ground and shaking my head slightly.

Where Gerard and I are in a different league, I still feel cared for, even adored. But Alex. Alex equals one hundred percent pain. He calls me out on all my bullshit and it hurts. To fall in love with someone like Alex would be like raking myself over hot coals. Everything I am would be exposed. Every weakness would blister and come to the surface for me to deal with. All the disgust I feel about myself, my actions and the deceitful life I'm living would be exposed. Not because he would demand to know, but because I would want to tell him, to be transparent and still loved unconditionally by Alex would feel like a rebirth, complete with all the pain.

"Are you sure about that, Princess?"

I'm so lost in my own head I didn't even notice he'd moved. Like a vampire, he is suddenly so close that his heat makes me break out in a cold sweat and all my insides tighten.

"Please don't torture me, Alex. I don't think I can carry around the guilt if I keep cheating on Gerard. I... I need to know we can just be friends. That you can respect me enough to keep your distance from now on."

"Is that honestly what you want?"

I nod. "It is. I know I need to be stronger toward Gerard, and it's up to me to ask him about Jolene. And I will. I just want to help here. Get my gallery up and running. It'll be good for me."

"It will." Alex nods, reassuringly. "Well, I guess on that note, we'll call it a day then and I'll see you tomorrow."

"You will." I smile, as something like black goo clogs up my heart. I turn to leave.

"Hey, Paige."

I turn so quickly I haven't time to rearrange my sullen face and he looks at me curiously.

"So—why do you hate me?"

Because you're gorgeous, kind, talented, and great in bed. That you're so damn sexy you're all I can think about. But mostly it's because you treat me like an equal. But I can never be with you because if you knew everything about me you'd hate me.

But I say none of that. Instead I say,

"Because you tell the truth. And the truth always hurts."

Alex's face falls and he takes a step toward me, his arm reaching out for me. My arms shoot up to stop him and for a moment he pauses, but then he closes the gap and wraps me in his arms, crushing me against his chest.

His smell is intoxicating and sets my heart racing, making me bury my head deeper into his chest and clench my fists to ward off the urge to reach up and grab his face. To kiss him and get lost in the moment. I need to be strong and fight this urge that will destroy us all. I can't do it. Can't live with the guilt of betraying Gerard again. He took me in and nurtured me. Showed me I was worth loving when I felt ashamed of myself. I owe him. I'm bound to him in a way I can't even begin to explain to Alex.

Finding the strength in me I push out of Alex embrace and look him in the eye.

"I'm sorry, Alex I just can't do this to Gerard."

"But, Paige. Look what…"

I shake my head wildly at him. "Stop. You don't get it. I owe him, Alex. And it's something you will never understand."

I cry all the way home. Then when I get home, I slam pots and pans around as I prepare dinner. Then when I shower, I scream. By the time I'm brushing my hair in front of the mirror, I'm finally exhausted. For a long time, I just stare at my reflection as the ugly truth about me surfaces.

When I was fifteen, and still at school, there was a gang of boys that used to hang out together. I had a crush for a long time on one of them. His name was Peter Moriarty. He was tall and freckle-faced with red hair. Sometimes I thought I must have crushed on him purely because we shared the same hair color, because it wasn't like he was nice to me or anything. The other boys in the gang are faceless to me now, but I'll never forget the way they smelled. They reeked of cigarettes and fuel. They rode trail bikes at Hogan's Hangout, a section near the garbage dump just out of town.

I'm not sure who built the tracks, but that's where most of the kids hung out on weekends and during the school vacation. It's where Sheree and I would sometimes go. Mostly to bum cigarettes and sometimes we'd get lucky and score Red Bull energy drinks spiked with Vodka that were getting passed around. I liked getting drunk back then. It took me to that place where nothing mattered. Sheree always kept a level head on her, but I think I inherited my mom's genes. There were many things to be jealous about with Sheree. She got good grades and new things all the time. Everybody liked her, even all the teachers. Most of the boys followed her around and teased her, hoping to get a date. Tall with long blond hair and big boobs, she always dressed in tight jeans and a silly Broncos jersey that she got from an aunt or cousin or someone who lived in Australia, which everyone liked. Everyone was jealous that she had that jersey, because owning a football jersey from anywhere other than the States was a huge deal back then.

She never let me wear that jersey though, not once, and it made me question if our friendship was fake. Like she just had me around all those years so she would look better because everyone knew what sort of family I came from and who my mother was. I know better now, but back then, it started to eat at me that she was so loved and cared for and I was nothing and a nobody.

Peter Moriarty, I'd sigh, doing love hearts on my page. Then he kissed me. At the bike park, as all his friends watched. It wasn't my first kiss and Peter's kisses felt clumsy and too wet. His lips were floppy and lacked the experience I'd grown accustomed to from Sheree's dad's lessons.

When I told him not to kiss like a fish, he got angry, telling me it was because of my ugly lips or something stupid like that. I laughed because I thought he was trying to be funny. Then I said I could teach him how to kiss better. I said it quietly, so his friends wouldn't hear, but he still got angry and yelled out to his friends that I was a whore just like my mother. His comment shattered me.

My face fell and the next thing I knew, they were all there fighting around me, but I was in the middle and then they were tearing at my clothes and pulling my hair and slapping me. Sheree had not long gone, saying she needed to meet her father at the bakery, or she'd get grounded. I should have gone too, but I'd waited so long for Peter to notice me, so when he finally did, I got a rush from his attention and stayed behind.

Peter Moriarty was the first to let me go, but he was the last to leave. The others had run away and left him there. My torn shirt was gathered together to cover my exposed chest. My messy hair smoothed down, and one shoe needed picking up from several yards away. The whole time this was going on, Peter Moriarty was dangling by the scruff of his jacket by Sheree's dad, who by then, was letting me call him Richard.

"You dirty little bastards, just who do you think you are?" he swore, shocking me. "I should haul your asses to the police station, and have you arrested, or cut those dirty little peckers clean off, turn you into pussies, which is what you are. So, it takes four of you to get one girl, does it? You, pathetic scumbags," he hollered, checking me up and down, appearing relieved my jeans were still on and fastened. Peter Moriarty's face matched his hair color by the time Sheree's dad was through with him. "Now leave, and if you come near this girl again, I swear I will stab you with my goddamn scaling knife," he threatened before letting Peter go. I'd never felt so important before, someone worth fighting for.

I drew a line straight through Peter Moriarty's name over and over in my diary until the paper gave way, vowing to be forever grateful to the man who saved me, not just once but again, later that very same day.

23

HOOPS

The toothpaste lid is off, the hairbrush is full of hair, and there is dirty laundry piled on the upholstered chair. Two drawers have been left open in the vanity and there are water stains on what would normally be a pristine shower screen. I glance back at our bedroom, at the unmade bed. I've been both lazy and busy, choosing to spend my energy elsewhere for the entire week and loving it.

Downstairs, Gerard is slamming cupboard doors. I look at my paint-stained hands, then at my reflection. My messy hair, my casual clothes and the smile I can't seem to wipe off my face. Working with Alex has been strangely empowering. He seemed to trust that I knew what I was doing. Assigning me jobs then leaving me to it. It thrilled me whenever he asked for my input or liked my ideas. We've made good progress and the results are spectacular. I can't wait for Gerard to see the transformation.

With the coming summer heat settling in, the days have been long and hot. Most days, we finish by four so I can be home before Gerard. Tonight, however, after sharing well-earned beers with Alex on the deck, I'm late.

279

Gerard's cussing that he can't find something, drifts upstairs. I roll my eyes at my still-smiling reflection and stupidly decide my shower will have to wait.

"It looks amazing, Gerard. I think you'll be really pleased with what your brother has done so far." I watch as Gerard cooks steak on the barbecue, the smell wafting from the hot steel reminding me just how ravenous I am.

"Stepbrother," Gerard corrects, stabbing at the steak. "Hand me those onions please. I'm ready for them now." He gestures toward the bowl of rings I'd chopped earlier. Reaching over the table on the back patio, I grab the bowl and hand them to him. It's a beautiful night and we're dining alfresco.

"Next week, we will finish the prep and then we can paint the outside walls. I'm so excited. I think you'll love the color, it's a light beige with a hint of gray. Like the Heslop building on Beissel Street."

Gerard nods but stays silent.

"Are—you—still okay with me helping?" I take a sip of wine and lean against the table that's laden for our mealtime.

"Are you fulfilling your obligations for Harper's Bazaar? That really isn't something you want to jeopardize. Is it?"

"It's fine, I'm keeping up," I lie.

Donnie, my editor, had only just called today while I was sanding the wooden handrails. Covered in dust and sweat, I'd answered my phone to a ranting and raving editor who was screaming that his young, dumb assistant, "Can't find her way around an empty parking lot with a seeing-eye dog leading the way, let alone around my damn inbox," and how they couldn't find my submission. I was tempted to let his assistant take the heat for my tardiness and regretted I didn't when, after admitting I hadn't sent it in yet, he said, "Well for flying fuck's sake, Paige. Since when do you not understand the word deadline?"

Alex had thrown me a concerned look when I held the phone at arms length. When I explained what happened, he suggested I stay away for a couple of days to catch up on more important things. But I was enjoying myself. It was nice being in Alex's company. I felt unrestrained and useful. It was exciting to see the transformation knowing I was partly responsible for breathing new life and energy into the tired, neglected treasure and I was more determined now than ever to carve a business out of my passion for photography.

"Can you believe, it's only weeks until the Brave Hearts function? Annabel has been doing an amazing job," I say to Gerard, changing the subject to something more neutral. "Can you believe she has secured over one hundred donations to auction so far, including two Honda Civics?" I try snatching some half-cooked onion rings off the barbecue with a wine in one hand. It's my third and I'm getting a little tipsy. Gerard raps my knuckles with his tongs.

"Are we donating anything?"

"Well," I begin, getting rid of the one onion ring I'd pinched into my mouth. "Do you think I'm being conceited if I donate one of my own photo series?"

"I don't think so. What subject were you thinking?"

"I got an idea from something I saw on the news the other night. There was a report on a group of young homeless kids and the amazing street art they're doing. Some organization commissioned them to do their murals on a row of shipping containers that face the highway. Have you seen them in your travels?" I ask, knowing Gerard often gets around LA.

He shakes his head and waves his tongs at a tray because the food is ready. I grab it for him then top up my wine before continuing.

"Anyway, amongst the row of containers I saw three that had a mixture of hearts painted all over them. All sizes with replicated textures. With a little tweaking, I thought they'd make a great abstract sequence."

Setting the food on the table, Gerard nods. "I don't want to discourage you, but that side of town is a little dangerous." Gerard puts the steak on our plates as I dish up the salad.

"I know, and I might need consent to photograph them, but that shouldn't be a problem, given it's for charity." I end my story and begin cutting into the juicy rib eye that Gerard has cooked to perfection.

"Please be careful if you go there," he suggests.

"Oh, I wouldn't feel comfortable going alone. Will you come with me?" I swallow down the mouthful I'm chewing on before continuing. "I was hoping we could do it this weekend."

I can tell I've caught him off guard. I see him thinking the invitation over. Not wanting him to feel pressured I add, "If you can't, Alex said he'd take me when I told him my idea." Appreciating the steak, I murmur, "This is beautiful, Gerard."

"It's just meat." His expression turns into a scowl. "And would you mind sitting up straight? You're hunching over and eating like a Neanderthal."

"Okay," I sit taller and frown, my chewing slows so I take another sip of wine. Sensing he would rather be center stage, I clear my throat. "How is work?"

"It's fine. So how much longer do you plan on working with Alex?" He turns the conversation back to where I do not want it to go. I can feel him working up to something that I will not like.

"I don't know, maybe a few weeks, and then there's the gallery to set up. I'll need his help with that."

"That long. Does that mean I have to see you getting around in tattered shorts like that when there is a closet full of beautiful clothes that you never seem to wear anymore?" He points at my clothing with his fork while he chews ardently on his steak. "Why do I have to look at you like that? And why don't you ask Annabel to help with the gallery? Alex isn't everything you seem to think he is."

I stop eating, sit even taller, and pin my shoulders back then place my fork on my plate so I don't stab Gerard in the eye. "What's the matter? Have I done something wrong?"

He keeps chewing and cutting into his steak roughly. Finally, he looks up at me. "I don't know. Have you? And no, I can't take you on a photo expedition this weekend. I've already arranged a game of golf with a client. You may as well take your boyfriend." He snatches up his drink and glares at me over the rim of his glass.

"Gerard."

"Well, is that what he is to you now?"

"No."

"Besides, don't you think you need to spend some time here? I'm appalled at the state of this house."

We keep to ourselves for several minutes then Gerard gets up to pour himself another scotch. I look down at my empty glass then glare at him as he sits. When he picks up his fork to eat again, I push my plate away.

After chewing some salad, Gerard looks at me.

"Have you had sex with him again?"

Pulling my mouth tight and shaking my head, it takes all my strength to stay calm. Deep down I knew this was coming. It was too good to be true. That he would actually be happy for me to be doing something other than waiting on him. He keeps looking at me expectantly like it's a perfectly acceptable question. Even the cicadas have gone quiet as though holding their breath.

I don't know where my cockiness comes from. Maybe it's something residual from my youth because suddenly he's reminding me of Carlos, my mom's boyfriend, or maybe it's because being around Alex has giving me confidence. Most likely it's because I know Gerard is hiding something from me and rather than call him out on it, I just want him to tell me it's over between us. I face him squarely, ready for the challenge.

"What would make you feel better Gerard, if I say yes or no? You tell me what you'd like me to say."

"I want the truth. That's all."

"Then no."

"Why not?"

"What do you mean '*why not?*' Are you saying you want me to? Did you let me work with Alex hoping to catch me or something? Who are you, and what have you done with my husband?"

"Like you're one to talk," Gerard snaps back.

"I haven't changed Gerard. I screwed up. Once. I confessed. You said you forgave me. We tried something. Why don't you just trust me now?"

"Because I know you'd rather be with him. Look at you. At this place. You've changed."

I cradle my now throbbing head. "I won't work with him anymore. It's obviously annoying you and this is you messing with me. I just wish you hadn't said you didn't mind in the first place, now I know the fun I'll be missing."

"Is that right? Are your referring to getting your hands dirty, or your cunt?"

"Gerard!"

Gerard's features soften and he looks at his half-eaten

meal. Ignoring it and me, he sips from his glass until the entire contents are gone.

"Why are you doing this to us?" I reach over to cover his free hand with mine. He puts his glass down with a thud. For what seems like forever we stay silent, just searching each other's eyes, looking for the people we once knew. Then slowly Gerard slides his hand away and interlocks it with his other, placing them purposely in front of him on the table, then speaks in an eerie controlled voice.

"No, you did this to us. I want you to tell me the truth. Did you fuck him without me because I think you're lying?"

Nausea sets in and my heart is pounding in my ears. God, how I wish I could draw my entire being inward and into a hole. He knows something. His lips are compressed, his jawbone knotted. The eyes I once fell in love with, their light guiding me to a safe place, are no longer the jewels they once were, but cold steel ice picks jabbing and chipping at what little self-esteem I have left. I flinch from the tightening in my chest, a squeeze that makes breathing difficult.

I don't know why I do it. Maybe because there is a part of me that wants to confess about the sex I had with Alex in the hotel when Gerard wasn't there. In case he knows. That maybe Alex told him and now it's up to me to be honest. Or maybe it's because I unconsciously need drama for things to make sense. But mostly I think it's because I am guilty. I do have feelings for Alex. Strong ones. And I may as well have cheated on Gerard twenty times over for all the fantasizing I've been doing, day in, day out. Then the masochist in me becomes curious how he'll react, what he'll say. Will he finally hate me like I expect he should? Tell me to leave. Or will he forgive me again? I swallow the lump my pounding heart created but cause a flush of heat to hit my face.

"What if we have? What will you do about it this time?"

It's nothing I expect, and everything, I fear. Gerard nearly rips his pants on the edge of the table in his rage and urgency to get up. Snatching my hand, he pulls me roughly to my feet. I stumbled and jerk behind him as he drags me across the lush green lawn. My heart is hammering and every cell that makes up the totality of who I am, is buzzing. I think I'm too scared to scream, so shocked I don't even cry, just let him take me, drag me forcefully to the house. Once inside, he locks the doors and turns off the outside lights.

I stand motionless for a moment before my hands go up in defense when he turns on his heel and charges at me. He snaps a hand around my wrist.

"I knew I couldn't trust you," he says, pulling me through the family room and toward the stairs. I try twisting my arm free, but his grip is vice-like, pinching and burning my skin.

"Gerard, stop, nothing has happened." But it's like he can't hear me through his ranting.

"I've been a fucking fool for too long. You were always out to hurt me. You're a stupid little girl."

Little girl?

"You could have had it all, but you had to go behind my back, leave me out of it. Have your own fucking fun and not give a damn about me."

"Gerard, stop. We didn't have sex, not since we were all together." It's the closest I allow myself in telling the truth. But again, it doesn't seem to matter. And just when he has me on the top of the landing, he says it. Words that crush me to the core.

"You're just a whore like your mother."

I tear up and my bottom lip quivers. His words may as well have been his finger closing in around my throat, strangling me. I stumble along behind him in defeat, lost for words and filled with shame.

"I can't believe you betrayed me twice, even after suggesting Alex again. Why can't you just fuck him in front of me like I want?" Gerard whines, stopping and shaking me. His eyes focus on me long enough to witness my tears.

"You haven't forgiven me. You just want to use me. Why would I make this worse by playing your filthy game?"

"My game? You're the one playing games. I gave you everything, everything!" He grabs my jaw and shoves me backward into the bedroom then slams the door behind us. I stand there like an idiot looking around the room, my eyes settling on the walk-in closet before I make a move toward it.

I don't even get close enough to open the door let alone grab a suitcase down before Gerard is spinning me around and holding onto my shoulders. I twist out of his grasp and go for the bedroom door. In an instant he is reaching over me and slamming it shut again.

"Did you fuck him or not?" Gerard is asking, but I don't think I'm there anymore. I'm trapped back in a dark past where I feel worthless.

"Are you going to answer me?"

"It won't matter what I say, you've already made up your mind about me."

"Well, are you sorry?"

"Yes, sorry I believed you. You said you wouldn't mind me working with him."

"I'm not the fucking liar!" He screams so loudly, I think he shocks himself because he crumbles onto the bed, holding his head and staring at the floor. Now that he has calmed, I don't dare move or provoke him, just stare at him from my side of the room.

"Go and have a shower," he shouts making me jump.

Still undecided what I should do, I don't move, barely even breathe. The only thing moving are my eyeballs which dart about the room, trying to gain a sense of what transpired, questioning who went too far and who is to blame. Gerard leaps up and balls his fists. "Have a fucking shower, now."

Having jolted me, I use the momentum and move to the bathroom, closing the door behind me. For a moment I pace the tiles, my mind still garbled. What just happened? What is happening? What do I need to do? Should I just turn around and say I'm leaving? Where will I go? To Sheree's? No Annabel's, she's closer. I'm still pacing when the door bursts open and Gerard storms in, scaring the shit out of me. Bypassing me he goes straight to the shower and snaps on the tap then spins around. Instinctively my hands go to my face but in a heartbeat, he is reaching for my shorts and unfastening them, jerking and pulling, making me stumble.

"You're still just a fucking child who can't do what she's told, aren't you? Now get undressed damn it. I'm tired of your shit and I'm tired of waiting. I've played Mr. Nice Guy for too long with you and look where it's fucking gotten me. Nowhere."

"I'm sorry Gerard. Just please, can we talk about this rationally?"

He doesn't answer. He has shut me out, his vacant eyes fixated on my shirt as he unbuttons me, yanks it down over my shoulders not even bothering with the last few buttons that get pinged to the floor when he rips it from my body. Leaning in, he reaches around to unfasten my bra. My hands get trapped between us. I reach up, try to stroke his neck to placate him, but having freed the clasp of my bra my arms are soon pulled away by his jerking movements and then he is bending and removing my underwear.

I think I'm in shock because I just stand there naked, not feeling a thing. Even when he shoves me under the shower, I don't know whether the water is too hot or too cold, because there is nothing in me to register the temperature. I've gone completely numb.

"Don't take too long." He slams the bathroom door on his way out.

Robotically I wash. Asking myself over and over what just happened, but still I can't seem to gather any thoughts to string together an explanation. It all happened so fast and I never thought he'd react like this.

I'm just about to switch off the tap when he bursts into the bathroom again, shoving the door so hard it bounces back and hits him in the face. My eyes fly open and the air gets so thick, I don't even try sucking in a breath. I'm so scared I don't even ask if he's okay, just push myself back farther into the shower.

"I said to fucking hurry, now get the fuck out." He rubs his cheek, his eyes staying locked on me.

I snatch up a towel and wrap it around myself, moving past him and toward the walk-in closet. I decide that if I want to survive the night, I can't provoke him. Tomorrow I'll make plans.

"You won't need any clothes." Gerard is suddenly behind me as I'm staring into the closet, lost in thought.

"What?"

From nowhere he has the belt tie from my silk dressing gown. I watch stunned as he binds my wrists.

"What are you doing?"

"This is how he does it because this is how you like it. Don't you?" His face contorts. "You're so messed up in the head you need it rough."

Oh God, Alex must have told him.

"Gerard—Please, please don't do this."

He pulls me along by my bound wrists, my towel now falling away. He doesn't even bother to pick it up, just kicks it out of the way, leaving me dripping wet. Then he's yanking on my hair, dragging me forward, then pushing me onto the bed face first. I start crying as the reality of what he's doing sinks in.

"No, Gerard, not like this, please," I beg. "This is not…"

"Not what? How Alex gets you off?"

He's lost his mind, doesn't know what he's doing. I pull at my restraints trying to get free. Why is he doing this? He must know it will freak me out.

"Please, please, please don't Gerard, please you're scaring me. You know I can't take this. It makes me remember, please, I'm sorry, I'm sorry, I promise nothing happened."

When I push myself off the bed and stand, he cusses then looks around the room frantically as if searching for something to assist him. I pull at the silk tie binding my wrists and head for the door. When he realizes he has no aids to help restrain me, he becomes more determined. Like he needs to put me back in my place to show me he is in control, not me.

With a shove, I'm on the bed again and in a flurry, he is on top of me pinning my still bound hands above my head.

"He said you liked it rough. So that's what you're getting. I found you first. You're mine and I only let you have him because I said so."

"Gerard. No, it's not like that. I don't like it rough, please stop." I sob as a dark cloud wraps around me, shadowing my rational thoughts. I can't do this. I can't be here. I need to block it out. But I can still hear him in the background as my mind tries slipping away.

"You like this, don't you. Should I call you *Princess*, will that help?" He leers down at me.

I wiggle and squirm beneath him, losing my strength with every tear sliding over my temples. He is taller and stronger and no match for me, and my will to fight melts into the mattress as demons drag me back to somewhere I can't go. A past I can't endure again. Gerard promised to care for me. To treat me right and now he's working his legs until they are between mine, forcing me wider, too wide that my hips protest. I scream out and try to get out of his grip.

"Please don't hurt me like this, you know it's wrong."

"Wrong is it? I bet it wasn't wrong when Alex was doing it." His free hand dives between my legs to feel me. My eyes widen, and his head snaps up to meet my terrified gaze. He shakes his head, then slaps my thigh. I yelp before he ploughs his fingers inside me causing my yelp to turn into another scream. I'm so dry he breaks my skin and I sob uncontrollably, pleading and apologizing. But he's still not listening.

Why, is this happening? What is he hoping to get from this? I ask myself this over and over my head thrashing and tears drenching my face as Gerard tries to penetrate me before spitting on his fingers, a vain attempt to lubricate his violation.

Then he is there sucking my nipples, pinning me down and sticking his finger inside me. I go numb. Everything is blurring.

"Please, I'm sorry, I'm sorry, I'm sorry," I sob over and over, clamping my eyes tighter trying desperately to curl into a ball, praying I can draw a cloud around me.

Gerard slackens and pulls me up roughly by my hands and unties me. "See, this is what you make me fucking do. I need to remind you why you're here. Because that's what men do out there, isn't it? How they treat their woman. They take it whenever they fucking want it. But not me. No, I'm Mr. Fucking Patient."

I wipe at my quivering face.

"This is your fault because you're a little liar," he seethes.

I nod, sucking in sobs.

"You say you don't want to sleep with Alex again, but you do. I said I didn't mind; I just want to be there that's all.

There's nothing wrong with that. Why make me angry over it?" He reaches for the throw rug on the end of the bed and tosses it at me.

"Because you'll hate me in the end," I mumble into the blanket then use it to wipe my face.

Pulling it tighter and getting to my feet, I wobble over to the upholstered chair in the corner of the room and curl into it, away from him. He's confusing me and my stomach is so tight, I feel like vomiting. Gerard finds a pair of boxers and a tee but I'm so drained, I can't get my brain to work or even get up, let alone put clothes on.

When he's done getting dressed, he sits on the bed, resting his face in his hands and looking at the floor. "I didn't mean to call you a whore."

"Yes, you did."

"Fuck." He gets to his feet and starts pacing. "You can't mess with me like this Paige. Fuck, fuck, fuck," he chants walking around the room. "See what you made me do?" he runs his hands over the top of his head vigorously and growls. "What is it you want from me then?"

"A divorce."

"You're joking?" He lets out a dry chuckle. "What? Over that?"

"Why would you do that to me?"

"Because you needed reminding, Paige. I'm one of the good guys you don't fuck over. I've given you everything, why can't you just give me what I want?"

"Because I can't be like that. Why would you want to share me?"

"I just want us to be happy. Tell me what you need, and I'll do it."

"I didn't need anything. I was happy but now you're different. It feels like you're just waiting for me to change my mind and agree to have sex with other people."

Gerard looks thoughtful, his eyes darting across mine, searching intently then frowns.

"You're right. The thought turns me on. And I don't know," he adds sourly. "I guess there's a part of me that's still angry at you. I want to see you get fucked hard by someone because—you fucking cheated and it softens the blow. If I'm there as a witness, it doesn't creep in my head and torment me."

I want to throw up. He's twisted in the head. "You want men to punish me by fucking me. Is—Is that what you mean?"

"I don't mean it like that. Look." He crouches down in front of me not answering, leaving me confused. "Do you want to go away together, just you and me? Should we go to counseling? Tell me how I can fix this, so it works for the both of us."

"I'll tell you what won't work. Me having sex with other men in front of you."

"You say that now. But I know you'd like to do it again with Alex, so what's the problem?"

I don't have an answer for him. Everything is swirling around in my head and I can't make sense of anything. He just tried to force himself on me and now... Punish me by letting other men... I cradle my pounding head and massage my temples.

Gerard pulls my arms away and makes me look at him. His eyes are glassy and he's pleading silently before he lets his head fall into my lap. I don't know what to tell him, don't know what to say. I feel like I've done this to him. This is all because I cheated on him. He was never like this before.

I place an unsteady hand on his head and sigh. "I don't know what to do anymore."

"Do you love him?"

"I don't know. No, I don't think so. It's just..." I moan

because I'm terrified to say what's really on my mind. Should I ask about Jolene so I have some leverage and risk getting Alex in trouble? Or should I just blurt out how I feel about him, and risk Gerard turning on me. Either way, Alex cops the fall-out and I don't even know if he feels the same way about me. And then, do I honestly want to jeopardize everything I have here with Gerard? And for what? Some hot sex. Oh God, why don't I just give in? But I can't live a life like that. I'll feel cheap and whorish. I'll become—my mother.

"Just what? Just tell me. Whatever it is. Just be honest with me," he mumbles into the blanket, content with me stroking his head absentmindedly.

"Well, I suppose I'd be lying if I didn't say I have strong feelings for Alex and that scares me."

He nods in my lap, lays there for some time before meeting my sorry expression.

"So, you've been lying." Gerard gets to his feet, dusts off his knees then sits on the edge of the bed, oddly his face is expressionless. "And if you're not interested in having the two of us together, it must mean you want a divorce so you can be with him. Is that what you're working on?" He doesn't even give me a chance to defend myself or correct him. "I can't believe you'd do this to me, Paige. I took you in. Cut ties with my past to be with you. Gave you everything. I forgave you when you cheated and now you want to run off with someone who has nothing and take my money with you. Nice piece of work you are."

Pulling the blanket tighter does nothing to block the sudden chill that runs through me. Gerard lured me into a false sense of security, and I fell for it. He has switched again. His eyes turn a stone-gray, making me hesitant to speak.

"What's so great about him, anyway?"

I'm not sure where to look anymore. My eyes dart around the room until I finally close them and let my head fall. "I guess maybe it's just because I feel I have more in common with him or something," I confess, mumbling at my lap, shaking my head slightly. I can't bear to look at him, but I can't handle the sound of his slow, controlled breathing and the feel of his eyes burning into my scalp either. I cradle my head, cringing. "But I never said I was going to leave you for him."

It seems like minutes pass without a word from either of us. What's he waiting for? Just tell me to go. I'll pack my bags, leave tonight. Surely Alex will... I stop my chain of thought. He has other women. He jumped Jenna in a heartbeat after me. Why am I making more stupid confessions when I know nothing about anything? I let out a groan and dig my fingers into my scalp.

"No, but you've fallen in love with him. How fucking perfect." He lets out a sarcastic chuckle. "That's why you won't let me be there. You think what you have is sacred or something ridiculous like that. No Paige, what we had was sacred and you're jeopardizing what's left of it."

"Just go ahead and hate me then," I whisper, slowly lifting my head, hoping his gaze has softened in understanding, praying my senses are incorrect. They're not. Gerard's complexion is gray and waxy, as though he has just witnessed the most horrendous accident and he's fighting the rising bile. I want to look away again, but the sight of his perplexed face has frozen me into a wide-eyed stare just waiting, my heart thumping erratically. It's as though I'm watching him unlock and load a gun—that I'm trapped prey waiting for his bullet because I know he knows how to hurt me, he always has.

"I don't hate you, honey, no not at all. Disappointed yes, maybe even a little hurt that you have become so flagrant, but no, I pity you." His tone is so condescending, I shift in my seat when he bends in front of me, his hands squeezing my knees. "Because sweetie," he strokes my hair, then his mouth closes in on my ear, "if you're thinking of leaving me because you're in love with Alexander John Perna," he whispers, his fingers digging deeper into my flesh, causing me to whimper and look down at his hand. "I think there's something you need to know."

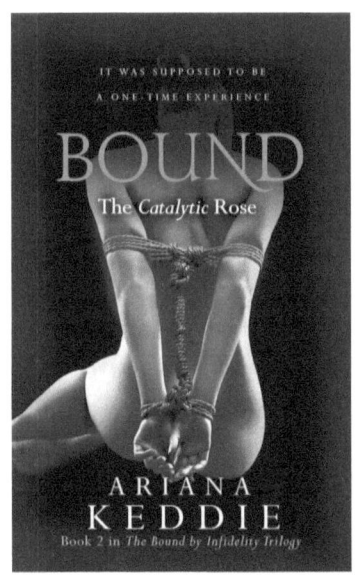

BOOK 2 BOUND - THE CATALYTIC ROSE

Turn the page for a preview

BOUND

THE CATALYTIC ROSE

1

YOUTH

I'm covered in perspiration. My joggers have caused blisters and my heart is striking so hard against my ribs, I'm surprised it hasn't given up on me entirely. Stripping off my running clothes to my underwear, I plunge into the freezing pool. This gives my body even more to deal with, but also makes it's impossible to cry. Last night's fight with Gerard had brought up memories of a past I'd successfully buried. All night I'd tossed and turned. Then every time I started to drift off to sleep, the memory of Gerard's forceful act jolted me awake. Although he seemed remorseful, I'm sure it was a deliberate act to traumatize me to my senses. His cruel behavior and malevolent words, a reminder—I am beneath him, and his love is something I should be grateful for.

I stay submerged until my lungs burn, and even then, once I break the surface, I only snatch a quick gulp of air before going under again. Exhaling, I sink to the bottom of the pool. For an indulgent second, I wonder what Gerard would do. How he'd react if he found me dead on the tiled floor, my body blue and lifeless but my eyes wide and haunting. A huge part of me wants to punish him with my death. But now I'm questioning, would he even care?

Even immersed in frigid water I can't get Gerard's voice out of my head. "I needed to pay Alex to have sex with you again, Paige. That's right—don't look so surprised. Do I need to remind you, you were a revenge fuck to begin with?"

I groan into the wet and curl into a fetal position before what's left of my rational mind slaps me into action. Springing from the bottom of the pool I burst through the water to suck in air so I can let out the trapped anguish via a sob.

"Don't you see it? You're getting yourself attached to a man who is not only a thief and a player, but he's also unscrupulous. Do you honestly think he's a good catch? He's got nothing, Paige. For Christ's sake, the man's been in prison. Is that who you want to spend your life with? A lowlife who will never love you or give you what I have. In some sick way, I think Alex must remind you of Carlos or something."

I dunk my head and scream into the water to stifle the noise. Gerard never really forgave me. He's punishing me. That's what this is. How dare he even say Carlos and Alex in the same sentence? The thought of me being attracted to Alex because of Carlos, makes me want to scrub myself. To stop the relentless chatter and flashbacks, I do laps until my arms are screaming and my heart gives off shooting pain. Exhausted, I roll onto my back and float, staring into the early morning sky. For a moment, I forget about the disgusting truth and just let my mind go numb.

Hours later, Gerard finds me sitting on the edge of the pool, dangling my feet in the water with nothing on but my underwear. I must look like a wax figure, given my blood is near frozen in my veins. Plastered all over my shoulders, my hair is like a dripping shawl and I'm staring off into space.

When Gerard sees me, he grabs a towel and puts it around my shivering body before pulling me to my feet.

"Paige, honey, what are you doing?"

"I have a headache," I whisper.

"So, you thought you'd go for a swim?" He cups my face with his warm hands then pulls me into a hug and rubs my back vigorously. I stand lifeless in his arms. "Come inside, you need a shower, you're freezing."

"I don't want a shower. I need to figure it out first. It needs to make sense." I don't even try stopping the tears anymore. Warm, they slide down my cheeks and land on my lips.

"What, what do you need to figure out? How long have you been out here? Come inside." He looks about the yard, most likely concerned the neighbors might see.

"I can't work out what's worse. What you did to me last night, or that you needed to pay someone to sleep with me, or maybe even that Alex took the money, or—or that you've just been pretending to love me because my past disgusts you. You're punishing me, and now there's someone else, isn't there? Why manipulate me into a threesome if… No. I know. You want me to be jealous. That's part of the punishment too. Isn't it?"

"I beg your pardon?" He falls away and steps back, his hands going on his hips. Dressed in his boxers and tee from last night, I figure it must still be relatively early. "Is that why you've been sitting out here, you think I have someone else in my life, that I manipulated the three-way to even some score?"

"Well, did you? Is there another woman? And is she the reason you turned my romp with Alex into a sordid... sordid —I don't even know what to call it... Sexcapade?"

"Look, Paige," he comes closer and takes hold of my arms, but I shrug him off.

"Are you seeing someone else?" I demand.

"Don't be ridiculous. I love you. Christ, I just wanted to see you—enjoy yourself, that's why I paid him."

"But what you did last night—what were you trying to do? Why were you saying all that stuff? You think I'm a whore," I scream, not caring if the neighbors hear. "You promised you wouldn't hold it against me but you do."

"I just wanted us to have an understanding, that's all." Gerard grits his teeth. "Now get inside and have a goddamn shower and discuss this like a fucking adult." He doubles up his insult by grabbing my arm like I'm a child. I pull away and storm off ahead of him.

Half an hour later, I come back downstairs in jogging gear again, still seething and intent on running away from my muddled thoughts—and Gerard. He's sitting at the dining table babbling on his phone about a stupid client and looking concerned. There's a breakfast of French toast and juice spread out for us, but the smell just makes me want to puke.

"Well, that's not what he told me." Gerard, hunched over his phone on loud speaker, glances up when I enter. When I go for the door he shakes his head, so I wait.

"I need to go. I'm having breakfast with my gorgeous

wife." He smiles but I don't smile back. Gerard ends his call and places the phone on the table. "Feel better?" He picks up his cutlery and gestures for me to sit.

"Not really."

"Please, sit down. Have some breakfast with me and we'll talk."

"I'm not hungry. I'm just going to run."

"No. You'll have breakfast with me, now sit down." His tone is a little firmer, but I still don't make the move to sit down.

"I'm—not—hungry."

"Sit, fucking, down," he snaps.

I'm stunned into silence and stare at him for a moment. Who is this man?

Using his knife, he tears into the toast looking like a demented med student dissecting a cadaver. Realizing I'm making things worse, or he might even turn the knife on me, I sit. I miss Gerard's genuine smile, his electric eyes. I miss my husband and want him back. But he's gone. And really, it's me who's to blame.

"I'm sorry I told you about Alex, but you needed to know the truth, Paige."

"Most people pay a lover to get out the way. Why did you need to pay Alex to join in on the threesome?"

"Because he wouldn't agree." He raises his eyebrows looking nonchalant then takes a mouthful of French toast with maple syrup and strawberries. Trickles of fruit pulp escape, leaving a mess on his lips before he licks it away. I can't understand how he can even eat. Watching him makes me feel putrid inside.

"But why wouldn't he want to do it?" My disappointment is audible. Gerard knits his brow and jabs his fork at my plate, wanting me to eat. "I thought…"

"What?" he snaps. "That he was in love with you? Oh,

come on, Paige, seriously? How many times do I have to tell you? He's a player. He had sex with you in the first place because he's a spiteful, jealous little shit who wanted to get back at me. And some men just don't go back for seconds. I'm sorry, but it's true." Gerard shrugs. "So, I had to pay him. It's no big deal and it was certainly worth it."

Shaking my head, I pick up my fork and stab at a strawberry, trying to make sense of what Gerard is saying because in the back of my mind, I'm reliving the private moments Alex and I had shared, making it difficult to know whether Gerard is playing mind games with me or Alex is toying with me, period.

"The way I see it…" Gerard continues,

"The way you see it? No! The way I see it is that I made a mistake and then you…"

"Shut up," Gerard callously cuts me off. "Yes, you made a mistake, you fucked a man who is a player. He was always out to use you. I simply took advantage of that, so sue me for wanting to see you fucking come. When are you going to understand how ridiculous this is? It's just sex for God's sake."

"Just sex?"

"Honestly, Paige." He pauses and shakes his head slightly for maximum intimidation. "I had hoped you'd be more open-minded about this. Christ, I didn't think you'd get attached. Were you honestly thinking of trading this for him?" He gestures around the room with his cutlery, looking mystified, then chuckles.

"I didn't say that. All I want, is for things to go back to normal." I place down my fork with the strawberry still attached.

"Normal is boring. Most women would jump at the opportunity of having their cake and eating it too."

"Having too much cake makes you fat and unattractive to your husband, eventually."

"Is that what you're afraid of? That I will discard you?" Gerard asks, leaving the table to pick up the newspaper he has spotted outside the French doors.

"I know you will. After a while, it will gnaw at you. You'll see me as a slut. You already do. Sex should be special. A one-on-one loving experience."

"Well, you changed all that when you cheated on me, didn't you?" Gerard glosses over the front page of the paper. I can't believe how matter-of-fact he is. It's like he's detached himself.

"What's that supposed to mean?"

"It means our relationship has become something more complex now. And come to think of it, I don't know why you're angry at me. I'm the one who should be upset. You admitted last night you have strong feelings for my brother. How do you think that makes me feel?"

"Stepbrother," I mumble.

He gives me a sarcastic look. He's right though. If the situation were reversed, I know I'd have trouble looking at Gerard again, let alone forgive him.

"And as far as discarding you," Gerard smiles, his muscles making the movement but there is no warmth in the gesture. "Not a chance. We made vows. Now, all I need is your willingness to grow up and accept the changes."

"What changes? And what do you mean grow up? This has got nothing to do with maturity. What happened was stupidity. I hate myself for being so easy and giving in now."

Gerard drops the newspaper on the table and glowers at me. "We both know you wanted to sleep with Alex again. So, you can stop the charade."

"I knew you'd end up holding this against me."

"I'm not holding anything against you. I'm just speaking the truth."

"Okay, great, fine. If that's how you want it. Set up another date with Alex. Pay him for all I care. You can watch, I'll be the dirty little girl you want me to be. Let's do it every night. Ask him to move in. Whatever. I don't care."

"Now you're sounding vindictive. You need time to cool down. I understand you're hurt about Alex, disappointed he doesn't care like you hoped. Now please, eat. It will make you feel better, and maybe it's best we keep Alex out of it then. We'll find someone else." His phone rings again. "I need to take this, Paige, I'm already late." Gerard gets to his feet, assuming he gets the last say in all this. But like hell there'll be anyone else.

"Who's Jolene?"

"Excuse me?" He takes a step back stunned then rolls his eyes at the ceiling. "That prick is trying to ruin me."

"Who is she?"

He glares at me with his phone still ringing in his hand and without answering it or me, he walks straight out the French doors, mumbling to himself. I don't know what to do. Should I follow or leave him alone? Standing, I see he is heading for the gazebo. He must feel my gaze because he turns and looks back.

After a few moments of questioning whether I should push the issue of Jolene, I zip up my jacket and follow him outside, tucking my hands under my armpits to stop them from shaking. When I'm close, I survey the dewy ground before settling my gaze on Gerard who is now sitting. He shakes his head and draws in a heavy breath.

"It was Alex who told you, wasn't it? Is that what you talk about while you work? Do you even work on the house or do you just fuck and then talk about me?"

I try swallowing, but I have no saliva.

"No, it's not, and yes we work. You can see for yourself, and I told you, I haven't had sex with Alex since the hotel." Which—is the truth.

"But you'd like to."

Ignoring him, I confess I overheard him and Alex the morning after Jenna's party.

He huffs loudly. "You were eavesdropping? Typical childish behavior."

I don't even need to nod because my flushed face is enough acknowledgment.

"How much did you hear?"

"Enough to know you didn't want me finding out about her."

Gerard keeps his eyes locked on me, his jaw balling at the edges before he clears his throat and looks away. "That's right. Because you of all people should know I hate discussing my past." Clasping his hands, he rests his elbows on his knee and stares at the ground. "Alex shouldn't have even brought her up. The past belongs where it is. We've talked about that."

I slip onto the bench opposite him. "So, you're not seeing anyone? You're not living a double life?"

Gerard snaps his head up. "No, I'm not living a double life. Honestly, Paige. Where do you come up with such stupid ideas? She's of no relevance to us, that's why I didn't tell you."

"But who was she?"

Stalling again, he looks over the yard with a passive expression. I join him and realize how unkempt it appears. It's not just the fact that the weather has changed, and leaves are littered everywhere, but there are weeds in the gardens too, and I've been so preoccupied I haven't even cared.

"I suppose I need to hire a new gardener," Gerard says offhandedly, I'm sure out of spite. It's my punishment, but it's Alex who will suffer. When will I ever learn to keep my mouth shut? But then, he's just as much to blame, so why should I be concerned about him, anyway.

"You'll miss him."

"Not anymore," I reply.

"I think you're lying, but whatever."

"Are you going to tell me about Jolene?" I pester, because he's trying to distract me.

Gerard takes a deep breath then stands. Smiling or smirking, I can't tell, but he takes my chin in his hand and looks down into my face. "She is an ex-girlfriend who…"

"You mean the one you stole from Alex?"

Gerard huffs. "So you're taking Alex's word on this are you? She damn well came willingly, Paige. Then she claimed the baby was mine."

My mouth falls open. I twist my face out of his hand that feels more foreign than ever. "You have a child together?" I get to my feet, a hundred questions going through my mind. "Oh my God, you *are* living a double life." I'm so shocked, I shove him. Gerard stumbles backward then grabs my readying fists. I just want to punch him.

"A double life? The child is six years old, Paige."

"But you told me we wouldn't have children." How is that fair? I rip myself free from his vice-like grip.

"I told Jolene the same thing, and the stupid girl got herself pregnant, anyway."

I force my eyes as wide as they can go. "You abandoned her when she became pregnant?"

Gerard points a finger in my face. "Don't you dare judge me. She knew I didn't want children; she was trying to trap me." He turns on his heels and marches away, back toward the house. My mind is calculating the timing. They must have broken up just before we got together. Was I the cause? Is that why Alex has been messing with me?

"Why did you abandon them? Was it because of me?" I

ask, chasing after him. Feeling so sick, my chest hurts. Please tell me it wasn't because of me. Not again.

Stopping, he faces me. "Because it turned out the child wasn't mine. Seems I attract sluts, doesn't it? Besides children are a nuisance."

"Children aren't a nuisance." Wait. Not his?

"Is that right, is it? Weren't you a nuisance to your father? Don't you ever stop to think that's why he left?"

Gerard may as well have physically punched me in the solar plexus because his comment winds me, forcing me to grab onto him. "That was a such a low blow, Gerard." My eyes burn, but I refuse to cry.

"I'm just stating that some adults find children a problem. I am one of those people. Now, I need to get ready for work." He sweeps his eyes around the yard again then lets his gaze fall on me, his brows raised. "Are we done here?" He tugs his arm and stomps away.

"Gerard," I snap, making him stop in his tracks. "After all these years, why wouldn't you tell me about this?"

Gerard marches back and grabs me by the arm, starts pulling me along. "Jolene and her little girl are part of my life from a mistake I made with a stupid young woman. This," he waves a hand around our property then gestures to the house, "is us. Why would I burden you with that mess?"

"So why is Alex still in contact with her?"

"Gee, I don't know, Paige. Maybe he's still fucking in love with her. Look," he grits his teeth. "I was trying to make amends with Alex by giving him work. I thought I was doing the right thing. If you hadn't had sex with him in the first place, then we wouldn't even be having this stupid conversation. So, I think it's fair to say you're to blame that this is becoming so damn ridiculous."

"Did Jolene let you watch? Did you do that with her?"

"Why are you asking such moronic questions? No, I did not."

"You didn't." My voice waivers slightly.

"You and Jolene are—different."

"Or is it you were different with her?"

"Don't try to psychoanalyze me. It won't work. I love you, not Jolene, and that's all that matters."

"All that matters! Is that all you can say about it?"

"I need to get ready for work. I've been late enough these last few weeks, this bullshit needs to stop. Do you understand? You're my wife and I need you to work with me, not against me." Gerard yanks the door open and pushes me inside, the warmth is welcoming against the cold hard reality that I know nothing anymore.

Dismayed, I pull out a chair and sit down, watch as he walks away then climbs the stairs and I don't move the entire time it takes Gerard to get ready. Before I know it, he's standing in front of the French doors in his suit, his hand poised on the doorknob looking at me. For a moment we just stare at each other, my lips trembling and tears resting on my eyelids, just waiting until he leaves.

Putting down his briefcase, he marches out the room and moments later he returns with a piece of paper in his hand. He places it on the table then slides it in front of me. It's a signed check. My focus dart to him, searching for answers in his furrowed face.

"What's this for?"

"If you're so in love with Alex, I'd rather you leave. I mean, you're not the only fish in the sea, are you?"

"You want me to leave?"

"I didn't say that. I love you, I want you to stay, but if you're going to become intolerable, like screw men behind my back without an invitation for me, or regurgitate my mistakes to punish me, then you should leave."

So now I've become disposable. He explains nothing else, just walks away, shaking his head and mumbling to himself. Then he's straight onto his phone again as if the last twenty-four hours' revelations, change nothing at all.

<u>BUY BOOK 2</u>

To discover more books by Ariana Keddie and be notified of new releases, deals and specials, visit:
<u>arianakeddie.com</u>

ACKNOWLEDGMENTS

I have so many people to thank for helping me get the Bound by Infidelity trilogy published, even those who indulged me without judgment when I began with, "Yeah, so I'm writing a book," and I can assure you, there were plenty of unsuspecting ears, too many to name. But to all those who listened and didn't roll their eyes, thank you. Your interest and encouraging smiles helped me to believe in myself.

Firstly, I'd like to thank my husband Mick. Wow, what a journey you took me on to get me where I am today. Thank you for all your support and encouragement. For believing in my talent regardless of the lack of evidence to support the fact I have any. You have come through for me in so many ways.

Jay-Jay, you brave, patient, indulgent little girl of ours. Thank you for giving me the space to find my writer's voice. Those red flowers truly were a gift from beyond this realm. Without you handing them to me, I wouldn't have persevered to live this, my passion, my dream. A big shout out must also go to you for compiling the playlist. Songs that evoke the true essence of my story. It was a huge task and your selections and ear for music is to be commended. The list can be found on Spotify.

Mare, I will never forget you. I dedicated this first book to you because you gave so much to me when I really needed the shove. Not just knowledge, praise, and encouragement but you also shared the pain of real-life tragedies that made me realize these stories need to be told and told in a way that brings empowerment to those who read them. While the topic of my story I know is too close to your bones to read, I hope I have done you proud. I feel honored that you shared so much with me even though we've never met face to face. I love you Mare, for making me forgive myself, for believing in myself, and most of all, for loving myself.

Kira, against your initial reluctance to read your mother's cringe-worthy erotic words, you sucked it up as my first reader. Thank you for being honest and then later, proud. It means so much to now have your admiration and constant encouragement.

To my beta readers that followed. Terrianne, Joy and Timma, thank you. Your feedback gave me more purpose, and my writing got better because I drew from all the experiences we women collectively share.

To developmental editor Cate Hogan. Thank you so much for pointing me in the right direction when assessing my first chapter. Your advice was paramount in crafting this novel to have readers wanting more.

Amber, thank you for beta reading and proofreading draft copies along the way. You did a great job daughter, and thanks for the deadly truth, "No mother. Never, ever use the word moist. EVER!"

To all my family members, thank you for your enthusiasm and undying encouragement. Tyson, my son, for taking me seriously and putting me onto a talented author by the name of Harry Colfer. While Harry's work is not in the same genre as mine, I drew inspiration from his talent then later got to know him which made the world of published authors not so intimidating. Note to mention he also loaned me his grammar guru wife to go over my work.

A massive big thank you to second editor Marni MacRae. Not only is Marni a published author herself, but a fantastic resource who goes above and beyond. I'm so glad I found you Marni. Getting praise and help from another author is truly a gift.

Thank you to those of you who received an ARC and said they loved it. I appreciate your interest and for reading my debut work.

Thank you, author Gerard Byrne for allowing me the use of an excerpt from his novel, © Nemesis Publishing Limited / Gerard Byrne - *No Man's Audience.* You can purchase his interesting and well written book here.

Thank you to all those authors, song writers, bloggers, platforms and writing aids that help writers become published authors. Your advice and online services have been a godsend and truly invaluable.

And finally, the biggest thanks need to go to you, dear reader. Thank you from the bottom of my very humble heart for buying my novel. I hope you enjoyed the fictitious representation of true-life drama as much as I enjoyed bringing it to life.

ABOUT THE AUTHOR

Ariana Keddie is the author of suspenseful, sexy, intriguing fiction. Growing up addicted to romance novels, it seemed a natural progression to hone her passion for writing to become a junkie of the craft. Spending most of her spare time researching the art of storytelling, Ariana hopes to resonate with an audience via her writer's voice. A voice she found while struggling with personal demons which became the inspiration behind her debut work, *Lured - The Unrivaled Serpent.*

In quick succession *Bound - The Catalytic Rose* was published followed by *Free -The Luminous Pearl* to complete the *Bound by Infidelity* trilogy.

A lover of animals, fine wine, and Byron Bay, when Ariana isn't behind her laptop, she spends her time helping her cowboy husband on their Queensland properties and creating memories with their family.

To find out more about Ariana Keddie visit
arianakeddie.com

facebook.com/ArianaKeddieAuthor
twitter.com/ArianaKeddie
instagram.com/ariana_keddie
amazon.com/author/arianakeddie